THE LANGUAGE OF

Divorce

Leanne Treese

Filles Vertes Publishing LLC

Coeur d'Alene, ID

Leanne Treese/Filles Vertes Publishing, LLC
PO Box 1075
Coeur d'Alene, ID 83815
www.fillesvertespublishing.com

Publisher's Note: This is a work of fiction. Names, characters, places, and incidents are a product of the author's imagination. Locales and public names are sometimes used for atmospheric purposes. Any resemblance to actual people, living or dead, or to businesses, companies, events, institutions, or locales is completely coincidental.

Book Layout © 2019 Filles Vertes Publishing

The Language of Divorce/ Leanne Treese. -- 1st ed.
ISBN 978-1-946802-39-2
eBook ISBN 978-1-946802-47-7

To Jake
Thank you for believing in me.

ONE

Will

Present day.

When the limousine door opened and Will Abbott stepped out, he could feel the hidden cameras bearing down on him, their lights bright in the darkness. Immediately, a director, unseen to the television viewers, signaled for him to stop. They'd make him wait; Will knew that. The beads of sweat on his forehead, which had started in the limo, now trickled down his face. He wiped them, skimming the bruise. The makeup woman had wanted to cover it; he'd insisted it stay. He dug his hands deep into the pockets of his khaki pants and wondered, briefly, if he should have worn the tux. Would Hannah have liked that?

Harry Stewart moved in front of him, the gel on his dark, graying hair shining in the moonlight. They shook hands, Harry holding on to Will's longer than necessary, long enough for good camera footage.

"Hannah's waiting for you." Harry gestured to a small, winding pathway lined with giant red hibiscus and tiki torches whose sideways flames ebbed and flared with the breeze. Will's gaze fell on the path and beyond. Not more than two hundred feet away, he could make out Hannah's dress through the foliage. The floral blue one she'd gotten on their honeymoon. His favorite.

"How do you feel?" Harry asked, dragging out the moment.

"I've been better, Harry."

"Any idea what this meeting will hold for you?"

He was supposed to play the game. He was supposed to have a conversation with Harry, reveal something about his relationship with his wife for the viewers at home. He opened his mouth, wanting to speak, then shut it. Another bead of sweat slid down his cheek.

"It's really up to Hannah," he said finally.

Harry waited for more, training a concerned look on Will. The hidden director signaled with frantic, exaggerated hand gestures for Will to speak. He stayed silent.

After a moment, Harry nodded as though he knew exactly what Will was going through. He patted him on the shoulder. "Well, America is waiting, Will. We all hope that you and Hannah get the closure you need." He stepped back, allowing Will a clear path to the walkway.

Will took a step forward. As he did so, his heart pounded, his footsteps heavy on the asphalt path. The intensity of the sensations made him stop. He took a deep breath, shutting his eyes. When he opened them, a camera lens was trained on his face. He smiled reflexively, immediately regretting the gesture. Jesus. How would that look? He shook his head slightly and continued. With each step, more of Hannah came into focus. She was seated at a candlelit table on a small patio, her chair turned so she couldn't see his approach. Her hair fell down her back, straight and shiny. Her legs were crossed, arms resting gently on her lap. He stood, frozen at the edge of the patio, staring at his wife as he had fifteen years earlier—as though she'd dropped from the sky like a gift.

As if she could sense him, Hannah turned, her eyes meeting his.

This was it.

TWO

Fifteen years ago.

Will was alone. His mom had gone on a church bus trip to Long-wood Gardens. Nearly all of his friends from high school were in college. Marissa had broken up with him only two weeks before, and his sisters no longer lived at home. He'd spent the morning at the gym, then washed his car by hand. On a whim, he'd taken apart the dishwasher to determine the cause of its leaking. Staring afterward at the pieces laid haphazardly on the linoleum floor, Will regretted the decision. He picked up a gray piece and put it down. He was alone. And he hated it.

From the floor, he looked outside the sliding glass door, sun streaming through slits in the blinds. He should water the plants. And put in some more of those daffodil bulbs. His mom had been bugging him to do that.

He got up, abandoning the dishwasher—temporarily, he told himself—and slid open the glass door. He saw Hannah immediately. She was sitting in a plastic chair on her square concrete patio next door, engrossed in a thick textbook. A live person! He was no longer alone. He observed her, unseen. Every few moments, she highlighted a sentence in fluorescent green then looked up at the sky, her reddish hair dipping behind the chair.

Of course, he knew her. They had gone to the same high school. He'd lived with his family in the townhouse adjoining hers for nearly three years.

Had he ever had a real conversation with Hannah? No. Not really. It seemed, suddenly, a major oversight. He should introduce himself. He made his way toward her, bare feet crunching on the brown grass.

Hannah sat up, startled. "Hello."

"What are you doing?" Will rubbed the newly-grown stubble on his jaw.

"I'm studying."

"On this day?" Will gestured to the blue sky and the tiny grass plots surrounding the townhouse patios.

She let out a little laugh. "I have a test."

"When?"

"Tuesday."

Will looked at the sky and tapped his finger on his chin. "Tuesday. Tuesday? Why are you studying now? You're free until Monday evening, at least. Maybe even Tuesday morning. What time is the class?"

Hannah shrugged and smiled. "It's a lot of information." She held out the book.

Will extricated it from her hand. "Human anatomy." He stared at the cover a moment. "Come on. You know that. Shins, knees, elbows." Will pointed his elbow in Hannah's direction.

"It's on muscles."

"Well, biceps then." Will flexed his bicep in an exaggerated gesture, catching a glimpse of the box of bulbs in his yard. He should plant them. And fix the dishwasher. He thought of the parts strewn on the kitchen floor of the empty house. He looked back at Hannah. "Do you want to get something to eat?"

She paused. Too long. Was this a mistake?

"You do take a break to eat, right?"

"I'm kind of a mess," she said finally.

"You're fine. All you need is a break from this book." Will laid the book down on her lap. "Tony Luke's? Cheesesteaks?"

"Tony Luke's in the city?"

"Tony Luke's is the place for Philly cheesesteaks. Don't tell me that you have never been to Tony Luke's?"

"Actually, no."

"Never?" Will widened his eyes.

"No." She giggled.

"We must correct this." Will shook his head. "You know we must correct this, right?"

Hannah stood. "Okay. Give me a few minutes and I'll meet you out front."

Hannah emerged not long after in a T-shirt and jeans. They walked in silence toward his Jeep, the spontaneity of the yard encounter now gone. Will felt a twinge of regret for the invitation.

"So, how are things?" he asked, as they slid into their seats.

"Good. Studying." Hannah gestured back to their yards.

"Right. Human anatomy."

"Yes. Human anatomy."

Will drummed his fingers on the steering wheel. "Good class?"

Hannah twisted a lock of hair around her index finger. "It's a good class, but there's lots of memorization."

The conversation about Hannah's class was followed by one about the weather. "Yes, it does seem unusually warm for April." It was horrible. As he pulled onto Interstate 95, Will's mind was teeming with excuses to turn around. He could feign a forgotten appointment or say he didn't feel well. As he began to articulate a valid excuse, the car started vibrating violently. He immediately pulled to the shoulder.

"Sorry about this," Will called as he stepped out of the Jeep. He stared at the car. Staring back at him was a completely deflated tire.

In the next moment, Hannah appeared at his side, seemingly energized by the crisis. "Looks like a flat."

Will fumbled with his wallet without speaking. Of course it was a flat.

"What are you doing?"

"Calling Triple A." He pulled out the card and flashed it to her.

"For a flat?"

"Yes." It occurred to Will then that he should be able to change a flat. But his dad was gone by the time he drove. In a house of all women, Triple A was the gold standard. Now, holding the card, Will felt unmanly.

"Don't tell me you don't know how to change a flat," Hannah teased. She seemed to suppress a smile.

"Don't tell me you do." Will looked up at her, noticing, for the first time, she had stunning green eyes.

"The spare tire is on the back of your Jeep." Hannah pushed the spare wheel on the back of the car until it dislodged. She opened the trunk and folded back the carpeting. Then, like a magician, she pulled out tools, that, to Will's great embarrassment, he did not even realize were there.

As she removed the hidden tools, Will noticed that her legs were long and skinny. Her shiny, strawberry blonde hair blew slightly in the breeze. He watched as she put the jack under the car, spinning the attached clasp to lift it up. She started wrestling with the lug nuts, small but firm muscles bulging slightly. Will was so transfixed by the whole scene that he would have remained dumbly, silently watching had a car not driven by and honked.

"Why don't you help your girlfriend, asshole?" The driver threw a plastic Solo cup at his head.

"Geez!" Will touched his head where the cup hit him. He shook his head. He was such a moron. Will bent down to take the wrench. "Hannah, I'm sorry."

"I got it, pretty boy," she said and laughed. A lovely, infectious belly laugh. He smiled at the sound of it.

"I am so embarrassed." Will let go of the wrench and sat on the asphalt. "I can't believe I never learned how to change a tire."

"Well, my granddad owned an auto body shop. I can do all sorts of car repairs. You should see me fix a carburetor."

"I'd like that." Will pictured it in his mind.

The new tire firmly in place, she lowered the jack. "So, what do you think of Pat Burrell?"

Will looked more closely at her. "I like him. He's a solid left fielder. Good for the Phillies. You?"

"Hate him. My favorite Phillie is Jimmy Rollins."

Will smiled as they got back in the car. "Rollins is good. What do you think of Donavan McNabb?"

"Eagles quarterback? No opinion. I'm a Steelers girl."

Will pulled onto the highway again. "What? Traitor."

She shrugged. "My granddad, the one who taught me about cars, he's a Steelers fan."

Will spent the remainder of the ride listening to Hannah justify why the Steelers were a better football team. She knew her sports. How was it he had never talked to her? As Will neared Tony Luke's, the long line of patrons came into view.

"Popular place," Hannah commented.

"Philly cheesesteaks," Will responded as though no further explanation was required.

He pulled into the parking space then stepped around the Jeep to open the door for Hannah. She looked surprised for a moment, then stepped out. Her legs seemed even longer than they had earlier. She pushed a lock of hair behind her ear.

"So," Will started, "now that I know you're a Steelers fan, I'm not sure I want to take you to the real Tony Luke's." They took their place in the back of the line, puffs of air forming from their breath.

"Can't beat Primanti Brothers sandwiches anyway. That's what Steelers fans eat. They have coleslaw and French fries inside." Hannah rubbed her arms for warmth.

"We'll see about that." Will took off his sweatshirt and handed it to her. "And you can put French fries inside your cheesesteak if it's that important to you."

Hannah looked at the sweatshirt for a moment before putting it on. "Thanks."

"Just don't get ketchup on it." Will winked at her as they entered the building When they were almost to the order window, Will whispered to her. "You have to be fast. Know the kind of cheese you want."

"The kind of—"

"Let me." Will spoke as though he were offering to place her order at a five-star restaurant. He stepped forward and ordered two cheesesteaks with whiz.

"Did you really just order Cheese Whiz?" Hannah questioned. Will held his hand up. "Trust me."

Once served, they carried their food to one of the dozen red Formica tables in the eating area. Will brushed crumbs off their table in an exaggerated, gallant gesture.

Hannah laughed. "First the sweatshirt and now this."

"Hey. I know how to treat a girl." Will made a show of pulling out her chair. "Please." He gestured to the empty seat.

As they unwrapped and ate their cheesesteaks, Hannah told Will that she was taking courses to get into dental school. To help pay for classes at the community college, she worked part-time at Heritage House nursing home doing activities with the residents.

Will had been forced by his mother to go on two field trips to Heritage House. He had hated the smell, a combination of urine and disinfectant. The residents had seemed so old; he'd hidden in the bathroom nearly the whole time.

Hannah stared at him, seeming to read his mind. "Don't tell me you're one of those people who's afraid of the old?"

"Of course not."

She tipped her head forward, still staring.

"Okay. Maybe a little."

She pulled Will's sweatshirt down over her hands. "You're crazy. Old people are the best. I love talking to them. Someday, I plan to be the Anne Geddes for the old."

"Anne Geddes?"

"The woman who takes the adorable pictures of newborns." She said this as though her explanation would prompt obvious recognition. When it didn't, she pulled out her phone and showed Will a picture of a new baby, curled and sleeping inside a cut-out watermelon. Her head was close to his as they looked at the screen; he could smell her shampoo. Strawberry. He liked that. He fought the urge to inhale.

"See. Now what I want to do is capture people after they've lived a full life."

Will nodded. "So photography. That's what you do for fun?"

"Photography, school, work. That's it for me. You? What do you do for fun?"

"I take pretty girls out for cheesesteaks."

Hannah looked down and picked at her French fries. Had he misread her? The silence stretched out. Finally, she spoke.

"Just as I suspected, Will Abbott," Hannah said, her voice light. "I am just one of a long line of girls you have taken to the real Tony Luke's."

"But you are the only one who has ever fixed my car."

They both laughed.

An hour later, they stood on their shared sidewalk, in an uncomfortable silence. Will shifted on one foot. "Thanks for coming out tonight," he said lamely.

"Thanks for taking me, Will. I had fun." She started to walk up the path then stopped abruptly.

"Oh." She slid her arms out of the sweatshirt. "I almost forgot to return this."

Will waved his hand in a dismissive gesture. "Keep it tonight. It's fine."

"Thanks." She turned and started toward her townhouse.

Will watched her, panicked. The evening was slipping away; he didn't want her to leave. "Hey," he called out. "What's the verdict?"

She stopped and glanced over her shoulder at him, her expression confused.

"Primanti Brothers or Tony Luke's? Which is better?"

Hannah stood, contemplating, as though she'd been asked a terribly serious question. "Not sure. I think I need another Tony Luke's steak to make an informed decision."

"So we need to go again? So you can make the final verdict?"

"Right. It's a critical decision. I mean, I can't just base it on the one time."

"Of course. Makes perfect sense. I'll call you."

"I think you'll see me." Will watched her disappear behind her door. His future wife.

THREE

One year ago.

Will made a special trip to Philadelphia to get cheesesteaks. It was a small gesture, but meaningful. Hannah would remember. She'd love it. They'd abandon the nutrition plan and drink ice cold beers straight from the bottle.

As he drove home, Will could almost feel the Rolling Rock sliding smoothly down his throat, taste the warm cheesesteak, whiz seeping from the sides of the crusty steak roll as he bit down. Hannah would be cheered by a night together like it was in the beginning. They would laugh as they remembered their first date. And they needed that. They'd been subtly off for a while now. There were no screaming matches or long arguments, just an underlying discontent, easily hidden behind the bustle of daily family life. Pick ups and drop offs. Lunches and sports games. Homework and bedtimes. Good stuff. It was all good stuff. But it would be good to remember, for one night, how it was at the start.

Will was so cheered by the thought of a fun night with Hannah that he didn't notice the cars parked in the front of their small ranch, the telltale bike propped against the garage. It wasn't until he opened the side door and heard Trent's unmistakable Australian accent that he realized the error. His body slumped. He'd forgotten. Again. Childishly, he considered sneaking out, but before he could move the back door slammed shut behind him, its unmistakable clank reverberating into the family room.

Hannah's response was immediate. "Will? Is that you?"

Will paused, thinking he could somehow escape without notice. Then, realizing the futility of the thought, he answered, "It's me." He wiped his feet and walked through the narrow hall which adjoined the family room. What excuse could he possibly provide? This was the third fifth-grade committee meeting he'd forgotten. But Hannah already knew he didn't want to be on the committee. It seemed too much hoopla to plan an entire year's worth of events just to commemorate finishing elementary school.

Still holding the bag from Tony Luke's, Will stepped into the family room, the meeting clearly underway. He waved to the group which had, at the start of the year, included a dozen or more parents. It was down to four, not including him and Hannah.

John, one-half of Jess and John (both in attendance and both very, very into the fifth-grade committee) greeted him first. "Hey there, Willy." Jess followed with her own greeting as though failure to do so would throw her and John out of sync.

Charlotte, the mother of their daughter's best friend, held up a glass of ice water in greeting. Probably her latest diet fad.

Trent was the only one to stand. "What you got there, mate?" He stepped toward Will who now stood in front of the kitchen door.

For no reason he could consciously state, Will intensely disliked Trent. He carried a burlap knapsack and rode his bike instead of driving. Will would see him along the side of the road, legs pumping, sack bouncing along on his back. Will was certain that if he caught his eye, he'd wave and say, "Hey mate! I was just on my way to a poetry reading in an organic garden. Want to tag along?" It was the kind of joke that used to make to Hannah laugh, the kind that would engender the coveted belly laugh. But the last time Will had said something in jest about Trent, Hannah had become irritated. "He's a lot more help than you are, Will," she'd said. The comment had made Will feel like a scolded child; it made him like Trent even less.

When Trent reached him at the door, Will reflexively held the bag tighter. "Just some cheesesteaks." He tried to make eye contact with Hannah. "From the original Tony Luke's." Will set the bag down on a side table.

At the mention of Tony Luke's, Charlotte got up and joined them. She peeked inside the bag. "Whoa." She stepped back, as if it contained a toxic substance. "Those must be really high in calories."

Jess and John joined them by the door, followed by Hannah. Will made eye contact with her. This was it. She'd clear the group, tell them that she needed to end the meeting early. They would sit together and eat and talk about their days and maybe—possibly—more. Anxious to begin their night together, Will opened the door to the kitchen to get beers.

Then Hannah spoke, her voice clipped and unnatural. "We've got a bit more to cover. Let's finish the meeting." She turned her attention to Will. "Why don't you join us when you're finished eating." She tapped on the yellow pad where she kept meeting notes.

Before Will could respond, Jess spoke. "I know this probably seems rude, but I haven't had a cheesesteak in forever." She paused. "If you really don't want it, Hannah, would you mind terribly if I ate a little bit?"

Hannah turned, her eyes distant. Jess opened her mouth as though she might retract the request. Hannah seemed to snap back to the present. "No, no, of course not." She turned to Will. "Do you mind?"

Did he mind that he was thinking about her all day? Did he mind that he wanted to have a special night with his wife? Did he mind that, in a stupid way, these cheesesteaks were a kind of peace offering?

Will took a wrapped cheesesteak out of the paper bag and held it out to Jess. "Knock yourself out."

Jess unwrapped the cheesesteak with the same excitement as a little kid opening a birthday present. She took a bite then fed one to John. In the span a minute it was decided that they would divide the cheesesteak into appetizer-sized pieces so the whole group could "taste a bit of heaven." Jess took the steak into the kitchen.

Will stood on the outskirts. He knew he should cut up his own steak, offer it to the group, and participate in the discussion about the fifth grade. He could even offer help with some activity. That would be the right thing to do. Or would it? Hannah should have known why he went to Tony Luke's. Couldn't she have postponed the meeting? Didn't she want to?

Hannah ignored him.

It was just a silly committee. Why did it matter so much? Hannah laughed at something Trent said, touching him lightly on the shoulder. Trent laughed back and they put their heads close together, looking at the same paper. Trent made a note on the pad.

Will watched the exchange, feeling like an intruder in his own home. Hannah laughed for the second time and her hand skimmed Trent's as she took his pen. Will stared at the two of them, anger snaking up his body. He tried in vain to catch Hannah's eye; she remained focused on Trent. Will shook his head and stepped into the kitchen. He grabbed a Rolling Rock from the refrigerator and popped it open. He carried the beer and the giant cheesesteak to the family room and sat in the recliner, five feet from Hannah's meeting. He switched on the television and took off his shoes and socks, dropping them on the floor next to his chair. That's what he would normally do, after all.

Hannah stumbled over her words as Will pushed out the recliner to elevate his bare feet. He rested the unwrapped cheesesteak on his stomach and leaned back, grabbing the remote to turn up the volume.

"Will," Hannah said in the tone she used with their children when she was trying to be very, very patient. "We still have a bit more of our meeting."

"That's alright," Will said, pretending the concern was for him. "I don't mind."

"Do you think you might watch upstairs?"

"Television's broken up there. Remember?" Will leaned back and took a swig of beer. "Don't worry about me. I'll be able to hear fine."

"Hannah," Trent started. "Will just got home. No harm with a little baseball in the background."

Will glanced in their direction, confused as to why Trent was trying to defend him.

Hannah nodded at Trent and continued.

Will should have felt vindicated, but the exchange didn't feel right. It was as though Trent were giving Hannah advice on how to handle her jerk of a husband. What was that about? He found himself unable to concentrate on the game; his cheesesteak grew cold.

The meeting adjourned thirty minutes later. Charlotte remained behind. She and Hannah stood in the kitchen. "I burn over 300 calories every time I run. That's like half a muffin with peanut butter or two scrambled eggs with a piece of plain toast."

Normally, Hannah would have made wide eyes at Will over Charlotte's head as if to say in secret: "Do you believe this?" Instead, she gave Charlotte her full attention. "That many calories? Just from running? I never would have guessed."

Will balled his fists. Did Hannah not care about the effort he'd gone to? The meaning behind it? He moved to the dishwasher and loaded dishes with loud, exaggerated clanks. Charlotte got the hint.

Once she left, Hannah went upstairs to check on the kids, a clear message that he should have checked on them instead of watching baseball. She returned, holding a blanket and pillow.

Will stared at her. "You're not going to sleep upstairs?"

"No, Will, I'm not." She tucked the sheet into the couch with quick, angry gestures. Will watched her in silence.

This was big.

Hannah had always been incredibly fussy about sleep. She was not particular about clothes or cars or jewelry, the last of which she declared "useless," but insisted that their first big purchase as a married couple be a top-of the-line mattress. "The average person spends one-third of their life asleep," she'd argued. Will had been unable to counter and didn't really want to. If his beautiful wife wanted a comfy mattress, she would have one. Thrilled with the purchase, Hannah had dressed the mattress with 1500-thread-count cotton sheets, a comforter lined in fleece, and memory foam pillows. On her side table, she'd placed a scent diffuser which steeped the room with lavender each evening, a scent shown to evoke deep sleep. They'd often joked that, in a divorce, the biggest argument would be over the bed.

It wasn't.

As he watched Hannah smooth the sheets, Will ran over the evening. His intentions had been good. He had only wanted to spend time with her. It shouldn't end like this. "So I went to Tony Luke's…" He left the sentence open, waiting for Hannah to fill in the rest, comment upon the gesture.

She answered by patting the couch cushions.

"I'm not sure why it was a bad thing," he said.

Hannah stood straighter. She put her hand on her hip. "It wasn't the cheesesteaks, Will. It was forgetting again. I know you think it's dumb—"

"I never said that."

Hannah rolled her eyes. "I'm in charge of the committee, Will. I want it to be a success. I wanted you to help me make it a success. I thought it was something we could do together." She slumped on the couch. Will fought to find words.

"And the whole television thing. And taking off your shoes and socks! How embarrassing. For both of us."

Will pictured the scene as it must have looked to Hannah, to her committee. She was leading a meeting and he was sitting watching television with a cheesesteak on his stomach. God. He was an asshole. "I'm sorry."

She shook her head. "It's fine. I just want some space."

Will looked at the made-up couch and at the worn face of his wife. "I'll sleep down here."

She shook her head. "No, I–"

"No, really. I want to." Will picked up a pillow and fluffed it. "See? Perfect." It was the kind of thing that used to make her laugh, but she stared at him, silent.

"Okay," she said finally and started up the stairs. Will heard her footsteps in a steady climb. Then, abruptly, they stopped. No sound as one moment strung on the next. She would come back down.

"Mommy. My throat hurts." Their son Charlie's small voice sliced the silence and the footsteps started up again.

Will stretched out on the couch and grabbed his phone, mindlessly scrolling through various social media accounts, stopping at the latest post from Jess. It was a picture of a cheesesteak with the caption: "Tony Luke's cheesesteaks are to die for. Thanks Hannah Abbott!"

Will shook his head and laid the phone back down. He waited up for Hannah, thinking she might come down after tending to Charlie. She didn't. It was his first night sleeping without his wife.

FOUR

Nine months ago.

Hannah let her anger subside relatively quickly. Will resumed sleeping in the bed. He and Hannah watched television, spoke normally, and managed the kids' schedules. Will was even early for the next fifth grade committee meeting. And, though it seemed normal, it wasn't. Their conversations lacked intimacy; his attempts at humor failed. They slept fully clothed, side by side, like siblings sharing a bed. If Will—and it was almost always Will—made an overture for more, the gesture was met with a promise of "later" or, occasionally, an unsatisfactory, transactional experience.

It felt like he and Hannah were bobbing along a stream in the same direction but simultaneously floating apart. He tried to express the sentiment; she dismissed it. "We're just busy, Will."

So, when Hank, Will's landscaping business partner and best friend, offered box seats to the Phillies game, Will jumped on it. A group of their friends would be there.

The day Hank gave him the tickets, Will found Hannah in the kitchen making dinner. He fanned the tickets out and waved them in front of the skillet. "How would you like to go to a Phillies game?"

Hannah glanced at the date on the tickets, a look of regret momentarily crossing her face. "Will. I have the photography shoot that day with that nice woman, Dorothy Vanderlippe." Her tone took on an edge of irritation. "Remember I met her daughter at that school concert?"

Will had forgotten.

Two years back, Hannah had started a small business photographing elderly people, the first step of her dream to be the Anne Geddes for the old. They'd used nearly all their modest savings to buy photography equipment and print up brochures, the latter of which she'd dropped off at every hospital and nursing home in the area. Charlotte helped her set up a website. She made a Facebook page. For a few weeks, she'd even started a blog. Still, almost no one called. She'd had two clients in two years. So this one, the third, was a big deal. Will should have remembered.

"And Amanda has that swim meet, remember? She qualified with her relay?"

Will leaned against the counter. "Oh. Right."

Hannah put chicken in the skillet. The grease sizzled; Hannah turned the heat down.

"Maybe I could take Charlie?"

Hannah moved the chicken around. "Why don't you just go with the guys? I can take Charlie to the swim meet. Your mom could watch the kids during the photo shoot." She flipped the pieces over.

It was a grand gesture. Hannah would take care of everything and he would enjoy a night with his friends. But there was more to it. To Hannah, Will was a parental doofus, incapable of watching a seven-year-old at a baseball game. He would feed Charlie the wrong food, let him get sunburned. He might even lose him! Will believed that, in Hannah's mind, it was entirely possible that he would drive halfway home alone, thinking, "I feel like I left something at the ballpark..."

It was an unfair assessment of his parenting abilities. "I'm okay to take him."

Hannah cut into the center of a chicken breast. "Maybe we could all go another time," she offered. "That would be fun. Remember last year?" She removed the breasts and put them on a plate.

They went a few more rounds until, finally, Will relented. He'd go by himself and she'd stay with both kids. "Perfect," she'd said with a perfunctory kiss on his cheek. "You'll have a blast."

On the day of the game, Amanda sat at the kitchen table in her swimsuit eating an egg salad sandwich. Next to her, Charlie dipped celery in cream cheese. Hannah stood in the kitchen, phone to ear, cutting up oranges for a team snack. "Have fun," she mouthed at Will. Will nodded at her, then turned his attention to the kids.

"Good luck, A," Will said, punching Amanda lightly on the shoulder.

"Thanks, Dad."

He rumpled Charlie's hair. "Should we see the Star Wars movie tomorrow?"

"Yes!" Stray bits of cream cheese and celery flew out of his mouth and landed on the table.

"Gross, Charlie," Amanda yelled. "You shouldn't talk with your mouth full."

Charlie opened his mouth wide, a mass of chewed up celery visible.

"Oh my God, Charlie, stop it." Amanda turned to Will. "Dad, make him stop it."

"Charlie, stop," Will said.

Charlie stuck a celery-covered tongue out. Will gave him a "you better not do that again" look.

"Wh'd I do?" Charlie asked, his expression innocent.

Before Will could respond, Hannah hung up the phone. "Enough, you two." She pointed her finger at Charlie. He shut his mouth with an audible click.

Hannah kissed Will on cheek. It felt like a dismissal. "Have fun," she said cheerily.

"Thanks." Will reluctantly turned and walked out of the room. When he reached the door, he stopped. "Hey, good luck with the shoot."

There was no answer. He stood for a moment, debating if he should say it again. When the blender started up, he left. He could text Hannah from the game.

By the time Will arrived at the stadium, Hank's second-level club box was filled with a dozen high school friends and acquaintances. At the top of the box, several people sat at a covered bar next to a buffet of hot dogs, chicken fingers, and fries. Steep stairs led down to the seats for the game. The box looked out on third base.

Kat saw him first. "Well, if it isn't William Abbott," she said in a flirtatious tone.

"Hey, Kat."

He reached her and gave her a kiss on the cheek. She dipped her head toward the group seats. "Scotty saved a seat for you." She winked.

Will looked at the empty seat next to Scotty. "Lucky me."

Scotty had spent $15,000 on his two-year divorce, and every conversation snaked back to his ex-wife. The last time they'd been out, he'd cornered Will for nearly an hour.

"I'll have a drink first." Will said. He ordered a Rolling Rock, then a second, half-watching the game, half-talking to Kat. He was about to go sit with Scotty when a girl, no older than twenty-five, made a beeline for Kat. She had ringlets of long, dark hair and wide brown eyes. Large breasts spilled out of her V-neck, black sundress. She embraced Kat.

Will's eyes widened. "Who is that?" he mouthed.

Kat let go of the girl and smiled. "Amber Mitchell, this is Will Abbott. Will Abbott, this is Amber Mitchell."

"Amber," Will repeated. "Pretty name." He could kick himself. Pretty name? Who says that?

"Thanks," Amber said. They stood in silence.

Will searched his mind of a topic of conversation. Finally, he cleared his throat. "How do you know Kat?"

"We met at the gym. We're in the same spin class. I'd seen Kat before but, one day, she dropped her bag in the locker room and it spilled everywhere." She gestured her hands in demonstration. "I was helping her clean it up and I picked up her license and saw that we live in the same neighborhood." She spoke with such enthusiasm, Will half expected her to clap in delight.

"I see Amber almost every day," Kat interjected, with a quick, private wink for Will's benefit.

Just then, Scotty joined their group. Will was about to greet him when he sidestepped Will's extended hand to hug Amber. "Amber! Great to see you."

Scotty released Amber and turned to Will. "How do you know Amber?" Will asked.

"Amber runs a support group for a local divorce attorney. I've been attending for a few months. She does a great job, a fantastic job." Scotty gave Amber a double thumbs-up.

"I don't really run it," Amber corrected. "I usually just stop by with food."

"Well it's great food and there's always tons of it." Scotty clapped her shoulder.

Amber smiled, her teeth a ridiculous shade of white.

Kat gestured to a table overlooking the field. "Should we sit?"

They carried their drinks to the table and sat. Scotty ordered a pitcher of beer and Kat got a plate of food for the group. Congenial conversation passed as they watched the game. Scotty ordered another pitcher and Kat replenished their plate of food. Will lost track of how many drinks he'd consumed.

By the seventh inning stretch, he was drunk.

As the four of them left the stadium after the game, Scotty rapped Will on the shoulder. "You should come out with us." He gestured to Kat and Amber.

Amber pulled on his arm. "Yes! You should come." Her lips pouted slightly. Was she flirting with him?

He should go home. But what was one more drink? Hannah had given him the night off responsibilities. He should take advantage of that. Right?

He looked at Amber, whose brown eyes now seemed to have a pleading expression. "Okay," he said finally, "just for one more." He'd text Hannah when he got to the bar.

The smoke-filled bar near the stadium was loud and crowded. Will forgot about texting Hannah. After navigating the mass of people to find an open spot, Kat went to the bar and purchased a round of shots. They downed them; Scotty brought a second round. After finishing the shots, Amber suggested they go to a different bar and they collectively agreed. Once outside, Will heard the familiar ping of the text message. He pulled out his phone. He'd missed seven texts and two phone calls.

Stopping mid-stagger, Will held up his phone to the group. "Wait, wait. I just got a text message." The group stopped. "It's from Hannah." He pointed to the phone. "It says, 'I'm getting worried. Where are you?'"

"Where are you?" Scotty said in a mock tone. Amber punched him on the arm.

Will wrote Hannah a message and sent a selfie of the group. She never responded.

FIVE

At the second bar, Will squeezed into a booth next to Amber; Kat and Scotty sat across from them. After a round of beers, one of Amber's friends, also in a black dress, showed up and slid into the booth. Amber introduced her as Raven and Scotty made a stupid joke about Edgar Allen Poe. Not long after the Poe joke, another of Amber's friends appeared in a black dress. Then a third. They ordered another pitcher of beer. More girls came. They squished into the booth and surrounded the sides of the table.

Scotty and Kat left together. Amber's friends filled in the space they'd left vacant. Will was now alone with ten girls. To his surprise, they seemed to want to talk to him. He showed them pictures of Amanda in her swimsuit and of Charlie on the high dive. He showed them the family selfie on the giant Ferris wheel in Wildwood, taken during their vacation last summer. Finally, he pulled up a picture of Hannah which had been his screensaver for years. It was a close-up of her in their yard, hair gently blowing, on one of those perfect sunny days where the sky was so blue it almost seemed fake. "This is my wife."

"She's beautiful," one of the girls proclaimed as she passed the phone.

"Stunning eyes," said another.

"How long have you been married?" Raven tipped the phone forward as she asked the question.

"Fourteen years." Will said it with pride.

Raven handed Will his phone just as an employee tapped a microphone. "Ladies and gentlemen," he started. "It's time for Karaoke Cuts! I see a lot of groups out there. This should be good! I'm psyched! Are we ready to rock and roll!?" The patrons cheered; a few girls at Will's booth banged the table. "Our esteemed judges are in the house!" The man pointed to three individuals behind a long table. "We're looking for skill, originality, humor. And keep it clean, y'all. Winning group gets a thousand bucks!" Cheers erupted around the bar. The girls in Will's booth began to high five one another.

Will took in the girls' reactions. The black dresses made sense now. The girls were there to perform.

"Let's go, Singing Sisters," the announcer called out and a group of women wearing yellow raincoats headed to the stage. Once in formation, "It's Raining Men" blasted from the speakers. Will sang along from the booth, nodding his head to the beat. Amber smiled at him.

When the group finished, the announcer took the stage again. "Diamond Girls. You're up!"

The girls in Will's booth stood. Amber grabbed his hand, pulling him up in the process. "Help us win," she whispered as she led him toward the stage. "Just follow along."

Intoxicated beyond the point of either embarrassment or reason, Will followed the group up on to the stage. There was light applause as they took their places. Amber moved Will to the center and shifted to his left. "Single Ladies" by Beyoncé roared from the speakers. Will smiled. He knew this song. He bobbed his head to the beat and moved in the same way as the girls. At the refrain, the girls held their hands out and sang. Will followed along, moving his hands from side to side in the same way as the girls. He belted out the next part so loudly the girls stopped their own singing to defer to his. He was in the center now, singing and choreographing his own moves. He was so lost in the song and the moment that he didn't notice camera flashes or iPhones on videotape. At the end of the number, the girls clustered around him as though he were the beloved lead in a high school musical.

The karaoke routine was Will's last recollection.

Will woke with a start. He blinked, trying to get a fix on his surroundings. He lay on hard couch with a handmade afghan pulled over his fully-clothed body. He sat up. His head pounded. Where was he?

A glass of water sat on an end table next to his cell phone and wallet. Instinctively, he reached for his phone and pulled up his messages. The "group" selfie to Hannah filled the screen. He could see now it was just he and Amber in the picture; Kat and Scotty had been cut out. The message underneath was gibberish. No.

No. No. No.

Will put the phone down and pushed himself up from the couch. He blundered to the bathroom, trying to recall the events from last night. After a brief fumble with the light switch, he moved to the bathroom mirror and did a double take. Jesus. Someone had taken markers and drawn orange and black lines all over his face. He looked like a tiger. In a different circumstance, Will would have thought the whole thing a great crack up. He'd have played the part, found the culprits, and roared at them, raising his hand in a mock territorial gesture. But, today, he felt sick. Physically sick and sick about Hannah. God! What was she thinking? How would he get all the marker off his face? How could he even explain where he'd been?

And where was his car?

Will closed the bathroom door behind him and looked around the apartment. It was clean with heavy, expensive-looking furnishings. Fresh flowers sat on a mahogany table. Will looked around for mail or some other indication of the owners. Finding none, he started up the stairs. Midway, he stopped himself. He should just go home. Will stepped outside and found the house number and street. He took out his cell and called Scotty.

"Hang tight," Scotty said after Will's explained the situation. "I'll be there in ten minutes."

Will sat on the step of the brownstone, tiger-faced, and waited. Several joggers ran past. Some of them didn't notice him; others did a double take. After what seemed like much longer than ten minutes, Scotty's Mustang pulled up. Will stood. He felt like a teenager being picked up by his parent after a party.

Scotty rolled down the window. "What's up, pussycat?"

Will shook his head and opened the door to the car. "Not funny, Scotty." He slammed the door. "I really need to get home."

Scotty snorted. "Like that? What do you think Hannah will say?"

Will put his head in his hands. "I have no fucking idea."

Scotty put his hand on his shoulder. "Alright. Calm down. You can clean up at my place." He started the car. "It will be alright, man. It's not a CATastrophe or anything."

Will glared.

"You're just FUR-tunate that Hannah hasn't seen you yet," Scotty joked.

Will leaned his head back on the seat. "Come on, man."

"Alright, alright. Sorry." Scotty drove Will to his apartment in silence.

Will scrubbed the Sharpie marker off his skin, red patches of irritation left behind from the effort. Once his face was clean, Scotty delivered him back to his car at the stadium. On the way home, Will stopped and bought Hannah a bouquet of purple irises. Her favorite. Was there a chance she'd find the whole thing funny?

Will crept in the house and stopped at the kitchen door. Hannah and the kids were in the middle of breakfast. He hovered on the outskirts, watching. When Hannah glanced up and saw him, her face registered relief. Then, too soon, the expression was replaced by one of disgust.

Will stepped forward and handed her the flowers. "I can explain," he said in a low voice.

"Dad!" Charlie ran over and hugged him. "We made the daffles!" He pointed to a plate of waffles immersed in powdered sugar. Will shut his eyes. Shit. He usually made waffles on Sundays: Dad waffles. Daffles. It was his thing. The existence of the waffles, made without his presence, made him feel worse.

"That's great, buddy," Will said, trying to catch Hannah's eye as she put the irises in water. "They look delicious."

"Have one!" Charlie slapped a waffle down on a plate.

"In a minute, buddy," he said, moving toward Hannah.

"Where were you?" Amanda asked.

Will didn't answer. He moved toward Hannah. "Can we talk?" he whispered. She arranged the irises. "Please," Will whispered.

She looked up at him, then nodded imperceptibly.

"Just going to talk to your mom for a minute," Will told Charlie. "Then I'll come back and have one of those daffles."

Will followed Hannah into their bedroom and shut the door. "I'm so sorry," he started. "I got drunk." Hannah stood at the door, her arms crossed, staring at the floor.

"Who was the girl?" she asked, finally, her voice measured.

"The girl?"

"In the picture?"

Will remembered the selfie. "Oh. A friend of Kat's. I don't know her."

"Well, where've you been?

"Scotty's." Will looked down. He had never lied to Hannah before.

"And why didn't you call?

"Because I was passed out."

"Why didn't Scotty call?"

"I don't know, Hannah. We were drunk, okay. I'm sorry. I can't remember the last time I was drunk." Will's head pounded. He should have taken a Tylenol at Scotty's.

Hannah began to twist her hair, a sign she was thinking. Will's heart lifted. Maybe it would be okay.

Amanda's voice pierced the moment. "Give it back, Charlie!" Hannah turned toward the door.

"Hold on," Will said. "They'll work it out." Heavy footfalls sounded outside their door. Then Charlie's voice. "Okay, okay. Do you want to play Mario Kart?"

"Yes," Amanda responded, and the footsteps retreated back down the stairs.

"Hey," Will said, remembering. "How did the photo shoot go?"

Hannah's face lit up. "It was amazing. The lighting was perfect and Dorothy looked beautiful. I think they were happy." She paused. "It might be a breakthrough."

"Awesome! You deserve it." Will crossed the room to hug her. Hannah held her hand out.

"You stink of cigarettes and beer."

"I guess I should shower then."

"I think you should." She smiled. Will exhaled. She wasn't mad. He felt ten pounds lighter as he pulled his T-shirt over his head.

Hannah's eyes widened. Will looked down. Written on his chest, in red, were eight pretty signatures with the caption "Diamond Girls."

SIX

Hannah

A week after the incident, Hannah invited Charlotte over for coffee and explained what had happened.

"So, do you believe him?" Charlotte asked when Hannah finished the story.

"I don't know. I think." Hannah clicked the YouTube video again. Will was clearly drunk.

Charlotte tipped the screen toward her. "Who was that girl in the selfie again?"

"A friend of Kat's." Hannah watched her husband weave about the stage on the small screen. She shook her head. "He's such a man-child."

Charlotte leaned closer. "But he's your man-child." She picked off a piece of coffee cake and popped it in her mouth. "And he doesn't usually drink, right?"

"No," Hannah admitted as Will slurred on screen.

"And he asked you to go to the game?"

"Yes."

Charlotte pushed the coffee cake away with an emphatic gesture. "So he couldn't have planned it. I mean, it wasn't premeditated or anything." She stressed the word premeditated.

"Look," Hannah said, clicking off the video. "All I know is Will didn't come home on Saturday. When he finally showed up, he had a bunch of girls' signatures on him. Don't you think I have a right to be upset?"

Charlotte tilted her head. "Well, have you told him about Trent?"

Hannah went still. "What do you mean?"

"About the photography classes you two are taking together."

She hadn't. She had asked Will to take one with her; he wasn't interested. Trent jumped on the idea. It wasn't her fault Trent liked photography.

"It's not the same thing. It's just a class."

"Which you are taking with another man." Charlotte reached across the table and took another chunk of coffee cake. "Ugh!" she said after swallowing. "This thing has to be a gazillion calories. I'll be on the Stairmaster forever."

Hannah picked up the coffee cake and grabbed cellophane from the cabinet.

"I think you should tell him."

"He'll just think it's weird. He has this thing about Trent."
Hannah recalled Will rolling his eyes when she'd mentioned that
Trent had started composting.

Charlotte shrugged. "All the more reason to tell him." She
looked at her watch and then stood. "I better get going."

Hannah walked her to the door. "I'll consider it."

"He's a good man, Hannah. Don't forget that."

Hannah bristled at the comment. Her husband gets drunk and
fails to come home, yet somehow, she's the bad guy. That was the
magic of Will Abbott. Everyone loved him. No matter what.

"Bye, Charlotte. Thanks for listening."

Hannah closed the door behind her friend then watched the
video again. As ridiculous as he looked, she had to admit Will was
handsome. Tall with broad shoulders, easy happy smile, tiny lines
of middle age around his striking blue eyes. Underneath his shirt,
Hannah knew, lay rippled muscles and a perfectly haired chest.

She watched him among the cluster of women on the video.
They appeared to like him. Of course they did.

Hannah clicked off the video and started in on the breakfast
dishes, her mind on Charlotte's words: "All the more reason to
tell him." Really. Charlotte should have been outraged by Will's
behavior, not hers. He was the one weaving about drunk with a
bunch of young women. He was the one who arrived home with
signatures on his body. He was the one who hadn't called.

She was only taking a class with a friend.

Hannah scrubbed a nearly-clean pot, intense hot water red-
dening her skin.

She hadn't done anything wrong.

Had she?

Trent had come to Dorothy's photography shoot at the park
on the night of the Phillies game. He'd insisted that she needed

help setting up. And she did need help. It wasn't as though Will had remembered it or would have wanted to go if he had. He would have stayed home and watched the Phillies on television. She was sure of it.

Hannah registered that her hands were starting to burn from the hot water. She pulled them back and waved the water off. She examined the pot. It was more than clean. As she dried it, she remembered Trent's gentle manner as he escorted ninety-two-year-old Dorothy to her place on the stool, his tall body towering over her tiny frame. He'd stood under a tree with Dorothy's daughter, watching her work.

Hannah flushed at the recollection then shook her head as if to remove the image by force. Still, Trent's words formed in her mind as clear as if he'd been standing in the room. "That was amazing! The lighting was perfect. You really captured her. I love how you used the tree limbs as a frame." They'd stood in the park as the light faded, heads together as she showed him the shots on camera. He'd smelled like Irish Spring soap.

Hannah put away the pot, slamming the cabinet door shut with more force than she intended.

Did she believe him?

She picked up her phone and flipped on the video again, watching with scrutiny. She saw her then. The girl from the selfie. Kat's friend. Hannah took a screenshot and enlarged the image. It was her. And she was definitely staring at Will. Hannah watched the video anew, eyes now trained on the girl. She seemed to be watching Will throughout the routine; she was the first to encircle him at the end, her face next his, white teeth framed by red lips.

She went back to Will's text message. Same smile.

Did she believe him?

She checked the clock. Shoot. The kids' camp ended at three and she needed to get to the grocery store and the mall. She found her shoes and bag then picked up her phone, the strange woman's pretty face temporarily illuminating the screen. Hannah switched it off. She shook her head. Enough, Hannah. Enough.

But unease had already taken root inside her.

Once at the store, Hannah lost her grocery list and found herself walking haphazardly through the aisles, picking items at random. In the check-out line, she viewed the items in her cart as though they had been put there by a stranger. She'd picked Oreos? She walked out of the store in a daze. In the parking lot of the Acme, Hannah took a deep breath, loaded the groceries, and got in the car.

Get it together.

As she drove to the mall, Hannah tried to banish any thoughts of the video, the signatures on Will's stomach, the fact that he hadn't come home. She heard her mother's words: "You can never trust anyone, Hannah."

She recalled the day those words were uttered, the day she'd come home from school and found her mother forcefully cleaning with loud, erratic movements. "So your father's moving out. Apparently, we're not good enough for him." Her mother had continued to clean, her jagged movements and angry voice so foreign to Hannah's ten-year-old self that she'd started to cry.

"You can never really trust anyone, Hannah."

Hannah had never forgotten the words but, until now, she never doubted Will. What would she do if something happened to her marriage? She'd quit her job at the nursing home when the kids were small; they relied entirely on Will's income. And what would happen to Charlie and Amanda? She'd want them all the time. Will would too.

She drove, thinking of traumatic, post-divorce scenarios. In one she lived, destitute and alone, her time with her children relegated to token days here and there. In another vision, she worked full-time and assumed all responsibility for the kids, Will taking the role of the fun weekend parent. Significant others. Holidays. Vacations alone. Hannah heart quickened as she drove. It would be awful.

As she neared the turn off for the mall parking lot, a billboard came into view. It depicted three male attorneys. On the side, the firm's practice areas were listed in bold letters. Number three: divorce. Hannah pulled to the shoulder.

There was nothing wrong with getting information. It would make her feel better to be prepared. It didn't mean she was getting a divorce. Or that she wanted a divorce. All it meant is that she would know what to expect if the worst happened.

Which it wouldn't.

But if it did.

Cars whizzed by. Hannah stared at the three supersized men on the sign.

"You can never trust anyone, Hannah."

She dialed the number.

SEVEN

Well before the designated appointment time, Hannah pulled into the parking lot of Tremblay, Rubin, and Connors. She sat in her car and, for a moment, considered leaving. It seemed crazy. She didn't want a divorce. But things between her and Will weren't right either.

She would get information and leave.

That's it.

No harm.

As Hannah exited the vehicle, one of Charlie's art projects from camp fluttered out of the minivan to the ground. Hannah picked it up and, though she'd seen it before, looked at the drawing with new eyes. It was a fingerprint picture of their family. The fingerprint depicting Will was bigger and bolder than the rest, clearly made with Charlie's thumb. She noted that Amanda's print was set slightly further apart and that her own held Charlie's hand. Each tiny figure had a smile and stick legs and arms. Hannah hand shook as she held the photo; she visualized Charlie making it, his tongue out in concentration.

A car door slammed, and Hannah's attention was brought back to the moment. She folded the picture and placed it carefully in her purse.

She took a deep breath.

It was just information.

Hannah sat in the pristine waiting room for what seemed like an hour. She kept her head buried in a Cooking Light magazine, reading and re-reading the same paragraph about dream picnics. The man in the article looked at bit like Will. Hannah stared at the smiling stranger and pictured Will at their home barbeque, spatula in hand. She didn't want a divorce. Why was she here?

A woman in a fitted black suit came into the reception area and looked at her. "Hannah Abbott?"

Hannah resisted the urge to tell the woman to lower her voice. Instead she waved her hand in a limp gesture which, had she not been the only one in the room, may have gone unnoticed.

The woman, very young, extended her hand. "Hello, I'm Rachel Goldstein, an attorney here. Mr. Connors just called. Unfortunately, he's going to be a little late. He asked me to take your information." The woman gestured for her to follow. Hannah looked at the door to the office. She should leave.

"This way, please."

There was something about Rachel's voice that compelled Hannah to follow her. With a final glance to the door, she followed the Rachel's brisk, clipped gait. They reached a small office with black furnishings. Once inside, Rachel closed the door and sat in a huge leather chair behind a sleek, black desk. Two gold-framed photographs sat on the shelf behind her. One showed a fluffy white cat on a pink satin pillow. The other was of the woman with a man her age in Downtown Disney. Hannah's breath caught. It was "the spot."

A few months into their relationship, Hannah had booked a surprise trip to Disneyworld. She'd picked Will up at work and drove directly to the airport. When Will saw the planes and the twinkling lights of the runways, he smiled and shook his head.

"I don't know where you are taking me, Hannah Bennett," he'd said, "but I am all yours." Having limited funds for park tickets, they had spent an excessive amount of time in Downtown Disney eating greasy food from cheap carts and pretending to be in the market for expensive merchandise.

On the last night, after a full day of watching overstimulated children truck about after their parents, they'd sat at a shady table in comfortable silence at the end of the boardwalk. Hannah could visualize the moment as though it were happening in front of her: her slowly sipping a vanilla latte, Will licking a fat ice cream cone. A fiery red sun slid behind the landscape, the last rays illuminating Will's face.

He squeezed her hand. "I love you, Hannah."

She shut her eyes.

"So. You're here for a divorce." Rachel's voice assaulted the memory.

Hannah snapped back to the present, strangely alarmed by the word "divorce." "No, no. I told the assistant for Mr. Connors that I just wanted information."

"Information about divorce?" Rachel said, slowly.

"Well, yes. Just what would happen? You know. In case." Hannah fumbled with her words.

Rachel started with basic questions. How long had she been married? How many kids? How old were they? How old was she? How old was Will?

"What do you do for a living?" Rachel asked.

"I'm a photographer," Hannah said, though she had never once described herself that way. "I own my own business."

Rachel looked intrigued and, though she had no reason to care, Hannah felt gratified.

"How much did you earn last year? Approximately."

With the question out there, Hannah suddenly felt silly. She wasn't really a photographer. She'd earned less than a thousand dollars. "I'm not sure," she answered after too long a pause.

"I don't know what photographers make so just give me a ballpark figure. We can always change it later." Rachel tapped her pen on the desk.

Hannah picked a piece of lint off her pants. "It's a new business. I didn't make much."

Rachel waited, and when Hannah wasn't forthcoming with more, she moved on.

"Okay. Your husband, then?" She looked at the pad. "Will?"

His name felt wrong coming out of Rachel's mouth, and Hannah didn't respond right away.

"Will?" Rachel said again, pen poised.

The words came out in a tumble. "He owns a landscaping and contracting business with a friend. Studs and Buds."

Rachel's face broke into a smile. "Studs and Buds. I've seen their trucks around. I love that name!"

"The name was my idea." Hannah blurted out, having no idea why she felt a need to impress this woman. But it was true. They'd been drinking at Kat's house, brainstorming names for the new business. The proposed names ranged from boring (HC Contractors) to the ridiculous (Hosta Hotties). Hannah had come up with Studs and Buds to a flurry of high fives. "That's it!" Will had yelled excitedly. "That's it! You're a genius!" He'd kissed her full on the mouth.

"Good one," Rachel said, her voice carrying a twinge of pity. Hannah cursed herself.

Rachel asked questions about Will's income, their retirement assets, and their home, dutifully recording her answers. They didn't have much.

Rachel's phone buzzed and she picked up the receiver. When she put it down, she looked at Hannah. "Jack Connors is ready to see you now."

Hannah blindly followed Rachel past cubicles of suited office-workers surrounded by stacks of paper. She bumped into a water cooler, accidentally dislodging the cone-shaped cups affixed to its side. She bent down to pick them up. Rachel seemed not to realize and continued striding ahead. Hannah placed the cups on top of the cooler and stepped quickly to catch up to Rachel.

They stopped at a large corner office. When they entered, Jack Connors stood up from behind a huge desk. His reddish hair, tinged with gray, was slicked back with gel, his face wrinkled but tan. He looked like a man fighting the onset of middle age.

"Hannah." He smiled and reached over to shake her hand. "Jack Connors. Please sit." As she sat, Hannah scanned the office. Like Rachel's, all the furnishings were black. There were few papers on the desk and one photo of Jack fishing with two teen-aged children.

From her vantage point in the chair adjacent to Rachel, Hannah could see the notes she'd taken during their meeting. She'd written in large, swirly print, the letters "H" and "W" peppered throughout. "H" and "W"? For Hannah and Will? Husband and Wife?

"Rachel?" Jack Connors prompted.

Rachel consulted her notes and read through like she was reciting a grocery list. "Fourteen-year marriage. Two kids, ages seven and eleven. Hannah has a new photography business. Doesn't know what she made last year. Said it wasn't much. Her husband is part owner of a landscaping and home improvement business. His income varies. House has about seventy-five thousand in equity. There's an IRA with twenty-two thousand."

Hannah sat still, startled by the entirety of her marriage being summarized in a few sentences. She was still digesting why it bothered her when Jack Connors sprang forward in his chair. "Do you think he hides money?"

Hannah shook her head. "Will? No. I mean, I don't know. How would I know?"

Jack leaned back and made a steeple with his fingers. "It's just tricky, those guys with their own businesses. I represented the wife of a plumber and this guy, he managed to hide over a million dollars right under her nose." He paused. "We found it though."

"I don't think Will would hide money," Hannah said. "I don't think it would even occur to him." She pictured Will stashing money in some secret place. Knowing Will, he'd forget where he put it. She suppressed a smile then added, "Really. I don't."

"You'd be surprised," Jack said, unable to let the subject drop. "Keep your eyes open." When Hannah didn't respond, he continued, "Look. We'll get you permanent alimony. Do you want the kids?"

"Yes. Of course."

"Is your husband a good dad? Is he active with the kids?"

"Yes. I mean, I do most of the care but—"

"Look, we'll ask for sole custody. That way you can call the shots. And child support. We'll get that too."

A tall woman with bright lipstick entered the office. "David Dewey's here for the Knights dep." She handed a stack of letters to Jack.

"Court reporter?" Jack asked as he scrawled his name on each page.

"She's all set up in the conference room. The clients are here." The woman took the papers back.

Jack Connors stood up and adjusted his jacket. "Hannah, it was nice to meet you." He shook her hand again. "Rachel will take care of you. She'll get that complaint filed. You'll be fine." He tapped her on the shoulder. "We'll find any hidden money."

Hannah opened her mouth but, before she could formulate a response, Jack Connors breezed out.

Hannah looked at Rachel, who sat staring at the open door.

"Well, I guess that's it," Rachel said finally as she stood. "You'll call if you want to file a complaint for divorce."

"Right." It was all Hannah could manage to say.

Rachel led the way back out, Hannah trailing behind. At the front desk, Rachel handed her one of Jack's cards. Hannah stuffed it in her purse on top of Charlie's fingerprint family.

"You can pay the consultation fee here at the desk." Rachel smiled and gestured toward the receptionist.

"That will be three hundred and seventy-five dollars," the receptionist said sweetly.

Hannah pulled out her wallet, her fingers brushing the thick business card with Jack's name emblazoned in bold capital letters.

All she had wanted was information.

EIGHT

Hannah's feet pounded and sweat trickled down the side of her face as she ran through her small, tree-lined neighborhood. What kind of consultation was that? She had learned absolutely nothing. Three hundred and seventy-five dollars wasted.

Hannah continued past her normal stopping point, the pounding of the run cathartic. She looped around the neighborhood, bright sun warming her face. Birds chirped. She inhaled the scent of fresh-cut grass. She stopped in front of her house, breathless. From her vantage point in the driveway, she saw the package.

She stepped forward to get it, knowing without looking who it would be from. Rose Bennett. Her mother. Hannah had gotten used to her mom's packages, part of the latest Mom/Walter fad. She picked it up and went inside.

Her mother had met Walter when Hannah was a high school senior; they were now married and living in Florida. The two rotated passions regularly. There had been the composting fad and the organic garden fad. And the Christmas they had donated livestock in the children's names as a gift. It took forever to for Hannah to convince Charlie and Amanda that, no, there would not be real sheep under the tree.

Their latest passion was minimalism. "Excess belongings are a burden," her mother had informed her in a phone call before the first package arrived.

At least once a week, a box arrived containing relics of Hannah's childhood—the Christmas tablecloth, a pewter bowl, and old photographs. It had irritated Hannah that, in freeing her own space, her mother never considered that she was cluttering hers. She'd been set to say something, but Will told her not to worry about it.

"It's not worth an argument," he'd said. "Besides, I like seeing your old things. Like this." He'd pointed to a ladybug picture Hannah had made when she was six. She'd been so insulted that her mother had sent it back that Will taped it to their own refrigerator. "Look what your mother made," he'd told the kids that night. "This ladybug painting is going to be worth big bucks someday." He smiled at her over their heads and she'd felt better. Months later, it was still there.

Package in hand, Hannah grabbed a glass of water and sat on the back screened-in porch. She could hear the trickling water of the koi pond, the sound of the birds in the yard. A warm breeze blew through the small space.

Hannah peeled the tape off the package. She opened the box and felt dozens of tiny balls of bubble wrap inside. She pulled one out, unwrapped it, and took a breath. The crystal cat! From her childhood collection. She set the cat on the windowsill and unwrapped a crystal dolphin. She placed it next to the cat. Hannah continued the process until there were a dozen animals displayed on the windowsill. The sun hit the crystals and created small rainbows. Hannah sat in the midst of the thin bands of color and breathed in. She felt relaxed for the first time all day.

Hannah glanced down and noticed there was more in the box. She reached into the package and pulled a stack of letters. She paged through them and realized that they were the letters she'd written to her mother when she and Walter had lived in England. Her happiness over the crystal collection vanished. Really? It was too rude. Hannah found her mother's note on the bundle. "I found these when I was cleaning out old papers. I thought you might get a kick of out them. More to come. M."

Hannah shook her head. She opened the first letter and read:

March 20, 1999

Dear Mom,

Wow! You sound like you are having the best time. Thanks for the pictures. I think the ones of Buckingham Palace are my favorite. I love the one of you with the guards. I can't believe they don't move at all! Please thank Walter for the coins.

Things are fine here. I have A's so far in my core classes but a B in Archery. Can you believe that? The teacher takes it really seriously. I couldn't hit the fake deer so he gave me a C on the last assessment. He says if I were in the wilderness, I wouldn't be able to eat. I am not planning to live in the wilderness. I just want to be a dentist!

One exciting thing. Will Abbott from next door asked me to go out with him. We got cheesesteaks in the city. I think he was just bored but it was still fun. I changed his flat on the way down there. I think he was shocked! Well, back to studying. Love and miss you.

Hannah

Hannah shut her eyes and visualized Will on the day of their first date. He'd been so adorable in his gray T-shirt, newly grown stubble on his jaw. He'd been so shocked when she changed his tire! She smiled at the memory, opened her eyes, and read the next letter.

November 6, 1999

Dear Mom,

The Thames River cruise sounded fun! I am glad you are able to take a course at Oxford. That must be really cool.

I am doing lots of things with Will. We joined a rock-climbing gym. I am actually really good at rock climbing! We also got a six-game pack for the 76ers. I think they are going to be good. I included a picture from Halloween. I had to diet for a month to fit into that Catwoman costume. Isn't Will a great Batman?

I understand about Christmas. If you have a chance to go to Switzerland, you have to go! No worries. Mrs. Abbott invited me to come there so I won't be alone.

Talk to you soon. Miss you.

Hannah

Hannah put the letter on her lap and pictured Will in his Batman costume, running in the yard to show off his billowing cape. She could taste his mom's special Christmas cookies and remembered how kind she was when Hannah had spent Christmas there that first year. Will's mom always got three presents for each of her kids because, in the Abbott house, you didn't get more gifts than Jesus. That year, under the tree, there were three packages, wrapped and ribboned, with Hannah's name on them too. Hannah remembered she had cried.

Hannah opened the third letter.

January 15, 2000

Mom,

Your pictures from Switzerland are unbelievable. Maybe you should be the professional photographer! I see you went skiing. I did too. Will and I went to the Poconos after Christmas. We got one of those rooms with the heart shaped hot tub outside. Will is an amazing skier. I spent most of my time on the bunny slope, but I am improving. We are going to go again with his high school group at the end of this month. They all rented a big house.

We can talk about this on the phone next time you call but I am only going to take two classes at Mercer this semester. I picked up some extra hours at the nursing home.

Don't be mad but Will and I got a dog from the SPCA! He's a ten-year-old bulldog mix. His name is Newman. Don't worry. He lives at Will's Mom's house.

Love you, love you, love you. Hannah

Hannah pictured Will outside of Newman's cage, unable to move from the hopeful, wagging dog with the big cherry-sized tumor under his eye. She could hear his voice. "No one will pick him. We've got to save him." She could feel Will's muscled, tight body as they sat, entwined, in the steam-covered hot tub outside their Pocono room. She opened the last letter.

March 30, 2000

Mom,

We are back from Disneyworld! I know you will be happy that I finally got to go after I bugged you about it for so many years. Check out the pictures! I did get mouse ears. Will is set to surprise me back. I think he has something planned for this weekend because he is acting very strange. He is the worst secret-keeper.

Newman is good. Will and Hank are thinking of starting their own landscaping business. I am considering taking a full-time job at the nursing home. We can talk about it when you visit in May.

Cool that you got to go to St. Paul's Cathedral for Easter! I went to church with Will's family and then to a big celebration they have at his aunt's house. They have ridiculous relays like running with an egg on a spoon. I laughed so hard, I almost fell over. And I met tons of cousins I didn't even know he had.

See you in May.

Love, H

Hannah put the letters on her lap and squeezed her eyes shut. How had she forgotten so many good times? And, although she was too practical to believe in divine intervention, the arrival of the letters smacked of coincidence. On the day she'd gone to a lawyer to talk about divorce, she'd been reminded of the good times. In her own handwriting, no less.

The back door reverberated. "I'm home," Will called out.

"Hey hon." She held the letters behind her back.

"Hey, hi." Will brushed her cheek with a quick kiss. "I am in need of a shower." He gestured to his sweat-drenched shirt.

Without saying more, Will started up the stairs. Hannah wanted to stop him, to show him the letters, but Amanda charged down with a towel. "I'm supposed to go to Daria's house for her pool party, remember?" she said to both parents.

"Got it," Hannah said to Will. She put the letters in a drawer and went to get her keys.

Hannah drove Amanda to the party. When she returned, Charlie and Will were gone to help his sister fix her sliding glass door. He texted that they were grabbing a bite to eat on the way home.

The phone rang. It was Jess. Hannah was still on the phone when Will walked in.

She picked Amanda up.

Will put Charlie to bed.

He scheduled a few more jobs.

Hannah checked her emails.

When she came to bed, Will was asleep. Hannah stared at him, this version of her husband. He was so different from the Will in the letters. Less free, less spontaneous. Had she made him that way?

Hannah stared at Will's sleeping figure until her eyes became heavy. Right before falling asleep, she reached out and laid her hand on his.

NINE

In the early morning sun, the signatures on Will's torso had faded to a barely-perceptible outline. They would fade further and disappear over time. Hannah knew she should let the memory of Will's evening out fade along with them.

Will opened his eyes and reached for her. She laid her head on his chest and breathed in the cedar scent of his aftershave. He pulled her closer, burying his face in her hair. They laid there, holding each other in silence, until the sound of the alarm raided the moment.

"Why would you set the alarm on a Saturday?" Will asked.

"We..." She was about to launch into all the things they had to do, then stopped herself. "I don't know." She reached over him and turned the alarm off. A half hour later, both kids came in the room and jumped on the bed.

"What are we doing today?" Amanda asked. Will feigned sleep.

They snuggled around Will, leaving Hannah as the sidekick. She was the parent for Band-Aids and homework and teeth flossing. Will was the favorite. A carnival parent.

"Dad," Amanda shook him, and Charlie joined in. "What are we going to do today?"

Will snored louder, and the kids shook him harder. "Daaaad! Wake up. Mom." They turned to her. "Make him wake up."

"Raaah!" Will sat up suddenly and grabbed each of the kids with mock fierceness. The kids screamed. His hair was rumpled, his face showing new stubble. "How about," he started, "we go tubing." The kids cheered. "A day with nothing to do but float down the Delaware River," he continued. "What do you say?" He looked at Hannah, the gatekeeper to their schedule.

"Sure," she answered, her mind now focused on the practical. They'd need more sunscreen. And bug spray. And old shoes. Did they need reservations? Wouldn't it be crazy crowded on Saturday? What time did they open?

Will tickled the kids, while Hannah continued with the mental list of things they would need. A cooler for drinks. And rope to tie the tubes together.

Once awake and moving, Will made daffles; Hannah packed and checked the website. She even found an online coupon.

It was a perfect day for tubing—excessively hot with a blue sky peppered by puffy clouds. Will purchased the package deal which allowed them to stop at the river restaurant for hot dogs, drinks, ice cream, and a prize. The kids fist-bumped one another.

Floating in a rope-tied circle of colorful tubes, Hannah's shoulders unclenched. She closed her eyes and lay back, the sun warm. Her hands skimmed the cool water. She breathed deeply. This was a good day.

"Why was the broom late?" she asked.

"No, Mom," Amanda said. "Just no."

"Because it over swept!"

Charlie laughed. Will splashed her.

"What did Cinderella say when her photos did not show up?" she asked.

Amanda put her hands over her ears, but she was smiling.

"What?" Charlie asked.

"Someday my prints will come."

"Ohh!" Will said. "That's so bad."

"One more," she told them. "Why did the picture go to jail?" No one said anything. "It was framed!"

"Oh!" Will said again. "So bad. So bad, you need to be ousted. Doesn't Mom need to be ousted?" He looked for affirmation from the kids. They nodded.

"Get her, Dad!" Charlie yelled.

Laughing, Will got off his tube and pushed the bottom of hers, upturning it. She spilled into the river. When she broke the surface, they all laughed. Hannah jumped back on her tube, soaked.

"Just for that." She splashed water in Will's direction.

He swam way ahead, tanned arms slicing the water. "See if you can get me now," he called back.

An hour in, they stopped for lunch on the side of the river. They sat at a picnic table, each with cool drinks and warm hot dogs. After, they licked ice cream cones and skipped stones, Will's inevitably going the furthest.

"Seven skips! Dad, you got seven skips!" Charlie said excitedly.

Will took Charlie's hand in his and showed him the movement. His rock plunged. They did it again. Two skips.

"Good start, buddy," Will said, clapping him on the shoulder. "Try this one."

He held out a thin, triangular rock, and knelt beside Charlie. Charlie imitated the motion Will had shown him. The rock skipped three times.

"Awesome," Will said. "Way to go."

After rock skipping, they took turns on the rope swing—even Hannah.

"Wow, Mom! Go!" Amanda said.

"Don't act so surprised," Will told them. "Back in the day, your mom was quite the daredevil."

Hannah knew the statement wasn't true. She had always been an observer. The girl on the bunny slope, the one who held the coats. Still, she rolled with it.

"That's right," she said. "I did all sorts of crazy things."

"Like what?" Amanda asked.

"Never you mind, young lady." Will chased her into the water.

The day continued with one perfect moment linking to the next. Even the fights Amanda and Charlie had in the car on the way home seemed less an irritation and more just a part of a colorful, wonderful life. Here they were—the Abbotts—warts and all. How was it possible that she had seen an attorney for divorce? Hannah shook her head and spied Will drumming to the music on the steering wheel. She'd been crazy.

Once the kids had fallen asleep from all the activity and sun, Hannah waited for Will in the bedroom. It had been awhile since they'd made love, but it had not been only her fault. Neither of them had tried.

She mentally skimmed her dismal lingerie drawer. Should she put something on?

She was still contemplating the lingerie when Will walked in the room with an expression she could not readily place.

He held her phone. "Your phone was buzzing, so I got it out of your purse," he glanced down at it. "It looks like Trent would like to go to dinner after the photography class on Tuesday." He looked up at her briefly then continued to scroll through the messages. "Oh, and he wants to know if you've thought about what he said." He continued scrolling. "Looks like he has quite a few messages. Going back... going back, six months." His head shot up.

Hannah's heart plunged. "Will, it's not what it looks like."

"Isn't it?" He placed her phone and Jack Connors' business card on the bed. "I also found this. Legal help for divorce."

They both stared at the card.

Hannah's hands flew to her face. Oh God. No. Will couldn't believe she really wanted a divorce. Her heart accelerated.

"Will, it's not what—"

"What it looks like. Right. I'm sure. It makes perfect sense that my wife would carry around a card for a divorce lawyer." Will grabbed a duffel bag from his closet and threw it on the bed. He jerked open a dresser drawer and pulled out clothes with quick, angry movements.

Hannah stepped forward and grabbed a shirt from the bag. "Will. No. Don't do this." She held the shirt to her chest and choked back a sob.

Will put his hand on the shirt. "Hannah," he said in an uncharacteristically measured voice. "Let it go."

Hannah looked into Will's eyes. A combination of hurt, disbelief, and anger stared back at her. She released the shirt and watched as Will continued to pack.

Hannah felt defensive as she watched him. But she hadn't been the only wrongdoer. "Well, you had that night with those girls."

Will zipped the bag and shook his head. "That one night when I was drunk. That's your excuse to take a secret class with Trent? For months. I mean, week after week and you never told me. And the divorce." He picked up Jack's business card. "Why didn't you tell me?" He extended his arm to give her the card; she didn't take it.

"I don't want a divorce."

"Doesn't look like it." Will dropped the card on the floor and slung the bag on his shoulder. He started for the door then turned to her. "Look. I don't want to say something I regret. This is a lot to take in."

He stood still.

Was he going to change his mind?

Hannah opened her mouth to say something.

"I'm spending the night at Scotty's," Will said before she could speak.

"Will, wait. Please don't do this."

"Hannah. I need time to think."

He left the room and walked down the stairs. The front door slammed and, moments later, Will's car engine started with a roar. Hannah moved to the window. Her throat clenched as she watched Will pull out of the driveway and turn.

He was gone.

TEN

David

David arrived at his office in downtown Trenton, a run-down, house-turned-office sandwiched between two closed store fronts. He entered the door, sidestepping the plant Amber had placed on the step to make the space "more inviting." She stood near the door with a stack of papers when he walked in, almost as if she had been waiting for him. "Remember, my referral Will Abbott is coming in at 4 pm."

"I remember."

Amber had mentioned her client the day before. And the day before that.

"Be good to Will. He's a nice guy." Her curled ponytail swung as she spoke. She looked like a corporate cheerleader.

She handed David the stack of papers she was holding. David glanced at the letter on top. The words "abhorrent" and "unbelievable" jumped off the page. He shook his head and looked at Amber. "How do you know this guy again?"

"He's a friend of a friend. Oh, and Lorena is coming in at 9:15 to go over your marketing plan."

David nodded, then navigated to the kitchen. It was not an ideal setup for a big man. He had to crouch down on the stairs and, at least once a week, he hit his head on a door jamb. It was as though the house had been designed for a family of petite people; anyone above five-foot-ten would have trouble. For someone six-foot-two, it was a mess.

In the kitchen, a border of red roosters lined the ceiling and pink heart contact paper filled the drawers. Amber had suggested they paint over everything; David left it. It was temporary.

He observed the downtown Trenton traffic through the kitchen window, a maze of cars snaking their way to the courthouse two blocks away. Attorneys walked along the sidewalk. Brenden Bookman saw him through the window and waved.

David gave him the finger.

Black coffee in hand, David made his way to his office. He passed Whitney, his new receptionist, in the hall.

Morning, Mr. Dewey," she said in a Southern drawl. She pushed her blonde hair to one side and smoothed out a short, geometric-patterned dress.

"Whitney! So you came back for a second day? I didn't scare you too much, then?"

She smiled. "Of course not, Mr. Dewey." She leaned on one high heel.

"Please. Call me, David."

"David," she repeated. "Good morning."

"Better," David said, nodding.

David entered his office and sat in an oversized, wheeled chair behind a scratched, second-hand desk. He read the "abhorrent" and "unbelievable" letter. He was both of those things, according to Lewis C. Clark, Attorney at Law. And also "a disgrace to the profession." That was a new one. David yawned and took another sip of coffee. It was too early. Before he could do anything further, Amber buzzed. "Lorena's here."

David looked at his watch. She was early. He shrugged. "Let her in."

Lorena entered without speaking, shut the door, and fell into a well-worn chair from David's old family room. "So I see you got another Hooters girl? I like her Southern accent."

David rolled his eyes. "A friend of Amber's. It's not—"

She held up her hand, touching her straightened, jet-black hair in the process. "I'm not judging. I'm the marketing girl, remember? I love it. You cater to divorcing men and everyone on your staff is a young girl with—you know." She gestured to her chest. "It's genius, actually." She leaned back and crossed her legs. "How's the dad support group working out?"

"It's growing. Thirteen dads showed up at the last meeting."

"And business?"

"Up."

"Beautiful." Lorena paused long enough to signal she had something important to say. "So, listen." Though it was only the two of them, she had lowered her voice. "I wanted to have this meeting because I heard about a big opportunity that would be perfect for you. What do you think of... reality TV?" She waved her hands as if she were underscoring the words.

David half listened, half mentally scoured his to-do list. Lorena was always onto something big. "What about it?"

"You on a reality TV show. They're going to take a bunch of divorcing couples to an island somewhere and let them have at it. Like a reverse Bachelor. They are calling it Divorce House. They're looking for ..." She pulled out her phone and started reading, "spontaneous and engaging attorneys who are not afraid to mix it up." She paused again. "David, it's you. This show is made for someone like you. It would be a gold mine. You would get ten grand an episode, but that's just to start. And your practice? It will explode. It will absolutely explode."

David said nothing. Ten grand an episode? He could finally get out of this shithole.

"You have to apply," Lorena said.

"It's intriguing," David agreed.

"You have to find a client willing to be on the show with you. Try not to pick an asshole."

David laughed. "You expect me to find a nice guy getting a divorce?"

"As nice as you can get. So you'll do it?" She leaned forward in the chair.

"I'll think about it."

"Do more than just think, David. This is a golden opportunity for you. Don't miss it."

ELEVEN

After Lorena left, David put the meeting out of his mind and focused on the emotionally-charged legal battles which framed his daily existence. He picked up a letter from a firm he used to battle against as a trial lawyer. He stared at the letterhead, thinking of the old days. He missed that job.

His mind went back to Lorena's offer.

Ten grand an episode.

David drummed his fingers on the desk. He could get back to it, the trial work. If he built up a cash reserve, he could do it.

He tried to concentrate on his work, but his mind kept returning to the idea that he could be a trial lawyer again. He stood up and paced the room, orating a mock closing argument. At the conclusion of his pretend summation, he banged his fist on his desk and said, "Not guilty." Amber opened the door.

"Are you alright? I heard you talking."

David willed himself not to look embarrassed. "Fine. Just practicing an argument."

"Do you have one coming up? Should I put it on the calendar?" Amber looked alarmed.

"No. Not yet. It's fine." David waved her away and sat back in his chair.

"Will Abbott's here," she said, a small smile flashing across her face.

"Right. Your referral. Bring him in."

Amber ushered Will Abbott into his office. Will was a tall man in his thirties with beach-colored hair, matching stubble, and blue eyes. His shoulders pulled tightly on his t-shirt and David immediately felt the weight of the extra pounds around his gut.

He sat up straighter. He wasn't that much older than this guy. He should look better.

"This is Will," Amber said. She waited as though she hoped to be asked to stay. When David said nothing, she spoke again. "Well. I'll leave you to it." She stepped backward out the door and closed it.

Will stood, frozen, near the doorway.

David waited. Most clients came in oozing information. Will's silence was unnerving.

"How can I help you?" David said finally, gesturing to a chair.

Will stepped forward and sat perched on the edge of the chair. He spoke quickly. "My friend is in your dad group. Scotty Mahoney?"

David nodded.

"Scotty thinks I need to protect myself." He pulled a card out of his jeans and tossed it to David. "I found this in my wife's purse."

David picked up the card, the name in black letters jumping out. Jack Connors. He worked to keep his voice level. "And since your wife spoke to a lawyer, you want to speak to one also, right?"

"Right."

"Do you know what your wife talked about with Jack Connors?"

"No. She said she just wanted information. Things have been strained, I mean, not so much that I thought it would come to this. But I don't know. I don't know what he told her. I don't know what she wants."

"Okay." David leaned back, pushing Jack Connors out of his mind. "Anything else?"

"I found a bunch of messages on her phone from a guy we both know. She says they're just friends, but Scotty says I'm crazy to believe that."

"And do you believe it?"

"What do you think? In your experience?"

David paused. "Well, if it looks like a duck," he started.

Will was silent a moment. "So you think there might be something there?"

"I don't know your wife, but I think you're right to come here."

Some men were stupid like this. Wake up, David wanted to shout.

Will stared at the floor for a long moment. "Scotty said I would lose my house if I moved out for a bit."

"Nope. Wrong." David put his feet on the desk to illustrate his lack of concern.

"He says I'll pay alimony forever."

"Nope."

"But Scotty said that he pays…"

David sat up and leaned forward. "I didn't represent your friend. You won't pay alimony forever."

"But."

"No buts." David held his hand out.

"What about my kids?"

"How old?"

"Charlie is seven and Amanda is eleven."

"Do you want them?"

"Yes."

"Enough said."

The conversation continued, and David explained his philosophy. Women, in his opinion, had the major advantage in any divorce. They got alimony. They got the kids. Generally, they stayed in the house. And the men, they just worked and paid for it all.

"I level the playing field," he told Will. "I fight for the guys."

He waited for Will to have the typical reaction. Most men got revved up at this point. Yesterday's client even repeated back to David what he had said, like an echo. Almost always, testosterone reached new heights as the conversation went on, the men willing to pay almost anything to be under David's promised protection.

David waited. Will Abbott sat unmoved, his gaze on the floor.

"So I'll fight for your rights," David repeated. "You won't get taken with me at the helm."

Will looked up and met David's eyes. "If our marriage has to end, I want to be fair to my wife."

David was silenced.

Will continued, "And I want to do what's best for my kids. Which is probably Hannah." His shoulders slumped as he said the words; his demeanor struck a chord.

"I understand," David said, working to keep his tone professional. "But just know that this man—" He picked up Jack Connors' business card, "—doesn't play fair. He doesn't know how. And the decisions you make now will have long lasting effects. Some you can't even imagine. So don't just think you're going to play nice and it will all be okay. Divorce doesn't work that way." David paused, lost in his own emotion. "Don't even try to be fair."

Will said nothing. David couldn't read his expression. He had been too personal, he'd let his feelings get the better of him. He gathered himself. "I'm just saying, you may want to be fair, but not everyone does."

Will nodded. "I understand." He stood up.

David cursed himself as they said their goodbyes. He was certain Will Abbott would not be back.

TWELVE

The meeting with Will did not leave David much time to get ready for Wednesday dinner with his kids. He left the office and returned to his home, one of hundreds of identical apartments in nondescript tan buildings. He did have a pool view which, when he signed the lease, he'd believed would be a plus. But it turned out that the only pool-goers were the ten or so older ladies that did an aqua-fit class. Like clockwork at 10 a.m. in the summers, the overweight lifeguard would lumber off the stand, turn on an old radio, and lead the class. David had taken to closing his shades.

He unlocked the door and entered the beige space. The walls were bare, the furnishings sparse. Against one wall sat a large cage. David rapped on it.

"Hey, Bolt," he said. The tortoise looked up slowly and David dropped kale in. Almost imperceptibly, Bolt's pace quickened toward the food.

David pulled on jeans and an Eagles sweatshirt and drove to his former home. He rang the doorbell and waited. When there was no immediate answer, he walked back down the driveway, leaned against his beat-up Accord, and stared at the immense structure. It was a real estate agent's dream: spacious five-bedroom home with three full baths, finished walk-out basement, gourmet kitchen, and in-ground pool on an acre in the Princeton School District.

David texted Lauren. No response. He walked up the path and rang the doorbell again. Nothing. He returned to his car and lit a cigarette. He inhaled slowly, then puffed out the smoke in a ring. After ten minutes, he saw the glimpse of a heart-shaped face behind a lavender curtain. Then a text.

Go home, David. The girls do not want to go to dinner tonight.

David stared at the message a moment before texting back.

It will just be an hour.

Doesn't matter. They don't want to go.

David shook his head at the phone.

What about Ryan?

He's at baseball.

I thought that ended.

You've got the schedule.

And that was it. He could picture Lauren inside. She'd have on khakis, a blouse, pearls. Her shoulder-length blonde hair would swing as she moved. She'd tuck it behind her ear, a nervous habit he'd once found endearing.

Though it had been David's former job as a trial lawyer at Trembley, Rubin, and Connors that had given them the financial wherewithal to live in Princeton, Lauren was the one who blended with the Princeton elite. It was as though Lauren had grown up with private schools, nannies, and summers abroad instead of down the street from him in South Philly.

David walked to the mailbox and put the notes inside, one to each child. Then he slid in the envelope with the five-thousand-dollar check for Lauren, one of two monthly installments of alimony and child support.

David's mind flashed back to the day he signed the agreement at the courthouse. He had been so sure that Lauren, upon seeing how kind and generous he was, would have a change of heart. He remembered the feeling when his signature was the only one on the document; he'd expected her to push it away and take him back. Instead, she grabbed it, scrawling her name in swirly black ink.

David shut the mailbox. He'd done this every Wednesday for the past year. His fifteen- and sixteen-year-old daughters, Hailey and Sienna, had never bothered to acknowledge his presence. Ryan, at twelve, wanted a relationship, but there was always a conflict with Wednesdays. Of course there was.

David started his car, taking one look back at the house before starting down the winding, gravel drive. Every week, it amazed him this could happen and that no one cared. The court order allowing him this small window of time with his children would not be enforced by the police because they "don't get involved with custody matters." If he filed a motion to enforce his rights with the court, he would only get another paper order the police couldn't enforce.

David pushed his frustration aside and drove the familiar route to St. Paul's Lutheran Church. He saw Jenny's red Mustang in the parking lot and pulled in next to it. He entered the old structure and pushed open the second-floor door.

A dozen people sat in a circle. Jenny saw him and removed her purse from the seat adjacent to hers. As David sat, he made brief eye contact with the familiar faces and looked about for the inevitable newbies. A man he recognized but did not know stood, sharing. There was light applause as he finished.

He sat and scanned the room. A woman stood up and spoke.

"Sorry." Jenny mouthed, knowing that his presence at the meeting meant the kids had refused to see him.

He shrugged.

"Homeland?" she whispered.

"You bet."

The woman was followed by a man unable to succinctly describe his feelings. After the designated five minutes, the moderator interrupted. "Bob, thank you so much. We have to allow others to share." The man took his seat, his body language that of a scolded schoolchild. After a polite applause, David stood.

"I'm David. And I'm an alcoholic."

THIRTEEN

"Hi, David," the group chimed.

"So I tried to see my kids again tonight..." He told the story. Since becoming a regular at the meetings a year ago, David had found the shares cathartic. At the beginning, his confessions were designed to shock, to test the acceptance of the group. Would they accept him if he had...

Passed out at a school concert.

Showed up in court drunk.

Struck his wife.

Lost his job.

Week after week, the group accepted him. In fact, it seemed, the worse the offense, the greater the cushion of support. It took him some time to realize that everyone in the room had done the same or worse, and, by accepting his transgressions, they accepted their own. It had been, for David, a lifeline. To know that people saw the worst of him—the underbelly of his soul—and didn't turn away in disgust, it saved him.

And, of course, it's where he'd met Jenny.

When the meeting concluded, David watched her interact with the others. Jenny was so petite that, looking at her from the back, it appeared that a small child had snuck in by accident. But her face was more aged than her size let on, and her left eye was damaged, half-closed and framed in scars. The eye was all David noticed when he first met her. But she didn't hide it and David no longer noticed it, seeing only Jenny's unblemished olive skin, high cheekbones, and thick dark hair worn long about her shoulders, her pride and joy.

David watched as Jenny squeezed the hand of a new woman. "I hope to see you here next week," she said, her voice peaceful.

Three people stood rapt in conversation. Jenny smiled as she joined them. It amazed David how she instinctively knew how to do it, how to act. Jenny knew how long you should hold someone's gaze, the right words to say, when to be silent.

He'd long lost the ability to know how to behave outside of an adversarial context. As a lawyer, he knew when to be a bastard (always) and when to give in (never) but, as a person, he could no longer figure it out. He spoke loudly when silence was called for; he made demands when any normal person would know to let go.

He wished he could be more like Jenny.

He straightened and moved to her side, but his presence seemed to end the conversation, the two women speaking to Jenny nearly stopping mid-conversation to look at him. After an awkward exchange, the group shifted to goodbyes. If Jenny noticed the abrupt transition, she said nothing.

They walked to her Mustang. "I am so sorry you were unable to see your kids tonight," Jenny said quietly. "You deserve better than that."

David shrugged. "Not sure about that but I'd like to see them anyway. Maybe the notes will help."

"They will."

The notes had been her idea. If the kids wouldn't see him, drop off a note each week to let them know he cared. Jenny was confident it would work; David was confident in the opposite. Still, it was something.

As was the Wednesday routine, David left his car at the church and went home with Jenny. He squeezed into her Mustang and she drove to Giovanni's Pizzeria, chattering about her most recent watercolor painting.

She pulled into the parking lot at Giovanni's and they climbed out of the car and entered the building.

A new woman with large hoop earrings and a T-shirt with the caption "Wanna Slice?" stood behind the counter. After a quick glance at Jenny, she began to clean the countertop.

David tensed. It's just an eye, lady. Look the fuck up.

Jenny reached a slender hand over the counter. "You must be new. I'm Jenny."

The woman met Jenny's firm handshake with a limp one. "Can I help you?"

"Is Giovanni here?"

As if prompted by his name, Giovanni came from the back with a pile of pizza boxes. "Hello Jenny, David. I have ten pizzas for you tonight." He placed them on the counter.

"Thank you so much. I really appreciate you helping out," Jenny said. She and David each took a stack.

Giovanni moved to grab the door for them. "Always willing to help a good cause."

They piled the pizza into the trunk of Jenny's car and got in. Jenny gave Giovanni a friendly wave as she backed out. She drove to the women's homeless shelter. She brought leftover pizza there every Wednesday.

A few women were waiting out front; Jenny greeted each by name. They entered the building and Jenny immediately introduced herself to a new woman. They spoke a few moments before the shelter director found her and took the pizzas. Jenny smiled and said her goodbyes.

After leaving the shelter, Jenny drove David to her house. They climbed out of the car and walked up the path. Jenny pushed open the front door and her black lab, Moxie, jumped up on David, all eighty pounds pushing against his belly.

"Moxie!" Jenny scolded in mock shock. "You get down now."

David petted Moxie's head and stepped over a pile of clothes that Jenny intended to donate to Goodwill. He made his way into the small kitchen. He swept aside beads and cords and half-done necklaces scattered on the table.

"Diet Coke?" Jenny had started keeping some in the fridge for him.

David nodded. "This is new." He held up a box of calligraphy materials.

"Thought it would be fun." She met his eyes and seemed to read his mind. "Don't say anything."

"No. Wouldn't dream of it. Seems like great fun." David put the kit down. "Almost as much fun as soap sculptures."

Jenny stamped her foot. "Shut up. That soap rose was beautiful and you know it."

"Mmm. Was it now?"

"Yes." She handed him his soda and he followed her into the family room, Moxie trailing behind. David sat next to a pile of clean laundry and began to fold a T-shirt.

"David. Don't fold anything. You'll make me feel bad about all this." Jenny gestured around the cluttered room.

"Never."

Jenny's unexpected sloppiness was one of the things David liked most about her. It had been such a surprise. The first time he came over, he'd expected serene lighting, soft music, and a bonsai tree. Instead, there was Moxie, piles of half-done projects, and dishes in the sink. David loved it.

He folded another shirt.

"No," she said. "Really."

"It's fine." He held up a pair of tiny satin briefs and raised an eyebrow.

"Stop it." She grabbed the underwear out of his hand and moved the pile of clothes to a nearby table. She fished around for the Homeland DVD under piles of magazines and books with titles like Living your Best Life and Awaken the Power Within. Once found, she held it up, victorious.

She flipped on the show. They'd binge-watched five episodes of season one the first night and had held themselves to just two per night since. Aside from Jenny periodically saying, "oh my God," they were silent. At the end of the second episode, she looked at him. Then she started the third.

It was past midnight when they finally went to bed. David took his place in the spare room. From Jenny's master bath, he heard water running. He imagined Jenny's tiny form at the sink in the old T-shirt and sweats she always wore to bed. He held his breath, waited a moment, then heard the door to her room shut.

David exhaled. He could not be disappointed. They were friends. No more. That's how Jenny wanted it.

He was pretty sure.

As he began to fall asleep, David's mind drifted through the day's events.

Lorena's Divorce House idea. Ten grand an episode.

And Will Abbott. The only man in the world who wanted to be fair to his wife. Besides him, of course. And he knew how that ended. David thought again about Will and his affable manner.

Jack Connors would eat him alive.

FOURTEEN

Rachel

Rachel Goldstein spotted Hannah Abbott at the bar in McCourt's as soon as she walked in. Her stomach fell. Rachel knew she had come off as cold and impassive at the legal consultation. But it hadn't been entirely her fault. It had been her first day in the divorce rotation at the firm; Jack Connors shouldn't have left her to start that meeting alone.

Unlike most of her clients, Rachel liked Hannah Abbott. She was warm, but not saccharine sweet, and had a practical air which Rachel had found impressive. And she was a photographer. Rachel had always been in awe of creative people.

From her vantage point behind the hostess desk, Rachel studied Hannah. She wore a striped sundress, no jewelry, and stirred her drink in a methodical, unthinking manner. A man on the bar stool next to hers leaned over and said something. Hannah smiled politely, continuing to stir. Then, abruptly, she raised her head and looked in Rachel's direction. There was a flicker of recognition before her eyes dropped back down.

Rachel's face reddened. She immediately pulled out her phone and stared at the home screen. Should she apologize? Find out how things are? She took a step then stopped herself. For all she knew, Hannah's husband was in the bathroom and would return just as she approached. Rachel knew she would try to explain her presence away with a string of barely believable lies. And she was a horrific liar. She should say nothing.

And she had other things to think about. Rachel held out her hand. Light hit the huge diamond and Rachel moved her wrist. The diamond shone differently depending on the angle. She stared at it. It had only been five days since the proposal.

She was brought back to the present by the sound of her name in a chorus behind her. "Rachel, Rachel!" Lexi and Samantha surrounded her.

"Let me see it!" Lexi commanded, pulling on her hand. Oh my God, it's gorgeous! It's got to be three carats." The two of them bent down to examine the ring.

"It's huge." Samantha added. "And look at those giant diamonds on the side. It must weigh a ton."

Lexi dropped her hand. "I can't believe you're engaged to Aaron Weiss." Her voice was obnoxiously loud.

A few patrons peeked in their direction and Rachel sneaked a glance at Hannah. She was motioning to the bartender for another drink. The man next to her leaned in and spoke to her. Maybe he was her husband?

"You must tell us everything," Lexi continued. "Every detail."

"Wait until we sit down." Rachel's voice came out strangely choked, but before either of them could comment, the hostess told them their table was ready.

Lexi linked arms with Rachel and Sammy as they walked through the bar to the dining area. They looked like a millennial version of The Wizard of Oz, bumping into patrons as they tried to maintain the trio. It felt like the whole bar, Hannah included, was staring at them. Rachel was relieved to get to their table.

"So give us all the details." Lexi said as she sat down. She adjusted her hair so that her blonde locks were evenly distributed.

"Yes. How did he ask you?" Samantha asked.

"He took me to Nineteen."

"Did you know?" Lexi leaned forward.

"Suspected. But he didn't ask me until the end. I was dying. I mean, we'd looked at rings so I kind of knew but, you never really know for sure, right?" Rachel's voice, even to her own ear, had a superficial quality.

"Did he get down on one knee?" Lexi leaned so close, Rachel thought she might topple into her lap.

"Of course," she lied.

"Oh my God." Lexi and Sammy squealed. The couple at the table next to them smiled politely.

"Did he ask your dad first?" Samantha asked, picking up her water glass.

"No. But he's okay with it."

Her dad was not okay with it.

"And your mom?" Lexi inquired.

"Over the moon." This was an understatement. Rachel's mother would have bottled up Aaron and sold him if she could. In fact, if Rachel ever criticized Aaron about anything, her mother's standard response was, "It's Aaron Weiss, dear. Let it go."

"Can you imagine the kind of wedding Aaron Weiss will have?" Sammy asked.

"I can't," Lexi said. "And the honeymoon. That's going to be insane."

"I'd go to an island and lie there all day and have my people fetch me drinks." Sammy closed her eyes and leaned back as though a drink might be delivered to her at any moment.

"Does he have people?" Lexi asked.

"I don't know."

Lexi and Samantha looked at Rachel, expectant.

"He has a couple assistants. But I don't think they would go on our honeymoon." Aaron's main assistant was a heavyset woman in her forties who wore only suits in shades of gray. A vision of her in her perfect suit, toppling over uneven sand with cold drinks, flashed through Rachel's mind. She suppressed a smile.

Lexi examined a long, red fingernail. "I just can't believe you are marrying Aaron Weiss."

It was the second time she'd made that statement.

The implication was clear: how did boring Rachel Goldstein land a young securities broker at Stockton Richards worth millions? Rachel wanted to give a pithy response, but nothing came to mind. In typical Rachel fashion, she'd think of the perfect thing to say tomorrow.

"When's the date?" Lexi flipped all her hair to one side.

"It's not set yet."

"Mmm…"

"They just got engaged two days ago, Lex. Really." Sammy took another sip of water. The waitress returned with three flutes of champagne.

As soon as it was in her possession, Lexi held up the thin glass. "To the future Mrs. Aaron Weiss." They clinked.

The night continued with more discussion about the wedding dresses and flowers and possible venues for the reception. Neither Sammy or Lexi bothered to ask for her opinion; it was as if Rachel wasn't there.

Rachel picked at her food. She was careful to drink only two glasses of champagne; Aaron didn't like it when she had more.

When dessert rolled around, Lexi got peanut butter cheesecake, Rachel's favorite dessert. "Want a bite?" She pushed the plate toward her.

"No." She patted her stomach. "I have a wedding dress to fit into."

"You've got time, Rachel. There's no date yet."

"No thanks. I've got a ways to go until I reach my goal weight."

Lexi shrugged and stuck a fork into the pie. She took a bite with slow exaggeration. "Oh my God. So good." She looked at Rachel and Samantha. "Divine," she added. Samantha picked up her fork. Rachel shook her head.

As they scraped the peanut butter and chocolate off the plate, the waitress came by. "Anything else?"

"No." Rachel spoke before there could be an order of coffees or after dinner drinks or, God forbid, another peanut butter pie. Willpower only went so far.

She handed the credit card Aaron had given her to the waitress. "Aaron insists," she told her friends.

Lexi tipped her head back. "And so it begins. As friends of Rachel, we'll be treated to everything from now on. Good thing we went to high school together." Lexi and Samantha shared a conspiratorial laugh.

On their way out, Rachel saw Hannah, still on the same bar stool but now engaged in a conversation with the man next to her. Her husband. She knew it.

Lexi and Samantha stopped at the door in direct view of Hannah. No. Rachel did not want Hannah to notice her. "Thanks for coming," she whispered.

"Wouldn't miss it for anything." Sammy hugged her.

"Congrats to you, Mrs. Aaron Weiss!" Lexi's voice carried through the bar. She made a show of giving her two exaggerated air kisses, complete with a "muah" sound.

Rachel looked in Hannah's direction. She was looking straight at her now. Rachel gave a small wave. Hannah smiled broadly.

Lexi and Samantha looked toward Hannah, vaguely interested, then they hugged Rachel and left.

Rachel glanced back at Hannah who was now motioning for her to come over. It would be rude to ignore her. Besides, she was curious.

Rachel took a step toward the bar.

FIFTEEN

Hannah started speaking as soon as Rachel reached her. "I re-member you. You're the lawyer I talked to a few weeks ago." She put her hand on Rachel's shoulder and took another sip of her drink. The man next to Hannah was portly with parts of his rear end spilling over the sides of the stool. The top line of his under-wear was visible when he leaned over. He was not who Rachel had envisioned as Hannah's husband.

"How are you?" Rachel asked, noting that Hannah's eyes were a stunning shade of green.

"How am I? Good question. I, I—am not so great." She leaned forward as if she were going to tell Rachel a secret. "You know what?"

Rachel said nothing.

"Will left."

"I'm so sorry." Rachel slid onto the stool next to her. So the man at the bar wasn't her husband.

As if cued by her thought, the man looked at Rachel; irritation flashed in his eyes. He stared at her for a moment, then held up two fingers to the bartender.

"Did you want to talk about it?"

"It's just temporary." Hannah said in a low voice. "He says he needs space for a bit. He's convinced I'm having a sordid, sneaky affair." She laughed. "And that I'm secretly plotting a vicious di-vorce."

Rachel opened her mouth to ask, "Are you?" then shut it again. The idea that Hannah would be having an affair was incongruent with the image she'd portrayed during the divorce consultation. She'd seemed like a woman still in love with her husband.

The bartender set down two shots and dipped his head toward the man at the bar. "From the gentleman."

Rachel nodded her thanks and took a small sip. Straight gin. She nearly spit it out.

Hannah picked up her glass, drained the contents, and then smacked it back down on the bar. "So you're engaged. It's a beautiful ring." She bent down to look at it more closely. "Wow. That is really big." She rapped Rachel on the shoulder like they were old friends.

"Thanks." Rachel glanced at Hannah's wedding ring. It looked to be a half a carat, princess cut, on a single gold band.

"I can still wear my ring, right?" Hannah looked at her, concerned.

"Your ring? Yes. Of course. It's yours. Even when you get divorced, you get to keep the ring. It was given to you as a condition to marriage and you fulfilled that condition…" Rachel let the rest trail off, realizing how inappropriate the legal explanation was at that moment. "Not that you're getting a divorce. I mean, just if you did."

"Right." Hannah looked at her empty glass.

Rachel tried to think of something to say and failed. When silence hung in the air so long it became uncomfortable, she announced, "Well, I should get going." She slid off the stool.

"Me too." Hannah reached for her purse and got off her own stool, stumbling as she landed.

Rachel reached out to help steady her. "Do you think you're okay to drive?"

"I think so." She took a step and swayed. "Maybe not." She leaned against the bar.

"I can take her home." The man who had bought the shots of gin stood up. He put his hand on Hannah's arm possessively.

Rachel looked at the man and then Hannah. "Do you guys know each other?"

Hannah put her hand on the man's shoulder. "This is Burt. He agrees with me that Will is acting like a complete ass."

Burt shifted, taking a step back.

"But do you know each other? Before tonight."

Hannah didn't answer. She turned and directed her attention to the bartender. "Do I need to pay my bill?"

"Paid for already. By that gentleman." The bartender pointed at Burt.

Rachel gave Burt a hard look. "I'll drive Hannah home."

"Really, it's on my way." Burt reached out his hand to steady Hannah.

Rachel moved in front of her. "No. I've got this. You can go."

Burt stood a moment then shook his head. "Just trying to be a gentleman," he mumbled.

Rachel snorted.

Burt shot her a look.

Rachel took Hannah's arm. She guided her out of the bar and toward her car. The navy blue Civic had been her first major purchase when she got the job as an associate at Trembley, Rubin, and Connors, and she was still firmly in new car mode. There were no bits of trash on the floor, no coins in the cup holder. A tiny air freshener hung from the rearview mirror.

Rachel helped Hannah into the car and set her purse squarely on her lap. She slid into the driver's seat and pressed the Start button. A picture of her cat, Snowball, illuminated the dashboard home screen.

Hannah closed her eyes and leaned back. Would she get sick in her car? How easy would it be to clean vomit off leather seats?

"So. Where do you live?"

"I can't go home." Hannah shook her head. "Will wanted time with the kids. He's still mad at me, says he needs time. Time." Hannah leaned her head against the seat. "How much time does he need? I didn't do anything." She sat up straighter. "I said I'd stay out tonight. I was going to call one of my girlfriends when I got to the bar, but I couldn't. I just—" She paused. "I just don't want anyone to know we're separated yet."

"I'm sorry." Rachel searched her mind for something more to say but, before she could think of the right words, Hannah spoke again.

"I guess just take me to a hotel."

Rachel glanced at her. Would she be okay at a hotel? A vision of Hannah passed out in a hotel lobby flashed through her mind.

"Do you want to stay with me?"

"Oh. No," Hannah stammered. "I couldn't. That would be too much. I'm okay. Really. Just take me to a hotel."

"It's really okay. I have a townhouse a few miles from here."

"Are you sure it's not too much trouble?"

"No, it's not."

"Alright then. Thanks." Hannah turned to the window.

Rachel immediately regretted the invitation. She barely knew Hannah. And what would she tell Aaron? She'd been staying in his Philadelphia apartment almost every night; he was expecting her. If she didn't show up, he'd automatically assume she drank too much, that she'd done something wild. In fairness, perhaps inviting a stranger to stay in her home qualified as crazy.

Hannah was silent. Rachel struggled to find something to say. She had a strong aversion to silence, often peppering conversations with inane commentary or meaningless questions. "What do you think is in those trucks?" she'd asked Aaron once during a car trip. He'd looked confused.

"The trucks up there?" he'd said. "How should I know?" She'd been unable to explain the reason for the question.

The car ride continued in silence. Rachel filled the quiet with a step-by-step commentary on how to get to her house. "So, we'll turn left on Main, then make a right at the McDonald's. Northampton Knoll is on the left after that." Rachel tapped the steering wheel. "It's just a few miles." Hannah said nothing. "Won't be long now."

When the townhouse finally came into view, Rachel shouted, "There it is!" as though they'd reached a much-anticipated destination.

She waited for Hannah to get out of the car and the two of them entered the home. Rachel removed her shoes and dug her feet into the plush carpet, wiggling her toes. She left her shoes in the front hall and dropped her purse on the floor, loving the freedom of those small acts. Aaron had a very specific entry routine: remove shoes and put on the left side of the closet, hang purse on designated hook, place keys in bowl by the door. His black hardwood floors were always cold on her feet. Rachel wriggled her toes again at the thought of Aaron's apartment.

"Make yourself at home." Rachel gestured to the small living space to the left of the door.

Hannah moved into the room and sat on the couch, the deep cushions sinking in as she did so. As Hannah looked around, Rachel felt a swell of pride. She'd decorated the townhouse in shades of tan and mauve. The room was centered by a custom, lighted curio cabinet with accent pieces she'd collected at stores like HomeGoods. Tables were adorned with stacks of books, candles, photo frames, and tiny vases. Afghans, blankets, and soft decorative pillows lined every couch and chair. The kitchen adjoined the small family room with an open counter; colorful mugs stood in a rack on the side. The space was lovingly cluttered. She was proud of it.

Snowball, curled up in her favorite chair, slowly opened her eyes and stared at Hannah. Apparently unimpressed, she resumed sleeping.

Out of habit, Rachel switched on the television and HGTV came on. Shoot. She didn't want Hannah to think she spent her time on frivolous house shows. "Want me to flip on the news?"

"No. I'm fine." Hannah paused. "Are you sure this is okay? I could stay in a hotel." She stood up. "Yes, I think I should stay in a hotel. This is too inconvenient."

"It's fine. Really." Rachel flipped off the television and went into the kitchen area. She put a kettle on the stove. "I couldn't have you going home with Burt now."

"I wouldn't have gone home with Burt." Hannah got up and slid onto a stool at the counter overlooking the kitchen. "I didn't drink that much. I mean, okay, I drank a lot. It's not like me to do that; it's just that the situation with Will is so crazy." She paused. "But I wouldn't have gone home with Burt."

Rachel took out two mugs. "I thought Burt was your husband."

Hannah covered her mouth with her hand in surprise and shook her head. She grabbed her phone. "No! Why would you think that?" As she said the words, Hannah pulled up a picture on her phone and tipped it toward her.

Centered between two children was a smiling man, tanned from the sun, with piercing blue eyes and new stubble on a firm jaw. The girl to his left was a cookie cutter of Hannah with long, strawberry blonde hair, green eyes, and a smattering of freckles. She reminded Rachel of a Strawberry Shortcake doll. The boy had bright blond hair and his father's eyes.

"This is my husband, Will. And my kids, Charlie and Amanda."

Rachel stared at the image, the emotional and financial impact of a potential divorce on this family becoming real as she did so. The kids were no longer "minor children, ages eleven and seven" but the little girl with the dimple and the boy young enough to be missing front teeth. Will was no longer "husband" but a flesh and blood man strong enough to hold a happy child in each arm. And Hannah, from the look of her expression staring at the picture, was, quite obviously, not ready to let him go.

"I took this the day Will left," she said. "We'd gone tubing down the Delaware."

Rachel slid a steaming mug of green tea across the counter to Hannah. She studied the picture again. How could the day portrayed in this photo possibly have ended in a separation? "What happened?"

Hannah took a sip of tea then placed the mug down. She leaned forward. "Can I tell you about it? I haven't told anyone. It would —" Hannah looked at Rachel. "It would feel good to talk about it."

"Please," Rachel said and gestured to the couch.

SIXTEEN

"Will found messages on my phone from a friend of mine," Hannah said, as she settled in on the couch next to Snowball. "A male friend of ours. But..." She paused and pet Snowball. "Really more mine than his. Will's convinced that we're having an affair." Hannah sipped her tea.

"Why does he think that?"

Hannah shut her eyes for a moment. She opened them and spoke. "Because I sort of was. Trent and I, we went to dinner, we went on outings together and I didn't tell Will. I'd convinced myself it was no different than if I was going out with my girlfriends." She cupped her hands around her mug, focusing on a spot over Rachel's head. "I never really wanted to leave Will, but things haven't been so great between us. It's why I came to see you. I just thought I should know what to expect if—" She trailed off.

Rachel tried to imagine the handsome man in the picture and Hannah arguing, but all she could envision was the two of them sipping wine in the evening on a suburban deck, watching their kids catch fireflies in the backyard. The image was so idyllic that Rachel held it in her mind, expanding it to include dripping ice cream cones and neighbors and games of ghost in the graveyard at dusk. She could practically hear the kids laughing, the clinking of their parents' wine glasses as another evening slid into night.

"I guess it was silly for me to come and see you," Hannah said, pulling Rachel out of her thoughts.

"Information never hurts, right?"

Hannah shrugged, got up from the couch, and walked into the kitchen. She turned on the water, filling her mug. "Do you have any dish soap?"

Rachel moved to the kitchen and opened a side cabinet. "Right here."

Hannah grabbed the soap and squirted it in the mug for cleaning. It was as if she'd been to Rachel's house hundreds of times. They felt like old friends.

"I'll fix up the spare room." Rachel walked toward the stairs.

"No need, Rachel. I'm good on the couch. You already have blankets and pillows down here. Don't mess up a room."

"Are you sure?" Rachel asked, lingering on the stairs.

"Absolutely." Hannah put her dried mug on the counter.

Rachel was secretly relieved. She'd turned the spare bedroom into a workout area, the giant treadmill taking up half the small space.

"At least let me get you some sweats and a shirt to sleep in." Rachel ran upstairs before Hannah could protest. By the time she returned, Hannah had made up the couch. Rachel handed her the clothes.

"Thank you," she said. "I realized that I've been talking about myself all night. I'm sorry. And here you are, newly engaged. What's your fiancé's name? What's he like? When's the wedding?" Hannah patted the couch for Rachel to sit.

Rachel joined her on the couch, pulling Snowball up on to her lap. She told her about Nineteen and the proposal. She told her about how her mother had arranged her first date with Aaron through a friend from the synagogue. She tried to make it sound like she and Aaron had a special, cosmic connection, but her descriptions came off as flat. The funny stories weren't all that funny, the romantic gestures, not all that touching.

When she was done speaking, it felt like Hannah was still waiting for the big reveal, the, a-ha moment, where she'd say, "Right! That's how it was with me and Will!"

Instead, all she said was, "Oh. Nice. Congratulations."

Rachel didn't know Hannah. She shouldn't care what she thought. But the banality of her comment hung between them.

"How do I know if Aaron is the one?" Rachel blurted out the question.

Hannah looked surprised.

Rachel tried to recover. "I mean, how did you know with Will?" Snowball adjusted herself and began to purr.

"Well, everyone knew the Abbotts. They were the perfect family. Three girls and Will. He was the guy everyone loved in high school. He was just so nice and friendly and handsome. I was two years behind him and he didn't know me at all. Still, I had a crazy crush on him." She drew her knees toward her chest and hugged them. "When he was a junior, Will's dad died in a car accident. It was awful. I mean the whole community couldn't believe it. His mother couldn't afford their house and they ended up moving next door to me and my mom. But he really didn't seem to notice me and I kind of just dropped the idea of him. But then, one day, he asked me to get cheesesteaks and, that was it, our first date."

"And did you know that he was the one?"

"By the end of the first date, I could think of nothing else but Will Abbott."

Rachel knew it. That's how it was supposed to be.

"Did you ever have any doubts? I mean, as the wedding got closer."

Hannah seemed to be in her own world. "No. Never. Will was surprisingly romantic. Once, a guy in one of my classes sent me roses for helping him study. Will was threatened by this, I have no idea why. When I came back from class the next day, he'd made a giant rose garden in my backyard. Every day they were in season, he'd pick a bunch and leave a vase on the counter with a little note." She laughed at the recollection. "The first one said, 'not too bad to be dating a landscaper.'"

Rachel visualized Will planting the rose bushes, his thick muscles flexing as he dug into the ground. She saw him picking the buds in the early morning, feet wet from dew, careful not to cut his fingers on the thorns. As Rachel held the image in her mind, Hannah spoke abruptly.

"But I don't think it's that way for everyone. I know lots of people who got cold feet before their wedding. My friend, Melanie, told me at her rehearsal dinner that she wanted to call it off. And she's been happily married for twelve years."

Rachel set Snowball on the floor. She lowered her voice and leaned closer to Hannah. "You know, sometimes I wonder if Aaron is the one." Her heart beat forcefully in her chest as she made this admission.

Hannah said nothing. Rachel knew she shouldn't have admitted her feelings. She hadn't told anyone her reservations about Aaron! Why would she confide in a complete stranger? Rachel opened her mouth to recant when Hannah spoke.

"Rachel, I know I don't really know you, but you seem like you know what you're doing. Trust your instincts. If it's right with Aaron, you'll know."

"Yes, yes." Rachel agreed quickly. "I'm being silly, I know."

The conversation turned from Rachel's engagement to first loves. Will was Hannah's. Of course. Rachel's was Greg Tisbury.

Rachel had not talked about Greg in years. But, once she started, the memories poured out as though they'd been released from a locked cage. She told Hannah how she met Greg when she was a freshman at Lafayette College.

"All the freshmen in Biology 101 were assigned a project where we had to catch butterflies. I think it was a rite of passage. Make the freshmen run around the campus with big nets." She smiled at the recollection. "Of course, all I could catch were the slow, white butterflies which flew close to the ground. Then, one day, I spotted a monarch in the middle of the quad. I dropped my books and ran after it with my net. I was so fixated on catching the butterfly that I didn't see Greg. I tripped over him, literally landing in his lap. 'Well, nice to meet you too,' he'd said. And then he went and caught the monarch for me."

"That is so cute. I love it." Hannah's sat up straighter, as if this were the type of story she'd expected Rachel to have told about Aaron. "And that's when you started dating Greg?"

"That's when it started," Rachel confirmed.

"And what drew you to him? Why did you like him?" Hannah put her chin in her hand.

"Greg loved everybody. He was so accepting. Greg was the kind of person who wouldn't care if you had a nose ring or purple hair or tattoos all over your body. People were just people to him."

"Mmm…" Hannah didn't ask the question, but Rachel could feel what she wanted know.

"I broke up with Greg at the end of my senior year. It was awful, but my parents just didn't approve. Greg wasn't Jewish. He was too liberal, he talked too much, he was vegan." Rachel shook her head at the memories. "I think they were the only two people in the world who didn't like Greg Tisbury." She recalled the arguments she'd had with them over the issue. "I should have been stronger. I should have stood my ground."

Hannah paused. "Well. Now that you're engaged, maybe you could reach out to Greg. Close that door and move forward."

"I haven't seen or talked to him in years." Rachel leaned back on the couch.

"It might help you move on."

Would it? Rachel considered. Before she could respond, Hannah yawned. It was nearly 2 a.m.

"You're tired." Rachel got up. "We can finish talking tomorrow."

"No. I—" Hannah yawned again.

"That's it. Go to bed." Rachel started up the stairs, taking a quick look back at Hannah with the same giddy feeling she'd had as a child when a friend slept over.

Rachel pulled on satin pajamas and climbed into bed. She closed her eyes and saw Greg's tall frame and mop of unruly black hair. She saw his loping form as he ran after the monarch; his crooked smile as he handed her the net with the butterfly, victorious.

In her final thoughts before falling asleep, Rachel wondered if Hannah was right. Did she need to close the door with Greg to before she could fully commit to Aaron?

The next morning, Rachel looked forward to a leisurely breakfast with Hannah. Maybe they'd go to Starbucks and get biscotti and lattes. Pumpkin spice was out.

Rachel came downstairs. Hannah sat perched on the edge of the couch, the sweat clothes Rachel had lent her folded neatly in a pile next to her. "I'm so sorry about last night," Hannah said quickly. "I don't know what got into me."

"No worries. Really." Rachel ran her fingers through her hair in an attempt to look more presentable. She hadn't dressed yet. "At least you didn't go home with Burt."

Hannah winced, the camaraderie of the night before clearly gone. "I've imposed on you enough. I should really get going." She looked at Rachel then added, "whenever you're ready."

"We could get Starbucks on the way?" Rachel said with a small smile. "They have great biscotti there."

"That's so nice, Rachel but you've been so kind to me already. I couldn't impose more. Really. I feel awful."

"It was no trouble. I enjoyed having you." Snowball came into the room and rubbed up against her leg, a subtle reminder for breakfast. Rachel moved to the kitchen and opened a can, the smell of tuna temporarily escaping. "Last call for Starbucks," she said, keeping her voice light as she dumped the food in a dish.

"No. Really. Thank you though."

Rachel got dressed in a hurry.

Rachel drove Hannah back to McCourt's to get her car. Hannah was quiet on the drive. Rachel, unable to stand the silence, prattled on about the weather until they pulled up beside Hannah's minivan.

Hannah put her hand on the door and looked at Rachel. "Thank you for everything. I don't think I'll need you to file a divorce. I think the situation with Will is just a temporary thing. But can I call you if something changes?"

"Of course. But I may not be doing divorces for long. It was just a temporary assignment." Rachel launched into an explanation about how all the associates at Tremblay, Rubin, and

Connors do a rotation in each department before they are assigned a permanent one. "I'm most likely going to be in the commercial department," she explained. "But Jack Connors can answer your questions."

A look of unease flashed across Hannah's face.

Rachel registered the meaning behind her expression. "Or maybe the firm would let me work on your case even if I'm not in the matrimonial department, since we already know each other."

Hannah looked doubtful. "Really?"

"I can ask. Here. I'll give you my cell so you can get me directly." Rachel pulled a note out of her purse and scrawled the numbers.

Hannah took the paper. "Okay. I probably won't need you anyway." She began to open the door.

Rachel put her hand on her shoulder and Hannah turned to look at her. "Thanks for listening to me about Aaron. And Greg. I haven't talked about him in years." She smiled. "I really appreciated that. I think I needed it."

"Of course. I enjoyed our conversation. And don't worry about having cold feet. That happens to plenty of people. I think if you trust your instincts, you'll be fine." She stepped out of the car and looked back at Rachel. "Really. It will all work out, Rachel." She spoke with such confidence that it made Rachel feel calmer.

After a final goodbye, Hannah got out of the car and made her way to her van.

Rachel watched as Hannah's car turned left out of the parking lot and disappeared into the mass of vehicles on the roadway. Will and her kids would be there when she got home. They'd spend the day at the zoo or flying kites in the park, stopping on the way home for dinner at one of the generic chain restaurants Aaron refused to eat in. And Hannah would wake up in the morning to a vase of fresh cut roses with a handwritten note.

At least that was what Rachel hoped would happen.

SEVENTEEN

The week after her chance encounter with Hannah had been all-consuming. In the matrimonial department, every day was an emergency, every issue impacting a core element of someone's life. Rachel would listen to the clients' stories with horror, her emotions readable on her face.

After a client with a heart-wrenching story involving potential abuse departed, Jack Connors had laughed at her: "Don't get drawn in, Goldstein. They're all crazy."

But they didn't seem crazy. They seemed like regular people going through a terrible time.

Rachel found the work exhausting and intense. Even when she left the office, she was unable to leave the clients there. She carried them in her mind, worried she hadn't done enough, unable to force a boundary between their problems and her own. And the persistent thoughts about Greg Tisbury! Somehow, the conversation with Hannah had brought up memories and feelings she had thought were long buried. It was unfair, too, the way the memories played out, always when she was irritated with Aaron. If Aaron was rude, she'd recall some distant event where Greg had been polite in similar circumstances. If Aaron was busy, she would remember long afternoons spent with Greg doing nothing.

Rachel had to remind herself that the Greg she'd conjured up was fictitious. She had no idea what he was like now.

Because things were so difficult for her in the matrimonial department, Rachel was looking forward to Department Day, the day new associates were given their permanent positions at the firm. She desperately wanted to be assigned to the commercial department; rumors were the assignment was hers. An assignment in the commercial department would give her certainty, clarity, and direction. Rachel highlighted the day on her phone calendar; she had an internal countdown in her head. Seven days. Five days. Two days. Day of!

Rachel spent the morning of Department Day going through her twenty files, putting a sticky note on each to let the permanent associate know what had been done. She stared at the pile, thinking about the lives contained in those manila folders. Parents. Small children. Babies. She breathed out, averted her eyes, and turned out the office lights. That was that. No longer on her.

The atmosphere in the main conference room was charged. The large table in the center was set with flowers and drinks, a buffet of store-bought sandwiches, coleslaw, and chips on one end. Rachel stood in line with the other first-years. The two associates in front of her talked incessantly about the Philadelphia 76ers, while two others discussed a new restaurant nearby. No one acknowledged the reason they were there; it was almost as if their sole purpose was to exchange banalities.

After the group had their food and sat at the table, Andrew Trembley stood up.

"Hello!" he said, pushing his glasses up on the bridge of his nose. "Congratulations to all of you. You made it through our training program. Well done!" There was a smattering of applause. "Every associate in this room will be offered a full-time position in one of our departments today."

More light applause filled the room. Two associates high-fived each other. Andrew continued his speech.

"Much thought has been given to where each of you will fit best, to where your individual talents will be most effectively utilized for your personal development and that of the firm. You each will be given an envelope with your offer and will have until Friday to accept or decline."

Andrew paused, and Rachel imagined herself opening the envelope with her offer to work in the commercial department. Her face flushed at the thought.

"The assignments made today are final," Andrew continued. "If you cannot live with your assigned department, then you can decline our offer. We believe in all of you, believe in your placements, and sincerely hope that you will become part of our Trembley, Rubin, and Connors family."

Partners stood up in turn, announcing their new associates. Rachel barely paid attention; she knew the commercial department would be announced last. She daydreamed about how she would decorate her office in that section of the firm. Would they let her repaint it?

"Rachel Goldstein."

Rachel sat up in her chair, orienting herself. Why was her name called already? Were they doing the assignments out of order? She looked around. Jack Connors stood with an envelope with her name on it.

No.

The other associates clapped loudly. Rachel forced herself to stand. She pasted a smile on her face and took the envelope from

Jack's hand. She knew what she looked like. She was the bachelorette without a rose, the runner up on American Idol. She sat back down, feeling the weight of a room of stares. She smiled weakly. After what felt like forever, the next partner stood, deflecting the attention away from her. Thank God.

After the ceremony, Rachel grabbed her belongings from her now permanent office in the matrimonial department. She avoided the forced congratulations from her colleagues, slipping out the door unseen. She drove directly to Aaron's. He would know how much this meant to her. He'd scoop her up and recite clichéd platitudes about what a mistake the partners had made. She'd be kissed and coddled and babied and asked what she needed to feel better.

Rachel flung open the door to the apartment, ready for open arms and empathy.

The apartment was empty.

Rachel threw her purse on the kitchen counter and watched as its contents spilled out onto the black granite surface. She stood in the foyer and for a moment before stuffing the contents back in and moving the purse to its designated hook. She picked up her shoes and placed them in their space in the front closet.

Rachel walked to the kitchen, the hard floor unforgiving. She pulled out the white wine she'd brought from home, careful to wipe away leftover fingerprints on the stainless-steel fridge. Wine glass in hand, she moved to the black leather couch in the adjoining room, surrounded by severe modern sculptures and minimalist paintings. She didn't bother to turn any lights on.

Rachel closed her eyes and could see the pity on the faces of the other associates as her name was called for matrimonial. Matrimonial! The worst possible assignment. And working for Jack

Connors? It would be awful. A lump formed in her throat. She squeezed her eyes shut tighter to prevent the onset of tears.

The door opened. Aaron flicked on the lights.

Rachel stood. "Aaron—"

"Unbelievable news," he said, interrupting her. "I closed the Bleaker deal!" Aaron put his shoes on the left side of the front closet, still talking. "Even with five firms pitching. I managed to get the deal." He pumped his fist in the air in self-congratulations. "Come on. Help me celebrate."

Rachel stared at him. Had he really forgotten about Department Day?

Aaron disappeared into the wine cellar and emerged with a bottle. "Let's break open this baby." He turned the label so she could see it. She shrugged.

He opened the wine and inhaled the aroma. He poured two glasses, crossed the room, and took the wine glass from Rachel's hand. He sniffed it. "Don't drink this crap." He took the glass into the kitchen and poured the remaining wine in the sink.

Aaron gestured for Rachel to sit on the couch. He handed her his chosen wine and sat next to her. "Now this is the wine for a celebration." Aaron clinked their glasses. He launched into painfully specific details about the Bleaker deal, punching the air for emphasis several times. He leaned back after the story, as if the retelling had made him exhausted. He turned to Rachel and looked at her for the first time since he'd walked in.

"Is something wrong?"

"We got the department assignments today."

His expression was blank. "What was that again?"

"Department Day! The day we get assigned to our permanent departments."

Greg Tisbury would have remembered Department Day.

Faint recognition flickered across Aaron's face. "Oh. Right. How was that?"

"I got assigned to the matrimonial department."

"Divorce. Like, who gets the TV? Seriously?" He snorted.

"It's not about the TV." Rachel crossed her arms.

"Right, right. Who gets the couch, then?" He chuckled at his own joke then quickly added, "Is that what you wanted?"

Rachel put her wine down and leaned forward. "No, Aaron, it's not what I wanted. I wanted to be in the commercial department."

Greg Tisbury would have known she wanted to be in the commercial department.

"Should I call someone? I'm sure I know someone with connections to the firm. Maybe I can get them to move you."

"No. It's embarrassing enough. I don't need my fiancé calling trying to get me moved to another department. That wouldn't look right."

They sat in silence.

"You should quit," Aaron said suddenly. "We don't need the money."

She hadn't thought of that.

"Sell your townhouse. Move in here. You weren't planning to work after the wedding anyway."

She had never said that.

"Really, Rachel. Move in with me. It'll be a little marriage preview." He smiled crookedly. It made him look vulnerable. She felt a swell of what she imagined was love.

He took her face in his arms and kissed her. "I love you Rachel. Please move in with me."

She found herself unable to speak.

Quit her job?

Move in with Aaron?

It wasn't the craziest of ideas. She would be living with Aaron in a year anyway, after the wedding. She tried to let the idea take hold. What would she do all day in this sparsely furnished, modern space? What would she do with all her things? Aaron wouldn't want them. And what if she wanted a reprieve from order? A day to throw shoes on the floor and leave dishes in the sink?

Plus, she was proud to be an attorney. She'd spent three years in law school and two at the firm.

"I'll think about it."

A smile stretched across Aaron's face. "I'll do everything I can to convince you." He refilled her wine.

Later, Rachel lay stretched out on the king-size bed. She pulled the black sheets up over herself, Aaron's breath loud in the silence. She looked at his nude form. He was short but fit and his light brown hair, ordinarily neat, was rumpled. He snored lightly and appeared to be dreaming, his mouth upturned in smile. He was probably dreaming about the Bleaker deal.

Quit her job.

Move in here.

Rachel visualized herself alone in the apartment while Aaron worked late when she heard a faint ping alerting her to a text message. She uncurled herself from the covers and found her robe on its bathroom hook. She walked into the kitchen and retrieved her phone from the charging station, the light of its screen illuminating the space around her with an eerie glow.

A text from Hannah Abbott.

Just checking on you. Did you get the legal assignment you wanted?

She stared at the message. Hannah had remembered Department Day. That was thoughtful. Would it be so terrible to spend her days helping people like Hannah?

She could always quit.

She texted Hannah back and told her that she had been assigned to the divorce department and to call if she ever needed anything. Which she wouldn't.

And then she googled Greg Tisbury.

EIGHTEEN

"Honestly, Will, just come home," Hannah said when he asked to have the kids at his mom's for the weekend. Will stood at Scotty's counter, phone to his ear. When he didn't answer, Hannah continued. "This is crazy. I'm sorry. Okay? It's not like I didn't forgive the whole 'girls wrote all over me' incident."

"That was once. It was a mistake."

"So was mine."

Will paused. "I need more time."

She exhaled. He could picture her face, tight and pinched.

"Alright. What time then?" Will heard her open a drawer. Most likely the one where she kept the schedule.

They agreed she'd drop off the kids at his mom's at ten o'clock on Saturday morning.

When Will told his mother about the visit, Constance Abbott flew into action as though Charlie and Amanda were a king and queen scheduled for a royal visit. She cleaned every conceivable surface, including areas no person would reasonably see, like the tops of light bulbs. She stocked the fridge with kid-friendly foods like Capri Suns and Gogurts.

When Will opened a box of Ho Hos, she slapped his hand. "Those are for the kids." She handed him a bag of nuts.

Will reminded her that Charlie and Amanda had been to her home hundreds of times and that they had, just a few months back, slept over.

"Well, it feels different now," she'd said, vigorously rubbing a stain on the couch. It was one Charlie had made last Christmas.

On the morning the kids were to arrive, Constance baked cookies. She put coloring books out on the kitchen table with a new box of sixty-four crayons, the kind with the sharpener in the back. Will thought of Charlie and Amanda and their electronic appendages. "I'm not sure the kids color anymore."

His mother looked at him like she couldn't comprehend what he was saying. "Nonsense, Will. Every child likes a new coloring book."

The doorbell rang exactly at ten. Will opened the door, Constance right behind him. Hannah stood with the kids on the doorstep holding a carrot cake in a covered Tupperware container.

"For you," she said, handing it to his mother.

Constance took the cake with a forced, uncomfortable smile. "Thanks, dear."

They stood, an awkward quintet. Will picked up the kids' duffel bags; Charlie's stuffed rabbit, Mr. Hops, peeked out the top.

Hannah broke the long silence. "Okay then, call if you need anything." She kissed the kids on their heads. They looked at her, eyes wide, like pets being dropped off at a kennel.

This was stupid. Will began to formulate something to say, but David Dewey's words echoed in his mind: "If it looks like a duck." He visualized Hannah and Trent, heads together, at the fifth-grade committee meeting, her playful punch on his arm. He pictured himself scrolling through all the messages on her phone.

"We'll be fine," he said suddenly and shut the door with his wife still on the step. Constance looked at the closed door as if trying to understand what had just happened. Will turned to Charlie and Amanda.

"So, I thought we would ride bikes, have lunch, and get some ice cream. How does that sound?"

Charlie and Amanda looked at one another. "What would we do for bikes?" Charlie said finally.

"Old bikes. There's two still in the garage from when I was little. Nothing like the old Schwinn ten speed! I pumped the tires yesterday. So we're ready to roll." Even to his own ear, Will sounded unnatural.

"We don't have rain jackets here and it looks like it might rain," Amanda said. As if to punctuate her concern, heavy wind rattled the door.

"Nana will find some rain jackets," Constance interjected, strangely referring to herself in the third person. "Nana has extras." She bustled away.

"I think the rain will hold off," Will said, though he hadn't checked the weather. That was the type of thing he ordinarily would have left to Hannah. "But let's leave right away. Get this biking in!" He could not find his normal tone of voice.

"Can I use the bathroom?" Charlie asked.

"Of course, buddy. You don't have to ask, you know."

Constance returned with two windbreakers. The one for Amanda was hers, too large, and had the emblem 'Garden Gals' on the front. Upon his return from the bathroom, Charlie stuffed himself into a jacket left behind by one of the other grandchildren.

"Oh dear," Constance said. "That can't be comfortable."

"It's fine," Charlie insisted even though the jacket was so tight it looked like it might rip across his back.

Neither bike fit. Like the windbreakers, Amanda's was too large, Charlie's too small. Still, they stood next to their designated bikes and didn't complain.

"No helmets?" Amanda asked.

Helmets. Hannah would have had helmets. She most definitely would not want the kids riding without helmets.

She was always too careful.

"It's okay," Will said with authority.

Amanda stared at him as though he had told her they planned to jump from a cliff. "Really," Will assured her. "No one wore helmets when I was a kid. You're not going to fall. You're an expert bike rider, right?" The false cheerfulness continued.

As if to spite his words, five minutes into the bike ride, Amanda fell. Will ran to her, crouching down to look at the arm she landed on. Don't be broken. Don't be broken. She was scraped and bleeding, but there were no breaks. Thank God. Will couldn't imagine the phone call to Hannah. The kids hadn't even been with him an hour.

Amanda pointed to the bike. "It's too high," she whined. "I don't want to ride this bike. I want my bike."

"My bike's okay," Charlie volunteered.

"Shut up, Charlie." Amanda said. "No one asked you."

They walked the bikes back to the house in silence. When they entered and told Constance what happened, she immediately examined Amanda's arm. She washed out the cut, put on Neosporin and a band aid, and ushered Amanda to the couch. She went to the kitchen and returned with a glass of water, children's Tylenol, and an ice pack. "Big swallow now," she directed.

Will watched, wordlessly, wondering if he would have done any of those things had his mom not been there. Hannah would have.

Amanda sat on the couch and closed her eyes. Constance set out to make what she called "nice grilled cheese." She had always done that, inserted the word "nice" in front of a noun for comfort purposes. After a long day, he didn't just need a tuna fish sandwich, he needed a "nice" tuna fish sandwich; not a sweatshirt, a "nice" sweatshirt.

It worked for Will. He felt comforted. Nice grilled cheese was on the way.

The nice grilled cheese was not enough. Amanda was clearly still in pain. Will took her to the minute clinic to get her arm looked at. They waited over two hours.

"Some minute clinic," Amanda whispered as they walked back to see the doctor. Will laughed. Amanda had always been quick.

At the minute clinic check-out, Will didn't have an insurance card. Hannah always handled the medical appointments for the kids. The check-out girl had no tolerance.

"No, you are not in the system, Mr. Abbott," she told him after he'd insisted she look them up. He was sure Hannah had come here before. A line began to form behind him as he explained that Hannah had the insurance cards.

"If your wife has the card, maybe you should call her." The woman's tone hovered between irritation and anger.

Call Hannah?

"No. I'll pay," Will said quickly. He handed the woman his credit card and paid $165 for an appointment which should have cost $10.

When they returned to his mother's, Constance immediately showed him the three pictures Charlie had colored in his absence. Charlie still sat at the table, tongue out in concentration, as he made black spots on a dog.

"See. All kids love to color," Constance said, her voice triumphant. Then she saw Amanda. "Oh no!"

Amanda looked pleased by the attention. "It's a sprain." She eyed Charlie at the table. "I don't think I'll be able to color. Right arm." She moved it slightly for emphasis.

No writing. And they had just started school. Will hadn't thought of that.

"Well come here and sit then, dear." Constance moved to the couch and fluffed a pillow. They sat. Once finished with the dog picture, Charlie joined them.

It was 2:38 p.m.

Will had the kids until tomorrow evening.

The minutes ticked by and, slowly, each of them gravitated to an electronic device. They sat, a grouping of four, each in a different world commanded by tiny screens. The sound of Mario music emanated from Charlie's device. He muted it. A minute later, Amanda guffawed and typed furiously on her phone.

"Something funny?" Will asked.

"It's nothing."

"Shoot," Charlie said keeping his focus on the screen. "I just died." He shrugged then returned to the game.

"Looks like Wendy Sparks just had twins," Constance said and flipped her iPad to show Will a Facebook picture of a woman he didn't recognize.

"Nice."

Will stared at his phone. This could not be it. This could not be his first weekend with the kids, sitting on couches, staring at screens.

Will leaned his head back, willing an idea into his brain. Then, he sat up, suddenly excited.

"Who wants to see an elephant?"

NINETEEN

Everyone stopped, the draw of electronics temporarily abated.

"Who wants to see an elephant?" Will repeated.

"I do!" Charlie said.

"Is it real?" Amanda asked.

"It's six stories tall."

"Six stories?" Amanda shook her head. "Then it's not real."

"It's made of a million pieces of wood."

"Definitely not real," she said with a satisfied air.

"I still want to see it." Charlie's voice hinted at a whine.

"We can go inside. It's at the beach."

At the mention of the beach, Amanda's expression changed. She put her phone down on her lap. "Okay. I'd like to go."

"Will." Constance said, concern in her voice. "There's supposed to be a big storm."

"We'll be fine, Mom." He was too energized by his new idea to worry about details.

"Well, at least let me pack you up a nice snack." Constance put her iPad down and walked to the kitchen.

"Lucy the Elephant is 135 years old," Will told Charlie and Amanda as they got ready. "It's the country's oldest roadside attraction."

"How do you know this, Dad?" Amanda questioned as she put on her shoes. "I've never even heard of Lucy."

"I have a client who was on the Save Lucy committee. She told me about her." Will glanced at Charlie and Amanda. "Ready?"

Constance handed Will three Ziploc bags with pretzels and goldfish. "Be sure to turn back if it starts to storm," she called as they got in the car.

Will gave her a dismissive wave. "It's fine, Mom." Amanda took her place in the front passenger seat, Charlie sat in the back. Once on their way, Amanda used the front controls to make Charlie's seat hot; he protested to Will.

"Come on, guys," Will said as he pulled into a Wawa convenience store.

Junky food on car trips had been a tradition of his Dad's. It was one Hannah had not embraced. Will hesitated as if Hannah might appear and scold him. He shook his head. Hannah wasn't here, and a little junk wouldn't hurt.

"Pick anything you want," he told the kids as they walked in.

"Really?" Charlie asked. "What about Nana's snacks?"

Will shrugged. "We'll eat those, too."

They stood at the counter ten minutes later with cookies, two large packs of M&Ms, and giant Gatorades. At the last moment, Charlie grabbed a pack of gum.

They scrambled back in the car. Distracted by food, Charlie and Amanda didn't fight. Will flipped on the radio; John Denver's

"Take Me Home, Country Roads" sounded through the car. Will sang along and drummed the steering wheel. He wanted to make the day as normal as possible.

Amanda gave him a sideways look. "You're silly, Dad." She handed him a cookie.

An hour later, they turned off the exit to Margate, the torso and head of a gray elephant visible in the distance. Both kids crammed toward Charlie's window to get a better look. "There she is!" Charlie yelled with excitement.

Will pulled into a parking space a block away.

Lucy stood on a concrete block surrounded by grass one block from the ocean. A tiny house, bright green, sat adjacent to her. Both Lucy and the house were enclosed by an aging, split-level fence.

"Look how huge her eyes are!" Charlie reached for the handle of the car.

As they bounded out, a gust of wind blew them back. Will looked at the sky. There were still specks of sun in the darkening clouds. It would be fine. Just a little wind.

Charlie jumped up and down; Amanda pulled her arms around herself for warmth. Will checked the car for the windbreakers. He'd forgotten them. Shoot. He took off his sweatshirt and handed it to Amanda.

Charlie looked as though he was about to protest Amanda getting the sweatshirt. Will shot him a look and Charlie nodded.

Will opened the gate in the fence surrounding Lucy and they made their way to the green building. A heavyset man stood near the doorway packing up Lucy memorabilia. He stood up straight when he saw Will and the kids.

Will glanced at the man's nametag. "Anthony, hi. We'd like to tour the elephant." Will reached in his back pocket to retrieve his wallet.

Anthony picked up a box of Lucy snow-globes. "We stop weekend tours after Labor Day." He resumed packing.

Will looked at Charlie and Amanda. They stared back at him.

"Is there any way you can make an exception? I'll pay for the tickets." Will flashed his wallet. "I'll even pay extra."

Anthony stood up and stretched. "We're setting up for a party tomorrow so no one's allowed in."

"Just a quick peek?"

"Sorry. My hands are tied." He held up his hands.

Will looked back at Charlie and Amanda who, bored with the logistics, were vigorously shaking the snow globes.

"Put those down." Will looked back Anthony. "You're sure?" There was a hint of desperation in his voice.

"Sorry."

Will turned to the kids. "Guys. We have to go. No tours today."

"You mean we don't get to go in the elephant?" Charlie put down the snow globe. Wisps of white confetti swirled and fell.

"Not today."

"Can we at least get a picture in front of it?" Amanda held out her phone.

The man looked up from his box. "If you stand in front of the tape, I'll take it for you."

They stood in front of Lucy. Amanda's hair blew into her face from the wind. Will squinted into the harsh air. As Charlie opened his mouth to say something, Anthony snapped the shot. He flipped the phone and they examined the photo. The only part of Lucy visible in the picture was her thick, gray legs. Charlie appeared to be crying; Will wincing. They looked like apocalypse survivors. Amanda posted the picture on her Snapchat anyway.

"Thanks, sir," Will said automatically. He looked at the kids. He had to do something. The day, his first day as a solo parent, had been such a disaster.

"Let's check out the boardwalk, guys."

They walked a block to the boardwalk. Wind blew in unrelenting gusts; sand swirled on the wood surface like mini tornados. The ocean waves, rough and white-capped, crushed against the beach near a few brave seagulls. Dark clouds covered all but a few bits of sun. Nearly all the stores on the abandoned boardwalk were closed, their merchandise visible through thick metal grates.

The wind pushed at their backs as they walked. Amanda said something Will couldn't make out.

"What?"

She repeated the statement, louder but still unclear.

"I can't hear you," Will shouted. "The waves are too loud."

Suddenly, Will stopped and squinted. Two blocks ahead stood a store with flag whipping on a post out front. OPEN. Will pointed at it. "Look! Let's go!"

They ran to the shop and stumbled through the doorway. It was crammed with junk—T-shirts, pens, keychains, stuffed Lucys, and flip flops. A metal bin of cheap buckets and shovels in mesh bags stood near the check-out counter. Tiny bathing suits hung throughout the store, their price tags dangling like little yellow flags.

"See anything you like?" Will asked the kids. He picked up a picture frame lined in shells. "For the Lucy picture?" He held it out to Amanda. She shrugged and Will put the frame back down.

"How about those!"

Will followed Charlie's gaze to a shelf of cylinder-shaped containers, each holding a small hermit crab with a painted shell. A tiny, plastic sign was affixed to the handle of each container: "Get Crabby in Margate."

"They're so cute!" Amanda chimed in. She looked at Will. "Can we get them, Dad?"

Will looked at her sling. He thought about the bikes and the jackets and the failed attempt to see Lucy. Outside, the wind whipped, and the sky darkened. "Why not?"

Will could think of one thousand reasons why not. The first one started with H.

"Really?!" Amanda seemed not to believe that Will was actually going to let them get the crabs.

Neither could he.

"Sure. One for each of you."

Charlie and Amanda charged the area with same enthusiasm they might have used had Will told them to pick two puppies from a litter, their reaction a testament to how bad the day had been to that point.

Amanda picked a crab with a butterfly on its shell. Charlie's had a dinosaur.

A young girl with giant hoop earrings smacked gum as she rang them up. "Do you need food for the crabs?" She pointed to a bottle of food which, ironically, cost more than the crabs themselves.

"Oh, right," Will said sheepishly. "I guess we have to feed them."

Will bought the crabs and two bottles of food and they left the store. The wind pushed at the crab canisters; both kids held them tight to their chests. "Don't worry, little buddy," Charlie told his crab. "I'll get you inside soon."

A block ahead, a lone woman stood holding out a tray of fudge samples. Her face was red from the harsh weather and the wind blew her hair back. Will had to look twice to make sure he saw her correctly.

"Fudge sample?" she yelled.

Will nodded. As they approached, she peeled back the cellophane on the tray, but a gust of wind picked up the loose plastic and sent it flying down the boardwalk.

Charlie ran after it, legs pumping, his crab bobbing up and down in the cylinder cage he still held in his hand. "Hold up, Charlie!" Will yelled but Charlie didn't stop. He had just reached the cellophane when he fell forward. Before he could catch his balance, the basket slipped from his hand.

It broke, its pieces, crab included, now swooping along the boardwalk with the wind. Will sprinted after the flying crab, catching him just as he was about to career off the boardwalk. Will walked back, smiling and triumphant. He handed the crab to Charlie.

Charlie cradled the creature in both hands. "I'm sorry, crab. I'm sorry. I'm sorry. I'm sorry. I'm sorry." His voice choked, tears streamed down his face. "I'm so, so sorry. I'm sorry." The last sorry turned into a sob.

Will bent down to look at Charlie. His face was contorted; snot ran down his nose. Will pulled him into an embrace. "It's okay, buddy. The crab's okay."

"I'm sorry," he said, voice muffled as he sobbed on Will's shoulder. "I'm sorry. I'm sorry." He lifted his head and looked at Will. "I'm sorry I made you leave, Daddy."

"Charlie thinks you left because he quit soccer." Amanda clarified.

No. Will had been disappointed that Charlie didn't want to play soccer, but he had reassured him that it was okay. Hannah did too. They'd had a long conversation in the kitchen. Why would Charlie think he left because of that? He looked at his son's anguished face.

"Charlie, my leaving for a bit has nothing to do with you. Nothing to do with soccer." He wrapped his arms around his son's small frame again. "You're a wonderful little boy. I am proud of you and I love you. You've done nothing wrong."

Will held out an arm and motioned for Amanda. She folded into the embrace.

They stood, a crying, hugging threesome in the center of the boardwalk, unmovable despite the wind and sand pelting at their skin. Will felt a raindrop. "We should go," he said, releasing them.

TWENTY

They walked back down the boardwalk, the wind whipping their faces. The rain, now heavy, pelted down on them, soaking their clothes. Amanda cradled the crab canister to protect it from the rain.

Near the entrance to the boardwalk, a soft-serve ice cream cone picture lit up the darkening sky. Will motioned to the kids and they dashed to the overhang, a temporary reprieve from the increasing rain.

"Food for the ride home?" he asked.

They ordered hot dogs, boardwalk fries, and cookies. The concession worker put the items in a in a large plastic bag and handed it to Will. They made their way toward the car.

As they walked the single block, thunder clapped and the rain turned torrential. For a split second, the entire area was illuminated by lightning. Will saw Lucy and her surroundings brighten for a moment, then it was dark again. They continued their steady pace, unable to hurry because of the food and the crabs. Thunder clapped again. Charlie jumped.

"Almost there," Will yelled.

As they passed Lucy, Will saw Anthony locking up the green building.

There was another bolt of lightning and their eyes met across the illuminated sky.

Anthony observed Will a moment then yelled. "Hey, do yous guys want to eat inside the elephant?"

"What!?" Will and the kids made their way toward him.

"Do yous guys want to eat in the elephant?" Anthony asked again when they were closer.

Will registered the offer. "Oh. Okay."

The man ushered them out of the rain, into Lucy's leg. He flipped the lights, briefly revealing a winding staircase.

They stood in the open doorway, shivering. Rainwater from their soaked clothes dripped on the floor.

"Wow," Charlie said. "This is cool."

Amanda took out her phone. Just as she did so, thunder boomed again. A gust of wind blew the door shut with a bang. The lights inside Lucy's leg flickered for a moment. Then it was dark. Charlie wrapped his arms around Will's waist.

"No worries," Anthony said. A moment later, a small circle of light illuminated the space. They followed it up the stairs. When they reached Lucy's belly, Anthony stopped and shone the flashlight around the room.

The walls in the long, oval space were reddish brown and lined with historical pictures of Lucy. At one end, a staircase led to a doorway which, Will imagined, connected to the deck he'd seen from the outside. On the other end, Lucy's oversized eyes served as windows, providing the only natural light. Throughout the room sat a dozen circular tables adorned with white tablecloths and centerpieces with tall candles, pink carnations, and glittery sweet sixteen signs. A tiny replica of Lucy centered each place setting.

Anthony lit the candles on each table, casting a ceremonial glow.

He pointed to a box in the far side of the room. "We have leftover sweatshirts from Lucy's 135 birthday bash. We're getting rid of them so feel free to take a few. They're mostly XLs but they're dry."

Will and the kids walked to the box and pulled out the giant sweatshirts. Stenciled on the front each was a monogram of Lucy with a red, pointy birthday hat and the inscription: "Happy 135th Lucy!"

"Thanks, Anthony," Will said.

"You looked like you could use a break."

Will smiled. "Thanks," he said again.

In the gentle glow of the candlelight, they sat in their oversized Lucy sweatshirts, finally dry, warming. The crabs were perched, front and center, on the table. Rain battered Lucy's back; thunder boomed in periodic bursts. Every few moments, lightning briefly brightened the surroundings.

Will passed out the food.

"Wow! It's awesome in here," Charlie said, breaking the silence.

"I love the decorations," Amanda said, looking around. "And I can't believe you let us get hermit crabs."

"I can't believe you sprained your arm. Mom's going to kill me." They laughed.

"Mom will be more upset that we didn't have helmets," Charlie said, popping a soggy fry into his mouth.

"And that you didn't use sunscreen," Amanda added.

"Or bug spray." Worry crossed Charlie's face. "We won't tell her. Just get them next time."

Will reached out and squeezed Charlie's hand. "Okay. I'll do better next time."

They sat in a comfortable silence, worn from the day's events.

Hannah should be here.

The thought popped in his head. Then Will reminded himself that, if Hannah were present, they would never have been at the shore to begin with because she would have known it was going to storm. She would not have made a series of errors so pitiful that it would cause a stranger to take mercy. She'd have thought it unsafe to follow an unknown man into a dark elephant. She'd have frowned on his choice for dinner. If Hannah were here, they wouldn't be having this moment.

The fact that Will's failure of a day had been transformed at the last moment to a memorable event actually proved what Hannah had always said: "You're a charmed man, Will Abbott. Everything just works out for you." When they had first met, she'd said it in a loving, teasing way; since the kids, it had a more caustic feel. In the spring, he'd forgotten Charlie's cleats for a soccer tournament and the coach happened to have an extra pair in his size.

"The stars align again for Will Abbott," Hannah had said. Meant as a joke, it came off as a criticism.

Will shook the memory from his mind and pulled out his phone. "Let's get a picture." He extended his arm to hold out phone and the three of them posed for a selfie. It was a great shot. Will started to make it his screensaver but, staring for a moment at Hannah's pretty outdoor picture, he left it alone.

TWENTY-ONE

At 5 p.m. the next day, Will drove Charlie and Amanda home. He sent them inside and typed a text message to Hannah from the car.

Kids coming in now. Heads up that Amanda sprained her arm.

He pressed send and waited. He imagined Hannah reading the text. She'd shake her head and mutter about his parental incompetence.

His phone pinged with her response; he braced himself.

Things happen.

Pause.

Do you want to come in for dinner?

Will stared at the message. It was not what he expected.

Did he want to come in for dinner?

Yes. He did.

No. Too soon.

Will sat in his own driveway, a mass of indecision. He typed a response.

Can't tonight. Next time?

The stared at the words, unable to press send. He could almost hear his dad's gentle voice: "Just go in, Will." Then, as he had done dozens of times since finding the messages on Hannah's phone, he pictured Hannah and Trent in their photography class, discussing where they'd go to dinner. They'd have sat at a wiry table at one of the outdoor cafés Hannah liked, sipping wine, comparing notes. Had she talked about him? Was he the subject of some secret joke?

If it looks like a duck...

Will pressed send, drove off, and forced himself to not look at the house in the rearview mirror.

He drove to Scotty's who had, since Will's separation, appointed himself as a type of mentor, imparting unwanted advice about divorce and the dating scene. For the past two weeks, he'd begged Will to go with him to his men's divorce support group meeting. He promised it was more of a guys' get together at McCourt's.

As expected, Scotty accosted Will about attending the meeting as soon as he entered the apartment. "Come on now. Come to the meeting. If nothing else, you can get a drink." Scotty dangled his keys in front of Will like some kind of treat.

Will considered. He could use a beer.

"Okay," he said finally. "But I'm bringing my own car."

When they arrived at the meeting in the back room at McCourt's, half a dozen men sat around a pocked table centered by pitchers of beer.

"Scotty!" The chorus of greetings suggested Scotty was the leader among this small group.

"This is Will," Scotty said as they pulled up chairs to the table. "Soon to join our ranks."

Will started to correct the statement then stopped himself. It didn't matter. He wouldn't be back. The meeting started after a few late arrivals.

There was no real organization; it was more of a roundtable of outrage. One man was fixated on not paying for college. Another was incensed that he wouldn't get his children for Halloween. The most vocal of the group was a heavy man named Frank who was convinced that the family court judges were conspiring against him. Frank punctuated his sentences by banging his fist on the table, mugs reverberating in the wake, gold liquid sloshing about.

But no matter what the issue, the men were collectively aggrieved, their anger amplified through the shared experience. It was nothing like what Will had expected. It put him on edge. He had just wanted a beer and some camaraderie.

"So what did yours do to you?" Frank asked, staring at Will.

It was almost as if Frank were testing him. Was he angry enough? Bitter enough? Should he be admitted passage into this small club of outraged men? Will took a sip of his beer.

Scotty looked between Frank and Will. "Will's wife is having an affair," he volunteered.

"I don't know that," Will said quickly. The men laughed. Will's face flushed. "She said they're just friends."

The group laughed again; one man actually slapped his knee.

"Right, right," the knee-slapping man said. "The 'we're just friends' bit. Right. Okay." More laughter.

"That's just wrong!" Frank banged his fist again.

Will got up. He'd had enough. He didn't need to be here.

He started toward the door just as it swung open and a stunning woman wearing high, pointy heels hobbled in carrying a tray of hoagies. Will ran to grab the tray and realized it was Amber, the girl from the Phillies game.

"David wanted me to check up on you guys," Amber said then looked at him. "Will! It's nice to see you." Her face broke into a smile.

She remembered him. His heart quickened. Why? What did it matter? "Nice to see you too." Will kept his voice calm.

The men collectively said hello. Amber smiled as if seeing them was the highlight of her day. She perched on a chair and retrieved a yellow legal pad from her oversized bag. She crossed one leg over the other and her tight, auburn dress slid up her thigh. A set of silver bangles jiggled as she grabbed a pen.

"What are you doing here?" Will asked, taking a seat next to her.

"Dave wants to make sure men's rights are being protected. He wants to know how divorce impacts them in their real lives. So I come to the men's group to get a feel for what's happening."

Will nodded. He looked at her lips. They were full and dark red.

Amber turned to the group. "So? What can I tell Dave?"

She listened to every man's burden, sometimes shaking her head slightly in support, shiny hair bouncing with the subtle movement, eyes wide with concern.

Will wondered if it was an act. It seemed impossible that this angelic-looking woman could care that much about the lives of these angry men. But they loved it, seeming to take pride in their individual miseries, basking in her concern. At the conclusion of the meeting, most had issues they had to discuss with her privately.

For reasons he could not explain, Will found himself among the men waiting. She caught sight of him, her attention momentarily diverted from Frank, and winked.

"Ready to go, Willy boy," Scotty punched him on the shoulder.

Will glared at him. "I'm good. I got my car here, remember?"

"Want to grab some—"

"No. I'm good."

Scotty glanced at Amber then back at Will. A salacious smile crossed his face. "Okay, Willy." He raised his eyebrows and tilted his head in Amber's direction. "I see what's going on."

"Nothing is going on."

"Okay, then," Scotty said. "I'll see you later." He took a step toward the door then turned back to look at Will. "Maybe."

Will watched him walk out. Scotty's assumption that he'd stayed behind for some untoward purpose unnerved him. Yet, he couldn't fully explain why he was waiting to talk to Amber. He should leave. He felt his keys in his pocket and glanced in Amber's direction. "Hold up," she mouthed.

Like an obedient pet, he waited. Amber finished her conversation and walked toward him. "Will!" She motioned for him to sit. He sat and she took her place across from him. "How are you doing?" She grabbed his hand and squeezed, long nails momentarily digging into his skin.

Will looked at her. Her eyes, absurdly beautiful, were pools of dark brown. "I'm alright," he told her. "Hannah and I are taking a break for a bit."

"Is that going alright?"

"It is what it is."

It is what it is? Will never said things like that.

"Mmmm. And the kids. Are they okay?"

"They're okay. I just had them for the weekend."

"How was that?" She pulled her hair over her shoulder and leaned forward.

Will told her about the weekend, making the whole event seem like a hilarious comedy of errors. The bikes, the sprained arm, the storm.

She loved the part about the crab. "You saved it from flying off the boardwalk?"

Will didn't tell her about Charlie's meltdown.

She seemed intensely interested in the description of them eating in the elephant. Will pulled out his phone to show her the selfie he had taken of him and the kids inside Lucy. Hannah's image filled the screen when he turned on the phone. Will closed his eyes. What was he doing? He shook his head and pulled up the Lucy picture.

Amber shifted closer, placing her head next to his as they looked at the image. Her hair fell on to his shoulder; she smelled like lilacs.

"You seem like such a good dad," she said. He looked over at her. Her eyes glistened. Was she crying?

Without warning, Will heard his Dad's voice in his head: "Go home and be with your kids, Will."

He sat a minute, visualizing Hannah and the kids at home eating pizza and playing a silly board game. This was crazy. Why was he sitting with Amber? What was wrong with him?

"I should go," he said finally.

They left the bar and Will escorted her to a silver coupe. She stood next to it, the streetlamp overhead casting a celestial glow on her body.

"Will I see you next week?" she asked.

"Sure," Will said, unable to move away from her.

After too long a pause, he stepped back. "Well," he said as she got into her car. "It was nice seeing you again."

"You too, Will."

Amber shut the car door and drove out of the parking lot. Will held his hand up in a tiny wave.

He visualized Amber on the stool, thigh peeking out from her tight dress. He recalled the feel of her hand on his at the table; the light scent of lilacs on her skin. He shook his head as if doing so would make the image of Amber disappear.

Come on, Will.

He wouldn't be back.

TWENTY-TWO

Will went back the next week. And then the week after. After a month, it seemed Amber expected him to wait for her. He stayed; Scotty smiled perversely. Will ignored it. There was nothing going on.

He just liked talking with Amber. The conversation was easy, and she was unsparing in her compliments. Amber was not frustrated by him; he was not incompetent in her eyes. She looked at Will the way Hannah used to.

After the end of a particularly long meeting, Amber and Will sat at their usual table in the back of McCourt's.

"I'm starving," she announced. "But I'm not eating these."
She picked up a tray of half-eaten buffalo wings. "Would you
want to get something in the bar?"

She tilted her head to the side. Will watched as she twisted a
lock of hair around her finger. He should go home.

But it was just food. And he was hungry.

"Sure. I'll never turn down a good meal." Will forced his tone
to be light. He stood and Amber walked forward, high heels clicking on the floor. Will followed her. She paused and pointed to her
boot. "This darn zipper always comes loose." As she bent down
to adjust it, her blouse fell open. Will caught a glimpse of black
lace and looked away. He should really go home.

Amber stood and continued toward the bar. Despite his reservations, Will followed. At the hostess table, he asked for a table
for two.

The hostess seated them at a dark booth in the corner illuminated by a candle in a mason jar. She took their order. At the last
moment, Will ordered nachos to share, then immediately regretted it. He and Hannah always ordered nachos to share. He almost
called to the waitress to cancel the nachos, but it seemed silly to
do so. It was only chips and cheese. It didn't mean anything.

Bar workers cleared a large space in the center of the room. A
chubby man in an oversized cowboy hat rolled in a sound system.
Dozens of McCourt's patrons wearing brimmed hats and plaid
shirts congregated on the floor.

"It looks like the bar has been invaded by a dude ranch," Will
whispered to Amber.

She laughed. Will scoured his brain for something else funny
to say.

"Testing, testing, one two three," the chubby man, clearly the
MC, said into a microphone.

"Oh wow," Amber said, "I think they are going to have square dancing. I haven't square danced since elementary school!"

"We did that too. I was dying to dance with Donna James. I still remember it, our gym teacher pairing us up. I kept hoping I'd get with Donna. I never did. All six years of elementary school, I never once got paired up with Donna James."

"Oh, poor baby."

"You sound like you don't feel bad for me?"

"Oh, I feel bad for you." She smiled and took a sip of wine. Will watched her lips pucker around the glass, leaving tiny red prints.

Twenty or so square dancers gathered in the center of the room. The MC called out. "Alright y'all. It's time for a hoedown!"

Everyone clapped. One man yelled, "Yee Haw!"

"Get in groups of eight, y'all!" directed the MC. "Grab those pretty little ladies and come on down." The square dancers assembled into two groups of eight, one group of six.

The MC studied the groups. "Alright McCourt's. We need two more! Who's ready to go for a whirl?" He began to circle the room for volunteers.

Amber stood up and pulled at Will's arm. "Let's do it."

Will began to protest. "I don't—"

"I know I'm no Donna James," Amber teased.

Will looked at her and the group of patrons waiting. It would be rude to say no. It was just a silly dance.

"Alright, alright," Will responded, sliding off his seat. He followed Amber to the floor. They stood with their group and he received a few raps on the shoulder. This may have been for volunteering or because he was paired with Amber. It was hard to tell.

The MC bought them each a cowboy hat and tied a bandana around Amber's neck. Once they looked sufficiently Western, he returned to his station and started the music. His voice boomed over violin and banjo sounds. Neither Will nor Amber were prepared for the rapid commands and they laughed as they attempted to follow along.

"Change partners," the MC bellowed.

Will bowed to the middle-aged woman to his left. She leaned forward and whispered to him. "Your wife is stunning."

Will looked at Amber, charming the woman's husband. He thumbed his wedding ring.

The woman's words stayed with him for the next song, spilling over into the break. Your wife is stunning.

"Are you alright, Will?" Amber asked as they headed to their table.

Will forced a smile. "Great. Just have to use the bathroom." He walked to the back.

It was getting too real.

He'd tell Amber he had to go.

Will left the bathroom and walked toward the table with every intention of leaving. As he neared, he saw an older man sitting across from Amber, his face in a scowl. Will came up behind her.

"It's for medical bills," the man said.

"No." Amber's tone was harsh.

"You don't even know, Amber, you don't know." The man curled his knuckles around the table.

"I said no!"

Will stepped into view. "Is everything alright here?"

"Will!" Amber jumped up. "Let's go." She grabbed his hand and led him toward the door. Will glanced back at the man.

"You'll regret it, Amber," he called after them. "When she's gone, you'll regret it."

Amber kept walking.

When they got outside, she dropped Will's hand and walked briskly toward her car.

"What's wrong?" Will asked, hurrying to catch up. "Who was that? Can I help you?"

She turned to face him, her face wet with tears. She took a deep breath and said, "That was my dad. He wants money." She sat on a cement parking divider and put her face in her hands. Will sat next to her. She looked at him. "He says my mom is sick. He needs money for medical bills."

"Oh. I'm sorry." Will paused. "Do you need money?"

"It's a lie." Her voice was cold. She started to stand. "I don't want to keep you."

Will took her hand and pulled her gently back down next to him. "I have time."

"My parents are drug addicts," she explained, putting her hand on Will's. "They have been for my whole life. Sometimes, they'd be fine for a few months, but they always went back to using. The school nurse called DYFS when I was ten."

"DYFS?" Will asked.

"The Division of Youth and Family Services. DYFS put me in a foster home with the goal of family reunification." Amber made air quotes as she said the last words. "The idea was to put my parents in a spot where they could take care of me. They actually got better for a few years and I returned home."

"Well, that's good," Will said, believing this to be the end of the story.

Amber laughed derisively. "It didn't last. I was placed in a different foster home at age sixteen. The son in the house walked in while I was in the shower then I found him in my room one night. I complained and the court appointed David Dewey as my guardian ad litem."

"David Dewey was your child advocate? I can't see that."

Amber laughed. "David's a lot nicer than people think but don't tell anyone. He says it will ruin his image. Anyway, Dave was great. He got me emancipated and set me up in a girls' apartment with a house mother. He bought me things for my room and gave me a $100 gift card to Target." She smiled at the recollection. "I remember I was so excited about that gift card. When I went to use it, I just walked through all the aisles, thinking 'I can get that. I can get that.' I ended up leaving with nothing."

"And you started working for him then?"

"No. We lost touch. I was working at Hooters after high school to support myself. One night, David came in and I was sure he was going to hit on me. Instead, he said: 'so what's the endgame here?' So I told him that I wanted to be a lawyer and advocate for foster children, to help kids like I was."

She paused and Will tried to digest this new version of the woman sitting next to him. Amber wasn't just beautiful, she was complex and warm-hearted.

"David told me he'd just opened a new firm and needed a paralegal. He offered tuition reimbursement; I couldn't believe it. I'm almost done with my four-year degree at Mercer. Then I'll apply to law school."

Will felt inadequate. And foolish. He thought Amber had looked up to him, a wise, older guy.

Will stood and reached down to grab Amber's hands. He pulled her to her feet and they stood, their faces inches apart. "Impressive," he said finally.

In the next instant, her lips were on his, soft and moving. Will acquiesced. He put his arms around her waist and she opened her mouth.

Will pulled back. "I'm sorry."

Amber looked stunned.

"I can't—" Will took another step back.

"I understand." Her voice caught as she said it. She felt her cheeks then turned and reached for the car door. "Thanks for listening." She slid into the driver's seat and flipped on the headlights. Will stepped out of the light as Amber removed her cowboy hat and placed it on the passenger seat. She gave him a tiny wave and drove away.

Will stood in the dark parking lot thinking about the foster kid with goals to become a child advocate. And it scared him.

Because Will could have easily walked away from the first Amber.

But the new one?

That would be a whole lot more difficult.

TWENTY-THREE

Hannah

Hannah pulled into the parking lot of the Newtown Historic Church, the agreed upon locale for the fifth-grade spring carnival. The small stone church stood back from the street, a grassy plot in the front. A tiny graveyard encompassed by a small, wrought iron fence sat on the left, trees on the right.

Hannah got out of the car and scanned the surroundings. Jess's voice rang out. "Hannah! Over here!" She waved frantically from twenty feet away. John put his hand on her arm.

Hannah waved and saw Charlotte's car pull into the lot. Hannah waited and caught a glimpse of Trent's tall figure through the trees. He was walking the property line, his gaze buried downward.

The five of them assembled on the church steps to start the discussion about the carnival. Trent avoided looking at her; Hannah stiffened at the slight. She should have known it would be awkward. Since the fallout with Will, she'd cancelled on Trent twice and didn't return his texts. Hannah glanced at him out of the corner of her eye. His lanky body was perched on the edge of a step.

"So, healthy food carts are out," Charlotte started. "I mean, we could get any number of fried Oreo vendors, but I could not find a single group that had fair carts with healthy food. Unless you count popcorn. Which is laden with butter. So nothing." She took a sip of sparkling water. When no one joined in her outrage about the food vendors, she spoke again. "Fried Oreos? Who eats fried Oreos?"

Will loved fried Oreos. Of course he did. Hannah remembered him giving her a bite of one on the boardwalk just as an angry seagull swooped down to grab the treat. They'd both found it hysterical.

"We could do a trunk-or-treat, like the school does at Halloween," Trent said. "Parents could volunteer to prepare healthy treats and decorate their cars like booths. I could make my homemade granola."

"And I could make kale chips," Charlotte added.

"Count us in for oatmeal bars," John offered.

"I'll make fruit kabobs," Hannah volunteered knowing as she did so how much Will would hate the idea. She could practically hear his voice: "Kale chips? Really? What's wrong with kids eating hot dogs at a fair?"

They brainstormed more about the food, Charlotte making a copious list of options. Then Trent took them on a walk around the grounds, pointing out his thoughts about what activity could go where. Each time he turned and spoke to them, Hannah could not figure out where to put her eyes. One moment, she'd feel like she was staring and look down, the next, she'd feel rude and look up. She was so distracted by the whole encounter that she didn't process a thing Trent said until the mention of Will's name.

"Is Will going to make the booths, Hannah?" Trent looked as though he expected the answer to be no.

"Of course! He's pumped about it." Pumped. It was not a word Hannah would normally use. And, she was certain Will was not "pumped." He likely didn't remember he agreed to make the booths in the first place.

"Alright then. Here's a list of the booths we need built." Trent handed Hannah a list, his handwriting in perfect rows.

"Super! I'll get it to him so he can start right away." She smiled widely, knowing that, even in the best of circumstances, Will would not start right away. He would wait until the last minute, enlisting Charlie and Amanda's help. They'd follow him around the garage like ducklings. He'd be patient and allow the kids to take their time. She'd be the naysayer, constantly pointing out how many days to the fair, how much was left to do. Ultimately, she'd take over the kids' jobs so the booths would be finished on time.

And, in to her need for perfection and timeliness, she would ruin the moment.

But maybe she could be different this time. She'd let Charlie and Amanda paint the booths in spotty lines and nail on crooked signs. She wouldn't mention the deadline. Instead, she'd let the task unfold in its own time and celebrate its success with dripping ice cream cones. Hannah was visualizing the celebration when she heard Trent say her name.

"Hannah? Any thoughts on advertising?"

"Facebook, PTO website, flyers. I thought we could make cards and give them out at kids' sporting events. I'm working on the design now."

"Great." He held her gaze a moment before looking back at his notes.

Jess and John had been entrusted with prizes. John spoke at length about their research while Jess remained unusually quiet.

When the meeting dissolved, Charlotte reminded Hannah that she'd agreed to pick up her daughter, Grace, from school. "I have that doctor's appointment. Remember?

"Of course. I'm on it." Charlotte turned toward her car Hannah eyed Trent's figure as he walked toward the parking lot. "Trent, wait," she called.

He turned, his face unreadable.

Hannah stepped toward him. "Sorry I've been off the grid for a bit. I've been—"

Trent held out his hand, stalling her next words. "Look," he started, his voice low and distant. "I get it. I pushed it too hard a few weeks back, insisting I go to your photo shoot. I'm trying to lay off. Sorry if I'm not doing it well." He looked down and kicked a few pebbles. After a moment, he looked back up. "I'm working on things with Christine."

"Oh. Good."

It was good. He was working things out with his wife; Hannah was working things out with Will. Whatever they had or, whatever she thought they had, was over. It should have been a relief.

"Good," she repeated, unable to think of something else to say.

"So, let's try to move on, not make things strange." Trent's eyes caught the sun as he squinted at her. "I didn't sign up for the next photography class," he said, finally.

"Me either."

They stood in silence before Hannah realized she was standing in front of his car. "Oh, sorry!" She stepped aside and Trent entered the vehicle. Hannah watched, feeling strangely melancholic, as he drove away.

When she turned around, Jess was standing under a tree near the parking lot, staring at her. John stood by her side, arms crossed. Jess started toward her. She appeared to be angry or worried or both. When she was close enough, Hannah touched her arm. "Are you alright?"

Jess looked at the ground and twisted her watch. She looked up. "Hannah, I have to tell you something," she said quickly.

"What is it?"

"John and I saw Will with another woman."

"Oh. It was probably our friend, Kat. Or maybe one of his sisters." Hannah waved her hand to signal that she was unconcerned. "What did she look like?"

"I've never seen her before." Jess paused. "Hannah. It looked like a date."

Hannah stepped back. "What do you mean it looked like a date?"

"They were square dancing and having dinner and—"

"Square dancing? Are you sure it was Will? He hates to dance."
Hannah recalled that Will had barely danced at their wedding. She
was about to share this detail when Jess produced her phone and
handed it to her.

And there he was.

Will and the brunette square dancing in cowboy hats, heads
back in laughter.

Will and the woman sitting, side by side, on a parking divider.

Will kissing her.

"Hannah, I'm sorry. I thought you would want to know."

Hannah couldn't speak. She scrolled through the three pictures again.

"They didn't leave together," Jess added.

Hannah barely heard her. Who was this? Where was this?

She zoomed in on the perfect, laughing face of the woman
who held Will's hands in the photo. She had seen her before, she
was sure of it. Hannah could hear Jess babbling in the background
but didn't register her words. Where had she seen this woman?
Who was she?

Oh God.

Hannah pulled out her own phone and found the text messages from Will, scrolling months back to the baseball night. She
put the phones side by side, inspecting the dual images.

Unmistakable.

Indisputable.

It was her.

TWENTY-FOUR

"Hannah, say something," Jess urged.

Hannah forwarded Jess's photos to her own phone and handed it back. How many months ago was the baseball game? More than three. It had been going on all that time, maybe longer. She didn't know. She thought about Will's harsh words about Trent.

Hypocrite.

The hours she had spent feeling guilty. The number of times she'd apologized.

Jess placed her hand on Hannah's shoulder. She brushed it off with a quick, strong movement.

Jess stepped back. "Sorry. I—"

Hannah shook her head. "I have to go." She walked toward her car, unable to fully register her own movements.

Hannah could hear John's whispered criticisms behind her. "See. You should have stayed out of it." Jess and John continued to argue; Hannah ignored them.

She got in the car, started it, and gripped the steering wheel. She drove toward Scotty's house making decisive, angry turns. How could Will have done this to her? She cursed under her breath.

She stopped at a red light, thoughts churning. Her phone pinged a reminder. She glanced at it.

Shit. She was due to pick up her kids at school. And Grace for Charlotte.

Hannah took a deep breath. She couldn't just leave the kids at school to confront Will. She exhaled and switched her blinker to go left, signaling to the woman behind her the intent to change lanes. The woman beeped. Fuck you, lady.

Hannah drove to the school pick-up line and idled her car. She was early. She looked at the pictures of Will and the woman again. Her heartbeat accelerated. This could not be true. Will would not do this to her.

The car behind her beeped.

Hannah looked up and saw the car line had moved forward. She pressed the gas. Ahead of her, Charlie's face came into view.

Get yourself together, Hannah. She shut the phone off and shoved it in her purse.

She'd been that kid, the one in the crossroads of divorce. "Fifty-seven calls!" her mother had said, waving the highlighted phone bill. "He called her fifty-seven times last month!" Hannah hadn't known what to say. Her mother's anger had made her seem like a frightening stranger.

Hannah wouldn't do that to Charlie and Amanda.

The cars moved forward in turn, kids piling into each. When Hannah reached the designated spot, Charlie, Amanda, and Grace piled in, throwing down backpacks and water bottles.

"Hi guys! Hi Grace! How was your day!?"

Each child gave a different variation of "Fine."

Hannah launched into an inquiry about gym, recess, lunch, and classmates. She never fully processed one line of questioning before starting another.

"Are you alright, Mom?" Amanda finally asked.

Hannah drummed her fingers on the steering wheel, flipped on the radio. "Great. Why do you ask?"

"You're more talkative than usual."

"Am I?"

"Yes."

"Oh." She let the music fill the space.

Hannah dropped Grace off and they started home. Once settled inside, Hannah got the take-out menu and found the kids in the family room. "I thought we'd do pizza for dinner."

Amanda glanced up from her phone. "But it's Dad's night."

Will's night. She'd forgotten.

"No dinner with Dad tonight." The words tumbled out.

"But it's culture night!" Amanda stamped her foot in a preteen gesture of outrage.

"Culture night?"

"Grandma makes meals from different cultures on Wednesdays. Aunt Cammy comes over with her kids."

"Last week was Mexican," Charlie volunteered.

"This week is Chinese," Amanda said. "Dad's getting chopsticks."

The two of them looked at her expectantly.

Culture night.

Hannah rarely asked the kids what they did when they were with Will. She thought she was abiding by some code of good conduct, not pressing for details, not making the kids feel in the middle. But she'd imagined the Wednesday dinners as a sad event: the three of them sitting at a dirty, Formica Chick-Fil-A table or wrapped around Constance's kitchen in silence, Charlie picking his food. She'd believed that they missed her, that their conversation had been forced and dull without her presence.

Clearly, she had been wrong. Her absence was fun; Will had made it a celebratory event. He probably went to see the woman afterward.

Hannah pulled out her phone.

Too much going on tonight. No dinner.

Will responded immediately. What's going on? Can I help?

No. I got it.

I'd like to help.

It's okay.

I'd like to see them.

Not tonight.

The phone rang, and Will's face filled the screen.

"That's Dad's ring!" Amanda tried to grab the phone. Hannah held it out of her reach.

"I said no." Hannah visualized Will and the woman. "No," she repeated.

"I want to go to Dad's tonight." Amanda pulled out her own phone. Hannah grabbed it from her, barely registering her startled look.

"No!"

Charlie crouched in the corner of the room. Will called again. Hannah put her phone on silent.

"You can't keep us here against our will!" Amanda ran upstairs. "This is bullshit!" she called down before slamming the door. Hannah hadn't heard her curse before.

"Watch your language, young lady!" Her words sounded scripted and false.

Still in the corner, Charlie hugged his knees and put his head down.

Hannah took a deep breath and tried to regain control. She walked toward Charlie. "Do you want a snack, buddy?" She ruffled his blond tufts.

Charlie looked at her, eyes wide.

"Peanut butter crackers?"

He nodded, got up, and followed her into the kitchen, backpack in tow. He took his regular seat at the round table and tapped on the small fish tank, momentarily startling the betta fish.

"I got a hundred on my math test."

"Oh! I forgot to ask. That's wonderful!"

"I brought the test home to show you and Dad." He pulled it out of the backpack. There was a tiny sun sticker on the top. Next to it, in nearly illegible handwriting, was the teacher's notation, Great job!!!! "I guess I can't do that."

"Not tonight honey. Next time."

"But I have to bring the test back."

"Mmmm." Hannah picked up her phone. "Let's take a picture of it."

She snapped a shot of the paper, making sure to get the teacher's words and the sun sticker in the picture. She showed it to him. "See, there it is."

He nodded, a solemn expression on this face. Hannah put the plate of crackers in front of him and poured a glass of milk. "Can you text it to Dad?"

"Sure." Hannah grabbed her phone. She had been looking at the picture of the woman earlier and it flashed on the screen. Her frozen figure leered at Hannah. She swallowed. "I'll send it in a few minutes. Do your homework."

Charlie pulled out his spelling book and began to work, saying the words under his breath as he wrote. Hannah sat down at the table and closed her eyes. Images of Will and the woman invaded her thoughts. She stood and moved to the sink. She set about cleaning a ceramic vase she'd set out in the morning, filling it with scalding water. It didn't need to be cleaned, but dishwashing had always been cathartic for her. She allowed her hands to soak in the soapy water, felt the outline of the small piece with her hands, inhaled the scent of lemon from the soap. When she couldn't drag out the task out any longer, she unplugged the stopper from the sink and watched as it drained, tiny bits of soap bubble left behind. She dried the vase and left it on the counter. Now what?

Amanda entered the kitchen, dressed in a too-small kimono she'd gotten in Chinatown a few years back. "I'm going to Chinese night. I called Dad on the upstairs phone. He should be here any minute." She tapped her finger on the table in front of Charlie's spelling book. "You should get ready too. Dad's coming."

Charlie looked at her.

"Amanda," Hannah started.

Someone knocked at the door. "Hey. Open up." It was Will.

"See," Amanda said as she turned and left the kitchen.

"No." Hannah pushed ahead of her. She reached the door first and braced herself against it. She closed her eyes and felt the reverberations of Will's knocking.

"Open up!" he said again.

Hannah narrowed her eyes and pointed at Amanda. "No," she whispered. After a deep breath, she turned and opened the door, intent on telling Will that there would be no dinner with the kids tonight.

She opened the door a crack. Will burst in, his face unapologetic.

He wasn't alone.

TWENTY-FIVE

The woman from the picture followed behind Will on thin high heels.

Hannah stood back.

She was here.

In her house.

"Daddy!" Amanda ran to Will, stopping short when she saw the stranger.

Will bent down. "Hey, Pumpkin. Go get your stuff for dinner."

Then Will looked at Hannah. "I have a right to see my children." His voice was robotic and strange. "Where's Charlie?"

"Who is this?" Hannah pointed at the woman. Will didn't answer. "Who is this, Will? Who IS this?" The woman took a step toward Will.

"My witness." He sounded proud.

"Your witness?"

"That I am taking the children peacefully. I have a right to see them. Where's Charlie?" He started toward the kitchen.

"Don't go any further." Hannah's commanded. She eyed the woman again. She remained standing in the foyer, her expression serene.

"I'm getting Charlie." Will pushed by her toward the kitchen. Hannah followed.

In the kitchen, Charlie sat in his chair, eyes cast downward on the half-finished spelling sheet.

"Time for dinner, bud," Will said, putting his hand on his shoulder. Charlie looked up at him.

"No dinner, Charlie," Hannah countered, taking in Charlie's pained face.

Calm down, Hannah. Stop this.

"I am taking my children to dinner," Will said. "It's my night." He stood calmly.

Hannah heard the woman talking to Amanda, her voice low and raspy. No. She was not okay with this. She drew herself up. "And I said no. You are not going to take my kids with that woman. I know all about her, Will. I know everything."

Will said nothing. He stared at her, his expression unreadable.

"I know everything!" she repeated.

"I am taking them, Hannah." Will pulled Charlie's arm slightly and he stood.

She was losing. He was taking them. "Stop! I'll call the police!"

Will turned. "And tell them what, Hannah? That the kids are having dinner with their dad?"

It was the sound of his voice that did it. Calculated and mean. Not like Will. A stranger was taking her children away with that woman.

"Stop!"

They took a step toward the kitchen door. Charlie looked back, his eyes big and round. He was afraid.

"Stop!"

A second step. Charlie's face turned away.

Hannah grabbed the vase she had left on the kitchen counter. She held it behind her head like a weapon. "Stop!"

They were almost at the door.

"You can't take them!"

Charlie stopped and ran toward her. Hannah released the vase. She watched in horror as it turned over and over, flying toward Will's turned head. Before she could yell out a warning, the vase smashed into the side of his skull, a loud thump filling the room as it made impact. Will's hand went up to the point of the blow as he slumped to his knees. Around him, the vase smashed into bits of ceramic pieces, scattering on the floor.

"Dad!" Charlie ran toward Will. Hannah followed.

"Oh my God, Will." She put her hand on his head where the vase had hit him. He crouched downward, still holding his head. There was no blood. Thank God. "Are you alright?"

Before he could answer, Amanda and the woman were in the kitchen, the four of them clustered around Will. She was inches from Hannah, from her children.

"Will, are you alright?" The woman spoke calmly and touched his head.

Hannah slapped her hand away. "Get out," she hissed. "Just get the hell out!"

The woman ignored her; her focus remained on Will.

Hannah stared at her in disbelief. "Get out. You're trespassing." When the woman didn't move, she spoke again. "If you don't get out, I am calling the police." She pulled out her phone.

"I called them already," the woman said.

Sirens wailed in the background.

Amanda started to cry, her kimono now askew. Charlie ran toward her. They cowered together, jagged pieces of the broken vase around their legs.

"It's alright, guys," Hannah said from Will's side. "It will be alright."

There was a rap on the door. "It's the police." Amber got up.

Hannah could hear her speaking in the foyer. She looked at Will. He was still holding his head.

Two police officers, a male and a female, followed the woman into the kitchen.

"Stand aside," the female officer stated. "We've received a report of domestic violence." She spied Will on the floor, still clutching his head. Sir, are you alright?"

Will looked up at her. "I, I think I'll be okay."

The woman gestured to her partner and he stepped toward Will. "I'm Officer Merkle," she continued. "And that's Officer Bright." She pointed to the young officer who was now examining Will.

"This woman is trespassing." Hannah pointed at Amber.

"As I explained," Amber said coolly, "I'm an invited guest of Mr. Abbott, an owner of this home. I'm Amber Mitchell."

Will nodded. "That's true."

Hannah shook her head. She looked at Charlie and Amanda, now in the corner. "Can I take my children to their rooms?"

"I'm sorry, ma'am, but these children are witnesses. I'll take them to another room." She gestured to Charlie and Amanda who remained frozen on the floor.

"They're terrified." Hannah moved toward them.

Officer Merkle blocked her path. "They're witnesses. This is an investigation."

"An investigation of what? This woman is trespassing. That's all you need to know." Hannah moved to block the officer's path to her children.

"Again, we've received a report of domestic violence." Hannah opened her mouth to say there was no domestic violence, then she looked at Will, still holding his head. Did this count? Was this domestic violence? She stepped aside and watched as Officer

Merkle led Charlie and Amanda out of the kitchen. Charlie glanced back at her, eyes wide.

"It's okay, guys," she called after them. "It's okay." She put her hand over her mouth to stifle a cry.

When Officer Merkle returned, she directed her attention to Hannah. "I need to take your statement, ma'am."

Hannah let out a breath. Okay. She would let Officer Merkle know exactly what happened. Surely, once she explained that she didn't mean to hit Will, it would all be OK.

She followed Officer Merkle out of the kitchen, taking a quick glance back at Will. The male officer was helping Will into a chair while the woman—Amber—typed furiously on her phone.

"Please sit," Officer Merkle said, pointing to the couch. Hannah sat and the officer retrieved a pen and pad from her bag. The officer sat in Charlie's normal spot. Hannah suppressed the urge to ask her to move.

"So what happened?" Officer Merkle asked.

"Will came to get the kids for dinner. I told him not to come but he came anyway. He pushed through the door and was taking the kids. I told him to stop but he wouldn't listen. He was pulling on Charlie and Charlie looked scared. I threw the vase." Hannah took a breath. "I didn't mean for it to hit him. It was an accident."

"So, you threw the vase," Officer Merkle clarified.

"Yes. But I didn't mean for it to hit him."

Office Merkle looked up from her pad. "Are there any court orders?"

"No."

"Anything else to add to your statement?"

"That woman is trespassing."

Officer Merkle made a notation on the pad. "Thank you," she said and stood.

It felt wrong. She thought the officer would give her some assurance that this was standard procedure, tell her what would happen next. Hannah opened her mouth to ask her just as she disappeared behind the kitchen door.

Should she follow her?

No. She shouldn't look like she was trying to interfere. It would all be fine. Will would tell the officers to leave. She just had to wait a minute.

She stared at the ceiling and wondered what Charlie and Amanda were doing? Were they being questioned? Were they alright? She glanced at the kitchen door. What was taking so long?

Hannah sat back, rested her head on the couch, and forced herself to breathe. It would be alright.

The kitchen door swung open and Officer Merkle took a step toward her. Hannah sat up straight. Thank God. It was over.

Officer Merkle stepped toward her. "Hannah Abbott, you are under arrest for violation of the New Jersey Domestic Violence Statute and simple assault. You have the right to remain silent. Anything you say can and will be used against you in a court of law. You have the right to an attorney. If you cannot afford an attorney, one will be provided for you. Do you understand these rights?"

Hannah's hands few to her mouth. What was happening? She was under arrest? Why didn't Will tell her what happened? "No. It was an accident."

"Do you understand these rights?" Officer Merkle repeated.

"Doesn't it matter that it was an accident?"

"You'll have to talk to a lawyer ma'am. Right now, I need to know if you understand the rights that were just read to you."

Hannah lifted her head up. "Yes." Her voice came out small and choked.

"Please stand up and turn around."

Hannah slowly stood. She felt wobbly and held the side of the couch for balance. "Where are my kids?"

"They're safe, ma'am," Officer Merkle said as she clasped the handcuffs on Hannah's wrists.

"Can I see them?"

"They're safe," she repeated.

TWENTY-SIX

In the police car, as the final glimpse of her home drifted from view, Hannah panicked. How could she have left without checking on Charlie and Amanda? Without checking on Will?

"My kids and husband are back there. We have to go back."

Officer Merkle spoke firmly. "The kids are with their father, ma'am."

"But I want to see them. I need to make sure they're alright."

"They're alright."

"Take me back!"

"We can't go back," Officer Merkle said in a neutral tone.

Hannah felt desperate. "My husband doesn't even live at the house. He has no right to be there!"

"You said you didn't have a court order. Was that inaccurate?"

"No." Defeated, Hannah sat back and watched the staples of her life roll by: Mr. Printer's Graphic Center, the Carriage Shop, Kevin's Auto. A group of teenagers congregated outside of the

Dunkin Donuts. A tall man pressed numbers into an ATM machine. Life as usual.

Hannah shook her head. She was on her way to be booked. Hannah Abbott, President of the Fifth Grade Committee, mother of two, soccer team parent, booked. It seemed, suddenly, funny. She snorted and then laughed. Eventually, the laugh morphed into a mangled cry. She wanted to cover her mouth to stop the crying but couldn't move her arms because of the handcuffs. She moved her face on her blouse to try to wipe the tears, ultimately giving up.

When they arrived at the police station, Officer Merkle removed the handcuffs and escorted her to the booking room. Hannah scanned the narrow space. A computer monitor stood on top of the white cabinets lining one wall. At the end of the cabinet row, there was a seat in front of a beige backdrop, presumably for mug shots. Hannah shut her eyes.

A thin woman with clear blue eyes stood up. Her name tag read "Millie." Millie patted Hannah down then took her vital information before pointing to the chair in front to the backdrop. Hannah sat. Bright light flashed and Millie inspected the image on the computer screen.

"You blinked."

"Sorry."

Before Hannah could say anything further, the bright light flashed again. Millie looked at the image before taking Hannah's fingerprints. Then she opened the cabinet and pulled out a plastic bag. She wrote Hannah's name and booking number on the front.

"I need you to remove your shoelaces," she instructed. Hannah looked down at her sneakers and back up at Millie. Millie nodded.

Hannah bent down, untied the laces to her sneakers, and pulled them out. She stood up.

Millie held out a plastic bag and Hannah dropped the laces inside.

"I need your earrings," Millie said.

Hannah's hands flew to her ears. The diamond studs had been a wedding present from Will. For a moment, she could picture his face as he held the box out to her on their wedding night. She hadn't taken them out in thirteen years.

"No."

"I need your earrings, ma'am. You'll get them back when you are released."

"They're hard to get out." Hannah took a step back.

"Try," Millie commanded.

Hannah felt her left ear, carefully pulled off the back and removed the earring, then repeated the gesture with her right ear. She held the earrings in her hand a moment then dropped them in the bag. They fell loose in the bottom, overwhelmed by the plastic. Millie produced an inventory list; Hannah signed it.

"Make your call," Millie said, pointing to a black dial-up phone in the corner of the room.

Hannah paged through the giant phone book. She couldn't remember the name of Rachel's firm. She flipped to the attorney section. The firm was depicted on a full-page ad with the same picture that had been displayed on the billboard. Hannah dialed the number.

"Trembley, Rubin, and Connors," the woman said.

"I need to speak to Rachel Goldstein."

"I'll see if she's available."

Hannah took a deep breath.

The receptionist returned to the line. "She's left for the day. May I take a message?"

It never occurred to Hannah that she wouldn't be there.

"My name is Hannah Abbott and I'm a friend, client of Rachel's. I'm in jail. I really need help. Can't anyone help me? This is my only call." The last words came out in a panicked blurt.

The woman paused. "I'll put you through to Mark Ennis. He's in the matrimonial department."

Mark Ennis came on the line a moment later. He was silent after Hannah told him her circumstances. "I think you should talk to Rachel," he said finally. "I'll track her down."

Hannah protested, but it was clear Mark Ennis did not want to be involved. She hung up and looked at Millie. "Can I make another call?"

"It's police procedure that you get one call."

"But I didn't get anyone who could help me."

"Guess you should have made a different call then."

Millie escorted her to a dim, gray cell with a metal bench against one wall and a toilet in the corner. There were no windows. A large woman with caked-on makeup lay on the bench. Her white blouse fell open on either side, revealing a bra with leopard spots. She turned her head as Hannah entered, opening a single eye. She did not make room on the bench.

Millie stepped out. Hannah's heart accelerated as the lock clicked. "What happens now?"

"We process your information and the prosecutor will decide what charges should be filed."

"When does that happen?"

"Depends." Millie checked her watch. "It's late."

Hannah couldn't formulate her questions fast enough. She watched Millie walk down the hall and disappear through the door. Her breath became shallow and she fought for control. Instinctively, she felt in her pocket for her phone; it wasn't there. She eyed the woman in the leopard bra and moved quietly to the far end of the cell so as not to disturb her. She slid down the wall. The cell was probably a hotbed of germs. She looked for a hand sanitizer dispenser on the wall. There was none.

What happened next? Did she post bail? Was there a hearing? Would Rachel even come? What about her kids? She visualized Charlie and Amanda. Were they okay? And Will? Was he alright?

As the questions churned in her mind, she found it difficult to breathe normally. She pulled her knees to her chest and put her head down. She tried to breathe deeply, but a cry escaped instead, followed by sobbing. She covered her mouth to stop the sounds and looked to see if she'd disturbed her cellmate.

The woman was sitting up, staring at her. "Hey."

"Sorry," Hannah choked. She tried to control the crying.

The woman stood. She was giant, nearly six feet, and had to be over 200 pounds.

"Get up," she commanded, taking a step toward Hannah.

Hannah shielded her face with her arms.

"Oh, for God's sake, get up." She reached down and pulled Hannah to her feet. "Now, tell Layla what's going on," she said, her voice now soft.

Layla pulled Hannah to the bench. Hannah told her the story, her words emptying out in a bitter monologue. When she finished, Layla clapped her on the shoulder and said, "You should have killed them both." Hannah couldn't tell if she was joking.

"Do you know what happens now?"

"When your lawyer gets here, you get to go in a room and talk. The lawyers for the State have forty-eight hours to determine if they have enough on you to charge."

"Forty-eight hours? Do I have to stay here forty-eight hours?"

"No baby. Your lawyer can get you out while you wait."

"When? When can I get out?"

Layla looked around the cell. "It's late. You may have to stay tonight."

Hannah blinked. She would have to stay here tonight? In jail? "Are you sure?" She must have looked horrified, because Layla put her hand on hers and spoke again in a soothing voice.

"It's not all that bad baby, really."

"And if I have to go to the bathroom?" Hannah looked at the toilet in the corner of the room. Stains marred the now-gray surface. A half-used roll of toilet paper sat on the floor.

"Don't use that," Layla said, following her gaze.

"Where do I go then?"

"You gotta pee?"

She nodded.

Layla yelled for the guard. The door opened and Millie made her way to their cell. "She got to go to the bathroom."

"So go," Millie said.

"She got feminine business."

Millie opened the cell door and escorted Hannah through winding corridors to a bathroom. "Products in there," she said.

After using the restroom, Hannah was taken to a small room. Rachel was waiting inside.

TWENTY-SEVEN

"Will's wife won't let him see the kids for dinner. He doesn't know why," Amber told David.

David stared at the closed door of Lauren's house. "Does he normally have dinner with them on Wednesdays?"

"Yes."

"Then he should go get them. Go as a witness. This is how it starts. He has to set a precedent now. Tell him to be calm and to say, 'I have a right to see my children.' Tell him not to take no for an answer."

Amber repeated the advice. He pictured them standing together; it irritated him. Amber seemed so different around Will Abbott. He was glad when she hung up.

David walked to the front door, expecting, again, to be turned away. Instead, Lauren flung open the door just as his hand hovered over the bell.

"David!" She said it as though he had shown up by surprise.

"Lauren!" He met her ridiculously happy tone. "Are the kids ready?"

"Yes and no." She pushed her hair behind her ears. "Come in."

David walked into the foyer. It felt strange. It had been years since he'd been allowed across the threshold of the home he had once owned. Lauren had changed the paint on the walls. Tan, not blue. There was a new area rug, a patchwork of muted flowers instead of the stripes. Their wedding picture was gone from the front table, replaced by a thick, crystal candy dish. David reached over and took two mints, the plastic loud as he unwrapped.

"I have a proposition for you."

David leaned against the wall and popped both mints in his mouth. "A proposition? I'm all ears." He lifted his eyebrows.

"David, be serious."

"I am serious," He said, his voice garbled from the mints.

"Brett has a work function in Italy. It's a seven-day trip and I'd like to go with him."

"Sounds fun. Eat lots of pizza. Are the kids ready?" David bit down on one of the mints.

"I need someone to watch the kids. Can you—"

David's heart leapt but he kept his demeanor steady. "Watch my own kids. Yeah. I can do that."

"It's serious, David. I'll be abroad."

"Oh no! How will I reach you?"

She stomped her foot. "Come on, David. You're making this difficult."

"Okay. Fine. I would love to do it. When?"

"We leave Tuesday."

Tuesday? It was outrageous, the short notice. Wasn't he the one with the job that supported them both? "Tuesday as in six days from now? You just thought to ask now—"

Lauren interrupted before he finished the sentence. "Brett's mother, she got sick and couldn't come. We thought—"

"Thought I'd want to see my own kids."

She kept his gaze. He wanted to say no, just to spite her. But this could be it. His chance. "I can do it. But my place is small."

He visualized the kids in his tiny box apartment overlooking the sad, debris-covered pool. "There may not be room for all of us."

"You can stay here." Lauren spread out her arms in a grandiose manner.

"Really? I can stay in the house I pay for? Wow. That's unbelievably generous of you, Lauren."

"David." She fiddled with her earring.

"Sorry. It's fine. I'll be here Tuesday. No kids tonight?"

"They're not here. They're—"

David held his hand out. He didn't want to hear it. He turned to leave, then stopped himself. He looked at Lauren, the light catching her eyes, reflecting back pools of blue. "I haven't had a drink in more than a year."

She nodded. "I'm trusting you, David."

TWENTY-EIGHT

David drove directly from Lauren's to St. Paul's. He couldn't wait to tell Jenny about Lauren and her asking him to watch the kids. He swung into the parking lot and searched for her tiny red Mustang. Nothing. Maybe she got a ride. He climbed the stairs and walked into the room. No Jenny.

David pulled out his phone and texted. Where are you?

No response. He took off his jacket and put it on the gray folding chair next to his own. Jenny would creep through the door any minute. She'd whisper "traffic" or "phone call." He'd remove his jacket; she'd take her place next to him.

He texted again.

Meeting's about to start. Have a seat for you.

Still no response.

David half listened. He didn't share. He looked at the door and the empty seat, his mind adrift in horrific possibility. Halfway through the meeting, he excused himself and called Jenny from the parking lot. Pick up. Pick up. Pick up.

"Hello, it's Jenny. Leave a message."

David clicked the phone off and drove directly to her house. The Mustang sat in her driveway. Thank God. He pulled in, got out of the car, and made his way toward the door.

"Jenny," he called as he knocked.

Moxie barked. David saw her frenetic wagging through the window.

Jenny opened the door. "David?"

"It's Wednesday," he said by way of explanation.

Jenny shook her head. "I'm sorry. I forgot. Please come in." She swung open the door. Moxie bounded out, circling David, her tail wagging. "I'm a bit distracted."

David stepped into the foyer and tripped lightly over a pile of used children's books.

"Sorry. I'm collecting these books for a book drive." Jenny pushed the books aside with her foot and gestured toward the kitchen. "Come in. I need to tell you something."

David followed her into the kitchen. Jenny grabbed a Diet Coke and slid it across the table to him. David sat down; Jenny took the seat across from him. Her hair, normally curled, was pulled back in a tight ponytail, her face makeup free.

"Is there something wrong?"

Before Jenny could answer, his phone rang. It was Amber. David switched the phone to vibrate.

"Okay," Jenny started, her voice low. "You are the first person I am telling." She pulled in a deep breath, letting it out slowly, as though she had to gather herself to say the words. "I have Hodgkin's lymphoma."

David processed the words. Hodgkin's lymphoma. Cancer? Jenny had cancer?

"It's treatable," she said quickly. "It's Stage II and the prognosis is good."

"Still. God," David said, still processing. He put his head in his hands, then looked up at her. "Why didn't you tell me?" He immediately regretted the statement. He had just made this about him. He put his hand over Jenny's. "I'm so sorry."

"It's okay. I should have told you. I just, I just didn't believe it myself. I felt fine. I found a little lump in my neck a couple months ago. I went to a doctor and he recommended a biopsy. I thought it was overkill." Jenny got up and filled a glass with tap water.

David's phone vibrated. Amber. Again. He turned the phone over.

"Do you need to get that?" Jenny looked at the phone, concerned.

"Of course not," David responded. "You were saying?"

Jenny sat back down. "The biopsy came back positive a couple weeks ago. Obviously." Her demeanor changed a bit.

David's phone pinged. He flipped it and saw Amber's name. He shook his head. Enough already. He directed his attention back to Jenny. "I'm so sorry. I can't imagine what you must be going through."

Jenny took a sip of water. "It's been a shock, that's for sure. There have been a lot of appointments."

David stared out the window, processing. "Jesus. I can't believe this. I wish you had told me."

Jenny shook her head. "It's not your problem, David."

David put his hand on hers. She looked up. "It is my problem, Jenny. I'm not letting you go through this alone. Tell me what I can do."

"David. No—"

"Please, Jenny. I want to help."

She adjusted her ponytail. "Actually, there is something."

"Anything."

"Can you take me to the first chemotherapy? It's Tuesday at ten o'clock."

Tuesday would be David's first day with the kids. But they would be in school during the day.

"If you can't—" Jenny started.

"I can. Absolutely."

The phone vibrated again. Amber's face filled the screen. David shook his head at the phone, looked up at Jenny. "I think I have to get this. I'm sorry."

Jenny nodded and stood up, gathering David's empty can and throwing it in the trash.

David answered the call. "What?" His voice was harsh.

"It's about Will."

"I'm in the middle of something, Amber."

She told him about Will's altercation with this wife. David barely listened. His focus was on Jenny. He watched as she put a pot of water on the stove. She looked fine. How could it be that she had cancer?

"Dave. Are you there?" Amber said. "Jack Connors is her attorney. Should I call him? See if we can work something out?"

David stood up, barely registering Amber's words. Jenny shouldn't have cancer. Could there have been a mistake?

"David," Amber said, irritation evident in her tone. "Should I call Jack Connors?"

David forced Jenny from tempohis mind and visualized Jack's typical, smug look. He remembered the expression on Jack's face the day David had packed up his office, the day the partners at Trembley, Rubin, and Connors let him go.

"We don't negotiate with Jack Connors."

"Well, what then?"

David thought about how Lauren never allowed him to see his kids. How he stood in front of the closed door of his former home, week after week, like an outcast. No man should have to go through that.

"Tell Will to file for a temporary restraining order."

TWENTY-NINE

Will got the temporary restraining order that night. David wasn't surprised. All you needed for a TRO was breath and a believable story. Will had both. He got custody of the kids and possession of the house for five days. In one week, the court would hold a final hearing and listen to Will's wife tell her side of the story. Will wouldn't win. David knew that. But it gave him time with full custody to prove himself. And David would have to have the final hearing date moved anyway; he was taking next week off to be with his kids.

David found Amber at her desk going through a stack of bank records for a client. "You have to adjourn the Abbott final restraining order hearing," he said as he approached her. "I'm taking next week off."

Amber didn't look up from the monitor. "David, you can't do that. Will doesn't want to postpone the hearing. He feels horrific about Hannah going to jail."

David tapped on her computer monitor. She looked up. "Amber. I haven't had an overnight with my kids in almost three years. I haven't taken a vacation in more than five. If Will Abbott feels bad, regrets his decision, whatever the problem is, then that is too fucking bad. He doesn't know what's good for him anyway. All I know is that I am taking the week off and I need you to get that hearing adjourned."

Amber stood up. "No, David. You can't."

"I can. I'm taking the week, Amber."

She opened her mouth then shut it. "He won't be happy," she said under her breath.

"Oh no," David said, not hiding his sarcasm.

David pulled his car to the side of Lauren's street and checked his watch. He was twenty minutes early to start his time with the kids. He idled the car, pulled out his phone, and checked his emails. After three angry messages, he shut the phone off. His clients could wait a week. David leaned his head back as a white Audi drove past his car, the tiny pebbles from its wake scattering on his window. Screw it. He could be early. David sat up, started the car, and drove to up the street.

After parking the car, David grabbed his duffel bag and picked up Bolt from the back seat. The tortoise retracted his head with the movement. "It's okay, buddy," David said as he walked up the path. "This will be fun."

David rang the doorbell. Lauren swung open the door, her eyes falling on Bolt. "No."

David stepped inside and put Bolt on the floor. "You're welcome."

"No," Lauren repeated.

Ryan ran down the stairs. "A tortoise! Dad! You brought a tortoise." He bent down and ran his hand over Bolt's back. "What's your name little fella?"

David squatted and held Bolt up. "Hello Ryan. I'm Bolt," he said in a deep voice.

Lauren stamped her foot down. "Seriously David!"

David looked up at her. "Careful, Lauren. If you startle him, he pees."

"I don't have time for this, David. I never said you could bring a pet." She looked at Bolt and shook her head. "I have a flight to catch." She waved her hand in Bolt's direction and then motioned for David to follow.

David followed Lauren into the kitchen, Ryan behind them with Bolt. She pointed a shiny red fingernail to the three spreadsheets on the granite countertop, one for each kid. The sheets listed activities, food likes and dislikes, emergency numbers. He felt like a teenage babysitter.

Lauren's phone pinged; she peeked at it then directed her attention to Ryan.

"Brett's waiting in the driveway, sweetie. I have to go."

"Alright." Ryan kept his eyes on Bolt as he said the words.

Lauren stepped forward and kissed Ryan lightly on the head before turning to David.

The girls get home around three," she said matter-of-factly.

She walked toward the door, high heels clicking on the floor. An overstuffed Fendi bag stood in the entryway. Lauren reached down, tried to lift it, then set it down again. She stared at the bag.

David looked at Ryan. "Go help your mother," he mouthed as he took Bolt from Ryan's arms.

Ryan stepped forward and picked up the bag. "I got this, Mom."

"What a gentleman." She cast a backward glance at David. "See what a polite son I've raised."

David watched her through the front window. Brett remained in his black BMW, head down looking at his phone. Ryan hurtled toward the car struggling with the oversized bag. Nice. And David was the one with no class.

After Lauren and Brett drove off, he and Ryan settled in the kitchen.

"What do you normally eat for breakfast?" David stood in the kitchen he'd designed. He pulled open the drawer where they'd kept the silverware. There were take-out menus there now.

"Oatmeal with flax. Sometimes fruit and wheat toast."

Healthy. Okay. He could do healthy. David opened the fridge. Neatly stacked, labeled Tupperware containers for all the meals sat inside. He digested the meaning behind the perfect rows. Lauren did not trust him to feed the kids.

He shut the fridge door. "How about... donuts?"

"We don't have donuts."

"Dunkin?"

Surprise flashed across Ryan's face. "Alright! Let me get my bag."

Ryan grabbed his bag and David drove him to Dunkin Donuts. They sat at a small table in the back. Ryan spread his donuts out liked prized possessions. He picked one up and took a bite. "I can't believe you let me get three," he said, mouth full.

David eyed the three icing-laden pastries, one of which oozed cream. It wasn't the healthiest way to start to the day. "So you got a good lunch, Ry?"

Ryan looked up and wiped chocolate from his mouth. "I dunno. What'd you pack me?"

Shit. He was supposed to make lunch? David pulled out his wallet, handed him a twenty. "Get something at school, okay? With fruit or protein or something."

Ryan nodded, staring at the twenty.

"Is that enough?" David asked. How much were kids' lunches these days?

Ryan nodded again as he chewed. "More than enough."

David drove Ryan to school. The cars in the drop off line snaked toward the school entryway. Each child was greeted by a frantic-looking woman who directed them inside with the same intensity as an air traffic controller.

David was ten cars back. He checked his watch. Shit. He was going to be late picking up Jenny. David pushed on the gas and pulled around the cars in front of him.

"Dad. What are you doing?" Ryan asked.

"Dropping you off."

The frantic woman yelled as he pulled up.

"Get out, Ry," David instructed.

Ryan opened the door and got out. David saluted the agitated woman. She shook her fist at him and started yelling. He suppressed the urge to give her the finger and drove straight to Jenny's.

Jenny stood in front of her house with a giant backpack, looking more like a schoolgirl than an adult woman about to start chemotherapy.

"I'm not going to lose my hair," she announced as she entered the car.

David glanced at Jenny's hair. It fell around her shoulders in fluffy, shiny waves.

"I've done my research. I've rented a cold cap." She patted her backpack as if to signal its presence there. "It's supposed to reduce the blood flow to the hair follicles so less of the chemo can get there."

"That's good," David said distractedly. Jenny spoke more about the cap; David half-listened. Was hair loss really her biggest concern right now?

"I know it probably seems stupid."

"No," he lied.

She pulled her hair forward and ran her fingers through it. "My hair has always been my best feature." She pushed it back behind her shoulders. "It's just, I already have this scarred eye. My hair makes me feel like maybe I could be a little bit..." She paused. "A little bit pretty."

The words came out before he could think. "You are pretty. Beautiful, even." He flushed, then glanced at Jenny; she seemed not to notice.

"You have to say that. You're my friend."

Friend. That's how she thought of him. He had to remember that.

David drummed the steering wheel as he drove. "Well, anyone would think it." He gave her a sideways glance. She was pretty.

The GPS announced their arrival: "The destination is on the right."

David pulled into the parking lot and turned off the engine. Neither of them moved. He squeezed Jenny's arm lightly. "It's going to be okay," he whispered.

They exited the car and walked into the waiting room. Empty black chairs lined yellow walls with floral paintings. A fish tank stood at one end, the check-in desk at the other. A man with a crew-cut smiled from behind it.

Jenny stepped forward. She looked tiny and vulnerable and it was all David could do not to pull her back and prevent whatever pain lay ahead.

He wished he could take her place.

"Jennifer Turner," she said in a voice so small it was almost inaudible.

"Hello, Miss Turner. We're all ready for you. I just need you to fill this out." He handed Jenny a clipboard.

Jenny took the board, and she and David sat in chairs adjacent to the fish tank. As Jenny began to fill out the form, David tapped on the fish tank glass. The nearest fish jerked.

"Stop it," Jenny whispered. The corners of her mouth upturned as she said the words.

David looked at her. Had she almost smiled? David tapped the fish tank again, harder; several fish twitched.

"David," Jenny mouthed, her eyes light. "Stop."

David lifted his hand again. Jenny grabbed it and let out a giggle. "Honestly. You're like a child." She dropped his hand and resumed filling out the form.

The door to the waiting room swung open and they both looked up. A woman walked in carrying a large bag and a blanket. She was completely bald.

Jenny stared at her. Then she picked up David's hand and squeezed.

THIRTY

David was late getting back to the house after Jenny's chemotherapy. He hadn't wanted to leave her alone.

Ryan had Bolt on the foyer floor when he walked in. "I'm teaching him to shake hands. Watch."

David crouched down.

"Shake Bolt. Shake." Ryan held out his hand. The tortoise walked in the other direction. Ryan stopped him, took a front leg and waved it. "Like that Bolty. Shake." He looked at David. "He's still learning."

"I see. School okay?"

"The same."

"Sisters home?"

"They're in the kitchen."

David got up and braced himself as he walked into the kitchen. Both girls tapped on PINK-cased phones, briefly looking up as he entered.

It was shocking. They were grown. He knew it, of course. He'd seen pictures. He'd seen them, on rare occasion. But it was different somehow. He hadn't expected makeup and jewelry and tight jeans. The girls he remembered wore friendship bracelets woven from bits of colored yarn.

He shook his head and started in.

"Sorry I'm late. How was your day?"

Hailey looked up. "It was fine."

Sienna pecked at her phone, not responding.

"Anything happen?"

"No."

"Anything good happen for you, Sienna?"

She looked up, her eyes the same blue as Lauren's. "No, nothing." She stared at him. It seemed like she was going to say something and David felt a strange anticipation. Did she need help with her homework? Teacher issue? A ride somewhere?

"What's for dinner?"

Dinner. Right. David checked Lauren's list.

"Chicken, asparagus, quinoa."

"KEEN-WAH," Hailey corrected.

"Okay. KEEN-WAH," David repeated.

She smiled, but barely.

He pulled the Monday Tupperware container out of the fridge. Typed cooking instructions were taped on the top. My God. He had a headache and his muscles ached from tension. The last thing he wanted to do was make or eat naked, skinless chicken and KEEN-WAH. And he hated asparagus. Had Lauren remembered that? Was it a little joke on him? Screw it.

"I'm getting takeout."

Both girls looked up from their phones.

"But Mom made us dinner." Sienna stared at him, a challenge in her expression.

"And you're free to eat it. And make it. I'm getting takeout." He walked to the foyer. Ryan was on the floor with Bolt. "Let's go get some grub, Ry."

He looked up. "But I'm in the middle of training." He tapped his finger on Bolt's shell.

"Bring him."

"Really?"

"Why not?"

Ryan piled into his car with Bolt. He held him up to the window. We're going on a trip, Bolty. See outside."

David drove to Applebee's, the last place he remembered all the kids had loved. Not knowing their taste now, he ordered all nineteen appetizers and was promptly informed by a snarky clerk at the take-out counter that he should have called ahead. It would be forty-five minutes. Fine. He and Ryan would get breakfast for tomorrow and come back.

"What about Bolt?" Ryan asked as David swung into a parking space at Acme.

David glanced at the tortoise. "Take him in the store."

"Do you think he's allowed?"

"I'm sure Acme has no rules about tortoises whatsoever."

They got out of the car and entered the store. In aisle three, a white-haired store employee tapped Ryan gently on the shoulder with a bony hand.

"I'm sorry, young man, we don't allow pets."

Ryan hugged Bolt to his chest.

David stepped in front of Ryan. "My son is training this animal as a guide tortoise."

"A guide tortoise?"

"Yes. It's the same idea as a seeing-eye dog. But here's the thing. Dogs pull on their leashes. And they're boisterous. It's a very dangerous situation for blind people. Tortoises are calm. And they have an innate sense of direction. That's a little-known fact."

The employee said nothing for a moment. "Still, sir, we don't allow animals in the store."

"Look. My son and I need to shop. I'm a lawyer. If you're going to discriminate against me and my son and our guide tor—"

"No one said anything about discrimination."

"Asking us to leave a public venue where my son is training a guide tortoise? That sounds like discrimination to me." David pretended to check something on his phone, then asked the woman, "Could you give me your last name?"

"Look, sir, I didn't mean to offend you. We don't usually allow pets. I didn't know this was a guide tortoise." She gestured to Bolt then added cheerfully, "I didn't even know there were guide tortoises."

"Well, look it up."

As they walked away, Ryan whispered, "Is Bolt really a guide tortoise?"

David laughed. "No."

"But you said he was."

"Just wanted you to be able to keep him in the store."

Ryan grinned. "Thanks, Dad."

They arrived at the house with the nineteen appetizers. David spread them out in a buffet on the kitchen island and called the girls. He threw away the Monday Tupperware container.

During dinner, Ryan couldn't stop talking about David telling the employee that Bolt was guide tortoise. "Then Dad told the lady to 'look it up'...."

Finally, Sienna said, "We get it, Ryan. Geez."

Hailey told David about the crush she had on a boy named Sam who she was hoping would ask her to the Fall Ball on

Saturday. Sienna, using air quotes, told him about her social studies teacher who "despised joy." And Ryan, apparently, liked
reptiles.

It wasn't perfect.

But it was something.

THIRTY-ONE

David got up early to cook the breakfast foods he made when the
kids were young: stuffed omelets, chocolate chip pancakes, hash
browns. He hummed as he flipped pancakes and pushed scrambled eggs in the frying pan. He placed the food in serving bowls
and set them on the kitchen table next to a stack of plates.

When Sienna woke, she walked by his display of breakfast
foods and shook her head. She pulled out a cereal called FLAX
and poured herself a bowl. "We don't eat like that anymore, Dad."
She sat at the table and pecked at her phone.

David said nothing.

Sienna stared at the pile of chocolate chip pancakes. After a
brief hesitation, she slid one onto a plate, poured syrup over it,
and took a bite. David watched her chew, her expression unreadable. He expected her to push it away and tell him it was terrible
and fattening and how could he think she would ever eat anything
so vile?

"They're just like you used to make." She took another bite.

It was enough.

David got the kids off to school and went to check on Jenny.

As soon as David walked into the house, he heard retching. He followed the sound to the bathroom and looked in. Jenny sat on the floor in a T-shirt and sweats.

He squatted down. "Oh, Jenny. What can I do?"

She looked up, her face pale. "I don't know. I feel really sick." She laid her head back on the bathroom wall and closed her eyes. "I'm really tired."

"Let me move you to your bed." David scooped up her small, paled frame and carried her into her bedroom. He set up her with blankets and pillows. "Should I call the doctor?"

"No. I already took the drugs they gave me for nausea."

David called the doctor anyway. A nurse told him to give Jenny a Popsicle. A Popsicle! David looked at Jenny's pained face. Really? He hung up the phone.

He propped Jenny's pillows and turned on soft music. She closed her eyes and began to breathe more deeply. Once she was asleep, David called the office. Amber spoke without introduction. "Will is very upset. He wants to drop the restraining order— he can't wait a week for the hearing. He didn't know—"

"Amber," David interrupted. She stopped talking. "Tell Will Abbott to enjoy the week with his kids."

"But—"

"No buts. We've been through this. I am sorry Mr. Abbott is upset, but I am not coming into the office. I'll be back next week." He hung up and took a seat in Jenny's family room. Moxie jumped up beside him. He stacked up the magazines on her coffee table.

Mid-afternoon, Jenny woke up with another wave of nausea. She sat in the bathroom, face over the toilet bowl. David crouched next to her and pulled her hair from her face as she vomited.

"Thank you," she whispered and leaned back against the bathroom wall.

David looked at her small frame. He couldn't leave her here. But he couldn't leave his kids alone either. David visualized Lauren's huge house. He looked again at Jenny. Why not?

"I'm taking you to my house."

"No, David. I'm fine. Really." She sat up straighter in demonstration.

"Jenny. I insist. Please let me do this for you."

David left the room before she could answer. He found a duffel bag, threw in clothes, and put the bag in his car. He returned to the bathroom. "I'm taking you, Jenny."

She looked up at him, her face pale. "Alright."

David bent down and put his arms under Jenny's arms and legs. He lifted her up and made his way toward the door. Moxie followed them.

David adjusted Jenny so he could open the door. He looked at Moxie. She looked back, her tail wagging slowly. What the hell. "Come on, girl." Moxie bounded out the door in front of them. David stepped carefully. When he reached the car, he placed Jenny in the passenger seat; Moxie jumped in the back.

When they arrived at the house, David guided Jenny to Lauren's room and helped her into the double-poster, king-sized bed. Moxie jumped up and settled by her side.

"Thank you," Jenny said. She squeezed his hand, holding it a moment longer than necessary.

The front door opened. Moxie jumped off the bed and flew down the stairs, her entire rear-end wagging. David followed her.

"You got us a dog!!" Ryan jumped up and down. The girls looked stunned.

"No, no," David said. "This is my friend's dog." David explained about Jenny.

Sienna stared at Moxie. "Mom's not going to like this. A dog and a stranger in her room. The shit's going to hit the fan." She took out her phone.

"You don't have to tell her," Hailey quipped. "Dad's trying to do something nice." Hailey bent down and nuzzled Moxie's head.

"Come on, Sienna, don't tell her." Ryan pet Moxie; the dog rolled on her back. "You're the one who's always asking for a dog."

"A little dog. Not this." She gestured to Moxie with a look of disgust but put her phone away.

Hailey's phone pinged. She pulled it out and looked at the message. "Sam asked Gabby to the Fall Ball." She stared at the phone, frozen. "He didn't ask me," she said, almost to herself.

"Well, that's Sam's loss," David said weakly. He looked at Hailey's devastated face. "Maybe you could go with someone else?"

It was the wrong thing to say.

Hailey's face contorted. She spoke with slow, articulate words through clenched teeth. "I don't want to go with someone else. I want to go with Sam." She turned on her heel and left the room. David heard her footsteps on the stairs.

Shit. He started to follow her, then stopped himself. He was not equipped for this.

David left Sienna and Ryan with Moxie and quietly opened the door to Jenny's room. In the huge bed surrounded by pillows, she looked like a tiny, eccentric queen. David explained the situation.

"She should go anyway," Jenny said. "You should get her a fabulous dress and have her hair done at a salon. She'll feel beautiful and she'll forget all about Sam."

David adjusted her pillow. "You think so?"

"Absolutely. In fact, you should take both girls and make a day of it. They'll love it."

Doubt flashed over David's face. "I have no idea where to go for things like that."

"We'll figure it out."

We'll. David liked that. He wasn't alone.

That night, he didn't intend to sleep next to Jenny. He checked to make sure she was okay. She was curled on her side. David watched her breathe, her chest rising and falling in small movements, her face slack and peaceful. She let out almost imperceptible snores.

David laid down next to her and put his hand on her shoulder. "Please be okay, Jenny," he said, before drifting off to sleep.

THIRTY-TWO

"Okay, I found the places for dresses and hair," Jenny announced the next afternoon. She sat at the kitchen table, looking at her phone. The color was back in her cheeks, her eyes no longer glassy.

David handed her a cup of tea. "And?"

"You should get the dresses at Lulu's and their hair done at the Sweet Pixie Salon. I've been told the salon is expensive, just warning you." She blew on her tea.

"And how do you know all this, Miss Turner?" David asked in a playful tone.

"I have my sources," Jenny said with a smile. "And I can watch Ryan. He's already promised to teach me how to play Fortnite."

"Lucky you."

As Jenny predicted, Sienna and Hailey were thrilled by the idea of shopping and lunch. As they got ready to go Saturday morning, Jenny and Ryan sat side by side on the couch, Fortnite on the screen.

"Press "X" to search the chest," Ryan instructed. Jenny's avatar held out its hand and the chest opened, revealing a gun and a bottle of blue liquid.

"We're going," David announced to their backs.

"Bye," Jenny called.

"Now press "X" again to pick up the gun," Ryan said, seemingly oblivious to David's departure.

David and the girls piled into his car and he drove to the dress store. Lulu's was a tiny, yellow house set back from the street on the outskirts of Princeton with a brick path covered in moss. The doorframe was buttressed by two lion statues, mold in the crevices. An array of pots with plants in varied states of distress lined the doorway. A faded doormat read "Behave or Be Gone." No one said anything. David's heart sunk. This was not what he had envisioned.

David tried to think of an alternative but, before he could do so, the door flung open and a middle-aged woman with uncontrollable dark, frizzy hair stood in the frame. "I'm so sorry, loves, if you've been waiting. I'm Lulu." She had a trace of a British accent.

Lulu ushered them into a small living room crammed with racks of dresses and piles of fancy shoes. A green parakeet sat in the corner.

Sienna and Hailey headed to the racks. Lulu rushed over to them. "Don't touch the dresses," she commanded. She took a deep breath, exhaling slowly before speaking again. "The dresses will choose you. Please sit. I need a minute." She plopped down the floor and closed her eyes.

The three of them stared at her still figure. Sienna stifled a laugh.

Lulu jumped up unexpectedly. "You doll," she said to Sienna and pulled her forward. Lulu picked up a lock of Sienna's hair and then dropped it. She leaned into her face. "Blue eyes." She repeated the process with Hailey, noting aloud: "Tall. Tiny waist." She picked up Hailey's hand then let it drop. "You should be a hand model," she said randomly.

Lulu lost herself in the racks of dresses, whispering under her breath. A few minutes later, she emerged with two. Sienna's was navy blue and cream; Hailey's, in gold, was tight with cut-outs in the waist area.

"These dresses have chosen you," Lulu said seriously.

Hailey and Sienna looked at each other.

"Should we try them on?" Sienna asked finally.

"Yes, yes. Right there." Lulu pointed to an accordion divider in the corner of the room. The girls disappeared behind it. Lulu stood with her hands clasped as though she were waiting for a divine surprise.

When the girls emerged, Lulu clapped. "Beautiful dollies, absolutely stunning."

"Those dresses look amazing," David said truthfully. The dresses were perfect for each, as if custom made.

"I love it!" Sienna cried and spun around. "And you look gorgeous," she said to Hailey.

"You too," Hailey gushed.

Sienna took her phone out. "Let's get a picture." They put their heads together; the camera flashed.

Hailey saw David on the outskirts. "Come on, Dad."

Sienna whirled around and looked at him. She paused and David braced himself for an admonishment. "Yeah, Dad, come on."

He stepped ahead. Each daughter put an arm around him, and they smiled as the camera flashed. David examined the picture afterward, a lump forming then dissolving in his throat. He looked like a real dad. He forwarded the image to himself and made it his screensaver.

The girls chose shoes and purses and accessories. As they piled the items on a stool under the parakeet's cage, it occurred to David that he had no idea of the cost of any of it. He directed his attention to Lulu. "So what do I owe?"

Lulu put her hand to her head and looked up as if the price would come to her from above. Then she stared at the pile of dresses and accessories. "Fifteen hundred dollars."

The parakeet squawked.

"But you…" David wanted to ask how she came up with the figure. He wanted to see her punch numbers into a machine and tally up a receipt. Then he saw the girls smiling in his peripheral vision.

He pulled out his credit card. He didn't have $1,500 in his bank account; his alimony check had just cleared. Plus, he had just paid the fall tuition for Amber's classes, part of the "firm reimbursement" program. He'd need to bill more this month.

After the dress shopping, the three of them sat at a The Princeton Cafe for lunch, laughing about their experience.

"You should be a hand model!" Hailey imitated Lulu's voice.

"The dresses have spoken!" Sienna said.

After they finished their meals, David ordered hot fudge sundaes.

"We'll never be able to fit into those dresses, Dad!" Hailey groaned. But she smiled as she said it. They finished the sundaes, Sienna even scraped fudge off the dish with her spoon.

They headed to the Sweet Pixie Salon and took their place in the waiting area, jammed with Fall Ball goers. As they sat, a half a dozen girls emerged with the same style: long, separated, spiral curls. David looked at his watch. It was fifteen minutes after the appointment time.

He stood to say something when a girl with heavy black eye makeup and combat boots stepped toward them. "Hailey and Sienna Dewey, you're up."

As the girls stood, David whispered to Hailey, "Don't do the curl thing. Try something bold."

David waited on a stool and checked his emails. He saw a message from Amber. He didn't open it. He knew it would be about Will Abbott. Why was Amber so obsessed with that guy? He responded to a few emails, then Sienna came out, her hair curled and long in the exact style of everyone girl in the salon.

"Beautiful," David said.

Then Hailey came out.

Her long blonde hair had been cut into an elegant, close-cropped pixie emphasizing high cheekbones. She smiled, her teeth a perfect row of white.

"Wow!"

Hailey twirled around. "I know, right! I love it. I absolutely love it." She looked at herself in the mirror and turned side to side. "Thank you, Dad. Thank you so much."

Sienna chimed in. "Yeah, Dad, thanks."

David felt his eyes grow wet. "You're welcome. Now let's get you to that dance."

THIRTY-THREE

When the week was up, David didn't want his old life back. He wanted to hear the sizzle of bacon in the morning, see the sleepy-eyed looks of his children as they tumbled down the stairs. He wanted to bring Jenny her green tea and honey in bed, hear her quiet voice say, "David, good morning." He wanted Moxie to follow him around the house. He wanted to watch Ryan try to train Bolt, cheering when the tortoise inadvertently followed his command. He wanted to know what happened with Sam and if Sienna still hated her social studies teacher.

But, mostly, David wanted to be on the other side of the door when someone came home.

Instead, he was completely alone. He'd given Bolt to Ryan and dropped Jenny off at her house the day before. David stood in front of his apartment, the morning sun rising behind him. He pushed open the door and stepped in. The walls seemed duller, the couch even more tiny and rigid. There were dishes in the sink, empty Diet Coke cans on the counter. A lone saucepan stood on an electric burner, residue from pasta sauce now congealed on the stove surface and laminate counter. David's single plant stood upright, amazingly, still alive.

Frustrated, David threw the Diet Coke cans in the trash, filled the saucepan with soapy water to soak, and watered the plant. He piled up old newspapers and put random, mismatched socks from the floor on top of his closeted washer/dryer set realizing, then, that there were still towels in there from a week ago. He opened the dryer and smelled the dampness. He wasn't surprised. The dryer never worked. The clothes never dried. Cycle after cycle.

It felt suddenly outrageous that he should live this way, without the simple amenity of a working dryer. David banged on the appliance with his fist, the surface surprisingly unforgiving. He waved his hand in pain; a primordial sound emerged from his chest. He slid down the wall and cradled his face in his hands. Holy shit. He couldn't do this anymore.

David sat by the dryer, a new resolve forming. This was his life. He had to accept that this was his life. He did not live on 52 Cherry Hill Lane anymore; he would not be getting pizzas or helping with homework or returning work emails amidst the bustle of family life. His only familial role was to make money.

He needed to do what was expected. Slowly, David got up off the floor and got ready for work.

Will Abbott was in the waiting area when David arrived, his body rigid as he sat on the edge of his seat.

Will stood up when David entered. "We have to do something," he said in a rush. "I never wanted this to happen." He blocked David's path.

David stepped around him. "I'll be with you in a minute." He made his way toward his office door.

Will followed him.

David spun around. "Excuse me; I said I would be a minute."

"You've been out of the office for over a week. I don't want to wait another minute."

David's mind flashed back to how Will looked at their first meeting. He remembered his words: I want to be fair to my wife. He seemed different now.

Amber walked into the area. "Oh good, you're both here."

Will's shoulders dropped and his eyes slid toward her.

"I was just telling Mr. Abbott that I would be a minute." David stared at Will.

Amber nodded. "I'll get him set up in the conference room." She put her hand on Will's, gently guiding him away from the stairs. She whispered something David couldn't make out.

Once in his office, David took a deep breath. Will's file was on his desk. Exhaling in the way Jenny had taught him, he peeked in it. The file was thin. It was always that way at the start of a case; empty files ready to explode with emotionally charged paperwork.

David grabbed a legal pad and a pen. He scribbled loopy spirals on the pad until the ink came out. He started toward the door, then stopped. He pulled out his phone and looked at the pictures from the past several days. Ryan holding Bolt on the back deck, sun streaming down behind him. A close-up of Moxie, pink tongue out, eyes bright. Jenny, recovered, giving the thumbs up. And the one of he and the girls at Lulu's, his face in the center of their smiling ones.

He switched off the phone and looked up. He had to do this. But for how long?

When David entered the conference room, Amber and Will were huddled together. They had pulled two chairs away from the table and sat facing each other, Amber's hand on his knee. She bent forward, her hair falling in long pieces around her face.

"David." Amber stood up abruptly. She smoothed her skirt.

David stood still in the doorframe. Did he just see Amber with her hand on Will's knee?

"Will is very upset," Amber said. Her face reddened and she moved her chair back to the table.

"I understand. Tell me what's happening." David sat, leaned forward. He directed his attention to Will but could not stop thinking about Amber's demeanor.

"I didn't know that my wife would be banned from the house or that she wouldn't be able to see the kids," Will said in a rush. "Charlie and Amanda are a mess. Both of their teachers called. Amanda failed a test and isn't handing in homework. At night, Charlie just lies in his room." He looked down, then up again. "His friggin' fingernails are bloody from biting, but I can't ask Hannah about it because I don't know where she is. I asked her friends. She's not with them. I tried to call her cell, but she didn't answer."

"She can't, Will." Amber's voice was soft. "Remember?"

"Right. That's the problem. I didn't know what this all meant, this whole restraining order thing."

David stopped writing. He looked at Amber. "Did you try calling her lawyer? Settling the case through him?"

Will looked like he might explode. Amber put her hand over his; they exchanged a quick glance. "You told me not to negotiate with Jack Connors."

Had he said that? David tried to remember.

"Okay. Okay. When's the final hearing?"

"Friday."

"This Friday?"

"Yes." Amber said. "That's why I've been trying to get in touch with you."

All the texts and emails he ignored. David leaned forward, thinking. "Has a divorce complaint been filed?"

"Wife filed, last week."

"Right, that's another thing," Will interjected. "While you were on your vacation, Hannah filed for divorce." He threw his hands in the air. Amber moved her chair closer to his.

David held his hands out, palms down. "Alright, alright. Right now, the divorce is a good thing. We can incorporate restraints from the DV into civil restraints under the FM."

"What are you talking about?" Will looked at Amber. "What is he talking about?"

"Will, it's fine. He's just telling you what I did. We can negotiate temporary visitation and custody as part of your divorce. You can drop the restraining order without worrying that Hannah won't let you see the kids again. We talked about this. It's alright. All David has to do is call the other attorney." She looked at David.

"I'll call Jack Connors today and tell him you want to drop the restraining order. Right now, in fact. I will negotiate visitation for you so you can see your kids." He got up to leave. "I got this, Will. Don't worry."

Will's eyes met his, untrusting. "I hope so."

David returned to his office and picked up the phone. He dialed the first three numbers for Jack Connors. Then he spied the fax that had just come in from Tookie Taylor. It sat ominously in his office machine, beckoning to be read. David hung up and reached for it.

Tookie Taylor was a ballbuster attorney who routinely wore hiking boots and legal suits. She was an avid hunter; it was rumored that she had a gun rack on her baby's stroller in case an errant animal happened by during a leisurely walk.

She had been Lauren's divorce attorney.

David had received dozens of letters from Tookie on Lauren's behalf over the years. In each, she had been outraged, disgusted, shocked, dumbfounded, aghast, astounded, offended, and dismayed by his horrid, reprehensible, disgraceful, shameful, and otherwise unlawful conduct. Those were the words she used. Many in combination and usually with modifiers: not disgusted, utterly disgusted; not offended, highly offended. David knew the language. Hell. David used the language.

It was the language of divorce.

David pulled the letter from the fax. It couldn't be about him. Lauren had been back less than forty-eight hours. He flipped over the fax cover page. The caption of his divorce case stared at him:

Re: Lauren S. Dewey vs. David R. Dewey

Docket No.: FM-11-3345-12A

It was about him. He read the letter:

Dear Mr. Dewey:

This letter is in relation to your recent exercise of parenting time at the former marital residence. As I understand from my client, there were numerous breaches of good judgment on your part in this timeframe, many of which will have a long-lasting negative impact on the children and some of which may require court action as explained in detail herein.

First, it is completely outrageous that you would leave your tortoise with Ryan without my client's permission. Ms. Dewey has a firm household rule against live animals which you surreptitiously undermined. Moreover, Ryan has become excessively attached to the animal, insists upon telling teachers and peers that he is a "guide tortoise," and has requested to bring him to school for "training." When questioned by a staff member about the guide tortoise program he shouted at her to "look it up!" This behavior is disturbing, to say the least. If this animal, who I understand is unlicensed, is not removed from the premises by the end of the week, please be advised that Ms. Dewey will effectuate its removal through animal control.

Second, Ms. Dewey understands from the children that a strange woman was housed in her bedroom with a large dog for a good part of the week. This is reprehensible, a complete violation of my client's privacy, and clearly adverse to the interests of your young and impressionable children. It is only because of Ms. Dewey's insistence that we keep things civil that criminal trespassing charges have not been filed. Nonetheless, as a result of this incident, Ms. Dewey is in the process of having her bedding professionally laundered. The bill will be forwarded to your office. Please pay same forthwith.

Third, Hailey is beyond distraught over your inexplicable insistence that she cut off her long hair and get a severe haircut. She has been unable to style it and, accordingly, is in tears every morning. She has been placated only by Ms. Dewey's suggestion that they get hair extensions until it grows back. As the entire situation emanates from your wildly poor judgment, it is expected that you will pay for same in full. A bill will be forthcoming.

Fourth and possibly most shocking, it is understood that you spent close to $2,000 on dresses, shoes, hair, and makeup for Hailey and Sienna for a high school dance in the gym. However, days before, you indicated to Ms. Dewey that firm funds were low and you could not pay the full support amount for the month of October. Clearly, this obviously false statement was an attempt to take advantage of my client's good nature. If arrears for October are not paid by the end of this week, a court action for enforcement will be filed.

A final example of your disturbing and erratic behavior is your encouragement that the children cheer at the disposal of the healthy, nutritious food prepared by my client and subsequent replacement of same with excessive, fattening appetizers. In addition, you did not enforce bedtimes, encourage completion of homework, or, as stated, follow the meal plan meticulously prepared by Ms. Dewey.

As a result of this five (5) day odyssey of unfathomable bad judgment, the children, quite frankly, need a recovery period. Ms. Dewey has scheduled additional therapy appointments for each. Until the therapy is completed and the situation normalized, please respect my client's wishes that you refrain from any and all contact with the children who, again, are understandably traumatized. You may call my office to arrange a time to remove the tortoise when the children are not present.

I expect your full cooperation with the above as I believe Ms. Dewey would prevail in an application to the court for this same relief.

Thank you for your attention to this matter.

Very truly yours,

Tookie Taylor, Esquire

David held the letter, frozen. The week had gone so well. The kids hugged him when he left, even Sienna. For a moment, David could feel the warmth of his children around him; the interlocking of limbs. They'd made plans to go to Applebee's tonight, a secret joke to remember the nineteen appetizers.

David crumpled the paper. He felt pulsing in his neck, the beginning of rage boiling in the pit of his stomach. He would go anyway. He'd stand in the driveway until the kids came out. He'd ring the doorbell, knock on the windows, call the house phone. He wouldn't take no for an answer.

And Lauren would call the police.

David would be told to leave.

Anger snaked up David's body. He picked up the pen holder from his desk and threw it. It hit the wall with a thud then dropped unsatisfactorily to the floor, pencils and paperclips scattering. He picked up a paperweight, one made by Sienna as a kindergartener; it felt heavy in his hand. Someone knocked on the door. He put it down.

Amber peeked in. "David, are you alright?"

"Fine. Dropped something."

"Are you—"

"I'm fine. I have work to do."

Amber looked closely at him then shut the door.

David sat at his desk, unable to move. With a sudden jerk, he threw the crumpled letter in the trash. His cell phone rang. He pulled it out. It was Jenny. The thought calmed him. He still had Jenny.

"Hello."

Her voice was muffled, like she was crying.

"Jenny? I can't hear you. What is it?" David's stood up and pushed the phone closer to his ear.

"My hair," she choked out. "I just lost a clump of my hair. I know it's stupid but—"

"Not stupid. I'm on my way."

David grabbed his keys and his phone and headed toward the door.

He didn't call Jack Connors.

And he didn't look at his messages.

Had he done so, he would have seen six from a woman named Rachel Goldstein.

THIRTY-FOUR

"Nothing from David Dewey?" Hannah called out the question from the couch as Rachel entered the townhouse. She had set out a bowl of candy by the front door. Rachel knew it was killing her not to be with her kids on Halloween.

"No." Rachel put her briefcase on the floor and kicked her heels off. Her bare feet sank in the carpet. "I left another message though." Snowball rubbed against her leg. She picked her up, kissed her head.

"And the hearing is still Friday?"

"Yes."

Hannah let out an indecipherable noise. "And if they don't want to settle?"

She knew the answer; Rachel told her anyway. "There will be a trial about the incident."

Rachel set Snowball down and sat next to Hannah on the couch. "Jack Connors is a fabulous trial attorney. He never loses." Hannah looked at her. "He never loses," Rachel repeated. "Try not to worry. And I'll call David Dewey again tomorrow."

Hannah took a deep breath, gave a glimpse of a smile.

But they both knew what was at stake.

Will had custody of the kids. If Hannah lost the domestic violence case, he'd keep custody, keep possession of the house. If that happened, Rachel would, of course, file a motion on Hannah's behalf to change custody. But the family courts took forever. The judge would likely order a custody evaluation; that would take months. And the longer Will had the kids, the longer that was the status quo, the less inclined a judge would be to change things up.

If Hannah didn't win the domestic violence case, she was screwed.

Hannah stood, the resolve to be strong evident in her tired features. "I made chicken parm." She clicked off ESPN. "And that salad you like."

As if her words prompted Rachel's senses, the smell of dinner flooded the room. The doorbell rang. Before Rachel could move, Hannah was at the door. She fawned over a tiny witch and a boy dressed as Batman. When she returned, she and Rachel sat at the table; her eyes were wet.

"I saw the kids' pictures on Facebook. For Halloween."

"Oh." Rachel knew the response was inadequate. "I'm sorry," she added.

Hannah said nothing. Unable to manage the silence, Rachel continued. "What were they? Did they look okay?"

Hannah pushed her chicken to the side of the plate. "Amanda was a candy corn witch and Charlie was a ninja. And yes, they looked okay. Better than okay. Happy, even."

"I'm sorry."

"Better than upset, right?" She tried to make a joke of it, but Rachel had gotten to know Hannah well enough to know how much this hurt. She'd been staying with her since Rachel had gotten the prosecutor to drop the criminal charge two weeks earlier.

Outside of the courthouse after the hearing, Hannah had been ecstatic. Rachel had to explain twice before Hannah understood: throwing the vase at Will was the basis of two different legal proceedings—a criminal proceeding, which had just gotten dropped, and a domestic violence proceeding, which was still pending.

"So what does that mean?" she'd asked.

"It means until the final hearing, you can't contact Will or your kids or go home."

It sounded awful. Hannah had stared at her, uncomprehending, before her hands flew to her mouth. She had fallen to her knees in front of the courthouse, fall wind whipping leaves around her balled body. Rachel had to help her up.

"Where do I go?" She'd asked, face stricken.

Rachel took her to her townhouse. It was meant to be temporary; a reprieve to figure out what to do next.

But she never asked Hannah to leave.

Rachel should have told Aaron. Or Jack Connors. But it felt strange, like she was overstepping an ethical boundary of some kind. So she lied to Aaron, told him she was swamped with work. She didn't tell Jack. It was almost as though Hannah was a secret friend Rachel had stored away. She felt strikingly similar to the way she had felt as a small child when she'd hidden a stray orange cat in her bedroom. Every time she'd left and come back home, Rachel had been surprised to find him there, curled up in the sun.

Hannah's voice interrupted her thoughts.

"So we'll have the meeting with Jack Connors tomorrow?" She put down her fork.

Rachel swallowed. "Yes. Nine a.m."

Rachel had set the meeting, personally put it into Jack's calendar in large block letters. He would take it seriously; she would make sure of it. This was not a fly-by-the-seat-of-your-pants kind of hearing. There was too much at stake.

The doorbell rang. Again, Hannah opened the door and gave appropriate, motherly comments. Rachel had always made boring comments like "nice costume" or "looking great." She'd remember Hannah's words for future Halloweens.

Once the trick-or-treaters left, they cleared the table like two friends who had lived together forever.

"That was delicious, by the way." Rachel motioned to her plate as she cleaned it. "Thank you."

"It's Amanda's favorite." Hannah's face clouded.

She left the kitchen and switched on a 76ers game. Rachel assumed it was to ease her mind about the upcoming events and she assured Hannah there was nothing she'd rather watch. In truth, she'd come to enjoy sports in the background. It was nice reprieve from Aaron's stock market ticker tape and the muted vanilla commentary from varied financial hosts. Aaron and Hannah watched their respective channels with a similar fervor, each cheering at symbols or numbers or plays Rachel didn't try to understand. But the sound of the basketball game soothed Rachel and she found herself drifting off notwithstanding the continued knocking from the trick-or-treaters.

Hannah shook Rachel gently. "Rachel. You should go to bed."

Rachel sat up and oriented herself. "Oh, thanks." She got up and walked toward the stairs then stopped. "Sixers win?"

"Of course," Hannah said. "Now go to bed and get some rest." She spoke in a soothing tone Rachel imagined she used with her children.

The tone made Rachel feel calm and reassured and she wondered, briefly, how nice it would be to have Hannah as a mother. At the thought, a vision of Charlie and Amanda materialized in her mind.

How were those poor kids doing without her?

Rachel awoke the next morning to the smell of blueberry muffins. She headed downstairs and found Hannah in the kitchen mixing more batter.

"Couldn't sleep. Sorry." Dark circles underscored her eyes, tinged in red.

"Please stop worrying," Rachel told her. "Like I told you, Jack Connors is an amazing attorney. You have nothing to worry about."

Rachel ate a muffin, then got ready for work. She arrived at the office early and settled in at her desk. She picked up a letter and tried to read. The words made no sense; she couldn't focus. She tried again, then dropped it, giving up. She checked her phone. It was ten to nine. Jack should have called her down by now.

As if he read her mind, Jack called her name. Rachel exhaled. Finally. They would come up with a strategy for the case. She expected he'd have the game plan etched out on a yellow legal pad and they'd work with Hannah to refine the details. What to ask, what to avoid. How to make sure she got the kids back. Rachel had expected he'd be hunched at his desk, surrounded by scrawled thoughts and used post-its.

Instead, when she entered his office, Jack had his feet up, shiny black shoes perfectly tied in symmetrical bows. He was leaning back in his chair, finishing a call. He seemed unmoved by her arrival.

Come on. Hannah will be here in ten minutes.

Finally, Jack hung up the receiver and removed his feet from the desk in a single, sweeping motion. He turned to look at her. "So, listen. You have to do the Abbott DV hearing Friday. There's a big deposition in the Thornton case."

Rachel stepped back. She must have misheard. "I can't do the DV hearing. I've never done one."

"You'll be fine. You've observed trials as part of your rotation."

"But it's not the same. I don't know what to ask and I don't fully understand evidentiary procedure."

Jack motioned for her to close the door. She got up and shut it. "Look, Rachel," he said as she turned. "I've got to take care of our big clients. This is your case. You need to be responsible for it."

Jack's phone buzzed, and his assistant's voice filled the room. "Hannah Abbott's here."

"Send her down," Jack looked at her again. "What's the worst that can happen?" He stood up and opened the door.

Rachel's mind raced through infinite horrid possibilities. Hannah appeared in the doorframe. She clutched her purse, her knuckles white around its handle. Rachel saw her inhale.

"Ms. Abbott," Jack said, his voice taking on the obligatory client-oriented tone. "Please have a seat."

Hannah sat in a chair, Rachel sat adjacent to her—the same chairs they had sat in a few months back. There was so much more at stake now. Back then, Hannah was just "wife"; her kids, ages and sexes, nothing more. Now Rachel knew Hannah. She knew that she loved sports, drank vanilla lattes daily, and cooked when she was nervous. Charlie, her youngest, was a people-pleaser; Amanda was strong-willed and would be her challenge. Will was her first real love and her voice changed when she spoke about him.

Rachel glanced at Hannah sitting straight in her chair. She couldn't do the hearing. She'd mess it up. She'd ruin Hannah's life.

"So, I've had something come up," Jack started. He crossed one leg over the other. "Rachel's going to handle your domestic violence hearing." He gestured at Rachel as if to clarify who she was.

Hannah looked at her, eyes wide.

Jack took a swig of water then glanced at their empty hands. "Drinks? Water, tea, coffee?"

Hannah shook her head. She looked at Rachel again before redirecting her attention to Jack. "Aren't you supposed to do it? It's been on the schedule for over two weeks." Her voice was strong, like a consumer who hadn't gotten what she paid for.

"That's just the thing. Something's come up. It's emergent. You'll be in fine hands with Rachel here. She's—" His voice trailed off a moment. "She's one of our best lawyers. Plus, David Dewey's on the other side. Man's a putz." Jack leaned forward and whispered. "He used to be a partner here, you know. He drinks." Jack pretended to put a cup to his lips. "He may even stumble in drunk. Who knows? With Dewey, anything can happen!" It was clear he intended his words to be humorous. When neither woman laughed, he continued.

"Why don't you tell me again what happened, and I'll make sure Rachel knows exactly what to do. It will almost be like I'm there."

Hannah explained what happened. When she got to the part about throwing the vase, Jack stopped her.

"Wait, wait," he said. "Before you picked up the vase, he charged at you, right?"

Hannah shook her head. "No. He was by the kitchen door. He was eerily calm."

"He wasn't angry? You weren't afraid?" Jack's eyes widened.

"No," Hannah said flatly.

"Well, if you weren't afraid, if he didn't charge at you, if he wasn't acting crazy, you don't have a good defense."

"She was angry," Rachel volunteered, too eager. "About the woman."

"And I was concerned he was taking the kids," Hannah added.

"His kids." Jack reminded her. "His kids." He pulled the trial notice out of the file and scanned it. "And your judge is a man."

Outside the sky darkened.

Jack shook his head. "Your defense would be better if he charged at you. And you were afraid."

THIRTY-FIVE

As soon as Hannah left, Rachel shut Jack's door. "I can't do this."

Jack looked at her, his expression incredulous. "You're a lawyer, Rachel. What did you expect you would be doing?"

Jack's assistant hurried into the room with a pile of documents.

"But—"

"We're done here, Rachel."

She stared at him; he looked at a paper on his desk. Rachel finally left and returned to her office, shutting the door. She sunk into her chair and, like a child having a tantrum, pushed a file off her desk, letting the papers crash to the ground in an unsatisfactory expression of rage. What if Hannah lost custody because of her? Rachel put her head in her hands and sat in perfect stillness, then jerked up.

She could still settle it.

Rachel fumbled through the file for David Dewey's number and dialed. A cheery receptionist with a Southern accent informed her that Mr. Dewey wasn't there, but she'd leave him a message.

"Tell him it's Rachel Goldstein. I'm the attorney for Hannah Abbott. I'd like to talk to about the domestic violence matter."

Rachel hung up the phone and tapped a pen on her desk. Could she do the hearing? She'd gotten the criminal charge dropped. And she had observed a bunch of trials. All she had to do was ask Hannah what happened. That was it. Attorneys, less capable ones, did it every day. She picked up the file and opened it.

Her cell phone pinged.

On my way! Almost there!

Rachel stared at the words. Shit. Shocked by the morning's events, she'd forgotten. How had she forgotten? She had been looking forward to it for days, the lunch she had planned with Greg Tisbury. Rachel had told Aaron about the lunch a few days before. She'd expected some type of reaction. When he did not look up from the paper, Rachel went on to add that she'd dated Greg in college. She gave him several details until he finally looked up and asked, "Why are you telling me this?"

"I just didn't want you to think it was weird."

"Should I?"

"No." The conversation ended, and she'd felt stupid then, her relationship with Greg somehow diminished by Aaron's lack of concern.

Still, as Rachel slipped on her coat and headed outside, her heart skittered at the thought of seeing Greg again. They'd pick up where they left off; she'd tell him about Hannah and the trial. He would reassure her, just like he had before her first-year exams at Lafayette. She'd been terrified, certain she would fail.

"You got this, Ray," he'd said. "You have the ability to do whatever you want. Always believe that."

The recollection of his words made her feel warm despite the cold. She weaved through the Princeton students laden with backpacks and laptops; she could see the smoky outline of her breath. It was getting colder, the forecast calling for a fluke November storm.

As Rachel got closer to the restaurant, she scanned the crowd outside, trying to get a glimpse of Greg. What would he look like now? What would he think of her? She spotted Greg at the door. Lean with a mop of curly dark hair. Dressed smartly, a briefcase at his side. She strode forward with such enthusiasm that she plowed directly into another man. The papers he was holding dropped and fluttered; they both grabbed at them as they flew about in the wind.

"Sorry," Rachel said, keeping her eye on the lean man by the door.

"It's okay."

The familiarity of the voice made her pause.

Rachel looked up. "Greg?"

THIRTY-SIX

"Rachel!"

They took each other in. Rachel glanced at the pseudo-Greg by the door then focused on the real one.

He had gained weight, not obese but much larger than the twenty-two-year old she'd last seen at Perkins. His hair was disheveled, unruly curls popping out haphazardly. He wore a faded army green coat with a tear in the sleeve. His glasses had a smear on one lens. Rachel observed the smear and thought, immediately, about how much Aaron would hate it.

Greg's voice interrupted her train of thought. "You look fantastic!"

Rachel struggled for something to say in return. "How are you?" She emphasized the word are with a superficial affect she didn't normally have.

204 · LEANNE TREESE

"Wonderful. Wonderful." His voice was the same. Her shoulders relaxed. It was Greg.

They walked inside the restaurant and checked in. The hostess showed them to an intimate table with a view of the sidewalk. A vase with a single carnation sat in the center of the table, tiny glass marbles like bubbles on the bottom. The sky darkened further as they sat. It felt ominous. Rachel brushed off the feeling.

Greg took a roll from the basket dropped off by a hurried waitress. After the niceties—the how are you and how was your trip and yes, it's getting colder, Greg plunged in. "So you're a lawyer? Is it great?"

Typical Greg. It made Rachel smile. He'd always been direct.

"It's good. I'm still learning."

She had an urge to tell him the truth—the snub by the firm's commercial group, her fear about Hannah's upcoming hearing. But it was too early. They hadn't even ordered their food.

"I remembered you always wanted to be a lawyer." He popped a hunk of bread in his mouth and spoke before swallowing. "Because it's what your parents wanted."

Rachel cocked her head. Was that a cut?

"The Goldsteins were pleased, that's for sure." She said it lightly.

"What kind of law?" His voice seemed unfriendly. Was she misreading him?

"Family."

"Divorce?" he snorted. A bit of the roll flew from his mouth. "Is that what you planned on?"

Rachel's back straightened, giving her all the stature her 5'3" frame could generate. Was he criticizing her? Or was she interpreting it wrong?

She held her head upright as though she were balancing a book on top of it. "Absolutely," she said evenly. "I love it. And you? Do you like Trending Now?" Her voice was dinner-party polite. The conversation was not going as planned. She'd thought Greg would be happy to see her.

Greg tipped the roll basket toward her. Rachel shook her head and Greg took the remaining roll. "I love Trending Now," he said as he smeared butter on the bread in thick, yellow layers. He gave her the premise of the show, but Rachel knew it already. Trending Now was a New York cable show which featured stories about ridiculous social trends, viral videos, and memes. Greg was a pro ducer.

As Greg gave her the background information, the hostess seated a mother and two children at the table next to them. Rachel glanced at them; they looked like a younger version of Hannah's kids. Lunch out. Something Hannah would probably do. Her heart plunged at the thought of her hearing and she forced her attention back to Greg.

"And your current project? What are you working on now?"

Greg took a swig of water. He leaned forward. His collar was unstarched. Something else Aaron would have hated.

"Right now, I'm doing a feature on Cowboy Pigs."

She laughed by accident.

"No seriously. There's this woman in Texas who dresses pigs in cowboy costumes and uploads them on social media. They've gone viral."

Greg handed her his phone and she scrolled through at least twenty photos of pigs wearing brimmed hats, tiny boots, checkered shirts, and bandanas.

"Oh my God. Who has the time to do this?" She scanned through the photos a second time, then zoomed in on one super fat pig with a leather vest, black cowboy boots, and a red hat. He stood behind a nameplate with Grimace stenciled in red.

Greg continued, the excitement evident in his voice. "The pigs are a thing now. She's making a calendar, greeting cards. People can't get enough. We're flying her in. She's going to make a costume live on the show." He said it in a manner that made it seem as though he had landed an interview with the Pope. "It's going to be lit."

Lit? Who uses the word lit? Rachel tried to imagine Aaron saying, "that stock trade was lit." She suppressed a smile.

Rachel closed out the pig pictures, handed the phone back across the tiny table. Just as she released it, Greg grabbed her hand. "Geez! What is that?!" He examined her ring. "Jesus. That's a rock." He looked up at her, the smear still evident on his glasses. His expression hardened. "You didn't think to tell me you were engaged?"

"Sorry. I didn't—"

"So who's the lucky guy?" Greg interrupted.

"Aaron Weiss."

"And what does Mr. Weiss do?"

"He's in finance."

Greg paused, then recognition crossed his face. "Wait. Aaron Weiss, the financial guy. The guy from Bennett Sterns?"

"That's him." Rachel was surprised at the pride in her voice. "That's my fiancé."

Greg put down his roll. "Wow." His voice was thick with sarcasm. "Your parents must be thrilled. Rich and Jewish. Plus, you're a lawyer. Just like they told you to be."

Before Rachel could formulate a comeback, their waitress appeared, pen poised for their order.

She ordered an oriental salad; Greg, a bacon cheeseburger.

Something about his order didn't seem right. As the waitress scribbled their choices and hurried away, it came to her. She'd never seen Greg eat anything from an animal, not even cheese. But that was eight years ago. "Are you no longer vegan?"

"I am vegan."

"But you just ordered a burger?"

"Right." He looked at her as though she would not understand what he was about to say. "I believe in vegan principles more often than I do not. But I am open to the idea that my body craves, from time to time, the non-vegan lifestyle. I listen to my body, my cravings, and I honor them. It's called fluidity." He folded his hands, as if he had just said something incredibly wise.

"Fluidity?"

"Yes. It a thing. It's trending."

Neither of them spoke. Rachel took a sip of water; the rattle of the ice cubes loud in the silence. She heard herself swallow. The reunion was a disappointment; Greg was not who she remembered.

"Sorry," he said finally. "I'm just having trouble digesting you, digesting this." He gestured at her with his hands.

Something inside her snapped. "Excuse me?"

"You. Playing the part. Lawyer. Jewish wife. I thought you'd be different by now."

The words hung there, stinging in their partial truth. The stress of the morning and the disappointment of the lunch ignited. Rachel spoke, her voice harsh and commanding. "You. Are criticizing me? You. Whose life work surrounds things like pigs dressed as cowboys. You. Who can't even bother to clean your glasses." She plucked them off his face and cleared the smear with her napkin. "You. A vegan who eats cheeseburgers. You. Are criticizing me?"

The people around them became silent. Rachel heard the mother next to them whisper to her kids.

Greg spoke in a tone with matched intensity. "I think you are whatever anyone wants you to be. You don't have a mind of your own. You never have. You're weak, Rachel."

Her mouth fell open for the second time.

It was too much.

"Get out." Her voice was unnaturally low.

Greg stared at her.

"Get out. You heard me. Get the fuck out." Her voice grew louder. The mother at the adjacent table looked alarmed. She moved closer to her kids.

Before Greg could respond, the waitress returned. "Okay now, I've got—" She looked at them and stopped. The tray with their meals balanced precariously on one hand.

Greg stood and patted the waitress on the shoulder. "No worries. I was just leaving." He grabbed the cheeseburger off the tray and took a bite.

"Yum," he said, as he stared at Rachel's open mouth.

And then he was gone.

THIRTY-SEVEN

What an asshole.

Rachel walked back to the firm in an angry daze, picturing Greg's face, mocking, mouth full of burger.

She couldn't go back to work. She found her car and started the engine with a quick spurt. Snowball's picture failed to comfort her. Rachel turned on the radio by habit. Upbeat Taylor Swift lyrics filled the car, the happy tune an irritation. She switched the music off with a sharp poke and banged her hand on the steering wheel.

And she had thought Greg might have been the one who got away! That she'd actually been nervous for the lunch! God. She was an idiot.

She didn't have a mind of her own, he'd said. Who was he to say that?

Stupid slob.

Asshole.

Rachel drove without thinking, her body on autopilot. Who could she call? Lexi? Samantha? No. They'd think she was absurd for meeting him for lunch to begin with. Hannah. She would get it. She'd be furious on her behalf! Once she thought of it, Rachel couldn't wait to tell her, to unburden the weight of it. She'd held on to the idea of Greg for a decade, even during her engagement. Especially during her engagement. He was out there. They'd find each other. It was meant to be.

Bullshit it was.

Asshole.

She pulled into her driveway and immediately noticed the absence of Hannah's car. Damn it. She took a deep breath.

Hannah's absence wasn't a surprise. She went to the grocery store almost daily. She'd be back soon, no doubt, laden with varied ingredients and spices Rachel had never heard of. She'd lay them on the counter and begin the process of slicing and dicing and adding herbs until the townhouse smelled like a home.

Hannah would be back soon.

Rachel walked toward the house, thoughts racing. What if she had lost Aaron over her stupid, girlish obsession with Greg Tisbury? A gallant version of Aaron entered her mind—taller, funnier, politer. As the vision became more vivid, Rachel increasingly felt it was imperative she act immediately, as though Aaron was, at that very moment, on the cusp of changing his mind. Who would blame him? His fiancée was an idiot.

As she stood at her doorway, the feeling of a crisis reached critical mass. She had to act. She couldn't wait for Hannah. This was serious. Rachel had nearly thrown out the best thing in her life. She dashed a text to Hannah and headed to the city. She needed to make things right.

Rachel got Aaron's favorite take-out, found good wine from the cellar (but not the bottles she had been instructed never to touch), and carefully set the table, placing a tall candle in the center. She struck a match and lit it, then commanded Aaron's smart home system to play soft dinner music. Sounds of light piano filled the room and she dimmed the lights. Rachel sat at the table and stared at the single, flickering flame. It calmed her in its simplicity. This was a good life. She shouldn't resist it. She took a deep breath. Why had she been so ungrateful?

"Rachel?" Aaron called out.

"In here."

He walked into the kitchen, looking perfectly groomed, excessively fit. A quick visual of Greg in his smeared glasses stuffing bread into his mouth popped into her brain. Idiot. What had she been thinking?

"Rachel! This looks great. What's the occasion?" Aaron kissed her on the top of her head and took the seat across. He lifted his wine and swirled the glass before holding it to his nose. "2009 Sequoia Grove Cambium?"

Rachel nodded.

"Nice." He raised his glass. "To this." The sound of glass hitting glass reverberated through the room, a festive addition to the soft background music. They each took a sip; Rachel allowed the liquid to warm her throat. She sipped again, smiling.

"This looks great," Aaron said again, gesturing at the steaks, bread, and wedges of iceberg lettuce slathered with blue cheese.

Rachel couldn't wait any longer.

"Let's set the date." The request came out rushed and, possibly, inarticulate. "Let's set the date," she said again, more slowly.

"The wedding date?" He looked surprised. Had she already ruined things?

"Yes." Rachel paused. The next part was big. "And let's get married on an island."

The corners of his mouth turned up. He chewed – and swallowed -- before speaking. "An island. Really?" Excitement filled his voice.

It was what he had wanted. Rachel had fought for a hometown wedding in the synagogue she'd gone to her whole life; Aaron wanted an exotic locale. He wouldn't give in. Even her mother had been frustrated. "A girl should be able to get married where she wants," she'd lamented.

Aaron put down his wine glass. "Are you serious, Rachel?"

"Yes. And there's something else." She leaned forward.

"What is it, wife-to-be?" He sounded suddenly silly.

"I've decided not to work after the wedding. Let's start a family."

"Really!" The timing of children had been another source of contention but, now, it seemed illogical to wait five years.

Aaron got up and came over to her, pulling her to her feet. "Rachel, you can't know how happy you've made me." He sounded like a little boy as he said the words. Rachel's heart swelled.

It felt like love.

They drank the whole bottle of wine and spent the night entwined, naked, in each other arms. They both slept in the next morning. Rachel felt like she had signed up for an endless summer vacation, no responsibilities in sight. She allowed herself to forget about the hearing. She was sure Hannah Abbott had not spent her time with Will worrying about work. Rachel visualized the picture of Will in his bathing suit, muscles flexed as he held a child in each arm. Definitely not.

Rachel took her time getting ready for work. It was just a pitstop now. After a proper bath, she luxuriated on the couch wearing a conditioning turban and watching a segment on the Today Show about fun gadgets for pets. The most intriguing feature was a talking, rolling mouse, called MOLEY, which retailed for $9.99. While Rachel was focused on getting the MOLEY information for Snowball (1-800-mym-oley), Aaron came over and said something. She couldn't really hear him through the conditioning turban but smiled as though he's said something of great importance.

"Any reason we couldn't do that?" he asked.

"No, of course not!" Probably a dinner or something.

It was 9:42 a.m. when Rachel finally rolled into the parking lot of Trembley, Rubin, and Connors. The big-windowed partner offices looked out on the front lot, each window telling a different story. Andrew Trembley was having a meeting, all attendees in rapt attention. Henry Rubin was typing what appeared to be an intensely important document, his face tight and serious. Annaleigh Finn was nodding, leaning forward, listening to a client.

And then, in Jack Connors window, stood. . . a giant. A HUGE man. With no hair. His face was contorted. All body language indicated rage. Jack, his six-foot frame dwarfed, was yelling back. Rachel stared at the scene. What in the world? She saw Jack pick up his phone. Thank God she wasn't involved.

A second later, her phone pinged. She pulled it out and saw the text.

Where are you Rachel?

Walking in.

I need you in my office.

Okay.

As soon as Rachel passed the threshold, the receptionist spoke in a hurried, worried tone. "Jack's been looking for you."

"Who's in his office?" she mouthed.

"David Dewey."

So that was the putz. Was he drunk?

"He's BALD," the receptionist added.

"Is that new?" Rachel asked.

"Well, he wasn't bald last week. He's always been—" She stopped herself. "Anyway, they're waiting on you."

As soon as Rachel entered, Jack started in, "Hannah Abbott is missing."

"No," David Dewey interrupted, "she's a kidnapper."

Jack shot him a look. "She apparently took her kids for pizza last night and disappeared. No one has seen her since."

"But there's a restraining ord—" Rachel started.

"She tricked an old woman!" David yelled, sounding more like an errant child than a lawyer. "She tricked my client's mother into letting her see them." He crossed his trunk-like arms and faced her.

"So here's the thing," Jack started, seeming to make an effort to keep his voice calm. "The girls," he pointed in the direction of the cubicles, "they don't seem to have an address for Hannah Abbott. Kelly said you'd been taking her mail. So," he said slowly, "we just need to find her, get the kids back, and it will be over."

Jack waited, expectant. It was a simple question.

"Rachel," Jack repeated. "where has she been staying? We need to start there."

She could not formulate words. Had she done something wrong in having Hannah stay with her? And where was she? This was unlike her. Or so Rachel thought.

David Dewey stared at her, his immense figure an intimidation.

"Rachel?" Jack said for the third time.

"I'm not sure where she's been staying." Why was she lying? What was wrong with her?

"Well, where are you sending her mail?"

"I give it to her at the gym." Rachel said the words like a question.

"At the gym?" Jack asked, incredulity dripping off every word.

"We belong to the same gym."

David snorted. "What kind of shit show are you running around here, Jack?"

"And she didn't mention anyone—mom, boyfriend, third cousin, whomever—while you were at the gym?" He stressed the word 'gym'.

"No." That much was true. "I know her Mom lives in Florida."

"Great," David said, his voice thick with sarcasm. "That narrows it down."

They stood a moment in silence before David spoke again. "Listen, my client's mother is in the hospital over this. Literally keeled over with stress. He does not want this to get any bigger or more stressful than it already is for her sake. Find your lady, get the kids, and we're done. No kids in twenty-four hours and we take this to the police. You got me?"

Rachel nodded, voiceless. He walked out.

As David Dewey retreated down the hall, Jack whispered, "At the gym. Why are you giving out legal documents at the gym?" When she didn't respond, he continued, "Listen, Rachel, you find her. We are not going to look like we can't control our clients."

"I'll find her," she promised.

Rachel drove directly home, her mind scattered. When had she last seen Hannah? Yesterday morning. At the meeting with Jack. She should have called her; Hannah had been upset. She'd gone to lunch with Greg Tisbury instead. And then went to Aaron's. What was wrong with her?

She put her head in her hands. It would be okay. They were probably just at the townhouse, eating cereal and watching cartoons. Hannah had probably just wanted to see them. That was all. In the short car ride, Rachel had managed to convince herself Hannah would be there. When the empty driveway stared back at her, it took her a minute to process. Had Hannah really just left with the kids? Rachel texted her.

Nothing.

She called.

Nothing.

Rachel entered the house. There was still a chance Hannah would be there. Maybe she'd hidden her car around the corner. She had made a mistake and didn't know what to do. Surely, they were holed up in a bedroom, waiting for Rachel's esteemed advice.

"Hannah?"

The only sound was Snowball jumping off the counter, padding toward her in greeting. Rachel picked her up and pet her distractedly as she sat down heavily on the couch. She didn't know much about Hannah Abbott. She didn't know the full name of any friend of hers. She didn't know the name or address of her mother. Rachel had no idea where she would go in a situation like this. She hadn't mentioned any fantasy destination or any hidden, family property.

Rachel's phone vibrated. She leapt up. A text! Hannah!

No. Aaron. It was a selfie of him holding a tiny yellow bikini.

Look what I got you, wifey-to-be!

Another vibration.

And this!

A second selfie with Aaron holding a pretty necklace that she had pointed out to him last time they were in town.

She didn't have time for this now. Someone's kids were missing. And every second that passed, Hannah got further and further away; she was sure of it.

Third vibration. Aaron AGAIN.

Can't wait to go away with you tomorrow.

Were they going away? She tried to calm herself enough to think in clear lines. Where were they going? Then she remembered the breakfast conversation. Aaron had said something, but she'd been distracted by the whole MOLEY thing. Where were they going? She pushed the question out of her mind. She'd have to worry about that later.

As she sat, it became clear, she'd have to tell Jack the truth. Hannah had been staying with her. She didn't know where she was. Didn't know where she'd go. If she got fired, so be it. Rachel Goldstein, Attorney at Law, was not long for this world anyway. She'd be Rachel Weiss soon.

Rachel got into her car and drove back to the firm, the first bits of snow starting. When she entered, it was quiet.

"Everyone's in the conference room," the receptionist told her. "Something is going on."

Rachel ducked her head in. All the partners, most of the lawyers, were transfixed around a television screen. A reporter stood in front of a hospital while pictures of Charlie and Amanda flashed on the screen. The reporter said, "It is believed that the children have been taken by their mother who was recently released from jail for a domestic violence incident on her own recognizance." A picture of the jail filled the screen as the reporter continued, "The mother, Hannah Abbott, is represented by the powerhouse law firm Trembley, Rubin, and Connors." A picture of the firm building appeared on the screen. "A source within the firm said they had no idea where Ms. Abbott may be hiding out and that the firm had no record of her address." The reporter paused then, letting the last statement sink in for viewers. "If you have any information about Hannah Abbott, please call our hotline." A number appeared on the screen. "This is Fannie Marcos, for the ABC twelve o'clock news." The show broke to weather coverage.

A cacophony of angry voices filled the room.

"No idea! Who said that we had no idea?

"Who's been working on this case?"

"Why don't we have an address for this lady?"

"I thought we were steering clear of DV matters."

"Who is Hannah Abbott anyway?"

Rachel froze, unable to speak or move.

Jack glanced at her. "Rachel." Everyone turned. "This is Rachel's case. What's the news?"

Dozens of eyes focused on her. Waiting.

THIRTY-EIGHT

Rachel took a step back toward the door. She felt like a small animal surrounded by large, starving predators. "I'm still looking for her." The words came out flushed and quick.

"Your department, Jack." Andrew Trembley threw up his hands. "This is bad press. We don't need that after Parker." They all nodded in grave agreement.

Rachel wanted to leave. She took another step back. No one said anything.

"Give me the weekend," she said finally. "I have some ideas."

Jack nodded and she left.

First, she swung by the townhouse, still holding out hope Hannah would be there; the whole thing a wild, crazy mix-up. No. Still no. She texted her. Called again. Nothing. Her phone rang. It was Aaron.

"Where are you, wifey?"

Wifey! Rachel had begun to hate the term. "I'm still at work," she lied.

"Good news! I was able to change our flight. We'll leave for St. John at eight tonight."

She pieced it together then. The morning's conversation, Aaron's texts while she looked for Hannah. Aaron was taking her to their wedding location for the weekend.

It was sweet. Something she normally would have mooned over. She was part of an elite, jet-setting off to the Caribbean for a weekend getaway. The thought was intoxicating. Still, how could she go? She had to find Hannah.

"You can be home in time, right? The driver is coming at six."

"I don't think I can go," Rachel stammered over the words. "Something has come up."

Silence. She waited. He said nothing.

"Aaron?"

Aaron spoke slowly, taking care to enunciate each word. "So, Rachel, again, the driver will be here at six."

"Right but as I—"

"And you'll be ready," he said, interrupting.

It wasn't a question. Rachel envisioned Aaron standing in his pressed suit, looking over correspondence, waiting for the expected answer. She heard the word "right" come out of her mouth.

"Good." He hung up.

Rachel drove to Aaron's and packed by rote, uncertain when she was done what she'd put in the suitcase. She zipped it blindly, her mind consumed with worry and guilt. Will Abbott's mother was in the hospital. A woman she had been hosting in her home had kidnapped her children. And where did that put her? Had she committed a crime by harboring Hannah, who was now a criminal? Had she done something wrong in not revealing where Hannah had been staying?

The answer came to Rachel as she mindlessly packed a second, smaller bag. Yes. By not telling anyone where Hannah had been staying, she was hindering a criminal investigation. Her mind raced forward; she saw images of herself in jail. Stop it. Stop it. Stop it.

"Ready!" Aaron stood in front of her, suitcase in hand.

"Ready!" Rachel tried to match his tone.

As Aaron prattled on, a heaviness cascaded from her chest to her stomach. Aaron's words were like pins in her brain. Please stop talking.

Twenty minutes before their flight was to take off, Rachel made the decision to call Greg Tisbury. He was an investigative reporter. Of sorts. Maybe he could help find Hannah.

Greg was surprisingly cordial, elated even, that Rachel had enlisted his help. He promised to use the databases and his "resources" at the station. He'd report back, he assured her, as soon as he found something. He sounded to Rachel like an overzealous boy scout who'd been given a pretend secret mission. A part of her regretted involving him.

Still, on the plane, she tried to relax. There was nothing more she could do. She couldn't make Hannah magically appear; she couldn't go back and redo all her mistakes. Besides, she was flying to an island for the weekend with her fiancé. They would be planning their wedding. Rachel wrapped her hand around Aaron's.

Warm, tropical air enveloped Rachel as she exited the plane, and the scent of hibiscus filled the air. The lights around the airport twinkled in the darkness, casting a fairy-like glow. The moon, round and full, centered perfectly over them as though it had been placed there personally by a meticulous deity.

After checking in, they walked down a torchlit path to their bungalow. Rachel opened the door. A warm breeze blew across her skin from an open window. She crossed the room and looked out at the white sand and lapping ocean water. The waves crashed in a steady rhythm, their sound filling the small space.

Aaron came up behind her and put his hands around her. "Not bad, wifey."

"No," she whispered. "Not bad at all."

He turned her and lifted her face to his. Rachel acquiesced to his kiss, forcing her worries about Hannah out of her mind.

The next morning, Rachel slept in, her mind lulled by the steady pattern of crashing ocean waves. She was awakened by a knock on the door. Aaron, already up, dressed, and reading, put down his financial magazine and opened the door. A uniformed bellhop wheeled in a silver cart adorned by a thick, white tablecloth. An array of breakfast foods stood around a tall candle: two mimosas in tall champagne glasses; wheat toast with strawberry jam; a tray of fruit in perfect, colorful lines. Aaron tipped the bellhop, closing the door behind him. It was just the two of them. A private paradise.

They had a meeting with the wedding coordinator at ten. Rachel felt, by then, how she imagined she was supposed to— delighted and blissful, a blushing bride. She and Aaron walked hand in hand to the wedding office and were immediately greeted by a tiny woman with cropped blonde hair named Susie. Susie told them she was "overjoyed" at the prospect of helping them plan their "special day." She carried a gold-plated clipboard and a pen with its own adorable bridal veil.

The meeting started well enough. "They" (really Aaron) decided on the location for the wedding ceremony—a grassy plot near the beach. He decided on the larger ballroom though they'd discussed a more intimate wedding. He wanted the guest chairs to be in straight rows, not at an angle. Susie looked at him quizzically, and he drew straight lines on her flowery pad. "Like this." She nodded cheerfully. "Straight, okay."

It went downhill after the chair row drawing, with Aaron asking multiple questions about even the smallest of details. Did he want a flowered archway at the end of the aisle? Aaron wasn't sure. How big was it? How many flowers? What kind of flowers?

Rachel tried to recapture what she had felt that morning, the relaxed feeling that this was right. That she and Aaron were meant to be together. Being particular was just part of him. A quirky, lovable trait they could joke about. Possibly. Or not.

"Don't fault me for having high standards," he'd said on that topic once before. Still. High standards were good. Right? They bred success. Clearly.

In the second hour, five hotel workers stood in front of them holding up different colored linens and plates for Aaron to see how they would look in varied combinations and different lightings.

"Most people do the white," Susie offered, running her hand through her short locks.

"I'm not most people," Aaron said evenly.

"I like the white linens," Rachel said, offering one of her only opinions of the day. "It's what I've always pictured."

Aaron didn't acknowledge her statement. "We'll do the blue."

Susie cast a pitied look in Rachel's direction. She stared at Aaron. Did she care? About the color of table linens? No. Of course not. It wouldn't be worth making a big deal about. "The blue is gorgeous," Rachel said quickly. "Better than the white, now that I look again." She looked at Susie, wanting to convey that she'd wanted blue all along.

After the linens, they continued to the selection of the appetizers. Susie's perfect pixie haircut became increasingly disheveled. The tiny veil on her pen had been tied and untied in a knot so many times that there was now a kink in the fabric.

"So we generally recommend at least one plate of raw veggies." She sounded tired. And she no longer seemed overjoyed at the prospect of helping them.

Aaron wanted to know if the tray was a circle or a square? Where was the dip in relation to the tray? Were the veggies laid out by type? Did they circle the dip?

"Of course, Mr. Weiss," Susie said, untying the tiny veil again and marking it down on the pad. She may have said, "Fuck you, Mr. Weiss." Rachel couldn't be sure.

By 1:30, they'd only gotten through half the options list with the meaty decisions left to be made (entrees, music, cake). Susie suggested they come back the next day. When Aaron hesitated, she added that she had another appointment, looking at her watch for good measure. "I wouldn't want you to feel rushed," she said sweetly. At that, Aaron agreed.

They walked side by side back to their room, Aaron oblivious to the change in Rachel's mood. He'd barely asked her opinion on anything. It was as if he had been planning a wedding for himself and she was an extra decoration, no different than the cake or the venue. Just something else he got to pick and control.

"That went well. Don't you think, wifey?"

Rachel wanted to scream.

"I have to make some work calls," he announced. "I'll meet you at the beach."

Rachel went to the beach alone. She sat close to the bungalow and could hear Aaron's voice slicing through the tranquil atmosphere. "Bullshit! That will never happen." She moved her chair out of earshot.

The peace Rachel had felt upon arrival at the island had eroded and she once again worried about the Hannah situation. She pulled out her phone and called Hannah again. No answer. She texted Greg Tisbury.

Anything?

She stared at the screen, willing a positive and immediate response. Nothing.

By dinnertime, Rachel had decided to tell Aaron what was going on. He had a lot of resources. More than Greg Tisbury. He could help. She vowed to tell him over dinner. They would leave immediately. She was crazy to be here. What had she been thinking? It was awful. She was awful. She had to tell Aaron.

They walked to the restaurant through winding tropical pathways lit with torches. The ocean remained in view, its vibrant blue dimming as the sun dipped behind red-hued clouds.

"Aaron, I need to—"

"I have a surprise!" he interrupted, grabbing her hand.

THIRTY-NINE

A surprise.

She didn't have time for a surprise.

"Aaron, we have to—" Rachel paused when she heard her mother's cackle followed by Aaron's mother's thick New York accent. When she and Aaron turned the corner, Shelly and Benjamin Goldstein and Sylvia and Stan Weiss came into view. Their parents. That was the surprise.

"Surprise!" the group shouted in unison as they engulfed her and Aaron in hugs. Aaron's mom pinched Rachel's cheeks like an old-fashioned grandma. Perfume from someone—her mother?—permeated the space.

"Did you know?" her mother asked, grabbing Rachel's arm. Her breath smelled like gin.

Before she could answer, Sylvia stepped in front of her. "My Aaron arranged the trip yesterday as a surprise for you, sweetheart." She waved an orange cocktail with a pink umbrella as she spoke. "And we're going tomorrow to meet with the wedding planner."

An image of Susie formed in Rachel's mind. God help her. Her tiny veil pen would be shredded.

Once they were finally seated, dinner was long. Rachel's mother was a notoriously big talker; Aaron's mother was worse. Each had strong opinions which they voiced with veiled commentary. When Rachel ordered her dinner—arugula salad—Sylvia's response was immediate.

"A salad? You'll waste away!" She put her hand up to the waitress and looked at Rachel. "Order something more, doll." The waitress stood, pen poised awkwardly.

"Rachel's trying to fit into a size four wedding dress," her mother countered.

Sylvia leaned over and whispered to Rachel while patting her hand. "You can get a bigger dress, sweetie. No one needs to be a size four."

"Rachel's a big girl, ladies," her father intervened. "She can decide what she wants to eat for dinner, for goodness's sake."

Rachel ordered the salad but picked up a slice of bread to please Sylvia.

After the main meal was served, the issue of where they would live after the wedding came up.

"Your mother would be over the moon if you moved back to New York," Stan Weiss volunteered.

"It's on the table," Aaron said.

It was? He'd never said that. Rachel stared at him. He did not return her gaze.

"New York! But the city is no place to raise children." Rachel's mother looked at her, wounded, as though she had knowingly kept the move secret.

"Aaron was raised in New York," Sylvia countered, curling her ringed fingers around a new cocktail glass. "He loved it." She turned to Aaron. "Didn't you love it, doll?"

"I did," Aaron responded. "I like being the center of everything," he said, then corrected himself. "IN the center of everything, rather."

They all laughed.

Stan looked down at his glass. "I remember taking Aaron to Times Square as a kid. He loved that stock tickertape. The day I explained to him what the letters and numbers meant, he went home and looked it up in the paper. He's looked at the stock page every day since." Stan rapped him on the back and Aaron smiled.

"And look where it got him," Sylvia added proudly.

Everyone grew silent. Rachel's phone vibrated. She pulled it out and looked at the text. It was from Greg.

I have news.

Rachel jumped up in surprise and the phone slipped out of her hand, skittering and landing next to Sylvia. Sylvia picked it up and inspected it. Rachel forced herself not to snatch it away.

"Aaron," she said, "Rachel's phone is cracked." She held it up for Aaron to see, Greg's text message still at the top.

"It's okay," Rachel said, reaching for the phone. "It works."

Sylvia was undeterred. "Aaron, look at this phone."

Aaron glanced at it, nodded. "We can replace the phone."

"See," Sylvia said proudly, "Aaron will get you a new phone." She patted Rachel's hand and slid the phone over to Aaron. "You just have to ask, sweetheart. She looked at the group. "Who uses a cracked phone?" she asked rhetorically.

"I can hold it," Rachel said, trying to appear helpful. "I have this whole purse!" She held up a tiny evening purse which could barely fit lipstick. No one commented.

"Let Aaron hold it, sweetheart," Sylvia said. "That glass may crack. You don't want to cut those pretty fingers." She squeezed her hand too hard, her rings pressing into Rachel's skin. "He'll get you a new one. He wants to take care of you."

"He's a carer." Stan reiterated.

"Indeed," agreed her dad.

"So caring," added her mom.

"To Aaron," cheered Sylvia, holding up a nearly drained glass. As the rest of them joined in the toast, Rachel heard the faint music from the Star Wars theme—the ringtone she had set for Greg.

Aaron reached into his pocket and pulled out Rachel's phone. "It's coming from this," he said, holding it up.

The Star Wars theme blared louder.

"It's a work call," Rachel stammered.

"On a Saturday?" Sylvia asked.

"Maybe an emergency. I should probably get that."

As Rachel moved around the table to get the phone, her mother asked, "Why the Star Wars theme?"

"I use that for work calls," she explained and as Aaron handed her the phone. "You know, May the Force Be with You!" She held up both hands in a grand gesture.

"Or may the firm be with you, is more like it!" Stan's sentence was met with cacophonous laughter. Rachel hurried to the ladies' room. Once in, she dialed Greg.

"So I've tracked down her mother," he said. "She lives in Palm Springs, Florida."

"Great." Rachel waited, expectant.

"So that's it for now."

Rachel's heart dropped. That was it? "Well, do you think Hannah's there?"

"Don't know yet. I got some guys on it." He said it in a way that made it seem like he was part of a gang, a force of tough guys.

"Did you find out anything else? Does she have any friends?"

"We are working on it. That's all I can tell you right now."

"But—"

"Rachel, it's better if you don't know everything."

Rachel opened her mouth to ask why, then thought better of it. Greg was the only one helping right now. If she questioned his method, he might get irritated and change his mind. And maybe he did have a lead. She would just have to be patient.

"Okay, Greg," she said. "Thanks for the update."

She switched the phone to off and returned to the table. The group was subdued.

"We were just talking about that case with your firm," her mom said. "The kidnapping."

"It's such a shame, the whole thing." Sylvia added before lowering her voice to a whisper. "She might be violent, the mom, if she was in jail. I just hope those kids are okay." She clasped her hands together as if she might pray.

"God bless," Stan said.

Rachel was unable to eat. The kidnapping was her fault.

And when they flew back on Monday, everyone would know it.

FORTY

Will

The twenty-four hours since Hannah's disappearance had been crazy.

"A cardiac event," the doctor had told them an hour before. "Precipitated by the onset of stress."

At the thought of the doctor's words, anger charged through Will. How could Hannah have done this to his mother? To Constance Abbott. A woman who, by all accounts, might just be the nicest in the world.

"She just wanted to see the kids, take them for pizza," his mom had told him. "It seemed the right thing." Then dusk turned to evening and then to night without a sign from Hannah. His mom had waited up, her hands wringing and twisting, the regret in her voice evident with every apologetic word. Will had told her it was okay; they'd find them, not to worry. But telling his mother not to worry was like telling an elephant not to be gray. He should have done more.

Cammy crossed the waiting room to sit next to him. "Hey, little brother. Are you okay? Are you worried about the kids?" She reached out and squeezed his hand.

"I'm alright. Hannah will be back. It's all just a mix-up." Will spoke with a stronger conviction than he felt.

"Did you talk to your attorney?" Cammy's obvious panic put Will on edge.

"Yes. David spoke to Hannah's attorney. He said they were tracking her down."

"Do you know where she's been staying?"

"No, Cammy, I don't." Will's voice came out harsh.

Cammy took a seat next to him. Will looked out the window. Light snow fell outside, the onset of the November snowstorm. News coverage about the storm scrolled across a large, flat-screen television mounted to the wall. But, even with the impending storm, well-wishers for Constance Abbott filled the waiting room, including six of the eight grandchildren. Will's two were glaringly absent.

Will and Cammy watched as "the grands"—his mother's affectionate name for the kids—congregated around a giant box of Dunkin Donuts munchkins. They were having a contest to see who could fit the most in their mouth. Will would have normally been involved, most likely the mastermind. Instead, he sat as an observer. Then Max, Cammy's youngest, appeared poised to put an additional donut in his already-full mouth. Cammy raced across the room toward her son. "No, no, no. Maxwell Sullivan. You put that donut down right now."

Just as Cammy reached Max, a hospital-employed clown arrived on the floor.

"Kids!" he said and walked toward them, oversize red shoes clopping on the antiseptic floor. "Who wants a balloon animal?"

There was chorus of cheers. With a flourish, the clown pulled a pack of balloons and a pump from a giant, polka-dot bag. He put a blue balloon on the end, pumped, then twisted it into a dog. He handed the dog to Max then repeated the gesture until every "grand" had an animal. For ten minutes, it was calm. But, then, one animal popped; others unwound. Max discovered that his unwound balloon made a wonderful sword. His siblings and cousins followed suit. Chaos broke out, the kids frenetically running and bobbing their balloons. Will saw two nurses frown.

Someone placed their hand on Will's shoulder. He looked up. A youngish woman with cropped dark hair and a black suit stood next to him. "I'm Frannie Marcos. I'm a reporter with ABC News. Are you William Abbott?"

Will stood and held out his hand. "I'm Will." Frannie took his hand in both of her own and squeezed.

"Will. I understand your wife and kids are missing. I am so sorry. You must be terribly worried."

"I've had better days, that's for sure." Will stepped away from the woman; she grabbed his arm. He turned to look at her.

"Mr. Abbott, we have to get your story out there now. Every minute you wait is a wasted one." She put her hand on his shoulder again as though he might need steadying.

Will shook his head. "I'm sure my wife will be back. Today even." But, as he said the words, the sliver of doubt he already felt grew larger.

"Do you know there are over two hundred thousand parental kidnappings per year?"

Two hundred thousand?

Frannie continued, "Many parents never return. You may never see your kids again, Will."

The words were jarring. Frannie looked Will directly in his eyes. "And even if Hannah is planning to come back, news coverage will accelerate that, Will. Wouldn't that be good for your mother's situation? Constance, right?" She took a step back, smoothed her skirt, then looked back up at him, blue eyes unwavering.

Will thought of his mother as she had stood in the doorway of his room the night before, hand clutched to her chest. "Something's wrong, Will," she'd said.

It was imperative they find Hannah and the kids as soon as possible. Will glanced around the waiting room, scanning for Cammy. She had the children corralled in a corner; the sword-balloons dormant on the floor. Her mouth moved with stern warnings.

"If you want to make a short statement, Will, I have a news truck out front. All you need to do is let Hannah know she needs to come back. For your mother's sake."

It made sense. And Hannah wouldn't know about his mother. She should know. Hannah loved Constance.

"Alright. I'll make a statement."

Will followed Frannie outside. The snow was heavier, the sky dimming to gray. A cool gust of wind surged as they made their way toward the news truck. Will wore only a sweatshirt; he'd forgotten a jacket in his haste. He rubbed his arms. It was freezing.

Despite the cold, a small crowd had congregated around the truck. They parted as he and Frannie neared. Almost instantaneously, a cameraman materialized and Frannie was handed a microphone. Will looked at the hospital and the truck and the crowd. It felt surreal.

Before he could ask a single question, the camera light switched on. A man said: "Live in 5, 4, 3, 2, 1."

Frannie moved so that there was a view of the hospital behind her. "This is Frannie Marcos. I stand here in front of the Capital Health Center with William Abbott. As reported earlier today, Mr. Abbott's estranged wife, Hannah Abbott, kidnapped their two young children. Ms. Abbott had recently been charged with domestic violence and assault and was released on her own recognizance."

Frannie turned to Will. He said nothing, still processing the words. The reporter had made Hannah sound so bad.

"Mr. Abbott, are you concerned about the safety of your children?"

"Yes." The response was automatic. What parent wouldn't be concerned about the safety of their children? But he wasn't concerned about them in Hannah's care. He started to say as much when Frannie fired off another question.

"And do you have any idea where your wife and children might be staying?"

"Not at the moment. I'm sure Hannah will—"

Frannie didn't let him finish the sentence.

"And your mother is inside this hospital, sick with grief over this event. Is that right?"

"My mom is really torn up about this." As Will said the words, the wind blew icy snowflakes into his bare face. He blinked; his eyes teared.

"Mr. Abbott, Will, if you could speak to your wife right now, what would you say?"

She held the microphone in front of him. His eyes teared again from the ice. "Hannah. Just come home. Mom's sick. We're all looking for you. We'll get this figured out. You need to come home."

Frannie retrieved the microphone, summarizing the story, making it seem as though a violent criminal was on the loose with Will's children. He'd correct that when she asked him again. But she didn't. The story ended, the camera flipped off. Frannie stepped back and retied her coat.

"What was that? I never said Hannah was violent."

"You filed for a restraining order, Will. A suburban mom leaving for an overnight with her kids isn't news." She paused for effect. "But a violent one is."

"I don't want it to air." A gust of snow circled; Will's words hung between them.

"Not your choice now, Will. It's news." She turned to the cameraman. "That's a wrap." The man shut off the camera and put it in the van. For a moment, Will considered surging at him, taking the camera and the tape but, before he could move, the man slid the door shut. Frannie stepped into the passenger seat, turning to Will just as she was about the close the door. "Call me if you want to make any more statements." She held out a card to him.

Will didn't take it. Frannie pulled it back. "It's news," she repeated and closed the door.

FORTY-ONE

Will walked back inside the hospital and sat in the first chair he saw. Had that just happened? Had he just been taped saying that Hannah was violent? Frannie's words echoed in his mind: "You filed for a restraining order, Will."

And he had. But he hadn't meant it. He hadn't understood the repercussions of that action. He had thought he was setting a boundary about his time with the kids.

Will pulled out his phone to call David Dewey then stopped himself. David's advice had started all this. Glancing at the phone, Will saw six texts from Amber. Will shook his head. This was not the time for his silly infatuation.

In a quick, frustrated action, Will dialed Hannah for what felt like the hundredth time. Nothing. He put the phone in his pocket and watched as people streamed out of the hospital, conversations peppered with references to the storm.

On the corner television, they were now projecting over a foot of snow. The gnawing worry Will had held at bay began to consume him. Where were Hannah and the kids? What if something had happened to them? Should he be looking for them right now? Should he call the police? His chest tightened, his temples began to pulse.

Maybe the television interview hadn't been a mistake after all.

Will sat immobilized until a woman accidently plowed a wheelchair into his leg.

"I'm so sorry!" she said.

Will waved her off but the brief distraction served as a catalyst. He had to do something. First, he would check on his mother. He walked toward the elevators but, in front stood a large crowd; a disordered scene of coats and hats and gloves as people readied themselves to take on the storm. It would be easier to take the stairs.

Will began the climb. He found the small physical effort calming. When he reached the third floor, he stopped and stared at the big number "3", his mind reeling back in time. He had forgotten. As he stood there, Will could almost feel Amanda's small hand in his. He could visualize the too large 'I'm the Big Sister' t-shirt falling about her knees like a dress. He could see her clutching "blue teddy," a gift for her baby brother.

Will traced their footsteps from that day, opening the third-floor door and stepping into the hall. He and Amanda had walked together, that same direction, all those years ago. They'd stopped to view the tiny, swaddled infants lined up in the nursery window.

"That's him!" Will had pointed to the rolling bassinet with the blue card, Charles Christopher Abbott. "That's your brother!"

Amanda had stared at the babies for a long time. "Do we have to take that one?" she'd asked finally. "The one over there is cuter."

Will followed her finger to a stunning baby with rosy cheeks, perfect pink lips, and wild hair. Her name card read, Jasmine Rose.

As Will stood there now, alone, he'd remembered squatting down to Amanda's level. "This one?" He'd pointed to the perfect infant and Amanda nodded, biting her lip. "She is pretty," Will agreed. "I like her hair."

"Me too!" Amanda said, hopeful.

"But our baby's cute. Look how little he is?" They both looked at Charlie's tiny blotchy form. "This baby," Will pointed to Jasmine Rose, "she has a mommy and daddy already. Our baby is Charlie. Do you think you could love Charlie?"

Amanda looked at Will, Hannah's green eyes staring back at him. She glanced at the pretty baby with the curly hair then focused on Charlie.

"I can love Charlie, Daddy."

They had spent the afternoon together in Hannah's room. She'd been radiant, holding Charlie, a possessive Amanda squished in the bed by her side. Their moms, the grandmother duo, had clucked about with tiny blue clothes, burp cloths, and a hand-knitted blanket. Will's sisters had strolled in and out, varied cousins in tow. He had held Hannah's camera, following her bedside instructions on how to use it. They still had those pictures. One was in their family room.

Will's vision of the day was so vivid that he found himself in front of room five, almost expecting to see them there, his intact family, waiting, ready to try again. The picture of them was interrupted by a woman's voice.

"Sir, what are you doing here?" the nurse asked, frowning.

She stood in front of the door like a shield, as though Will were a predator about to snatch an infant away.

Will shook his head. "I'm sorry. I'm here to see my mother. Wrong floor."

The nurse smiled. "Of course, sir." She pointed to the elevators; Will thanked her. When he reached the fifth floor, it was quieter. The grandkids had been taken home by their dads. The neighbors were also gone. There was a bold yellow sign in the center of the waiting room—

"Careful. Wet Floor."

Will pointed at the sign as he neared his sisters.

"Don't ask," Caroline said, rolling her eyes.

"Any news?"

She shook her head.

They sat in silence. After a few minutes, a nurse came out and told them their mother was stable and could have visitors. "But only for a few minutes," she advised. "Constance needs her rest."

They followed the nurse into a small room. Will's mother looked pale and fragile. Two IVs stemmed from her arm; a giant monitor sat in the corner with line indicators for blood pressure, heart rate, and temperature. They encircled her hospital bed.

"Well, that was something," Constance said, attempting a smile, her voice the same as always. Will breathed a sigh of relief. Something about his mother's voice had always been a comfort to him.

"Are you alright, Mom?" Cammy asked. "Do you feel alright?"

"I feel perfect. Just a bit tired." She paused. "Where's Hannah?"

After a long pause, Will said, "All is fine, Mom. Hannah and the kids are fine."

"Oh, thank goodness," she said. "Thank goodness. I knew it was a misunderstanding." Her face seemed to instantaneously gain color. Will couldn't correct her. It didn't harm anything for her to believe it was all fine.

His sisters widened their eyes. "Will," Cammy mouthed.

Will ignored her and directed his attention to his mother. "So your grandchildren had quite a day at the hospital. They had a munchkin eating contest and a sword fight. I think they might have made a nurse cry."

Cammy shot Will a look, but the intensity of the moment was broken, the focus off of him. The conversation turned to the storm.

Through the window, the heavy snow intensified, large white flakes illuminated by giant street lamps. "You should go now," Constance said. "I'm fine."

They kissed her, told her they'd be back in the morning.

"How are you going to explain where the kids and Hannah are tomorrow?" Caroline asked, as they rode the elevator down.

"They'll be back. No use upsetting her." But as Will said the words, he was gripped with his own worry.

Where were they?

FORTY-TWO

When Will reached his car in the hospital parking lot, it was covered in snow. He wiped it away with his bare hand, the cold burning his skin. Once inside, he started the engine. The car headlights illuminated the heavy white clumps still falling.

He drove slowly out of the parking lot and onto the main road. As he turned, the car skidded. Will jerked the steering wheel and the car fishtailed to the other side. He turned the wheel again, lightly this time, and the car straightened out. Headlights came into view behind him. He opened the driver's side window and motioned for the car to go ahead. He drove home at twenty miles per hour.

As he drove, Will's worry intensified. He should call the police. Why had he trusted that Hannah's attorneys would find her? Will pulled on to his street and decided to call the police as soon as he got home.

Will drove slowly toward his driveway. Was that what he thought it was? He craned his neck and looked through the front window. It was a car, its make and model unrecognizable under the snow. But it had to be Hannah! She and the kids were probably inside the house, waiting for him.

Will pulled into the driveway and thrust open his car door. He bounded toward the snow-covered vehicle with anticipation. Amber stepped out.

Will's face fell. He took a step back. "Amber. What are you doing here? Have you heard something?"

"No. I'm sorry." Her voice was hurried, her lips slightly blue from the cold. "I couldn't reach you so I came to see how you were doing. You weren't here and then I couldn't get my car to start. I've been trying to get someone to come out and jump me but no one is around. Then my phone died." She held up a blank-faced phone. "Can you jump me?" Amber wrapped her arms around herself and jogged in place on high-heeled boots.

Will looked at Amber. Her teeth chattered. He couldn't just leave her out here. But to invite her in his house? What if Hannah came home?

Will shook his head. It would be fine. He gestured to the house. "Come in and get warm first. We'll charge your phone and figure it out."

Will held Amber's elbow as he escorted her over the snow-covered walkway into the house. He led her to the kitchen and she plugged in her phone charger before taking Charlie's regular seat at the table.

"Coffee?"

"Perfect." Amber blew into her hands.

Will put on a pot of water then opened the cabinet where they kept the mugs. He touched Hannah's favorite—the one she had chosen on a trip to Cancun—then moved his hand. He reached behind Hannah's mug and pulled out one he'd received as a promotion from a bank. As the coffee percolated, Will's eyes focused on the cheerful pictures on his refrigerator: the four of them taken in front of a water park in Wildwood; Charlie holding up a bluefish he'd caught on a night fishing trip; a new picture of Amanda with her Alice in Wonderland script. The running grocery list hung in its regular spot. Hannah's neat cursive spelled out milk, Tide, and bananas.

Will poured Amber's coffee into the mug and handed it to her. He looked out the window at the front street. The snow fell in heavy clumps; an ambulance wailed in the background. Will looked back at the table. Amber blew on her coffee and fingered the pinch-pot that Amanda had made in first grade. Then she bent down to look at Charlie's betta fish.

"What's his name?" she asked, lightly tapping on the glass.

"Fred." Will recalled how the kids laughed whenever he used the "Fred" voice, the deep Southern accent he'd attributed to the fish. He resisted the urge to move the bowl away from Amber.

She put the mug down. Her red lipstick remained on the rim.

Will looked at the lipstick and the fish and Amanda's tiny pinch-pot. He glanced at the photograph of his family in Wildwood. This was wrong. Amber in his house was wrong.

"Let me drive you home," he said suddenly. "We should get going before it's too bad."

"I can't ask you to do that, it's terrible out there." Amber gestured to the window.

Will shook his head. "I just drove in this from the hospital. It's fine. I can get you home."

Amber paused. Did she expect him to ask her to stay the night?

"Really, Will—"

"I insist."

"Alright," she said, standing. "But you have to turn around if it's too bad." Will agreed and they made their way to his car. Will backed out of his driveway as Amber explained how to get to her house. Once on the main road, Will navigated around a car sitting with its emergency lights blinking in a steady pattern. Will skidded on a patch of snow; his antilock brakes made a loud grinding noise. The snow fell faster than his windshield wipers could remove it. Will gripped the steering wheel. Sweat beads formed on his forehead. He leaned forward, his posture rigid.

His phone pinged from its place in the console. Without thinking, Will glanced down.

Hannah!

We are okay. I'm sorry. I'll be back tomorrow.

Relief flooded his body. He looked back up, the road ahead seemingly clear. Then, without warning, his car spun around and Will jerked the steering wheel in the opposite direction by instinct. They turned, a full spin, his car ending up on the opposite side of the road. A truck drove toward them.

"Shit!" Will yelled.

"Oh my God!" Amber put her head in her hands.

"God. Sorry!" Will said, swerving the car away from the truck. He looked in his rearview mirror, panting. The other vehicle continued slowly down the road. He caught his breath and glanced at Amber. "Are you alright?"

"Yes." She took a deep breath. "I'm sorry you had to drive in this, we're almost back."

She gave the final instructions to her complex. Will pulled into the parking space in front of Amber's condo. He switched off the ignition. "I'm sorry again," he said.

"It's okay, but you shouldn't go out in that again. Come in. I'll make us something hot."

They walked up the path to Amber's apartment. Will looked at his phone again to make sure the text was real. He exhaled. Thank God.

"Hannah texted," he told Amber. "She and the kids are alright."

"Oh, that's good news." Amber opened the door.

They stepped inside her condo. Two beige couches sat on a bamboo area rug, a glass table between them. Black framed prints of flowers adorned the wall. A woven basket of books and magazines buttressed one end of the couch, a table with a glass lamp at the other.

Amber switched the lamp on, casting a gentle glow on the room. "You should call Hannah," she said, taking his coat and gesturing to the couch.

Will sat on the edge of the couch and dialed Hannah. He looked up as he waited. Pick up. Pick up. Pick up. The phone pinged. Will glanced down. There was no service.

He punched in a text. Undeliverable.

Will could feel Amber staring at him. He glanced over at her.

"The service is probably bad because of the weather," she said. "Why don't I get us a drink." She moved toward the kitchen before Will could respond.

Will leaned back on the couch and allowed his shoulders to unclench. God. He had been so worried. How could Hannah have done that to him? To his mother? "Unbelievable," he said under his breath.

Amber returned with two glasses of wine and the bottle. She sat on the couch next to Will, put the bottle on the table, and held out a glass. "I thought we could use a little alcohol after that experience," she said, gesturing to the storm outside. Light from the streetlamps shone on the steady white snow.

"Right." Will took the glass. Should he be drinking with Amber?

Will thought about Hannah taking the kids. And about his mother in the hospital. He recalled the harrowing drive to Amber's. He looked at the wine. What the hell? He lifted his glass. "To surviving the storm," he said.

"To surviving the storm," Amber repeated.

They clinked glasses. Amber took a sip; Will drained his. "I think I needed that," he said, placing the glass on the end table next to him. Amber reached over him to retrieve his empty glass, her body brushing against him.

"No so fast, Mr. Abbott," she said, sitting up and holding up the glass. "I think you have earned two glasses of wine today." Amber filled Will's glass and handed it to him.

Will took a sip. "If you say so."

Amber moved closer, her legs touching his. She put her hand on his thigh. "I do say so," she whispered. She took a long sip of wine then placed her glass on the table. Then she tapped Will's glass. "Drink up."

Will drank the wine. When his glass was empty, Amber extricated it from his fingers and put it on the table next to hers.

"I think I know something else you need," she said, moving her face inches from his own. Will drew back but Amber gently pulled him forward. She put her lips on his and moved his hand to her breast. Will felt his body respond. He tried to draw back, but Amber held him tighter.

Would it be so terrible to let it happen? Hannah had probably done worse with Trent.

At the thought of Hannah and Trent, Will moved closer to Amber, cradled her face in his hands, and kissed her.

FORTY-THREE

Will laid on the couch after, staring at Amber's naked form on top of him.

Had he really just cheated on Hannah?

Amber sighed.

Will recalled her body then forced himself to stop.

What the hell was wrong with him?

Will sat up abruptly; Amber shifted around him.

"Is something wrong?"

"I've never cheated on Hannah."

Amber pulled a blanket over herself. "No one has to know, Will." She sat up.

It dawned on Will that he hadn't used protection.

"Are you on—"

"The pill. Yes." She pulled the blanket up higher. "It's been a hell of a day for you, Will. It's no big deal. I won't tell anyone."

Will pictured Hannah, then squeezed his eyes as though to obliterate the image. How had he let this happen?

Amber got up, letting the blanket fall. She took his hand.

"We should get some rest," she said, as she pulled him toward her bedroom.

Will looked outside; snow still fell in heavy clumps. Hell. He had already slept with Amber. What difference did it make if he slept next to her? He would feel more clear-headed in the morning.

Once in the bed, Amber's body felt unfamiliar and, after she fell asleep, Will moved away. He closed his eyes. In a half-sleep, he dreamt he was back in his own home with Hannah, their kids sleeping peacefully down the hall. He'd wake up and make daffles.

Will opened his eyes in the morning and glanced at Amber, still sleeping beside him. He squeezed his eyes closed. God. What had he done?

His cell phone, left on the dresser, pinged. Will pushed the covers off and hobbled across the room, still naked. He picked up the phone; Caroline's name appeared on the screen.

Will put the phone to his ear. "Hey, Caroline."

"I'm at your house. Where are you? You know there are people on your lawn, right?"

He must have misheard her. "What are you talking about?"

"Check your Facebook. Or google 'Hunky Hubby ABC News." Call me back." She hung up.

Will sat on the edge of the bed and hit the Facebook icon on his phone. Scrolling down, he found a post entitled "Share if you want Hunky Hubby to find his kids." Underneath was a screenshot of his face from the interview with Frannie Marcos along with a link to the ABC segment. Will pressed play. Frannie stood on his street with a microphone.

"A local woman accused of domestic violence – and kidnapping her children – has now been missing with the children for twenty-four hours. The father of the children, William Abbott, is on a quest to find his children." A clip of Will from yesterday's interview, appealing for Hannah to come home, filled the screen.

Frannie Marcos continued, "Dubbed by social media as the Hunky Hubby, there is an outpouring of support for Mr. Abbott."

A woman outside a grocery store appeared on the screen. "I just want him to find them. It's so awful. And with the storm."

Frannie continued, "There is a concern that the woman in question, Hannah Abbott, might be unstable. Just two weeks ago, she was charged with domestic violence." Hannah's mugshot filled the screen. "Viewers are urged to come forward with any information concerning the whereabouts of Mrs. Abbott and the children." Pictures of Hannah, Charlie, and Amanda— all taken from Facebook—flashed in quick succession. "ABC News has set up a link for information. Go to ABC News dot com and click Hunky Hubby." Frannie paused, her expression grave. "This is Frannie Marcos, reporting for ABC News."

"Shit." Will's own Facebook was filled with personal messages of support. He had a dozen text messages on his phone. How had he missed all of this?

Amber put her arms around him from behind, her robe open. Right. That's how.

"What's happening?" she asked. "What's wrong?" Will handed her the phone. Amber watched the segment.

"Hannah's not violent," Will lamented. "She's not unstable. I never said that. I never said that about my wife. Look, I gotta go." Will stood up and found his found his clothes by the couch, their presence on the floor a testament to his infidelity. He pulled his pants on. What if Hannah got to his house before he did?

Amber tied her robe, her face now serious. "Can I do anything?"

"No. I'm going to go home and wait for Hannah and my kids."

"Maybe you should tell the reporter that she texted you."

Will considered as he pulled on his sweatshirt. "Good idea." Why hadn't he taken her card at the hospital?

Will kissed Amber on the cheek before leaving. He had slept with the woman after all.

Will navigated the roads, his thoughts on Amber and Hannah and the publicity. He pulled onto his street. A dozen people stood on his lawn. Amber's abandoned car stood in the driveway, brushed clean of snow. Shit. Would someone know that wasn't his car? Will pulled in behind it and stepped out. Half a dozen people held up their cell phones.

"Have you heard from Hannah?" called out a man in a parka.

Will put his head down and kept walking.

A blonde woman in a lavender pom-pom hat held up a sign: "Honk if you love Will Abbott." Will pushed past her. He made his way up the front steps and turned to the group.

"I have no comment," he said. Cameras flashed. Will turned, opened the door, and entered his house. He walked to the kitchen; the coffee mug Amber used still in the sink. He turned on the water and vigorously hand-washed Amber's lipstick from the rim. After putting the mug on the counter to dry, he slumped into a chair and looked out the front window. The pom-pom woman waved the sign at him. He got up, pulled the blind, and moved to the family room.

Someone pounded on the back door.

"Will, mate, are you in there?" Trent called out.

Will made his way down the hall to the mudroom and opened the back door. Trent stood on the step, his hand poised for a second knock.

"I'm sorry, mate, to impose like this."

Will looked at him. He thought of the texts; he pictured Trent touching his wife. "Why are you here?"

"I have news about Hannah."

Will gestured for him to come in. Trent stepped into the small area and brushed snow off his jacket; his cheeks were ruddy. His presence in Will's home felt like an intrusion.

"You have news about Hannah?" Will prompted, his tone unfriendly.

Trent rubbed his hands together for warmth. "Hannah came to see me Wednesday. She said she was going on a trip and wanted to borrow chains for her tires."

Chains? She must have known it was going to snow. Of course.

"She said it was a ski holiday," Trent continued. "I thought you were all going. I didn't know about the divorce, about any of this, until this morning."

Will hated that Trent had used the word divorce. What did he know about his relationship with Hannah? His words came out in an angry flood. "That's it? You came all this way to tell me Hannah needed chains? Did you see my kids? Do you know where she went? Do you actually have anything of value to say to me right now? Or do you just get off interfering with our lives? Again." Will kicked the dryer.

Trent stepped back and held his hands up. "Look. Will. I know it's not much, but I thought you should know."

Will stepped around him and put his hand on the knob to the back door. "Well, just so you know, Hannah texted me last night. She's coming home today."

Trent covered his mouth with his hand. "Oh, thank God."

Will swung open the door and gestured outside. "So, if you'll excuse me, Trent, I'm going to go wait for my wife."

Trent stepped outside then turned and looked Will in the eye. "Nothing ever happened between us, you know."

Will shut the door without commenting. He leaned against it and exhaled. Shit. Viscerally, he'd known Hannah hadn't cheated on him. But, in light of last night, he'd almost wished she had. It would have been a tit for tat, an equivalent transgression. Now only he was the cheater.

Will walked into the family room and closed the curtains. He slid down the couch and waited for his wife and kids.

FORTY-FOUR

Hannah

Hannah turned the car on to the highway. She glanced at Amanda in the passenger seat and then peeked in the rearview mirror. Charlie sat in the back, biting his fingernails. A nasty habit he had kicked. Now back again.

Amanda looked out the window, then sat up straighter. "Where are you going, Mom?"

Hannah drew in a breath then spoke with a conviction she did not feel. "We're going to go on an adventure. Dad's had a turn and now it's mine."

Charlie poked his head through the front two seats. "What kind of adventure?"

Before she could answer, Amanda spoke. "I don't think you can do that, Mom."

"I can take my own children on a trip, Amanda."

"I want to go on a trip," Charlie opined.

"How long is the trip?" Amanda flipped her hair back and checked her image in the passenger side window.

Hannah didn't answer; Amanda repeated the question. Still, Hannah said nothing.

"I have things to do this weekend, Mom. Play practice, Jessie's slumber party, and two tests on Monday."

Her voice had an air of impatience and the meaning behind her words had sliced through Hannah. She had spent three weeks obsessing about them. But their lives had gone on. Without her. Perfectly fine. She hadn't checked backpacks, made lunches, or marked the dry-erase calendar with color-coded markers. And the world didn't cave in.

"Well?" Amanda asked again. "How long is this thing?"

"We'll see."

"We'll see? You told Nana that we were just going for pizza."

Hannah gripped the steering wheel tighter. An image of Constance smiling appeared in her mind. Her heart plunged. She loved Constance like her own mother. She had betrayed her trust, told Constance she just wanted to have a meal with the kids. "Of course, dear," she had said.

"Well, Mom?" Amanda asked.

"We're just going on a trip."

The truth was Hannah had no plan other than to get to Rachel's family cabin in the Poconos. No one ever used it, Rachel had told her. In fact, according to Rachel, her mother absolutely detested the outdated kitchen, the tiny bathroom, and the drafts which blew through every window.

No one spoke. Hannah kept her foot steady on the gas. She couldn't risk losing custody of her kids. In the weeks since she'd been driven out, Hannah had been plagued with visions of Amber taking her place. She'd pictured Amber sleeping in her bed, arms wrapped around Will. Her clothes would be in Hannah's drawers; her skin products on the sink. Amber would make breakfast in her kitchen. She would be the one waiting when her kids got home.

No.

Hannah would not let that happen.

Silence permeated the car. It became palpable.

Finally, Charlie asked, "Do you want to sing a Wiggles song? Like we used to?"

They'd done that on long trips when the kids were young. She was surprised Charlie remembered.

Amanda snorted and Hannah shot her a look. "Sure, Charlie." She started the tune, one of his favorites. "Fruit salad. Yummy Yummy."

Charlie joined in, their two voices weak and hollow. "Fruit salad. Yummy Yummy. Fruit salad. Yummy. Yum—"

"It's not the same without Dad," Amanda interrupted.

She was right. Will, with his low baritone, had always belted out the lyrics, tapping his belly as he did so. Then he'd change the words. "Ice cream sundae! Yummy! Yummy!" The kids had always laughed wildly, and it became a contest to see who could insert the most ridiculous items into the song.

Hannah wanted to cry.

Upon arrival at the cabin, Hannah couldn't get the key to work. They stood on the step, a freezing trio, as she wiggled the key. When the door finally gave way, they tumbled into a small, freezing space that smelled like must. Hannah flipped the light. A wood-framed couch and chair sat centered around a fireplace adjacent to a small kitchen. A large loft overlooked the family room.

Hannah peeked out the A-frame window. "This will be nice," she announced.

Amanda slumped on the couch. "It's freezing."

Hannah looked for the heat, Charlie close on her heels. Amanda watched them from her vantage point on the couch, arms crossed as though they had been frozen in place. "Aren't you going to tell Dad where we are?"

"I'm not allowed to contact Dad." Hannah knew the response was childish. She immediately corrected herself. "I'll let him know later."

"What are we supposed to do here anyway?" Amanda asked.

Hannah spied an old jigsaw puzzle in the corner. It was a picture of hot air balloons, dozens of them, against the backdrop of a clear blue sky. Five hundred pieces. "Let's do a puzzle together," she announced, picking up the box. Amanda did not get up; Charlie immediately moved to the table.

Hannah dumped the box and stared at the pieces, bits of sky and cloud and balloon in what seemed to be a gazillion tiny parts. It felt like an overwhelming task. Charlie forced two pieces together which clearly did not go. "Look! A match." He held them up, but all Hannah could see were his torn up fingernails.

"They don't fit, genius," Amanda called from the couch.

"Shut up. They do so."

"No, they don't." She crossed the room and took the pieces out of his hand. "There is a cloud on this piece and this piece has no cloud. Idiot." She threw the pieces on the table. They broke apart on impact.

Charlie shoved her. She stepped back, then came toward him, hands raised.

"Stop!" Hannah yelled, moving her body in front of Amanda's a moment too late. She pushed Charlie; he fell to the floor, hitting his head on a small cabinet.

"Oh my God. Are you alright?" Hannah bent down.

"I'm okay, Mom." Charlie sat up, holding his head.

"What's wrong with you?" she hissed at Amanda.

Amanda moved so she was directly in front of Hannah. "What's wrong with me? What's wrong with you? Where have you been? What happened?" A tear slid down her cheek. She wiped it away with a defiant stroke. "Dad kept saying you'd be home soon. But you never came back. He kept talking to his lawyer. But nothing happened. We thought you were gone. We thought you'd left us."

Amanda's tears fell harder as Hannah reached out to her. "No, no, no. I'd never leave you." She grabbed Charlie. "Either of you. I'm so sorry." She let them go and explained, or tried to, that the police had told her she needed to stay away because she'd been so angry. They seemed to understand.

She wanted to scream at Will.

Why hadn't he told them what was happening!?

How could he have let them believe she had left them!?

Once both children were calm, the three of them crammed themselves into a single queen bed on the loft, Hannah in the center. Their small arms zigzagged across her belly. She willed herself to stay awake, to take it all in. Charlie's tiny freckle in the center of his hand. Amanda's ski-slope nose. The feeling of them close. The sound of their breath.

When it was clear both children were sound asleep, Hannah gently extricated herself from the bed. She pulled the comforter over Charlie's shoulders and kissed Amanda on the forehead. Small, motherly gestures. Ones she would have taken for granted three weeks ago.

No more.

She climbed down the stairs and sat on the couch. She had made a mistake coming here. She knew that had to take the kids back. Hannah found her phone and texted Will.

We are okay. I am sorry. I will be back tomorrow.

Hannah stared at the screen, expecting an immediate response. Wasn't he worried? She waited until it became evident that Will was not awaiting her text.

Hannah awoke to the sun peeking through the clouds. Shortly after, Charlie woke, stumbling down from the loft, hair messed, sleepy-eyed. Amanda followed. She took out her camera and snapped a picture of the two of them on the couch.

"Mom, no!" Amanda held her hand in front of her face.

"We'll start back after lunch. But first, let's enjoy this morning." Hannah forced herself not to cry. After a leisurely breakfast, they took a brisk walk. Animals, all kinds, emerged from snow-covered hideouts. Hannah snapped them all: cardinals, raccoons, and a family of white-tailed deer.

When it was time to go home, she wasn't ready.

"What happens now?" Charlie asked as they pulled out of the cabin's driveway.

"I don't know," she told him. It was the truth.

FORTY-FIVE

When they arrived at the house hours later, a smattering of strangers stood on the lawn, some with cameras, and others with signs. Hannah slowed the car. What was going on?

A heavyset woman with a sign that read "Help the Hunky Hubby" lumbered forward. She rolled down the window, intending to ask the woman what was happening. Upon seeing her, the woman shrieked.

"It's HER. It's Hannah. And the kids! Charlie and Amanda!" The group moved toward them in a collective mass.

"What's happening, Mom?" Charlie asked.

"I don't know." Hannah rolled up the window and locked the doors, unable to think of a better way to protect her children.

As they neared, the group-members yelled varied commands, the majority of which seemed to center on calling the police.

No!

Not the police.

Hannah's stomach lurched. She wanted to drive away, but the group surrounded the car, their faces peering in the windows, cameras flashing. One woman fell to her knees and yelled "Praise the Lord!"

Amanda moved toward the center of the car. "I'm scared, Mom. Who are these people?"

"I don't know." A man jiggled the car handle. Hannah picked up her phone. Maybe she should call the police. The crowd seemed dangerous by their proximity, like a mob.

"Go away!" Hannah shouted, waving them back. "Leave us alone!"

No sooner had she said the words then the crowd parted in two, making a path. It was almost as if a deity had arrived.

"It's Daddy!" Charlie cried, pointing at Will. And there he was. Face ruddy. Old sweats. Tousled hair. Typical Will.

Charlie opened the door and ran toward him. The crowd turned to them and cameras flashed, capturing their embrace. The same woman fell to her knees again. "Praise the Lord! Praise the Lord!"

Amanda put her hand on Hannah's shoulder, seeming, instinctively, to know that presence of the people signaled a bigger problem. She kissed her cheek. "I love you, Mom." Their eyes met. She squeezed Hannah's shoulder. "I'm sorry I was so rude. I just missed you."

"I missed you too." Her voice came out a whisper. Hannah wasn't sure Amanda heard the sentiment as she slid out of the car and into the fray. She joined Will and Charlie on the sidewalk. He ruffled her hair, kissed the top of her head.

"Oh my God, I might die that's so sweet," a young girl shouted out, filming the encounter with her phone.

Hannah watched them, her children, her husband, her home. Where did she fit in now? Or where would a court allow her to fit in? It wasn't her call anymore. She needed to call Rachel to find out how bad she had messed up. Hannah took a last glimpse and started her engine. It roared.

"Wait!" A man yelled. "Stop that car!" Hannah stepped on the gas; the car lurched forward. The man ran in front of it. Hannah slammed on her brakes. A woman joined him, both blocking her path. More of the crowd moved to the road.

"Let her go!" Will shouted.

Hannah looked at him. Their eyes met, a thousand emotions passing silently between them in an instant.

The group stepped out of the road just as a white van raced down the street toward the house.

"Go!" Will yelled. She hesitated. "Hannah, go!"

She pulled her gaze and sped forward, passing the van as it began to brake. There was a big 6 on the side of it. A news van. A news van? Why? What had she missed? She'd been gone less than two days.

Hannah drove to Rachel's.

She sat in her car in front of the townhouse, unable to move. What could she possibly say to Rachel? Hi! Sorry I disappeared.

But she needed to know what to do now. Hannah thought of the mass of people on her lawn. And what had happened in the past forty-eight hours? Slowly, she got out of the car, walked up the path to Rachel's door and knocked

Rachel opened the door and gasped. "Hannah! You're okay!"

She moved back so Hannah could enter. They stood inside the doorway. "So where have you been?" Rachel asked.

She told her. She told her about her panicked decision, about the Pocono cabin, about the kids' reaction, and the mob on her lawn. The story came out in a flood, words tumbling one after another without pause.

At the end of the monologue, Rachel said, "Hannah, maybe you should sit down."

Hannah removed her coat and sat on the couch; Rachel fixed her a cup of green tea, unusually silent. She handed Hannah the mug and sat adjacent to her.

Then she explained the Hunky Hubby phenomenon.

"So Will and I are actually trending on social media?" Hannah clarified.

Rachel nodded. "It will pass. It's just a fad."

The idea felt hilarious. She and Will, generic couple 101, the subject of trending social media. Part of Hannah wanted to call Will so they could laugh about the incredulity of it all. Instead, she reached for her phone to check the social media site Rachel had mentioned.

"Wait." Rachel said. Hannah ignored her. Hannah clicked the Facebook icon on her phone and searched Hunky Hubby. The most recent post was a picture of Will and the kids in front of the house. She scrolled down to view the other posts: one of her in the car, one of Will alone outside the house, and one of Will in front of a hospital, crying. Hospital? Then Hannah saw a photo of her, the woman from the Phillies game. Hannah enlarged the pretty image for a moment before scrolling down to the comments.

"Hannah," Rachel said again.

She couldn't stop herself. She read the comments. There were hundreds of them.

What kind of mother kidnaps her own children?

Hannah Abbott should be jailed.

Leave that shrew! Call me at 583-286-1104.

Hannah Abbott is a mother killer.

"Mother killer?" Hannah looked at Rachel.

"Will's Mom is in the hospital."

"Oh my God."

"She's stable," Rachel added quickly.

Hannah pictured Constance when as saw her last. She'd been wearing a sweatshirt with fall leaves embroidered on the front and comfortable shoes. What Constance must have felt when she didn't return! What had she been thinking?

Hannah looked again at the phone. More hateful comments. On and on and on.

After a moment, Rachel put her hand on hers. "Don't look at it," she said. "These people don't know you." She gently took the phone from Hannah.

Hannah leaned back on the couch, unable to speak. She'd been gone for less than forty-eight hours. She'd taken her own children on a short trip. She was not a villain. She didn't deserve this.

But even as Hannah thought those sentiments, the opposite ones creeped into her psyche. She was a terrible, awful, woman. She'd betrayed Constance Abbott, the nicest woman in the world. She'd scared her children. She'd trespassed. She'd broken the law. The last bit took hold in her mind.

"Will I go to jail for this?" Hannah blurted out.

The expression on Rachel's face changed from concern to confidence. She looked nothing like the woman who had stood in Jack Connors office stammering and twisting her hair as the thought of handling her domestic violence hearing.

"Not if I can help it," she said.

FORTY-SIX

A week later, Rachel handed Hannah a legal document titled "Consent Order." The three-page paper laid out how Hannah and Will would share custody and manage their finances until they were officially divorced. Under the order, Hannah resumed possession of the residence and primary custody of the kids. Will had visitation every other weekend and Wednesday nights. Appended to the order was a holiday schedule outlining where the children would spend each holiday. Hannah glanced at it. In odd years—this year—she would have the kids for Thanksgiving, and Will for Christmas. Her breath caught. She wouldn't see the kids on Christmas?

Hannah shook her head. Shared holidays were a reality of divorce. She'd have to get used to that. She read through the terms again. The order dropped all the charges under the domestic violence action. And she could go home. It was as good as it would get.

"I'll sign it," she said. Rachel handed her a heavy pen.

Hannah put the order in her desk when she moved back home. Home! For days, she basked in the simplicity of everything mundane: sleeping in her bed, eating off familiar plates, showering in her own bathroom. And the kids. She saw them every day. It wasn't perfect. She was still separated from her husband. She was still the subject of a trending social media story. But compared to the vision she had for herself—seeing the kids in jail once a week—it was heaven.

A week before Thanksgiving, Will texted her.

Kids can come to Cammy's for TG if you want.

Hannah considered the offer. She, Will, and the kids had spent Thanksgiving with Will's family every year for their entire marriage. Thanksgiving was big for the Abbott clan, the entire holiday steeped in tradition. The family game of touch-football. The mass of appetizers. The annual turnip vote—thumbs up if you liked it, thumbs down if you didn't. The evening kid talent show. Post-dessert card games for the parents, impromptu sleepovers for the cousins.

Hannah shut her eyes. She loved the Abbott Thanksgiving. Growing up with only her mother, their Thanksgivings had been non-existent. They went out to eat instead of making a big meal. When she was younger, she and her mother ate at restaurants which advertised traditional Thanksgiving meals but, eventually, that small effort died down. They went Italian on Thanksgiving; Hannah always ordered lasagna. Her Mom tried to make a joke out of it—Hannah's Thanksgiving lasagna—but it was never all that funny.

The first time Hannah celebrated with Will's family, she couldn't believe it. It was even better than the giant celebration she'd always wanted. In recent years, Hannah posted pictures of the event on her Facebook page.

Here we all are around the table.

Here we are playing football.

Here are my kids with their cousins.

Here I am with everyone.

Look at me. I'm part of this.

Now, Thanksgiving in odd years would be just Hannah and the kids. They would hate it. So would she. She texted Will.

The kids would love that. Thanks.

She waited, phone in hand, for the text back. For her invitation. What's one more in a group so large? She'd graciously accept. She'd be the perfect guest. She'd even bring pumpkin pie ice cream.

Her phone pinged.

Great. Drop them off at noon.

Her heart dropped.

In the days after, Hannah forced herself to be okay with the idea of Thanksgiving alone. She'd repaint the bedroom and put shelves in her office. She'd even make a lasagna for good measure. Hannah got so used to the idea that, when she told her mother, she was shocked by her horrified reaction.

"You're spending Thanksgiving alone?!"

Her mother couldn't get over it, seeming not to remember the years of their sad dinners out. She insisted Hannah come to Florida. Then, she insisted she and Walter come there. Hannah said no to both.

Two days before Thanksgiving, the doorbell rang. Hannah swung open the door. Her mother and Walter stood on the front step in pilgrim costumes. Hannah took a step back. Walter had on big-bucked shoes and knickers. Her mother wore a long, white apron over a full-length black dress.

"Surprise!" they cheered, peering under brimmed, black hats.

"Wow. This is a surprise!" Hannah moved aside and gestured for them to come in.

Walter spoke as soon as Hannah closed the door. "We have five tickets for the authentic Thanksgiving experience in Plymouth, Massachusetts!"

"The place of the first Thanksgiving!" her mother added. "We dress as pilgrims and Indians! Just like it's 1621!" She held up a bag. "I got you costumes! We've booked a hotel!"

When she said nothing, Walter added, "We have it all covered. No cost to you! Right Rose?" He tapped her mother who nodded and held out the bag of costumes.

Hannah took the bag and looked at her mother. It was exactly what she needed, though she hadn't realized that. Hannah wrapped her arms around her in a tight embrace.

"It will be okay, sweetheart," her mother whispered.

Later, Hannah gave Charlie and Amanda a choice. "You can go with Nana, Uncle Walter, and me and eat like the real pilgrims or you can spend the day with Dad and your cousins at Aunt Cammy's."

Both children looked at her, hesitation in their eyes.

Hannah fought the impulse to convince them to come with her. "There's no right answer. You won't hurt anyone's feelings."

"I'll go to Aunt Cammy's," Amanda said.

Charlie looked from Amanda to Hannah. "I'll go with you." He said the words like he'd drawn the short straw.

Hannah lifted an eyebrow. "Charlie?"

"I want to go with you, Mom," he said with more conviction.

Hannah's mother clasped her hands together. "Wonderful!" She pulled an Indian costume from the bag and handed it to Charlie. "Try it on, Charlie. See if it fits."

Charlie took the costume into the bathroom. He walked out, his feathered headdress askew. The pseudo-suede pants were too short, the tunic snug around his belly. He'd stuffed his feet into coordinating moccasins.

"It looks a bit snug. Is it comfortable?" Hannah felt the waistband.

"It's fine. I love it."

"Oh, Charlie! It's too small." Hannah's mother exclaimed. She stood back from him then stepped forward and inspected the seams. "I think I can let it out. Go ahead and take it off now. I'll fix it."

Hannah let her mother take charge. After letting out Charlie's costume, she made homemade mac and cheese with bacon, Hannah's childhood favorite. When dinner was done, she cleared the table, did the dishes, then put in a load of Hannah's laundry. Later Hannah found neatly folded clothes on her bed with the socks in balled pairs next to a typewritten itinerary of the trip. Her shoulders relaxed and her face softened. She hadn't realized how much she'd needed someone to take charge.

Thanksgiving at Plymouth was perfect. It was so different from Cammy's that Hannah wasn't nostalgic. They gathered for dinner in a converted barn on a wooden table adorned with flickering candles. Live violinists played period music. The servers, dressed in authentic clothing, spoke only old English. A fire burned in a real hearth. The meal consisted of the traditional favorites in addition to the dishes that historians believed were likely to have been served at the first Thanksgiving: venison, fruit, mussels, porridge. Charlie tried more food than Hannah ever thought possible—one previous Thanksgiving he'd eaten only bread.

At the hotel that night, Hannah and her mother sat at the indoor pool. Walter swam with Charlie and initiated a contest where each made ridiculous styles with their wet hair. Hannah had always thought of Walter as stiff and intellectual but, seeing him with Charlie, she realized that she'd been unfair. She hadn't given him much of a chance.

Sitting at a table near the pool, her mother squeezed her hand. They stared at Charlie and Walter.

"Have you seen all the posts? The social media stuff?" Hannah said finally.

"Some of it."

"People hate me. Will is cheating and people hate me."

"They don't know you."

"But it still hurts. One woman said she hoped I would get hit by a bus."

"Well, I hope she gets hit by a bus," her mother said. They watched as Charlie bounded off the diving board, making a small splash. Walter acted as though it had been a tidal wave. Mom leaned forward. "Can I ask you something?"

Hannah looked at her. "Of course."

"Do you still love Will?"

Hannah knew the answer but hesitated anyway. "I will always love Will." How could she not?

Her mother grabbed her hand and made eye contact. "Then fight for him." Her voice had a forceful tone, one Hannah had seldom heard her use. "You're letting that young girl get in the way of your marriage and your family. Being in a split family isn't easy. You know that."

Hannah looked at the floor. "But what if he loves her?" she asked, her voice quiet. "What if he doesn't want me?"

"Look at me, Hannah." Hannah turned toward her mother. "Of course he wants you. A few months cannot take the place of years of memories. I'm not excusing what he did, but there's a lot of good in Will Abbott, Hannah. Remember the cardinals?"

She did. Hannah's grandmother had always said that, when she went to heaven, she'd send cardinals to let her mother know she was okay. After she died, Hannah's mom confided to Constance that she hadn't seen any cardinals; she'd been waiting for the sign. She was devastated. From her bedroom window,

Hannah had seen Will in her yard hanging up bird feeders full with thick, black seeds. The next day, there were three cardinals. They ultimately made a nest in their yard.

"I remember the cardinals."

Her mother was silent a moment then grabbed Hannah's hand and squeezed.

"He's a good man, Hannah. Fight for him."

FORTY-SEVEN

In the weeks between Thanksgiving and Christmas, Hannah ruminated on her mother's words: "Fight for him."

Her emotional response to the idea was haphazard. In one moment, she'd think, "Yes! I will!" But then, moments later, intense anger would bubble up from her gut and she'd think, "Screw him. Cheating bastard!"

The continued coverage of their divorce by Frannie Marcos didn't help. The reporter continued to post pictures on the Hunky Hubby Facebook page and Hannah couldn't stop herself from looking at them. The most recent picture was of Will and Amber rollerblading.

Hannah asked Rachel about shutting down the page. "It's free speech," Rachel had told her. "They are in a public park. There's no expectation of privacy."

Hannah tried to keep all the Christmas traditions the same for Charlie and Amanda. They had cookie baking day. They shopped for needy children as part of the Angel Tree project at their church. They sent out Christmas cards and got chocolate advent calendars. They hung their stockings by the fireplace. It was all the same. And terribly different. Not knowing what to do with Will's stocking, Hannah hung it up. She was unable to duplicate his special Christmastime waffles, infused with a bit of mint. "They taste like toothpaste!" Amanda had complained. They had "Christmas Movie Friday" but, after the first movie, both kids asked to go to bed. She fell asleep on the couch with The Santa Clause on in the background.

Will did come to put up the outdoor lights and help with the tree. They all tried too hard to make it seem normal, speaking in forced happy voices, making unnatural comments about food and weather. Charlie told jokes. Amanda demonstrated an improved handstand. The kids were like dogs in a shelter. Pick us. Pick us. Pick us. It made Hannah sick.

As the month marched on toward the 25th, Hannah tried to come to terms with the fact that, for the first time in her life, she would have nothing to do on Christmas Day. Under the Mercer County Holiday Schedule, "Wife" had until 5:00 p.m. on Christmas Eve. She was thinking about what she should on Christmas—work in a soup kitchen, go to Jess and John's or Charlotte's—when Constance called.

"Hello, Hannah, dear," she said cheerfully. "It's Constance."

It was as though Hannah had never taken the children from her.

Constance's voice calmed her. "Constance! It's nice to hear from you."

"Listen, I am just calling to see if you might want to come for Christmas. We're not doing anything grand, but I'd really love it if all my daughters were here. If you don't have other plans."

Hannah digested her words: all my daughters.

"Wow. That's so nice. I don't have plans. I'd love to come."

"I am so glad to hear that you can make it," she continued. "It just wouldn't be the same without—"

"Constance, I'm so sorry," Hannah blurted out. "About taking the kids."

Constance was silent. Hannah gripped her phone.

"We mothers are all a little crazy," she said finally. "I'm not sure I wouldn't have done the same thing. We're all okay now, Hannah. Put it right out of your mind and I'll see you Christmas morning."

"Are you sure?"

"I am most absolutely sure. I wouldn't dream of it any other way. See you on Christmas, sweetheart." Constance hung up.

Hannah stood still in her kitchen. It felt like a weight had been lifted from her shoulders. She wouldn't miss Christmas! Hannah closed her eyes and visualized Charlie and Amanda running down the stairs to open their gifts. She saw family around the twinkling tree, busy with new gifts and books. She observed herself with Will's sisters in the kitchen chopping dinner vegetables, her annual Christmas chore. She could practically see the whole family sitting around the long dinner table, the atmosphere infused with laughter and stories. And Will would be sitting in his usual chair near the end.

Hannah opened her eyes.

And she would fight for him.

Hannah arrived early on Christmas morning. "Merry Christmas!" she whispered, letting herself in through the back door.

Constance and Will's sisters were in the kitchen making waffles, bacon, and eggs before any of the kids woke up, a family tradition. Hannah held up a bag of gifts and put a coffee cake on the table.

"Hannah!" Constance said loudly. "I'm so glad you accepted my invitation to come for Christmas." She emphasized the word "my" and Hannah—judging from the shocked looks on Cammy and Caroline's faces—realized her presence was a surprise. "Let me go get Will." Constance walked out of the kitchen.

Cammy poured more batter into a waffle maker.

"Hannah," Caroline said finally, "Merry Christmas." She kissed her on the cheek. After shutting the waffle iron, Cammy followed suit.

"Do you want to cut the fruit?" Caroline asked.

"Yes," Hannah said, exhaling. Anything but just stand there. She grabbed a cantaloupe and began to slice.

She'd cut up the cantaloupe and moved to a pineapple when Will walked in, clearly having been woken from a sound sleep. His hair was ruffled, and he had about four days of stubble on his jaw. He wore a tight-fitting T-shirt, revealing a more muscled physique than he'd had for some time.

"Hannah. Nice of you to come." He gave her a perfunctory kiss.

"Thanks for having me," Hannah responded, though it was clear the only person who'd wanted her there was Constance. She'd leave after the gifts.

The awkwardness of the morning was worth it when the kids woke up. Upon seeing her, Charlie cheered. "Mommy!" He squished himself next to her on the couch. Amanda was more understated but frequently turned and checked on her, ensuring that she hadn't ducked out amidst another round of opening. Will was in rare form, tickling the nieces and nephews, singing parts of Christmas carols, wearing all his gifts at once. It made Hannah angry that he could be so happy. But it made her miss him, too.

At the end of the chaos, there was a gift left under the tree. Will picked it up and handed it to Hannah. "This one's for you. Sorry the wrapping's so bad."

He looked sheepish and adorable. Hannah wanted him back in that moment, more than anything else, more than any other gift.

The room got strangely quiet.

Finally, Amanda said, "Well, open it already, Mom."

She slowly unwrapped the paper and turned it over. It was a painting of a bulldog with a big cherry under his eye. Newman. She met Will's eyes.

"It looked so much like him, I had to get it. Do you—"

"I love it. Thank you." She closed her eyes, wishing a gift from her would magically appear under the tree. Opening them, she looked at Will. "I'm sorry, I didn't—"

Will waved it off. "Don't worry. It's okay."

"Why a dog?" Charlie asked, now holding the small painting.

"It's a picture of our first dog," Hannah told him. "Newman. Daddy rescued him from an animal shelter."

"Sucker," Will said, shaking his head.

"Sweetheart," she corrected.

No one spoke. Hannah's face reddened. Mercifully, Constance clapped her hands—capturing everyone's attention. "Well, that's a wrap!"

Will excused himself so he could find a charger for Charlie's Nintendo DS. Hannah followed. "Thank you for the painting," she said once she'd caught up to him in his old bedroom. "I really love it."

"Yeah. It really looks like him." Will opened his old dresser drawer.

"It does," Hannah agreed.

Will fished through the drawer. He held up a charger. "Victorious!"

"Perfect. It would be a shame if we couldn't get that DS working." Hannah's heart pounded in her chest. She moved a step closer to Will and grabbed his arm. He looked momentarily surprised then leaned forward.

Was he going to kiss her?

Hannah moved closer. Will's phone rang. He pulled it out of his pocket.

Amber Mitchell's beautiful face filled the screen.

FORTY-EIGHT

David picked up his appointment book and saw that Amber had scheduled Will Abbott for 4:00 p.m. No. He couldn't do that. Jenny had gotten them tickets to see the impressionists at the Philadelphia art museum. He'd protested; she insisted.

"You're impossible and you're going," she'd said.

And, although he didn't know anything about art, he'd found he was looking forward to a whole night with Jenny. Will Abbott would have to wait.

David found Amber in front of an open filing cabinet. He handed her his appointment book. "You have to reschedule Will Abbott," he told her. "I'm leaving early today."

Amber retrieved a file and closed the cabinet. "David, he needs to see you. It's very urgent."

"But I'm leaving at 4:00." David knew he sounded childish.

Amber glanced at the book and pointed to a white space. "You have time at three." Before he could protest, Amber whipped her phone out of her pocket and pressed a single button. Will's face filled the screen. David stepped closer to make sure he saw it correctly. Was Will Abbott now a contact on Amber's phone?

Amber, animated during her conversation with Will, turned matter-of-factly to David when the phone call ended. "He'll be here at 3:00."

David opened his mouth to protest.

"It's urgent, David," Amber said as if reading his mind.

"What is—"

"It's better if he tells you," she interrupted and walked back to her desk.

David stood in the empty space, unsure how to respond. Had he just been dismissed? By his paralegal? He checked his watch. A few hours until he would see Jenny.

At 3:00 p.m., Will and Amber came into his office in tandem. They sat in chairs next to each other across from David's desk. Will held coffee in a #1 Dad mug Sienna had given David in kindergarten. He forced himself not to ask Will to put it back.

"So, Will," Amber started. "Tell David what's going on."

"Hank, my partner and Studs and Buds, dissolved our partnership. I don't have a job.

He got this in the mail."

Will handed him a standard subpoena issued by Jack Connors for business tax returns, check registers, profit and loss statements, and a host of other materials he needed to determine Will's real income. David had seen it.

"That's standard," he told Will, handing it back.

"It's a lot of documents," Will said.

"It's a legal proceeding. It involves documents."

Will paused. "Look. Hank didn't keep good records. He doesn't have this stuff. These requests freaked him out. He's worried he'll get in trouble." He paused again, looking down before continuing, "Now he's dissolved the business."

Amber patted Will's shoulder. Why did she keep touching him? David forced his attention back to Will. "So what are you doing now?"

"I'm looking for a job. But I don't have any money coming in. I can't pay Hannah the temporary support we agreed on." He looked as if he might punch something.

"If you don't have the money, you can't pay."

"But what about the bills?" Will asked.

Amber swept long pink fingernails across Will's back. "Will always pays his bills," she said, her voice taking on an air of familiarity, as if she had known Will Abbott for years. "He doesn't want to be delinquent. We have to do something."

"Look," David rolled his chair forward. "I can't make money appear where there isn't any. You can invade a retirement account. Or we can file a motion to reduce your support. Or maybe your wife needs to get a job to fill in the gap here. She's capable."

"No," Will said, shaking his head. "We agreed when Amanda was born that Hannah would stay home. She's needed at home."

"But Will—" Amber started.

"I said no." Amber drew back. Will looked at David and spoke again. "Okay. Understood about the money. But is there anything you can do about Frannie Marcos? The posts are crazy."

"No," David told him honestly. "I tried." And he had. He'd written Frannie a letter utilizing the full array of his divorce vocabulary. He found her actions "abhorrent" and "despicable" and threatened to come after her with "the full weight of the law." Frannie didn't budge and, in fact, posted his letter on the Hunky Hubby Facebook page with the quote: "Can't stop freedom of speech, Mr. Dewey." He'd felt ridiculous.

David explained why the posts could continue; Will left the office dissatisfied.

As soon as Will exited the building, Amber stormed back into his office. "You could have spent more time with him about the job loss, David," she admonished.

"And say what?"

"I don't know. Something encouraging."

David snorted. "What am I? A cheerleader?"

"Of course not. You just didn't have to be so rude."

David shook his head. "I wasn't rude. And by the way, what is going on with you two? Why are you so invested in this guy?"

"What do you mean?" Amber's eyes widened. David couldn't tell if the gesture was sarcastic or sincere.

"You keep touching him. You're always talking about his case." David paused. "Why do you keep touching him?"

Amber didn't respond. Her silence spoke volumes.

"Oh no. You're not—"

"What I do on my own time is my business, David." Amber pushed her hair back from her face and, for a moment, she looked as she did half a decade ago—the skinny, scared seventeen-year-old girl that he'd been appointed by the court to represent.

Like a permanent photograph, David could still visualize how she looked the day he dropped her off at The Girls' Home. She'd stood, alone, her belongings stuffed into a single plastic grocery bag. Her hair was knotty, her jeans too short and frayed from wear. She had no coat and had pulled an oversized sweatshirt around herself for warmth.

After leaving her, David drove to Target and loaded up. He dropped off bags of bedding and clothes and a coat and a $100 gift card. "It's part of the court program," he'd lied. Amber had stood in the center of the bags, holding the gift card as though he'd given her a key to a magic city. "I can't thank you enough, Mr. Dewey."

Amber's voice pierced his memory. "I know you care, David. But I'm okay. This is what I want. I'm in love with him."

FORTY-NINE

"So she's having an affair with him?" Jenny adjusted the temperature in David's car as they drove to the art museum.

"I guess. Or she's infatuated by him. The whole thing makes me angry. I can't really explain."

"Hmm." Jenny pulled on her headscarf.

"What?" David glanced over at her, then back at the road.

"Amber's like a daughter to you, David. Of course you're up-set."

"I have two daughters," David said emphatically. "Amber's a grown woman. What she does is her business. It doesn't concern me." Even as he said the words, David didn't believe them.

Jenny smiled at him. "Hmm," she said again.

"What?"

"You're just a big softie, David." She reached out and squeezed his hand. "And I love you for it."

She loved him. Did she mean that? The way he hoped? He glanced at her, but she was looking out the window. But her hand was still on his, small and fragile. He looked down at it and, as if she sensed he did so, she picked it up and punched him playfully on the shoulder.

"So, you big softie, would you be up for a vegan café before the exhibit?"

The question caught him by surprise; he laughed unintentionally. "Jenny, are you seriously asking me if I want to go to a vegan café?"

"Yes. Why?"

"Have you not eaten dinner with me almost every night for the past few months?"

"Well, you're stretching yourself with the exhibit so I thought, why not? Give the cows a break, David. Come on."

He agreed. Of course, he agreed.

They walked to the restaurant and were seated at a square table for two. Giant ferns hung in metal baskets from the ceiling; peace lilies stood in wicker pots on the floor. The bright green walls were adorned with framed pencil sketches of leaves.

Throughout the meal, Jenny chattered about the artists he would see, pulling up images of the paintings on her phone. The artwork all looked the same to David, all blurred pastel images. He announced each one as Jenny scrolled through: "a blurry bridge"; "a blurry night"; "a blurry dancer."

Jenny shook her head. "You're impossible, David."

After dinner, they walked from the café down the Avenue of the Arts, flags from countries around the world fluttering overhead in the cold wind. Jenny pulled her coat around herself for warmth. David thrust his hands in his coat pockets to stop himself from putting his arm around her. She turned to him and smiled, her face lit up by evening lights. "I love this view," she commented as they neared the museum.

"Me too," David replied, not looking away from her.

When they reached the stairs of the museum, the famed locale of Rocky Balboa's training grounds, they stood in front of the Sylvester Stallone statue. "Come on, David." Jenny pulled out her phone and motioned for him to stand next to her. He moved by her side and Jenny extended her arm to take the shot. The camera flashed, and Jenny showed him the picture.

"Can you forward that to me?"

"Of course." Jenny forwarded the picture then began to chant the start of the Rocky theme song. David smiled. She knew it was one of his favorite movies.

"I'm running up," she said suddenly, and, in a dash, her small figure was racing up the stairs.

David lumbered behind her tiny form. "I'm going to catch you."

Her laughter rang through the air, contagious. David laughed, causing him to fall further behind with each step. When they reached the top, both breathless, he stood facing her under a bright, full moon, the sky peppered with sparkling stars. Bits of tiny snowflakes fell, illuminated by street lamps.

David couldn't see the damaged eye, didn't notice the deepened wrinkles accentuated by Jenny's lack of hair. All he saw was the woman he wanted on the other side of the door when he came home every night.

He had to tell her.

"Jenny, I have something to tell you."

"I have something to tell you too." Her face clouded.

There was something wrong.

He grabbed her hand. "What is it?"

She looked down at the pavement then back up at him, "The tumors aren't responding the way the doctor thought they would."

David's heart felt like it stopped. "What does that mean?"

"I went to see Dr. Paz earlier this week. He was hoping for at least a partial response to the chemo—that the tumors would have shrunk. Instead, they're stable. They haven't shrunk or progressed."

David led Jenny to a nearby bench. They sat down. "What happens then?" he asked.

"I need another round of chemo."

David remembered how Jenny looked and felt after her first treatments. For her to go through that again. God.

As if reading his thoughts, she said, "I'm tired, David. I'm not sure how much more chemo I can do."

No. David felt like screaming. "Don't talk like that Jenny. You're a fighter." David made fists like he was about to start boxing. "Like our guy there." He gestured toward the Rocky statute adjacent to where they were sitting.

Jenny smiled weakly. "It's not like I have kids or a spouse or anything. I mean, it's a lot worse for other people. No one would really miss me."

David grabbed her hand. "Jenny, don't say that. I would miss you."

"You're sweet, David." She squeezed his hand then stood up. "Well, enough of that downer talk. We have some blurry pictures to see. Blurry bridge, blurry dancer…" She took a step toward the art museum.

David stood frozen, watching her.

She turned and a sudden realization crossed her face. "Oh. I'm sorry. Didn't you have something you needed to tell me as well?"

David took her in, wanting to speak but unable to do so.

A woman and her friend cackled as they passed.

The moon, bright a moment ago, slipped behind a cover of clouds.

The snow turned to ugly strips of sleet.

His moment had passed.

David shook his head.

"I can't remember," he lied.

FIFTY

David sat on the edge of Jenny's spare bedroom, hands clasped.

"Please, God, let her be okay."

David hadn't prayed since childhood; he felt strange saying the words aloud.

"God, don't let her die," he repeated, this time with more force.

"Please," he added, then dropped his head in his hands.

Prayers.

Something else he'd failed to do in his miserable version of a life so far. Would that be counted against him? Did God keep score?

David climbed into the bed and closed his eyes, images of Jenny an unstoppable parade in his mind. What if something happened? What would he do without her? He barely slept, and in the morning, David had every intention of having a conversation about her cancer treatment.

When he opened the door to the kitchen, Jenny was at the stove pushing scrambled eggs around a skillet while she hummed. At the sound of the toast popping up, she gave a jazzy little leap before retrieving it. When she saw him, her face erupted into a smile.

"Well, good morning, sleepy head."

He couldn't bring it up now. Not with Jenny so cheerful.

"Morning." David sat at the cluttered table and swept aside projects and papers to make room for the plates. As they ate, he looked at the sports section of the paper. Jenny skimmed the front page.

"Sixers won again," David commented.

"Nice. Who'd they beat?"

"Celtics."

"Awesome." Jenny poured more coffee. Then she showed him an article about a fundraising effort which allowed participants to name a venomous snake after their ex. "For your clients?" she suggested and handed him cream.

David took the cream. "Some of them," he laughed.

Moxie put her head on his lap. He fed her a piece of his toast when Jenny wasn't looking.

This is how it would be.

If they got married, if he lived here, this is how it would be.

David didn't want to get up. He read the entire sports section, the front page, and the business section. He drank two giant mugs of black coffee and poured a third.

"Won't you be late, David?" Jenny asked.

He checked the digital clock perched precariously at the edge of Jenny's kitchen counter. He would be late. Who cared really? Late for what? Helping angry men get back at their wives? Still, he had bills to pay, responsibilities to meet. Abruptly, he stood. "You're right. I'm not sure where the time went."

He stood and put his mug in the sink. He touched Jenny's shoulder. "We'll talk later?"

"Of course." She flipped a dish towel at him. "Now get out of here."

David got into his car and drove to his office. He checked the time as he pulled into the parking lot. Eight hours until he could leave.

David said a brief hello to Whitney and Amber then headed to his office. As soon as he entered, the phone rang. David picked up the receiver.

"Really, Dewey," Jack Connors started in. "I got your letter. Will Abbott lost his job. Thought you would be more creative than that." David could picture him, long fingers combing through his gelled hair as he leaned back in his leather chair.

"It's legitimate, Jack. Not sure what to tell you."

"He still has money."

"You're welcome to prove it."

Jack paused. David's finger hovered over the disconnect button.

"There's a picture of him on Facebook at a concert with your girl there." Jack said in a snide tone.

"Not sure what you're talking about."

"Your paralegal. They were at some concert. Looked like good seats."

"Doesn't mean anything." As he said it, David pulled up Amber's Facebook page on his computer. A friend of Amber's had tagged her in a post of she and Will at a concert. "Is that your case that Will has enough money to pay his support, Jack? This picture?"

"My evidence about Will Abbott and his ability to pay the support is not your business. Unless he doesn't pay, and we go to court. Which your guy doesn't want, trust me."

David leaned forward as if Jack could see him. "Is that a threat?"

"Interpret it how you want. No money by Monday, motion by Tuesday." Jack hung up.

David checked his watch. He'd only been at the office twenty minutes. The conversation with Jack would normally have fueled him; today, it felt draining. He spent the morning drafting a few letters, the effort interrupted by frequent internet searches about cancer treatments. Stem cell transplants. Immunotherapy. Clinical trials. Would any of these be good options if the next round of chemo didn't work? He'd started another search when his phone pinged.

Dad. It's Sienna. I'm doing a paper on the Constitution for social studies. Will you read it?

David sat up. Had Sienna really asked him for his help? Things had been going better with the kids. They were coming to dinner on Wednesdays. But actually reaching out to him and asking for help. This was huge. His finger hovered over the phone keyboard to type back a yes when another text from Sienna pinged.

It's law stuff. So I thought you would like it. We could talk about it at Applebee's.

David couldn't respond fast enough. I would love to. Let me know when and I'll be there. He looked at the message in satisfaction, then at the pictures that now adorned his desk. Ryan and Bolt. He and the girls in their dresses. And the selfie of him and Jenny in front of the Rocky statue.

David's phone rang. He picked it up.

"Your two o'clock is here," Amber said.

He looked at his appointment book. Ramon Quinn. Shit. David had handled Ramon's divorce several years ago but issues kept cropping up, most of them fueled by Ramon's own unreasonableness.

"Send him in," David told Amber. He took a gulp of coffee in an effort to garner more energy.

A scrawny man with thinning hair entered the office.

"David. Simoné is acting crazy again. She sent me these." Ramon laid out an array of disorganized receipts on his desk. "And she still hasn't given me my tools. The agreement says I get the Craftsman tools. Here, look." He handed David a photograph of tools in a garage. "That's her garage and those are my tools." He pointed to the Craftsman label in the picture. "And another thing. I think she got a raise. She's dressed all nice, got the kids new iPhones. My support should be reduced. I'm not paying for excess."

Ramon paced in front of David's desk. David looked at the pile of receipts and the picture of the Craftsman tools.

"So have you talked to Simone about any of this?" David picked up a pen and tapped it on the desk. "See if you could work anything out?"

Ramon looked at him as if he'd sprouted a second head. "Why would I talk to her? She's crazy. You know she's crazy."

David held up his hand. "Maybe there's an explanation? It might be worth talking to her first. I mean, are you sure she's aware those tools are yours?"

Ramon's face contorted, transforming from white to pink to red. "She knows. David, you know she knows. What has gotten into you? And what about these?" He picked up the ball of receipts. "Why should I have to pay these?"

David uncurled a few of the receipts. "They look like medical expenses for your kids."

"And I pay child support."

"It's separate."

"It's not."

Ramon's black eyes narrowed.

"Look, David. I come to you. I use you as my lawyer. I tell my friends to use you. Because you're tough. You're a shark. You fight for us guys." He paused, eyes still trained on David's face. "If I wanted to play nice, I wouldn't be here. Are you the lawyer I need or not?"

The question hung there. David averted his eyes from Ramon's. They fell to the pictures on his desk, the smiling faces of his children and Jenny.

He didn't want to do this anymore.

David pulled open his top desk drawer and retrieved a business card for Jack Connors. He slid it across the desk to Ramon.

"I think this is the guy you're looking for."

FIFTY-ONE

After Ramon left, David gathered up his belongings. Just as he was putting on his coat, Amber came into his office. She closed the door behind her.

David shook his head. "If this is about Will—"

"It's not about Will," Amber whispered. "Lorena Butler is here."

Lorena had left him several messages, all of which he had ignored. She helped him with marketing when he needed it; he had no obligation to call her. Still, he couldn't leave without passing her in the waiting room and he didn't want to wait long enough for her to leave on her own. He'd make it quick. "Send her in," David told Amber as he took off his coat and sat down.

Lorena stormed into office and began speaking immediately. "You could have told me I'd been replaced." She crossed her arms.

David took her in. "I don't know what you're talking about."

"Frannie Marcos?"

What did Frannie Marcos have to do with anything? "And?" David asked.

"She works for you, right? The Hunky Hubby Facebook page. It's a gimmick to generate business."

"Frannie Marcos is a reporter."

"Sure she is." Lorena stepped toward him. "And her beat is suburban divorces?"

David pushed his chair back and stood. "Look. I don't know why Frannie Marcos is reporting on the Abbotts. I don't know

why people care about the story or about Will Abbott. Frankly, I
don't like the guy."

David grabbed his coat. "Really, Lorena, I have to go." He
zipped his briefcase closed.

"Wait."

The way she said it made him freeze.

"Remember the show, Divorce House, I told you about?"

David hadn't thought about the show since the day she'd
brought it up. He turned to look at her. "Vaguely."

"Well. I contacted them." She paused. When David didn't
comment, she continued, "They want the Abbotts on the show."

David shook his head. No way was he going anywhere with
Will Abbott.

Lorena either didn't notice his reaction or ignored it. "David,
the network will pay double. David, think of the mon—"

"Money?" David glanced again at the pictures on his desk.
Then he thought about Amber's infatuation with Will Abbott.
The sooner that case was over, the better. "No. I'm not inter-
ested," he said with finality. He moved toward the door.

Lorena stepped in his path. "But—"

"I said no." David walked around her and out of his office.
When he got outside and into the fresh air, it was as though he'd
shed a heavy coat and was finally free. He drove to the book store
to get the Homeland DVD then picked up a few hoagies before
heading to Jenny's.

When he got there, David entered the house and found Jenny
on the couch trying to knit a blanket, her latest hobby. She
dropped the needles when she saw him.

"David! You're here early."

He liked the fact that, when she said the words, her voice
sounded like it was smiling.

"I'm the boss. I can play hooky when I want. Besides," he said dramatically, "I bought this." He pulled the second season of Homeland out from behind his back.

"Season two!"

"Binge watch?"

"Yes!" Jenny cleared a spot for him on the couch. David unwrapped the hoagies as she started episode one. They sat under Jenny's half-knitted afghan, eating and watching. During episode three, Jenny leaned her head against him. Moxie jumped up on the couch to sit on his other side. David felt, in that moment, buttressed by love. At least in Jenny's home, he wasn't despised.

Halfway through episode four, Jenny's breath deepened. He kissed the top of her head, skimming it so as not to wake her. Then he slowly got up, gently placing Jenny's head on a pillow and covering her with the blanket. David watched her breathe a moment before moving to the kitchen. The hoagie had been small; he was still hungry.

From the kitchen pantry, David grabbed a box of Fruit Loops and then rummaged around for a bowl. In the back of the cabinet, he spotted a single sheet of paper lying near a pile of dishes. It was neatly folded, but he could still see bits of Jenny's handwriting. He reached for it, then pulled his hand back. He shouldn't look. It wasn't his business. But the note wasn't hidden. David grabbed the paper and opened it.

It was a numbered list. His eyes strained to read Jenny's tiny handwriting.

In the number one space, it read 'swim with dolphins.' Number two: 'scuba diving in the Caribbean'. Number three: 'Paris!' The list continued, filling twelve spaces.

What was this? David stared at the items again.

God damn it.

It was a bucket list.

David held the paper in his hand, unable to put it back down.

A bucket list.

It didn't mean anything.

Did it?

David skimmed the list again. He could take Jenny to see the ball drop in Times Square. They could go ziplining. They could take Moxie to Martha's Vineyard. But he probably couldn't swing a trip to Paris or the Caribbean or a cruise to Alaska. One he could do. But not all three.

David put the list back where he'd found it and returned to the family room. He moved Jenny to her own bed, tucking her in with thick, heavy blankets. She acknowledged him with a tired nod; she was used to him moving her.

He sat on the edge of her bed and thought about how fun it would be to surprise her, to be the man who could meet every one of her requests. "Surprise! We're going to Paris!" "Surprise, I have tickets to the Caribbean. We leave tomorrow!"

He was lost with the thought of it. Could he make it work?

Maybe if he had a good year?

Took out a loan?

The idea came to him in a start. He could do it. Everything on the list. Easily.

David took out his phone and texted Lorena.

I'll do it.

FIFTY-TWO

Rachel

Jack Connors had given Rachel the letter from David Dewey about Will's job loss in the hall with an abrupt direction to "send it to the client and see what she wants to do." "She" being Hannah, of course. Rachel had read the letter immediately, then a second time. A job loss? No support? She thought of Hannah's carefully constructed life. This would cause even more of a strain, especially after what had happened.

Rachel tucked the letter into her briefcase. She'd break the news in person after dinner. Of course, it would be easier if Hannah was talking to her. Which she wasn't. But she couldn't very well shut the door in her face. Could she?

Rachel left early and drove to Hannah's house. She knocked then jogged in place on the front step. Her feet like blocks of ice. There was no answer though Hannah's minivan was in the driveway. Rachel texted her, hands freezing as she typed the words.

Please open up.

A swoop of cold air blew at her back. Rachel knocked again, more forcefully.

The door opened. Behind it stood a boy with sandy-colored hair and blue eyes. The spitting image of Will Abbott. Rachel smiled. His eyes widened and he slammed the door shut.

Rachel could hear him through the door. "Mooom! There's a lady here."

Hannah's face peered through the front window.

"It's important." Rachel called to her.

Hannah opened the door and peeked out. "What?" she said, not inviting Rachel in.

"I need to talk to you." Rachel shook her legs. A gust of wind blew bits of snow into the house. Hannah opened the door wider and stepped back. Rachel entered and stood awkwardly in the foyer.

"Make it fast." Hannah crossed her arms.

"Look, I know you're mad at me."

Hannah tapped her foot. She looked down at Charlie who lingered behind her legs.

"Go see your sister," Hannah told him gently. "This will only take a minute."

Once Charlie left, Hannah focused on Rachel. "Sorry," she said in a manner that indicated she was anything but. "He's a little spooked by strangers with all the news coverage." She crossed her arms again. "Oh. And sorry about the snow on the walkway. I can't get out there and shovel without someone taking a picture of me."

"Hannah," Rachel started. "Again, I didn't know he was going to report it. I am so deeply sorry."

Two days before, Greg Tisbury had featured the Hunky Hubby phenomenon on Trending Now. Prior to the show, he'd relentlessly called Rachel for an exclusive. After his fourth call, Rachel snapped and told him about Hannah's failed attempt to reconcile with Will on Christmas. She had intended it to be the final say, the words Greg needed to back off. Instead, Greg featured the story with the promo: "Wife of Hunky Hubby wants him bad!"

Looking at Hannah, Rachel felt a burning shame. How could she have betrayed her confidence like that?

"Please believe me," Rachel begged. "I told him about the reconciliation attempt so he would NOT do the story. The Greg I knew had real compassion. I thought if he knew how you felt, he'd drop it."

The words lingered.

"Is that why you came? To apologize?"

"Yes, but there's something else. Can we sit?" Rachel gestured to the living room couches.

"I think you can tell me here." Hannah didn't budge.

"Alright." Rachel reached into her briefcase, pulled out the letter from David Dewey, and gave it to Hannah.

Hannah read the letter. "So he has no job? What are we going to do for money?"

"Well, he's required by law to maintain the status quo." Rachel bounced from one leg to the other, trying to generate heat to warm up her legs. "We'll file a motion with the court to get an order that he has to continue to pay the support as agreed."

"But, if there's no money coming in, he won't be able to pay. Even with an order."

The statement hung in the air, the truth in it apparent. What was the point of an order if it couldn't be enforced?

Rachel tried a new angle. "Do you think he's lying? Husbands sometimes do this in divorce. We call it SIR. Sudden income reduction. Do you think he's, well, making it up?" Her voice went an octave higher.

Hannah walked from the foyer to the living room and plucked a large photo from a grouping of fancy-framed pictures. She walked back over and handed it to Rachel. It was a candid shot of Hannah and Will with their wedding party, outside, in a park with lush green grass and flowering trees. Hannah was stunning. She wore her hair long, slightly curled and pulled back with a modest tiara. Her dress had a tight, beaded bodice which flared into a full skirt. She wore no jewelry, her makeup subtle. She was leaning forward, laughing.

Next to her, Will filled out his long-tailed tuxedo with a muscular frame. He had deeply tanned skin and wore his hair cropped short. On either side of them were four girls in long pink dresses and four male counterparts in tuxes. Everyone smiling. It was a grayish day, but streaks of sunlight bore down through the clouds, illuminating the group. But it was Will's expression that stole the photograph.

Amidst the smiles, his attention was focused completely on Hannah. He looked like a man who had just opened a precious gift and couldn't believe his good fortune.

"Right after this picture was taken," Hannah said, "Will bent down and whispered to me 'I can't believe how lucky I am.'" She stared at the image a minute before continuing, "'We are,' I told him. 'I can't believe how lucky we are.'"

The sun dipped into the horizon outside, darkening the room.

"So," Hannah continued, "if you asked me if this Will would have SIR or whatever it is," she pointed to the picture, "I would say no." She pulled her phone from her pocket. "But this Will," she turned it around and revealed an image of Will and Amber, arms entwined, at a concert. "I have no idea."

Rachel gently took the wedding photo from Hannah's hand and looked again at Will's expression. Though she knew she should be concentrating on Hannah, she thought about Aaron. Rachel tried to visualize him looking at her that way, like she was a prized possession. Instead, his face in Rachel's mind was in a scowl, his words filled with criticism. Just that morning, she had failed to fold the newspaper properly. Stray newspaper pieces were a pet peeve for Aaron. He'd refolded it with crisp, loud movements.

Still looking at the picture, Rachel asked her, "So should we go ahead with the motion to maintain the support then?"

Hannah sighed. "Whatever's best. I don't really know anymore. This has all been so heartbreaking." She put her hand on the doorknob.

"Wait. Are you okay?" Rachel asked.

"Is it your business?" Hannah's green eyes flared.

"No. But I care about you. I'm sorry about Greg and the show. I didn't know. I swear it."

Hannah studied her face before responding, "I'm okay. I stopped looking at social media and deleted my Facebook account. Until the Trending Now story, it felt like it was all dying down."

"I'm sorry," Rachel said. She felt renewed shame at her part in generating the unwanted publicity.

"I believe you didn't mean to hurt me, Rachel." Hannah paused. "One good thing did come of all this, though. I got a part-time job at a photography studio to keep my mind off things. Hold on." Hannah left the room and returned with a half-dozen glossy photographs. "I mainly just make appointments and set up the shoots, but the owner lets me take some shots too. Here." She handed Rachel the photos, all black and white images of a mother and a newborn.

"Beautiful," Rachel said, looking through the stack.

Hannah's voice softened. "How about you? All good with the wedding plans?"

Rachel forced a smile. "Great."

"Is it really?"

"It is," Rachel insisted. "In fact," she pulled out her phone, "I picked my dress last week." She tipped the screen to show Hannah a picture of herself in the sample dress at the bridal shop, her mother smiling by her side. As they looked, Rachel realized that the dress was quite similar to the one Hannah had worn, billowing and princess-like.

"It's gorgeous," Hannah said. "And I love the picture. You and your mom look so happy." After a moment, she added, "Hey, can you forward it to me?" Rachel gave her a quizzical look. "I'm a photographer, remember? I live for good pictures."

"Alright." The swishing sound of a sent email filled the room. Rachel stepped outside. She turned to face Hannah. "Thanks for understanding."

Hannah nodded. "Of course. Stay warm." She shut the door behind Rachel.

Rachel walked to her car and thought again of Will's expression in the picture.

And how Aaron had never looked at her that way.

FIFTY-THREE

Rachel spent the next few weeks trying to push the image of the Abbott wedding picture out of her mind. The fact that Will Abbott was smitten on his wedding day was hardly a reason to doubt her own relationship. Aaron would never be caught, passed out, with a bunch of women's signatures on his torso. Aaron wouldn't be carrying on with a younger woman. He wouldn't lose his job. And, just because Aaron didn't look crazy in love, that didn't mean he wasn't. He had, just the other day, bought Rachel a fuzzy blanket because she complained she was cold all the time. If their love was more of a fuzzy blanket than a fairytale romance, there was nothing wrong with that.

Nothing.

Still, Rachel's doubts about Aaron became relentless as the wedding date neared. She almost didn't want to attend her bridal shower the following week.

Rachel hadn't expected Hannah to be at the shower. But as she stood at the threshold of Forrester's before her big entrance, she saw her amidst the familiar faces, standing alone by a flowing fountain of punch, one hand cupped tightly around her glass, the other holding a small, pink gift bag. Rachel stared at her, unable to move. She had told Hannah things about Aaron because she'd believed their worlds to be separate. She didn't want Hannah there. Her presence made it hard to play her part as the blushing, radiant, bride-to-be.

As Rachel stood in the doorway, Hannah turned and waved, pink bag swinging on her elbow.

Hannah walked over to her. "Your mom invited me," she said. "I hope it's okay."

"It's more than okay," Rachel lied. "Good to see you."

Samantha and Lexi ran over with a cluster of high school friends. "Rachel, Rachel!" They each kissed her cheek with "muah!" sounds. None of them acknowledged Hannah, and Rachel shamelessly allowed her to be pushed to the outskirts of the group.

"Show us that rock!" Rachel put down her hand in a dramatic gesture to the expected, collective exclamations.

Rachel looked at Hannah, mouthed "catch you later," and proceeded to whisk between groups of lively women standing in small circles about the room. Flitting from group to group, she chattered about her dress and the wedding plans. She bragged about the honeymoon—a villa on the water in the Caribbean. "Nothing but divine beaches and cocktails," she repeated to each group, putting her hands behind her head in a mock gesture of someone lying out. In truth, of everything wedding-related, Rachel was looking forward to the honeymoon the most. She couldn't wait to lie in the bright sun with Aaron with nothing pressing to do but, eventually, get up for meals.

As Rachel made her rounds, she found herself looking for Hannah. She was mainly alone, sometimes talking to a stray relative. She saw Aaron's niece, Madison, walk up to her. "Oh my God. Are you Hannah?"

Hannah looked startled. Rachel nodded absentmindedly in her own conversation as she eavesdropped.

Hannah said something inaudible.

"I can't believe it's you! I'm on Team Hannah at school."

"Team Hannah?"

Madison nodded. "Some of us, the nice girls, are on Team Hannah. The mean girls are on Team Amber. I'm on Team Hannah," she repeated, pulling out her phone. "Here we are," she said. Hannah stared at the phone. Rachel could only guess it was picture of Madison's team. She excused herself and walked over to them, hoping to intervene.

"Hey, can I get a selfie with you?" Madison asked.

Rachel strode faster.

"Sure. Why not," Hannah said, as a small smile creased her face.

They put their heads together and the girl held out the phone and snapped.

Madison asked, "Can I post it on my Snapchat?"

"Go for it!"

Madison rushed away, fingers flying over her phone.

"I'm so sorry," Rachel said, as she walked up behind Hannah.

Hannah whipped around and stared at her, her face unreadable.

"Hannah, I didn't know—"

"There are teams."

Rachel thought she was going to lose it. She braced herself for a torrent of emotion. Then Hannah laughed. A deep, infectious, convulsing belly laugh. Rachel put her hand on Hannah's shoulder. A giggle escaped, then another. Soon, they both were bowled over with laughter. Slowly, the room grew quiet as the groups of women turned their attention to Rachel and Hannah.

Rachel tried to compose herself but continued to laugh. It was as though the laughter came from a place deep inside of her that she could not control. Her stomach muscles ached; her bladder gave a little. She couldn't stop.

Rachel's mother rushed over and whispered harshly, "Rachel. Pull yourself together. You're causing a scene."

Rachel waved a "sorry" and excused herself to the bathroom. Hannah walked outside, her hand on her mouth to hold back the stray guffaws.

FIFTY-FOUR

When Rachel returned, calm and composed, her mother announced it was "time for gifts!" She escorted Rachel to a puffy chair dressed in white with a sign in fancy calligraphy: BRIDE.

The guests nibbled on artfully arranged finger sandwiches as they talked over pink centerpiece bouquets. Madison passed out papers with a shower game: How many words can you make out of Rachel and Aaron?

Rachel sat down in the puffy BRIDE chair. "Sorry for that, everyone! Just some pre-wedding jitters."

Everyone laughed.

Rachel spied Hannah coming in from outside. She sat at a table in the back. Madison sat next to Rachel with a straw hat, having been given the task of making a bow headdress. Rachel had been to enough bridal showers to know the drill. At the end of the present-opening, she'd pose in the hat, full of ribbons from her shower gifts.

Rachel's mother sat next to Madison, pen in hand, ready to write down every gift giver for the future thank you note. Ten gifts in, Rachel had yet to see an item that hadn't been selected by Aaron during their five sessions with the registry department at Nordstrom's. Eventually, Rachel opened the chip and dip server she'd picked and, holding it high for viewing, exclaimed, "Great! This will be perfect for casual get-togethers!" As she said this, Rachel remembered Aaron's words: "Put it on the list if you want, Rachel, but I can't imagine throwing a party with chips and dip. Can you?"

With two gifts to go, the overflowing, ribbon headdress could not fit another bow. Madison placed it on Rachel's head, and she posed, holding Hannah's pink bag up by her face to complete the shot. After, Rachel reached into the little bag and pulled out a framed picture. It was the one of her in her wedding dress with her Mom at the bridal shop. Hannah had removed some of the superfluous parts of the picture and blurred the edges, casting a fairytale glow on the scene. She'd touched it up, too; mother and daughter both flawless. Their heads were together, and Rachel had one hand around her mother, the other holding out the billowing folds of the skirt, Rachel's favorite part of the dress. She remembered twirling about in it in the dressing room, feeling every bit a princess, as her mother had exclaimed. "Beautiful. Just perfect."

Rachel turned the picture around. A chorus of "Awww!" erupted. She set the picture down on the table next to her.

"Thank you," she mouthed to Hannah.

The final gift was from Aaron. Rachel removed the card from the huge box and read: "Dear Rachel. A beautiful gift for a beautiful woman. Love, Aaron." A second, louder, chorus of "Awww!" broke out and a chant began: "Open it! Open it! Open it!"

"Should I open it?" Rachel asked, teasing, swept up in the moment. The women cheered and clapped and a few of them even sent out some catcalls. "Open it, Rachel!"

Rachel removed the giant bow, tore off the thick white wrapping, and carefully lifted off the lid. Reaching in, she felt heavy silk, jewels. Rachel pulled out a tight, low-cut wedding dress that flared out at the bottom. It looked like something a mermaid might wear.

No one said anything.

Sylvia broke the awkward silence. "Aaron had that custom made for you, doll. It's from Paris. Isn't it gorgeous?" She turned to the group and, in a louder voice, said, "Aaron had the dress made in Paris." When no one said anything, she added, "Custom made from a big designer. One of a kind."

"Beautiful," someone commented. "Exquisite," said someone else.

Rachel glanced at her mother, her mouth frozen in a fake smile. Hannah looked horrified. Sylvia stared at her as Rachel continued to hold the dress up wordlessly. Then, finally, she found her voice. "Two gorgeous dresses," she said. "I guess I'll have to marry Aaron twice." Laughter erupted, the tension broken.

"There's something else in there, doll," Sylvia said over the laughter. "It's at the bottom."

Now with trepidation, Rachel reached in and lifted out an envelope and held it up to the group. "Flat present," she said, trying to keep up the cheerful banter. "I like that." A few people laughed politely. Tension filled the room. Rachel sliced the envelope open with her finger nail and pulled out a brochure and itinerary for an exclusive honeymoon safari on the African plains. On it was a little, yellow sticky note with Aaron's handwriting: Thought this would be better than the beach. A.

Rachel stared at it.

The voices of her guests cut into her thoughts.

"What is it? Show us, Rach."

Rachel turned around the brochure and said with the voice of game show host, "We're going on a honeymoon to Africa!" Still wearing the ribbon hat, she held up the brochure with one hand and the dress with the other. Cameras flashed.

After taking photographs of Rachel in the hat, guests began to leave. She said goodbye to each, forcing herself to make enthusiastic comments about Aaron's gifts.

"I've never been to Africa!"

"I had no idea Aaron was having a dress custom made!"

"Yes, it is stunning."

"What a surprise!"

Her mother stood at her side and fawned about Aaron's dress as though the day they had spent together—their dress day—had been a silly sideshow. The fact that she'd spent several thousand dollars on the dress they'd chosen seemed not to matter either. Her mother actually seemed somewhat embarrassed that they'd chosen a regular, off the rack dress, when, clearly, a custom made dress from a top Parisian designer had been called for. "Custom made," her mother had repeated at least three times. "Custom made from Paris."

Hannah was one of the last guests to leave. She leaned forward and whispered in Rachel's ear: "Wear the dress you picked and go to the beach."

Rachel knew Hannah meant the comment as a show of support, but the words felt like a cut on her relationship. "We'll see," she said, smiling brightly.

After the last guest left, Rachel drove to Aaron's apartment building. Standing in the lobby, Rachel braced herself to march in and command: "Send back the dress!" "Cancel the safari!" She would admonish Aaron for not including her in such important decisions and say: "If this is how it's going to be between us, then I don't think I can do this." As she rode on the elevator, Rachel practiced the lines in her head.

"I don't think I can do this."

"I can't do this."

"I won't do this."

"I don't want to marry you, Aaron."

The silver doors slid open and Rachel strode out into the dimly lit hall, her resolve fully intact. As she neared Aaron's apartment, she heard a loud buzzing from inside. When she opened the door, a billow of smoke rushed out. Aaron stood in the kitchen flailing about with big mittened hands. It smelled like burnt steak. The sliding glass door was open. The smoke detector blared. The little table in front of the kitchen was set for two with a big candle in the center and a bottle of wine on ice.

Aaron was making dinner.

"What happened?" Rachel grabbed a chair, pulled it to the smoke detector, and removed the battery.

"Oh! Thank God." Aaron said with relief. "I've been trying to get that thing off." He gestured to the steak. "I wanted to make you a dinner," he said, his face obscured by the heavy smoke. "I think it may be overcooked." They laughed. It felt normal. "Pizza?" he said, holding his hands up like a question. She agreed.

As he grabbed the take-out menu from its specified drawer, he asked, "Did you have fun at the shower? Did you like my gifts?"

The question hung there, Rachel's rehearsed speech spinning about her brain as she assessed this version of Aaron. Humble. Imperfect. Sweet. Qualities made all the more endearing because of their rare appearance. In that moment, the words Rachel had practiced in the elevator seemed ludicrous. She pushed them away.

"I loved the gifts! The dress is gorgeous."

Aaron nodded with satisfaction. "A gorgeous dress for a gorgeous woman." He kissed Rachel on the cheek. "Oh, and I hope you don't mind about the safari. I know how much you like cats.

I signed you up for the 'cat watch', an exclusive excursion to see all the cats of Africa up close and personal—lions, cheetahs, leopards. I thought you'd love it. I wanted it to be a surprise."

Aaron's recognition of her love for cats, his efforts to give her a special surprise—how could she be mad? "I love it!" she said, meaning it now. "I love that idea."

"Oh," he said. "And speaking of cats, I have another surprise." He took Rachel's hand and led her to the spare bedroom. He opened the door and she stepped in.

Rachel's hands flew to her mouth.

Inside the room, a three-tiered cat gym lined one wall. On the other sat a scratching post, a basket of toys, a self-cleaning litter box, and a crystal food dish. A big screen television in the corner played a nature video. And, by the window, on a fluffy pink ottoman, lay Snowball.

Rachel screamed.

"Snowball! Oh my God!" She rushed toward the cat and grabbed her, holding her warm body to her chest, white fur clinging to her blue suit. Snowball purred.

Aaron smiled at her—almost a Will-worthy smile. "So you know I'm not really a pet kind of guy," Aaron started and they both laughed. He'd made his disdain for "fuzzy mammals" abundantly clear. "But I know Snowball is important to you. Is this room a good compromise?" He held out his hands.

"Yes, yes." The burned dinner, the cat watch—Snowball!—they had all served to buoy her emotions and she felt a rising tide of happiness, a feeling which lasted into the coming days and weeks and set a feeling of certainty in her gut where doubt had lain before.

FIFTY-FIVE

Rachel couldn't wait to tell Hannah about Snowball's room, Aaron's gesture somehow a validation of their relationship. They met for smoothies. Rachel told Hannah about the burned dinner, the candlelight pizza, and Snowball's room. She explained that Aaron changed the honeymoon so she could attend a safari featuring big cats. When Rachel finished the monologue, she leaned back in her chair and waited for Hannah's reaction.

Hannah sipped her smoothie.

Rachel leaned forward. She had expected her to yell out. "Wow! That sounds like me and Will!" or "Aaron must really love you!" or anything, really, that would acknowledge the realness of her relationship. She craved Hannah's acknowledgement that her love was just like the one she and Will had shared.

Instead, Hannah picked at a bran muffin.

Rachel laid on more details. "Our bungalow is right on an African plain! Snowball has her own television!"

With each additional detail, Hannah's expression became increasingly distressed until she finally touched Rachel's hand and said, "Hey, can I talk to you about something?"

She shut up.

Hands shaking, Hannah pulled out a paper from her purse. As she unfolded it, Rachel noticed the firm letterhead. It was a bill. Hannah owed $1,829.80 to Trembley, Rubin, and Connors. "It looks like my $5,000 retainer ran out," she said. "I don't have the money to pay this right now. I'm not sure how much more I can afford." She looked expressly uncomfortable. Rachel took the bill from her hand.

The bill included charges for phone calls between Jack and David, the time Rachel had spent preparing the motion for support, and all the time spent on the domestic violence incident. Plus, Will was part owner of a business. Finding out what he really earned was challenging. The bill was, Rachel realized, as fair as it was shocking. Fair because the legal work was necessary but shocking in its aggregate cost. Most people didn't have thousands lying around to litigate a divorce.

"Here." Hannah slid a check across the table. "It's $300, a start. And I don't mean to suggest that you're not worth it. It's just Will and I don't have that kind of money, especially with his job situation." She paused. "Any end in sight?" Her voice was hopeful but with a sadness that seemed to pour out into the space around her. When Rachel didn't respond she added, "We can always take out some retirement money. But we have to pay extra tax on that, right?"

"Right," Rachel said, her eyes on the bill. The check sat in front of her on the table, untouched. She didn't want to take it. "We have the motion hearing Friday," she said, looking back up at her. It wasn't an answer to her question. And they both knew the hearing and whatever result came of it was not a long-term solution. Whether the judge ordered Will to pay Hannah support or not, it didn't change the amount of money they had.

Gratefully, Hannah didn't call her out on her answer, instead, saying, "Okay. We'll wait until Friday then." She stood up and stuffed the bill back into her purse as she threw away the Styrofoam smoothie cup. "I'm so glad things are going better with Aaron." She squeezed Rachel's hand. "I'll see you later." She walked out.

At the office the following day, Rachel couldn't shake her conversation with Hannah. She couldn't bring herself to hand over the $300 check to Jack Connors to whom $300 was an insignificant, piddly sum. He charged more than that for an hour of his time. She thought about writing her own check, obliterating the balance. $1,800. Nothing to Aaron. Rachel had seen him spend more than that on a bottle of wine. But she'd already blurred the lines between client and attorney once. She couldn't do that again.

Mid-morning, Rachel poked her head into Jack's office with the intention of seeing if Hannah's bill could be reduced. David Dewey sat in a chair opposite Jack's desk. He and Jack were laughing.

"Rachel," Jack said as though she had just joined a party. "You're just the one I wanted to see. David has an intriguing idea for the Abbott case." He motioned to David.

David explained the concept of Divorce House. If Hannah and Will appeared on the show, they would each receive $10,000 with all legal fees paid by the network. The idea was to help them resolve their divorce in a peaceful, tropical setting. They would have a final opportunity to air their differences at a live last-chance dinner.

It was the first time Rachel had heard David Dewey speak without yelling.

"It's supposed to give emotional and legal closure," Jack said. The words, from Jack's lips, sounded ridiculous. "We go, too," he added. "It will be great exposure for the firm. Plus, we get paid by the network." He and David exchanged looks and Jack leaned back in his swivel chair. "So, you know Hannah. Do you think she'll do it?"

"I'm not sure," Rachel said, refusing to sell Hannah out again. Jack handed her an email describing the show. Rachel read through the details. Hannah would stay in a villa with two women and three men, one half of the twelve couples there for a divorce, the other half living in a separate villa. There would be downtime and activities for each house. Each couple would meet with their attorneys to try to settle the outstanding marital issues. Every couple, prior to the final divorce, had the option to have a final dinner together, aptly named the "last chance dinner," during which they could air their grievances. A judge would be available to complete any divorce and couples would leave the island free, their bonds dissolved forever. It would all be filmed – the villa activities, the attorney meetings, the last chance dinner.

Rachel looked up when she finished reading. David Dewey began talking immediately.

"The network really wants to feature the Abbotts in the first episode. They just love the Hunky Hubby angle."

Of course they did.

Rachel reread the email. It was possibly, she had to admit, exactly what Hannah needed; a chance to wipe the legal fees clean, speed up the settlement process, to confront Will for closure. Rachel looked up at them, their faces eager for her response.

"I think she'd be interested."

"Talk to her then. Put the dates on your calendar," Jack handed her a page with details. Rachel skimmed down to the dates and location: April 24th to April 27th, The Royal Caribbean Hotel, St. John. She stared, disbelieving.

In a strange twist of fate, Hannah would be in St. John to get a divorce the same weekend Rachel was there to get married.

FIFTY-SIX

Will

"So, she said yes," Amber said as she walked into her apartment holding a bottle of wine in one hand, Chinese take-out in the other.

Will barely registered her presence. "She said yes," he said without looking at her.

Will turned the statement over in his mind. Yes. Hannah would go forward with the appearance on the reality show. She was moving ahead with the divorce. Yes.

Amber smiled. "It's good news, right?" She stepped out of her heels and kissed him on the mouth, lingering there. Will pulled back. Jealousy and hurt flashed over her face. "I'll put this on ice." She held up the wine before moving to the kitchen.

Will put his head in his hands. The divorce was happening.

What had he expected?

He'd seen Hannah from a distance the prior week walking into a restaurant. As the last bits of her reddish hair disappeared through the door, Will had fought the urge to follow her. To ask questions. What are you doing? Who are you meeting? What do you think the Phillies' chances are this year?

That night, he picked up the phone to call. Just a quick "hey." No big deal. Will had dialed the first three numbers, then remembered their fight on Christmas and stopped himself.

He had just gotten a charger for Charlie's new DS. Hannah had moved in to kiss him when his phone had rung. They'd both seen it was Amber. He had accepted the call. The look on Hannah's face. The hurt. The betrayal. He hadn't talked to Amber long, but long enough. After, Will had found Hannah outside, forcefully jamming gifts into the car. "You forgot this." Will had held the picture of Newman out to her.

"Keep it," Hannah had said, then stopped and looked at him before speaking again. "You can't do this to me, Will. You can't be half in and half out. You can't give me a Christmas gift like this." She pointed to the painting. "And in the next breath be talking to your girlfriend. I deserve better than that."

"She's not my girlfriend."

Hannah rolled her eyes.

"You're the one who started it all. With Trent."

Hannah had gone rigid. "Trent was a friend."

"Amber's a friend."

"Really Will? She's your friend?" Hannah pulled up a picture of Amber in a seductive pose from the Facebook page and showed him. She got in the car and slid behind the steering wheel. Will watched her, limply holding the painting, trying to think of a comeback. Hannah shut the door. They looked at each other through the glass. Hannah rolled down the window.

"If you're not going to choose me, Will, you have to let me go." She drove away before he could respond.

Will called her Christmas night, the next day. She wouldn't take his calls. He texted. Nothing. Then a transactional text. Could he pick up Amanda from Lily's house? Then another. It was his turn to take Charlie to the math tutor. Then, please stop giving the kids sugar before bed. Charlie must do an extra sheet of math every night. Every purposefully mundane, contemptuous text was juxtaposed by a fun, sexy overture from Amber. Did Will want to get Thai food? How about they go ice skating? Wanna go to a concert?

Will had taken the path of least resistance. And, when pangs of guilt and regret surfaced, he'd look for Amber, his negative feelings temporarily eased by her enthusiasm for all things Will Abbott. He could do no wrong in her eyes and no right in Hannah's.

Will hadn't meant to choose Amber. It had just been too easy.

He sat on Amber's couch, in Amber's home, the vanilla scent of it suddenly bothersome. He stared ahead at a framed picture of the two of them. Will hated the man who stared back at him. Amber came up behind him and put her hands on his shoulders. He flinched.

"What's wrong?" Her voice had a babyish lilt and, though he couldn't see her face, Will could picture it, the sexy pout. She moved her hands down his chest, kissed his neck. "I thought you'd be happy."

Will pushed her hands away. "Hannah is my wife, Amber. Divorce is serious."

She stepped back from the couch. Will stood up. When he turned to look at her, she had a stunned expression on her face. They hadn't yet had a fight.

"I need some air." Will grabbed his keys and headed out. He didn't look back.

Will got in the car and started the engine. He had nowhere to go. His sisters thought he was—what was the phrase they used?— a total asshole. That was it. His mother was kinder, of course, but kept insisting Will was overtired, that he get some rest so he could think more clearly.

Scotty was pissed at him, too. He thought Will didn't treat Amber like the goddess she was.

With no better option, Will drove to McCourt's. As he walked in, a woman flashed a picture. He whirled around. Was it of him? He couldn't tell. Inside, he scanned the room before taking a seat at the bar. A woman across the bar smiled at him. To be nice? Or because it was him? The Hunky Hubby? Amber thrived on the attention; Will hated it.

Will sipped a Sam Adams, and the cold liquid slid down his throat. He took another sip, then downed it, slamming the glass on the bar. "Another," he told the bartender. Halfway through the second, Will saw her. Hannah. From the back. Red hair, a bit shorter. She'd lost a few pounds. It was a sign. This was it.

Will slid off the stool and strode forward. His heart pounded in his chest. What would he say? What could he possibly say?

Will reached her. He held his hand out and touched her shoulder. Instantaneously, he knew it. The woman was not his wife. A wrinkled stranger with red-tinged eyes and a pulled up nose turned to face him.

"Yes?"

"Sorry. I thought you were someone else." Will stepped back.

She looked at him, her eyes sweeping downward. "Well, we're both here now," she said, spreading her arms out like an invitation.

Will waved his hand. "No thanks. I'm looking for someone else."

"I'm here if you change your mind." She winked, alcohol seeming to make the effort more difficult.

Will left after the encounter with the woman and drove by rote to his own home. He parked in front. The windows were dark. Of course they were. It was a school night. He pictured Hannah inside, snug in their huge bed, the scent of lavender steaming out of the infuser in steady puffs. He could go in. But that would startle them. Ring the doorbell? At eleven at night?

Will drove to Amber's for lack of another option. He found her on the couch in a full regalia of sweats. She'd removed all her make-up, her red, puffy eyes exaggerated in its absence. A pint of ice cream sat on her lap. She looked like the star of a teen drama in a break-up scene.

"I'm sorry." Will's words came out by habit, a lifelong Pavlovian response to negative emotion.

"I thought you'd be happy."

"Look," Will started, then stopped himself. He couldn't verbalize his feelings.

Amber waited, expectant. She took a bite of ice cream.

"I'm sorry," Will said again.

Amber's voice grew harsher. "I know you're sorry, Will. But are you happy?"

It was the perfect opening. To say it. He'd made a mistake. Will opened his mouth.

"I—"

"Never mind," she interrupted, obviously trying to change gears. "Let's take a drive tomorrow."

"A drive? How do you jump from my divorce to taking a drive?"

"I just think it'll be good to get out and do something." She patted the couch.

Will sat next to her. Did he have anything to do tomorrow? Will tried to think. Amber stroked his leg.

"I think a day with no plans will do you some good." Her hand moved upward.

Will let Amber take over. Before he closed his eyes, Will saw it again—the framed picture of the two of them.

God, how he hated that man.

FIFTY-SEVEN

When Will woke up the next morning, he pledged he'd tell Amber how he really felt. During the trip. Or after. But today for sure.

After a light breakfast, they set out. After driving forty-five minutes on quaint backroads, they arrived in New Hope, Pennsylvania, a quaint Delaware River town crammed with shops featuring products made by local artisans. The sun shone brightly in a cloud-specked sky. Giant sunbeams highlighted the gentle current of the river.

Everything about New Hope reminded Will of Hannah: the hand-crafted jewelry, the wheel-spun clay pots. Will could picture her, camera bag in tow. She'd stop to take a shot; he and the kids would groan in mock frustration. Will was so deep in thought, the image so real, that he barely registered Amber.

She pulled on his shirt sleeve. "Let's do it! It will be fun!"

Will didn't know what she was talking about.

"You're not scared, are you?"

He looked around. Amber put her hands on his cheeks and turned his head toward the paint-peeled sign: Big Wanda Fortune Telling. A single, dirtied window displayed varied herbs and bottles. Amber grabbed Will's hands and pulled him toward the open doorway. A woman with gray frizzed hair peeking out of a turquoise turban sat at a table.

She stood when they walked in. "I'm Wanda. Fortunes are $20 apiece." Her voice was official, her handshake firm. The difference between the room and Wanda's corporate demeanor set Will off balance. He looked at Amber. She was smiling, apparently still thrilled. He pulled out his wallet, holding the two twenties a second too long. Amber reached for her purse. Will shook his head.

A round table sat in the center of a back room, the focal point of which was a glowing ball, emanating fog. Dozens of flickering candles lined narrow tables set against the walls; a reedy, earthy scent permeated the space. Amber put her hand on Will's shoulder and they made eye contact. Wanda motioned for them to sit.

She shifted her gaze to the crystal ball. She squinted, moving her head close, as though there were actual images inside. Next, she circled her hands around the ball and pointed at Will with a crooked finger. His heart quickened, and he reminded himself it wasn't real. Wanda didn't know him. There were no actual pictures in that ball.

"You have made a choice," she said, her voice now raspy and low. "But are unsure." She paused. Will found himself leaning forward. Amber's hand clutched his.

"A change is coming," she said. "A big change. I see a big change." She looked more closely at the ball, then added, "I see great sadness. I see tragedy." Her hands moved faster. Will was strangely transfixed.

"This change," she continued, "it will be the end of you."

Wanda turned to Amber. "And you," she said.

"Wait." Will put his hand out. "What do you mean the change will be the end of me? What did you see?" Will's words came out more urgently than he intended.

"It's another $20 if you want me to look for more specifics," Wanda said, her corporate voice back.

Oh.

It was a scam.

Will let out a breath he hadn't realized he'd been holding. "No thanks."

Wanda shrugged and continued with Amber whose fortune was the equivalent of rainbows and unicorns, most likely to contrast against his ominous fate. When they got up, Will looked back at the ball. It was white. He was stupid.

They stepped out into the sunshine. "Today may be the end of you!" Amber said, joking.

Will laughed but Wanda's words echoed in his mind. Great sadness. Tragedy. A change of heart. Was Wanda talking about his marriage? Will shook his head. He had just met the woman.

Amber's voice interrupted his thoughts.

"Join me, Will!" She motioned to a spot by the water and pulled out her phone. "Double selfie by the river!"

Will shook his head and held out his hand. "I'm good."

Amber took a selfie alone, then a second. She examined the pictures then held out the phone for a third shot.

It occurred to Will then that he'd never seen Hannah take a selfie. In fact, they had few pictures of her at all, as she was the photographer of the family. They'd have to change that. They'd get her in more of the pictures. Then Will suddenly realized the error.

There was no "they" anymore.

Even if he broke up with Amber, Hannah might not want him back. Why would she?

Will followed Amber the rest of the day in a daze, looking for a good time to bring up the obvious. This wasn't working. He allowed Amber to pull him into various stores, the last of which featured bohemian clothing for women. Will sat perched on an uncomfortable cushion while Amber tried on clothes. The owner's dog, a tiny pug with a leather studded collar, yipped at his feet. When Will went to pet him, he nipped his hand. Amber strutted out of the dressing room in a beige, tight dress, turning back and forth to admire herself in the mirror before turning to him.

"What do you think?" She cocked her head as if waiting for the expectant praise.

"Not the best color for you." Will picked up the pug.

Amber's face fell. The store owner swooped in. "Nonsense. It's gorgeous. She's gorgeous." He put a long, beaded necklace over Amber's head and stood back. "Perfect."

Amber looked at Will for approval. He shrugged.

"Will?"

"The necklace looks good with it," he said finally. "You should get it."

She looked at herself again, then at him. "The color? Okay now?"

"Beautiful. Not sure what I was thinking." Will tapped his foot. The pug wriggled out of his arms and pounced on it.

The store owner wrapped the dress and necklace in tissue and placed both gently in a reusable bag. "Gorgeous," he whispered to Amber.

They weaved through the town on their way back to the car.

"What's wrong?" Amber grabbed his hand. "You're so quiet today, Will."

"Just tired." He couldn't muster the energy for "the conversation."

They spoke little in the car. Amber drove while Will leaned back and closed his eyes. The sun began to dip as afternoon turned to evening. After twenty minutes, Amber flipped on music, Coldplay lyrics filling the car. He'd introduced Amber to Coldplay. She said she loved it. Did she? Who knew?

Will lost himself in the drive, eyes closing and opening at random. After too long, he realized Amber had turned off the highway. He sat up.

"I have to show you something." Amber navigated the car passed boarded up shops, abandoned factories, and the occasional store with an 'open' sign lit up in red neon.

Groups of people gathered on corners, on steps, in parking lots. Will sat up straighter. Where were they? Just as he was about to say something, Amber stopped the car in front of a worn-down brick building. A man with a pit bull and a group of teenagers stood out front. An overweight woman sat on the steps with a screaming baby, two toddlers in sagging diapers on the lawn in front of her. "Shut that baby up!" someone yelled. The pit bull growled.

After a moment, Amber spoke. "This is where I grew up." She pointed to a corner in front of the building. "That's where my mom used to get drugs. I used to watch her from my window." She paused, staring at the spot, then continued, "She'd hand over all our money for a little bag. I'd think 'no, no, no, don't do it.' But she always did. Then she would come back and lock herself in her room. And that would be it. We wouldn't see her for a day or more." She looked out the window. "I was only five the first time she disappeared like that. I ate stale bread for two days because that's all we had."

She stared out the window. Will opened his mouth to say something but, remembering his own childhood, shut it. His childhood experience was little league and after-school snacks, birthdays with homemade cakes. He knew nothing of this. He could offer nothing to Amber.

Almost reading his thoughts, Amber looked at him. "Have you ever eaten stale bread for a meal, Will?"

She drove him to Scotty's house in silence.

FIFTY-EIGHT

Will slept fitfully, his mind jumbling images of the needy woman in New Hope with a big-eyed child staring at the closed door of her mother's bedroom. There would always be pieces of Amber that he would never understand, layers of unstated experiences pulsing underneath, driving her actions. Her complex background made Will feel inadequate.

And he missed his wife.

Will had to act; yet, he sat on Scotty's couch, paralyzed. Amber's text came at 11:30.

I'm out front. Ready for the game.

Will looked out front. Amber sat behind the wheel of her car in a tight Phillies sweatshirt, her hair in two low braids. Shit. Will had asked Amber to the Phillies pre-season game weeks ago. He'd forgotten. He scrambled to get ready. He'd tell her on the way there. Or back. Today. Will said the word out loud. "Today."

Will got into the car. Amber had drawn a little P (for Phillies) on her cheek. Between the "P" and the braids, she looked years younger. Will stared at his own image in the side mirror. He might be mistaken for her father.

"About last night—" Will started.

"I don't want to talk about it." She waved her hand. "I just thought you should know."

"I'm sorry."

"Thanks." They drove in silence, the sound of the radio serving as a substitute for conversation. Twice Will tried to tell her.

At the ticket gate, the attendant gave them each bobbleheads. Amber was thrilled. "Which one is this?" she said, holding it up, its head wiggling.

"Aaron Nola." Will handed her his. "Here."

"Twins!" she yelled, holding them out in front of her as she walked. On the way to their seats, Amber stopped in front of "run the bases," an interactive game where four contestants run in place on mats while their corresponding digital players run on the screen. The winner of each round got a prize.

"I'm playing!" Amber insisted. She handed Will the two Aaron Nolas and got in line. When it was her turn, Amber stepped up with a bunch of ten-year-olds. Will stood with the parents. The irony was not lost on him.

Today.

When the game started, Amber ran in place and her digital figure ran around the bases. "I'm rounding third!" she called out, her legs pumping faster. Her avatar gained on that of a freckled kid in a Phanatic T-shirt. She edged him out at the finish line.

"I won!" she squealed. The attendant handed her a coupon. "Lunch is on me!" She showed Will the coupon for a free cheesesteak at the Citizens Bank Park location for Tony Luke's. She waved it over her head as she moved toward the Tony Luke stand.

"No cheesesteaks!" Will bit out the words before he realized how silly they sounded.

Amber turned. "But you love cheesesteaks."

"I'm just not in the mood for Tony Luke's. Let's try Chickie's and Pete's. We'll get crab fries." Amber looked at her coupon; Will could tell she was about to protest. "Save it for later," he said. She nodded and put it in the back pocket of her jeans, its white edge sticking out like a flag.

They got the food from Chickie's and found a standing table. They watched the Phillies warm up. When they were done eating, Amber bought herself a Phillies baseball hat with the same insignia that she had drawn on her cheek. She placed it on her head backwards. Will immediately noticed how much younger she looked wearing the hat. God. She looked like a teenager.

Will looked around to make sure there was no one he knew. He'd once been proud to stand by Amber. Now he felt ridiculous.

They walked down the aisle to their seats on the first baseline. A concession vendor walked down the stairs in front of them. "Popcorn here. Popcorn here." A man held up his hand, and the vendor stopped. They walked around him. Once in their seats, Amber took another selfie. Will texted Hannah on impulse.

What do you think of Nola?

Knowing how much she liked Cole Hamels, he smiled and sent another.

He'll be better than Hamels ;)

Her response was immediate.

No way!

Will smiled and typed his response. Yes way. BTW what do you think of Franco?

Hannah's response came back. He'll be good. Did solid in Clearwater.

Will began to type again. Engrossed, he barely registered Amber's question. "Whatcha doing?"

He looked up briefly. "Just texting a buddy." He resumed typing. I like Hoskins.

Charlie LOVES Hoskins.

Will paused. He didn't know Charlie liked Rhys Hoskins, the Phillies' left fielder.

"Everyone please rise for our National Anthem," the announcer said.

As a local school choir sang, Will thought about the fact that, a year ago, he would have known what player Charlie liked. He should know. He was his father.

After the song, Will's phone pinged.

Me and the kids are at the game.

Will read the text twice before digesting it. Hannah was here. His kids were here. His heartbeat accelerated as he scanned the crowd.

Amber put her hand on his thigh. "What's wrong? You seem nervous."

"It's nothing. Thought a friend of mine might be here." Will spun around to look at the people in the seats above him. A moment later, he received another text from Hannah.

I should have asked you to join us. Sorry.

Np. Will wrote back. He whipped his head around at the crowd again then responded to Hannah's text.

Where u at?

Third base line. Second level.

Will scoured the section. Because the crowds were sparse, he found them almost immediately, two redheads and a blonde. The kids had cotton candy, Hannah centered between them. Will imagined himself sitting with them, pretending he was about to take a huge bite of the puffy snack. As his open mouth neared their treat, the kids would squeal, "No, Daddy! Get your own!" And Hannah would smile at him with the exasperated look of someone who was not actually exasperated at all.

Will jumped when everyone started clapping. Bryce Harper had hit a triple. He watched Hannah high-five the kids.

Next to him, Amber clapped. "Way to go Phillies!"

The game went on with torturously long innings. Twice, Will suggested they leave early. "But it's tied, "Amber said, suddenly a fan.

After the seventh inning stretch, Amber grabbed his hand. "Ice cream?"

"No."

"Well just walk with me then." She tried to pull him up. "Come on, Will. Stretch your legs."

"I'm good here."

Her eyes flashed with hurt. "All right then. I'll be back."

As she bounded up the stadium stairs, Will looked at Hannah and the kids. He pulled out his phone. What a game.

Will watched Hannah begin to type. He couldn't make out her face, but imagined she was smiling.

Kids are loving it.

Great.

They got Aaron Nola bobbleheads!

Will looked at the two bobbleheads by his feet and texted back. They'll love those.

Amber returned with a waffle cone overflowing with chocolate ice cream. She licked it sensuously then tipped it toward him, raising one eyebrow. Will shook his head. She shrugged and took an exaggerated lick of the cone. The man next to them stared.

As the teams switched for the bottom of the eighth, a heart appeared on the massive stadium scoreboard with the insignia "Phils Kiss Cam." The Beatles song, "All You Need is Love" blared on the speakers. Will watched the screen as an older couple pecked each other briefly; then a Mom kissed a baby on the head. Two friends in Phillies shirts hugged.

Will didn't see it coming.

He and Amber were on the screen, supersized caricatures of a cliché. Amber smiled at the image before turning her head toward Will and leaning in for a kiss, her lips a red 'O'.

Cheers and catcalls erupted around them. Someone yelled out, "Hunky Hubby."

Oh God. No.

Will backed away. Amber looked shocked. Light laughter filled the stadium.

The camera moved to another couple but, a moment later, their side by side images were on the screen again. More cheers, louder now. Will pecked Amber's cheek.

When the camera moved away, Will looked at the spot where Hannah and the kids had been sitting. The seats were empty. Thank God. They hadn't seen it. Then, he spotted them walking up the stairs toward the exit to their section.

"I've got to go," he told Amber.

Will bolted up the stairs, two, three at a time and ran through the corridor of Citizens Bank Park. He weaved through spectators buying merchandise and spun around kids holding ice cream in plastic baseball caps. He knocked into a man holding two beers, the yellow liquid sloshing about his feet.

"Sorry," Will mumbled, not stopping.

He circled the dark space twice, his head pivoting as he ran. In a last-ditch effort, he ran outside the stadium.

"Hannah!" He wildly scanned the area. "Hannah!"

They were gone.

FIFTY-NINE

Hannah

They pushed through the crowd, Hannah holding Charlie's hand too tightly. Amanda trailed behind.

"Was that Dad?" Charlie whispered.

"Shh!" Amanda hissed.

"Who was that girl?" Charlie asked.

Hannah couldn't speak.

"Shut up, Charlie," Amanda hissed again.

They stepped out of the stadium. Hannah pulled in a breath. Charlie wrapped his arms around her waist in a tight hug; Amanda sat on a bench. Hannah struggled with the truth. Will had been texting her all day while he sat a few hundred feet away with another woman. In plain sight. What a laugh they must have had.

Stupid.

And to think she had thought about giving him another chance. To think that she had missed him. Hannah thought she saw him, weeks back, watching her as she entered a restaurant to meet Charlotte and Jess. She had wanted to stop and talk to him. But pride had compelled her forward. If he wanted Amber, well, what did she care? And, though she had said yes to the show, she'd been regretful. Her marriage was ending. She wasn't ready. Just yesterday, she'd called Rachel to express her reservations.

Amanda's voice pulled her out of her thoughts. "So when's the divorce?" She stared at Hannah, green eyes squinting in the sunlight.

Charlie let go, leaving a circle of warmth where his small arms had been. "What divorce?"

There was no escaping it now. Hannah may not have been ready, but Will certainly was.

"Mom?" Charlie prompted.

She and Will should be having this conversation together. Hannah looked away to gather strength. She gazed in the direction of the stadium and, through the open arcs, saw a man running. He looked like Will.

Hannah shook her head.

No. It was not Will. He was with Amber now. She needed to accept that.

Hannah sat next to Amanda on the bench and pulled Charlie down beside her. She put an arm around each of them. Skinny. They were so skinny. Had she not been feeding them these past months?

"Mom?" Charlie said again.

She could tell them the truth. Their father was a cheating bastard. An asshole. A liar.

She opened her mouth to say it.

She wanted to say it.

She couldn't say it.

Hannah's mother's voice echoed in her mind. Your father doesn't love us. Your father is a liar. Ask your father for the money. I can't believe you would want to see him.

No.

"Mommy? Are you alright?" Charlie's asked.

Hannah registered Amanda's hand on her back, gently stroking. She'd turned her eleven-year-old daughter into the parent. She had to retain control.

"Listen." Hannah moved from the bench and squatted before them. Their eyes were on her, intense, waiting.

"Daddy and I will always love some part of each other. And, for sure, we will both always love you." She took a breath. "But Mom and Dad are not going to live together anymore. We will still be a family but a different kind of family." Charlie opened his mouth, but Amanda put her hand on his shoulder to stop him. "It was nothing either of you did."

They said nothing, but the worry was apparent in their eyes.

"It won't be that different than it is now." Hannah had no idea how that could possibly be true. "Some days with Mom. Some days with Dad."

When neither child said anything, Hannah began to panic. Had she botched this, her first act as a single mother? Was there something else she should say? Then Amanda stood, pulled Hannah up, and wrapped her arms around her. Charlie followed suit. They stood, moored together, the three of them, in the sun. As they stood, a heavyset man sat on the end of the bench. A woman walked by with a dog. Cheers erupted from the stadium. Life moved on, their circle of change impacting no one around them.

"Will that woman marry Dad?" Charlie asked, releasing her.

Hannah stood back. "I don't know." A vision of it began to take hold and she shook it away. Nothing had happened yet.

Her phone pinged. Will.

I'm sorry.

Hannah stared at the two words and typed her response.

Me too.

Hannah switched the phone to off and took each of her children by the hand.

"Come on, now, let's go home."

SIXTY

That night, after the kids were asleep, Hannah called Rachel.

"It's happening," she choked out. "The divorce." Hannah explained to Rachel about the game and the texts and her false sense that Will wanted her back. "And then they were on the screen. It felt like a joke. They were there, huge, larger-than-life images. And the crowd was cheering."

"Oh my God, Hannah, I'm so sorry."

Hannah let the tears she held back all day trickle down her face. "So I definitely want to do the show," she said, collecting herself. "I know I said I might not want to but, clearly, Will does. So I'll do it. What do I have to sign?"

"Are you sure?" Rachel's tone sounded doubtful.

"Wouldn't you be?"

Rachel nodded. "Of course. I'll call David Dewey tomorrow. Do you need me to come over?"

"No. I'm alright."

Rachel protested; Hannah insisted she was fine.

"Call me if you change your mind," Rachel said. "I can be there in less than an hour."

"I'll call if I need you."

Hannah switched off the phone and trudged up the stairs. She put on old sweats, climbed into bed, and pulled the comforter so far up it almost obscured her face. When she closed her eyes, all she could see were the images of Amber and Will on the big screen. She didn't remember falling asleep.

In the morning, Charlie shook her awake. "Are you okay Mommy?" he whispered.

Hannah opened her eyes and saw his small figure, worry evident on his face. She sat up.

"I am okay, Charlie." She patted the bed and he climbed in next to her. "How are you doing?"

"I'm alright." Hannah fought the temptation to insist Charlie expand on his feelings. There would be plenty of time for that later. He needed to digest what happened. They all did.

Hannah ruffled his hair. "Do you want some pancakes, handsome?"

Charlie's face registered relief at the normal question. "Yeah, that'd be great."

"Okay. Go get dressed and meet me in the kitchen."

Charlie scrambled off. Hannah's phone buzzed. She grabbed it off the nightstand. Texts and messages from Will filled her phone. She deleted them.

The next morning, once the kids were off on the bus, someone knocked on the door.

Hannah looked out her bedroom window. Will stood on the doorstep, unshaven. "Hannah, are you in there?"

Hannah wanted to open the door. But she forced herself not to, remembering the image of Will and Amber at the game, at Christmas, from that karaoke night nearly a year ago. She would not be taken in again! Her psyche could not handle another Jumbotron moment.

Hannah stepped into the bathroom and turned on the shower. She could hear Will's knocking over the water. She removed her clothes and stepped inside. When she emerged, skin red and wet, he was gone.

Will showed up again the next day with a bouquet of irises. She looked at him in the driveway and shook her head. As if a few flowers could possibly serve as an adequate apology.

She called Rachel.

"Did you talk to Will's attorney? Did you tell him I want to move ahead?"

"Yes. I talked to him yesterday. Why?"

"Will keeps trying to contact me. He's here, right now, knocking."

"And you don't want to talk to him?" Rachel asked, sounding hopeful. It was almost as if she had a personal stake in Hannah's marriage.

"I can't talk to him, Rachel. If I talk to him, I'll cave. It's taken a lot for me to get to the point where I am okay with this. I can't get drawn back in."

As she spoke, Hannah looked out the window and watched Will walk back to his truck. She turned away then heard the engine start.

"Can you get him to stop coming here?"

"I can write a letter," Rachel offered.

That afternoon, Hannah and the kids sat at kitchen table, a plate of homemade chocolate cookies in the center. Amanda dipped one in milk. "They're good, Mom."

"Thanks." Hannah glanced at her computer. She'd left it on the counter so she'd wouldn't miss the email from Rachel. Nothing yet. She turned as Charlie stuffed a third cookie in his mouth. "I think that's good, Charlie," she said, picking up the plate.

The kids pulled homework from their backpacks; Hannah cleaned up the dishes she'd used to make the cookies. When she finished, Rachel's email was on her computer. She clicked on it. The email contained a draft of the letter she had written for Hannah's approval and read:

Re: Hannah Abbott vs. William Abbott
Docket No.: FM-11-3896-15A

Dear Mr. Dewey,

As you are aware and as I have informed you by telephone and by letter, my client, Hannah Abbott, wishes to pursue the divorce action on the Divorce House program as previously suggested by your client. Notwithstanding my client's clear intention to move ahead, Mr. Abbott has insisted upon harassing her with multiple texts, emails, and phone messages. More outrageous, he has come to the marital residence—of which my client has exclusive possession per the November consent order—on three occasions, unannounced, uninvited, and unwanted.

Please instruct your client to immediately cease and desist all contact with Ms. Abbott or she will file legal action against him. Please advise, also, whether Mr. Abbott is amenable to finalizing the divorce on Divorce House as travel arrangements to St. John need to be made in short order.

Very truly yours,
Rachel Goldstein

Hannah read the letter three times. It was strong. It was harsh. It was what she had asked for. It wouldn't go out without her approval. Hannah's fingers hovered over the keyboard. She shut her eyes. This was it. She typed the word.

Approved.

SIXTY-ONE

Hannah stepped onto her flight to St. John and found her seat. She put her luggage overhead and slid into her window seat.

She was glad she'd booked a different flight from Rachel's. Rachel was going to St. John for her wedding; she was going for her divorce. It was a strange dynamic that had strained many of their final conversations. And, since Rachel was leaving the firm, Jack Connors would be her lawyer on the show. Rachel had assured her she would be there if Hannah needed her, but they both knew she wouldn't call. This was the point, it seemed, at which their paths would diverge. Rachel would go on to a life of multiple homes and black-tie dinners; Hannah would return to her home in New Jersey, alone.

A silver-haired couple sat in the two seats adjacent to Hannah. After putting away their belongings and chatting about grandchildren and dogs, the man reached for the woman's hand. He interlocked his fingers between the woman's just as Will used to with hers. Hannah squeezed her eyes shut. She'd always thought she and Will would grow old together.

When the flight touched down, Hannah retrieved her suitcase from the overhead bin and exited the plane. Almost immediately, she saw a smallish man holding up a sign with her name. As she neared it, a camera flashed.

Hannah turned. A short woman with wild, black hair wearing a bright pink scarf waved at her. "I recognize you," she gushed. "I have tickets to the show finale. Good luck, Hannah! Go get him!" She raised her fist up in what Hannah imagined was meant to be a sign of solidarity.

Hannah smiled. She felt like she was embarking on an athletic endeavor, not divorcing her husband. But that's what social media and reality television did. It made the ordinary seem glamorous.

Hannah strode forward and shook the woman's hand. "Thank you for thinking of me."

"I'm divorced too," she whispered. "It's tough."

Hannah nodded. "Thanks for your support."

The woman waved and Hannah turned to follow the smallish man. He ushered her into a room with several well-dressed people. The network employees introduced themselves.

"I'm Lanie," a woman with bleach blonde hair wearing a tight green dress said. She spoke in a Southern drawl, friendly blue eyes meeting Hannah's.

"Nice to meet you. I'm Hannah."

"Come on. I'll introduce you to everyone here so far." Lanie took Hannah's hand and led her to the small group gathered in the corner. She pointed at a tall man. "This is Peter from Massachusetts. He's a Patriots fan. Don't hold it against him." Lanie moved and touched another man's shoulder. "This is Brad." She pointed to a small woman in an expensive-looking pantsuit. "And this is Tia." Lanie pushed Hannah forward. "Everyone, this is Hannah."

Brad shook her hand, and Tia waved an arm full of bracelets. Peter offered to get her a drink. She accepted and Peter returned with iced tea. "I can't believe they start filming the minute we get out of the limo," he said as he held it out it to her. "I thought we'd have some time to unpack."

Hannah took a sip of tea. "Yes. I have to admit I'm a bit nervous. I'd love to get my bearings first."

"Trial by fire," Peter commented, tipping his head.

The final villa member arrived and the limousine pulled up outside shortly after. The group piled in and took their places on the plush leather seats. Champagne and glasses were set in the center. Lanie popped the cork and poured them each a glass. She held up her own. "To us."

"To us," the group repeated back.

The limo wound through wooded streets, bits of ocean visible in the distance. Peter put on music; Tia poured herself a second glass of champagne. Lanie chatted with Brad about his job as a gastroenterologist. Hannah discreetly poured her drink out and sat back.

The limo rolled to a stop in front of a beautifully landscaped, red-roofed villa on the beach. The driver stepped out and opened the door. Fans lining the walkway screamed. Lanie got out first, followed by Tia. When Hannah emerged, someone yelled, "I love you, Hannah!"

Amidst cheers, Hannah made her way down a torch-lit path lined with fragrant island flowers. When she reached the residence, a uniformed man held open a heavy door with a lion knocker. Hannah stepped into a white-themed room. An arrangement of plush couches sat in front of a majestic fireplace. Porcelain plates of artfully cut fresh fruit, crackers, and cheese were set out on narrow table against one wall. Against another stood a fully-stocked bar with heavy crystal glasses. A sliding glass door to a patio had been left open and a gentle breeze filled the room.

The atmosphere was so relaxing, Hannah almost forgot why she was there.

She poured herself a glass of chardonnay and moved to the patio, only few hundred feet from the ocean. The warm air caressed her arms. Light classical music complemented the sound of gently lapping waves. Colorful flowers adorned every corner of the space in large, overflowing pots. The group shared a bottle of wine, then a second. One of the men got a bottle of vodka for shots. Eventually, complaints about spouses infiltrated the conversation.

Hannah stood at the edge of the group, the fleeting peaceful feeling now gone. She didn't want to be here. She moved to the edge of the patio and took off her heels. She skimmed her feet on the soft, white sand.

"Uh oh," Peter said, spying her. "We got a beach-goer."

Hannah smiled.

Lanie cocked her head to the side. "Well, should we take a swim?" She gestured to the ocean. "I'm game for some skinny dipping."

"Lanie!" Hannah scolded, as if Lanie had been her long-time, crazy friend whose antics she was accustomed to squelching.

Lanie downed her wine. "When in Rome," she said and trotted toward the water. Halfway there she turned, "Come on, y'all!" The group set out toward the water.

Hannah watched their retreating backs.

"I'm not one for skinny dipping."

Hannah startled at the sound of a voice. She thought everyone had gone down to the beach. She turned and Peter stepped into the light.

"No. Me either." Hannah looked again at the shore. "Though I'd like to be free like that."

They both focused on the beach.

"Swimming naked with strangers?" Peter said. "It's overrated."

They both laughed.

"Hey, can I refresh your drink?" Peter held out his hand for her glass. Hannah zeroed in on the white mark on his wedding finger. Peter followed her gaze. "Took the ring off a while back," he explained.

Hannah nodded then looked down at her empty glass, unable to uncurl her fingers from the stem. The overwhelming feeling of wanting to share this moment with Will overtook her ability to speak. She waited too long.

Peter held up his glass. "Okay then. I'm going to fill my own drink." He took a step toward the door then turned. "I wasn't trying to hit on you, you know." The door slammed shut.

Hannah's face reddened. She should just relax. If Will were here, he'd be skinny dipping. In fact, for all Hannah knew, Will was skinny dipping at that very moment. Hannah pictured him, face bobbing above the water, muscled frame blurry underneath.

Move on, Hannah.

She stepped on to the beach and started toward the water.

SIXTY-TWO

The next morning, Hannah woke early, giddy with the memory of the night before. She'd done it. The water had been warm, and Hannah had floated on the surface, feeling the bobbing lull of the waves as her muscles unclenched. The sky had held stars so bright it almost looked like a child's drawing, part of a fanciful world where there might be elves or unicorns. The group sat afterward on the patio, each of them wrapped in thick terrycloth towels. They each told their story. Hannah slept deeply, feeling a part of a community of souls with the same brokenness.

She and Jack Connors were to meet at 1 p.m. with David Dewey and Will for the first of their televised negotiations. Before Hannah left New Jersey, she and Rachel had gone over her settlement positions. Hannah felt prepared, but she knew she couldn't sit all morning and dwell. She put on hiking shoes, packed up her camera, and set out to explore the island.

Hannah walked along the pristine beach and marveled at how different St. John was from Ocean City, New Jersey, her lifelong vacation destination. Rather than a boardwalk teeming with greasy food, cheap T-shirts, and clanking rides, the ocean was buttressed by a forest with lush green trees and mountains rolling off in the distance. Rather than gray and chilly, the water was turquoise and warm with colorful fish visible from the surface. A gentle breeze flowed easily, filling Hannah's senses with the smell of ocean air. It was, in every sense, paradise. And, yet, she missed the familiar.

Hannah pictured herself as a child, parents still together, each holding an arm, as they pulled her up over the crashing waves of the Ocean City beaches. She visualized their rental home, two blocks from the beach, and remembered walking along, laden with beach gear, ready for the day's adventure in the surf.

Fast forwarding, Hannah pictured herself and Will, newly dating, lying on adjacent towels after having lathered each other with sunscreen. She pictured his retreating, muscled back as he ran into the surf without stopping. And she pictured them, years later, with tiny Amanda as she filled buckets with sand, her face fixed with great seriousness at the overwhelming task of getting all that sand into one tiny bucket.

And, like yesterday, Hannah could see the elated look on Charlie's face the first time he dug down by the water and pulled up a sand crab. She could practically taste the New Jersey boardwalk staples: fries, saltwater taffy, fudge. As if the image was in front of her, Hannah could see all of them as they walked along together, a happy family.

Of course, in the nooks and crannies of the good times, there were hard moments. Trying to change newborn Amanda's diaper—a seedy, wet mess—on the beach as sand flew about and fellow beach-goers stared at the crying baby and the frantic, new mother. The sunscreen which, despite heroic efforts to the contrary, would always melt into the kids' eyes. The feeling of impending doom that the surf would sweep Charlie and Amanda out to sea and the corresponding need to constantly look for their heads in the crowded ocean water.

But even these memories, the so-called bad ones, were not really bad as much as less good. They morphed with the fun times; creating a patchwork quilt of memories with happiness as the predominant, recurring theme. It had been, Hannah realized, a different kind of paradise.

But it was over now. She needed to accept that. Hannah pushed the thoughts from her mind, refocusing on the paradise before her. As she got further from the main tourist area, the landscape became rockier and ultimately morphed into giant cliffs along the sea.

Hannah stopped and looked up. If she could get to the top of the cliffs, she'd have a spectacular shot of the island. She climbed carefully, her camera swinging on her back. She lost her footing a few times. Her final step deposited her onto the summit.

Looking down, the scene was spectacular. A tiny, pristine beach in the shape of a triangle, was surrounded on every side by tall cliffs. Palm trees stood tall in front of the cliffs, creating a private forest area. One of the trees had partially fallen and was perpendicular to the water, a tire swing hanging from the end. Clear water lapped at the white beach. Boats peppered the landscape in the distance, looking like toys. Hannah took out her camera.

As she zoomed in, she heard someone giggling. Hannah craned her neck. A bald woman in bright pink bikini stood on the beach.

"Come on," she urged her unseen companion, gesturing to the water.

"Alright, alright," a man with a familiar voice said.

A massive man with no hair walked up to the diminutive woman. David Dewey. The woman ran into the water and David took off his shirt and ran into the surf behind her. He splashed her from behind then swam underneath the water, popping up next to her. They swam out into the cove, bald heads bobbing in the surface.

It was a private moment. She should leave. But she couldn't look away. It touched her, the image. She zoomed in and took a series of shots, stopping after a time to view them. They were good. Great, even. The expressions on their faces showed a complexity of emotion—happiness and sadness bound up together. Hannah felt proud to have captured it but, at the same time, guilty for having done so. It was not her place to make a record of this, to insert herself in the private moment of two strangers. She should delete them.

Hannah began to pack up the camera, but the sound of their laughter caused her to stop and look again. They were swimming toward the tire swing on the palm tree. The woman got on the tire first, flying off in a circle after a big push from David. After she splashed into the water, David climbed on, the tree bending from his weight.

"You're going to break it, Dave!" the woman yelled, and they laughed as he fell into the water, the tree springing back. And then they were kissing, intently, tenderly. Hannah picked up her camera and started shooting again just as David kissed her head and leaned in as if he was whispering something in her ear. The woman pulled back and said something to him and they both smiled. She took a final shot of their faces and left. Whatever happened next was not her business.

The entire walk back to the villa, Hannah thought about the silliness, the tenderness, and the unity David and his girlfriend shared. She found herself surprised that David Dewey was capable of such rich emotion, then thought the judgment unfair. She didn't know him as a man, only as a lawyer. And, while Hannah knew the moment had been theirs, it felt familiar. It had been the kind of love she'd once shared with Will.

By the time she reached the villa, Hannah had slipped into a crushing melancholy. The group greeted her as she walked in and made room at the kitchen table.

"You look like you're worn slap out, Hannah. You okay?" Lanie asked.

Hannah forced herself to speak. "I'm good. Just went for an early morning walk." She touched her camera bag. "I got some great shots."

Lanie narrowed her eyes. "You sure you're okay, sweetie?"

"I'm a little nervous about seeing Will at the negotiation today," Hannah admitted. It wasn't a lie. She hadn't directly communicated with Will since the final text she'd sent outside the stadium.

Hannah was quiet the rest of the morning; she picked at a muffin for lunch. Steven, a network executive, came to pick her up for the meeting a few minutes before 1 p.m. He led her down a twisting, floral-lined pathway. He chattered about it being his first day. Hannah wanted him to stop talking and was grateful when they arrived at a small cottage, their destination. They stepped inside a beautiful sunlit room with wall to wall windows. A circular table with fruit in a crystal bowl stood in the center. David Dewey and Jack Connors sat at opposite ends of the table. They rose as she entered.

"Hannah," Jack said, crossing the room. "This is David Dewey."

She approached David and he shook her hand. Hannah suppressed a giggle at the thought of him swinging off the tire hours earlier.

The three of them sat in silence as they waited for Will. Jack tapped his pen and checked his watch. David grabbed an apple and threw it up in the air like a ball. Hannah observed Steven out the window, pacing on the lawn.

Of course Will was late. Without her to remind him, he'd probably forgotten to set his alarm. Or believed, as he often did, that start times were suggestions, not mandates. At any moment, he'd saunter through the door, flash a perfect smile, and the world would forget they had been inconvenienced.

But he didn't.

Hannah turned and saw David pull out his phone and type a text, presumably to Will. He left the room. Through the window, she saw him on the lawn, talking briefly, then stopping to stare at his phone.

More time elapsed and Steven came in and asked Jack to step outside. The three of them congregated on the lawn with one of the cameramen. Hannah pulled out her phone. Rachel had sent her a message.

How goes it?

Okay. Waiting on Will for a meeting.

Typical.

Rachel's response made Hannah laugh. She sent a smiley face emoji.

The lawyers entered the room trailed by Steven and the cameraman.

"So," Steven started. We are going to have to postpone today's meeting."

"Why?" Hannah asked.

"You see," he said, twisting his hands. "And don't panic about this. But it seems." He stopped to gather himself, adjusting his glasses. "It seems that your husband is missing."

SIXTY-THREE

David left the meeting. He felt a little sorry for Hannah. She'd looked upset, maybe because she wanted to rid herself of Will as soon as possible.

Personally, David could care less where Will was. The man was an asshole. He was probably out with one of the women in the villa. And now, instead of sitting in a meeting, he could spend the afternoon with Jenny. On the beach? In their room? David's gait quickened as he thought of additional time with her. He started down the path to the hotel.

Jack Connors caught up to him, trailed by a cameraman.

"If he's a no-show, then it's a no-go," he said. "My client should just get what she wants."

David stopped, turned, and shook his head. "It doesn't work that way." He began to walk again. Jack followed.

"No guy, no try."

David stopped and gave Jack another long, hard look. "What's with the rhymes?"

"If he's not here, there is no deal," Jack said in response, the cameraman filing the encounter.

"That's not a rhyme," David responded. "Why don't you try this one: what the fuck, you're a schmuck." The cameraman guffawed.

"You're an asshole, Dewey."

David shrugged. "So they say."

David continued down the pathway, Jack and the still-laughing cameraman left behind. He smelled fresh bacon and followed the scent. Tucked away on a secluded path was a small building with a thatched roof and an array of lunch foods. A grill with bacon and sausage sizzled in the background, and fresh cookies laden with thick icing sat in glass covered containers.

"Lunch, sir?"

David thought of Jenny. They could eat on their small deck overlooking the water, read the paper, take a walk. He ordered two sandwiches. The woman behind the stand handed him the bag. When he turned, Hannah Abbott was standing behind him.

"Oh." David stepped back in surprise.

She gave a quick wave. "I know this may seem strange. But could you let me know when you find him?"

David was distracted for a moment. Her eyes were a stunning shade of green. "Sure," he said, stumbling over the word.

"My number," she said and handed him a small paper.

David stared at the numbers in neat penmanship.

She laughed. "Sounds like a proposition, doesn't it?"

David looked up from the paper. It took him a minute to realize she'd made a joke. He laughed, ashamed for having villainized this woman for the past nine months, for having encouraged Will to abide by his standard "no holds barred" approach. Part of him wanted to tell her that the whole "your husband is missing" thing was possibly staged by the network. That it was possible that, as they stood there, Will was safe and waiting, ready to reappear dramatically at the perfect time. But, having no evidence of this, it seemed reckless to say so.

"Look," she said, meeting his eyes. "I know we're getting divorced, but a part of me will always love Will. That might sound weird." She looked down then back up at David. "But I think you know what I mean. Some types of love will just always be a part of you. No matter what happens."

David thought of his morning with Jenny. The look on her face when he'd told her, "I love you," her small, pretty voice when she said it back. David could still feel her body hugged around him in the warm water. They had stayed on the beach for more than an hour afterward. They talked about their fabricated future together—where they would live, what they would do for vacations, their pretend, perfect jobs. Then, suddenly, Jenny had started to cry. "David," she'd said finally. "What took you so long?"

Hannah's voice brought him back to the present. "So, you'll call me then? When you find him."

"Yes," David held up the paper with her phone number then slid it in his pocket. "I will."

"Okay. Thanks." She grabbed David's hand and squeezed it briefly. "And good luck with everything." She winked at him.

They parted and, walking back to the hotel with the sandwiches, David realized that Jenny might be sleeping, getting the rest she needed to combat her disease. David changed course and walked toward the beach that they had found that morning. He'd take some pictures with his phone. To remember.

As David walked along the tree-lined path toward the beach, he thought about Hannah. She was what any man would want: pretty, quietly strong, caring. And then he pictured Amber: young, vivacious, ambitious. Two compelling women, neither able to let go of their love for the same man.

Like a jealous teenager, David began to wonder what Will Abbott had that was so spectacular. What about Will Abbott caused a woman like Amber—one courted and desired by dozens of men—to fall into sadness and depression after their break-up? What about him would make a woman like Hannah—a woman whom he had publicly left—continue to care about his well-being?

Still thinking of Will, David walked down the sunlit path leading to the small beach. His dislike of the man intensified to the point where it felt unnatural. He'd represented worse men. Men that wanted to level their wives financially and emotionally. Men that lied about their income. Men that cheated. Selfish men. Ugly men. David didn't like those clients, but he saw them for what they were: a means to an end. With Will, it had felt personal. Will was like a spoiled child who, having been given the world, had no appreciation for the precious.

David found a spot under a tree by the beach and sat down. He removed his shoes and socks and buried his feet in the warm, white sand. The area was more crowded than it had been earlier. Two kids swung on the tire, falling into the ocean with tiny splashes. A family picnicked on the beach; a couple lay on a single towel, their hands entwined. David forced Will Abbott from his mind. After this weekend, he would be out of his life for good.

David lay back directly on the sand, feeling the warmth of the sun that peeked through the tree limbs. He closed his eyes. In a half-sleep, David imagined Jenny getting stronger, the cancer shrinking smaller and smaller until, finally, it disappeared into nothingness. He visualized them walking on a beach—on this beach—a tiny, long-haired child trailing behind. David felt Jenny's body next to his and fought to stay awake long enough to keep the sensation present. Eventually, he succumbed to sleep, the happy pictures of the future falling away into the darkness of slumber.

David awoke with a start. He looked at his watch. Two hours had passed. David cursed himself as he ran his hands over his face. With his fair skin, he would be sunburned in the places not obscured by the tree. Jenny would tease him about it; he smiled at the thought. Gathering himself, David picked up his shoes and started toward the little path which led away from the beach. As he reached it, David saw a familiar figure standing at the entrance.

Will Abbott was waiting for him.

SIXTY-FOUR

"Good sleep?" Will asked, blocking the path.

David stared at Will, registering the sadness in his eyes. He resembled a hologram without its light source, a faint image of what he could be.

"Sorry," Will said, sheepishly. "Didn't want to wake you. Can we talk?"

David gestured toward a rocky ledge on a nearby cliff. Will followed him; they leaned back and looked at the still water.

"I'm sorry about this morning," Will said. "I just couldn't face her."

"The network thinks you're missing," David told him. "Hannah's worried about you."

Will shook his head. A ball from a game of paddleball rolled in front of him. Will picked it up and threw it back. "I don't want to have the meeting. I just want to give Hannah what she wants."

Waves crashed against the beach. David stared at the white caps on top, waiting for Will to continue.

"I don't want to get a divorce, but I think Hannah would be better off without me." He kicked his foot. "I've hurt her. I've been terrible. I've been selfish. I don't deserve her, even if she wanted me back. Which she doesn't, not that I blame her." He paused. "My father would be so ashamed of me," he said, as if talking to himself. "He always treated my mother like no one else in the world mattered." He looked into the distance for a moment before turning back to David. "So, can you just tell her lawyer that I'll sign whatever she wants?"

David remembered saying those exact words to his own lawyer. He had signed his divorce agreement, scarcely reading it. His lack of care in that moment cost him everything. Until Jenny. Forgetting his warm feelings for Hannah, David said, "Don't do it."

Anger overtook Will's features. "No. You will not talk me out of this. Hannah isn't going to screw me. Not every woman is a bitch." He stepped away from the ledge. "Half of the problems in this whole situation are because of you. Because of your advice. I did everything you said and look where it got me."

David paused. He recalled his earlier angry thoughts about how Will had taken advantage of Amber. "Really?" He pushed away from the ledge and stood directly in front of Will. "Did I force you to take advantage of a twenty-two year old? Have you thought at all about Amber?"

David stepped closer to Will. "Do you know who she called when you left her stranded at the baseball stadium? Me. Jesus. Who does that? Who do you think you are?" David pictured

Amber as she stood alone outside the complex, her hair in the same braids she had worn as a girl. "And I met your wife this morning. Lovely woman. Beautiful and kind. What exactly was it about her that wasn't good enough? Or did you just want to fuck around with a woman half your age?"

Will punched David's left jawbone hard. He stumbled back, stunned, holding his face.

Testosterone coursed through David's body. He made a fist and landed a right hook on Will's jaw. Will fell and David pounced, pinning him against the sand. "What was it?" David yelled as Will clawed at him.

Someone shouted, "It's a fight!" A crowded gathered.

"What was it!?" David yelled again. Will punched him on the mouth. He tasted blood. David lost his balance and Will pushed him away, jumping to his feet. David countered his move, the two of them now circling each other. Will jumped forward and David moved back. They continued their circle, neither of them making a move but neither of them stopping either. And then David saw Steven, a cameraman by his side. The camera light was green.

"Hey!" David said, stopping the dance with Will for a moment. "You can't do that. You can't film us. This isn't part of the show."

Steven motioned to the cameraman to cut. "You signed a contract," he said. "We... we can film you anywhere."

David took a step forward. Will put his hand on his shoulder. "It's not worth it."

David shrugged his hand off. Still pissed, he started toward the entrance to the beach.

"I'm sorry," Will said, catching up. "I'm not sure what happened."

David waved him away. "I provoked you. Forget it. It's not the first fight I've been in. You did knock my tooth loose though." David opened his mouth to show him.

"Jesus. I'm sorry. I—"

David laughed. "It was loose already. Like I said, this ain't my first rodeo."

Will fell into step with David and they walked up the path together. After a moment, he broke the silence. "I cared about her, you know."

"Amber?"

"Yes, Amber. And not because she's beautiful. I mean, that's part of it, but it was more than that. She was spontaneous, willing to take risks. And she was layered. You'd think you knew her and then she would say something, and you'd think 'I didn't see that coming.' She surprised me and I got drawn in. I couldn't think straight. I know that sounds cheap but it's true." He stopped. "Then, one day, I woke up and I really wanted to talk to Hannah. I'd wanted to before, but it was different that time. Like a need. I became fixated on it. I kept thinking that I saw her. In the store, on the street. I would catch up to the person and then it would be someone else. It drove me crazy." He paused for a moment before continuing, "I didn't want to hurt Amber so I just kept going. But all I wanted was my wife. And then we went to that Phillies game."

Will stopped walking and David turned to look at him. "Is she okay?"

David thought about Amber and, again, pictured her humiliated face outside the stadium. But Amber was strong and young. She would not let Will Abbott be the pivot in her life that changed everything for the worse. David would make sure of it.

"She will be."

"I know it's too late for me and Hannah. That's why it's so important to me that she gets what she needs, what she deserves. Can you talk to her lawyer?"

"As your lawyer, I have to tell you that—"

"I know. Just do it. Please." Will said, interrupting.

David remembered the look of concern on Hannah's face when she thought Will was missing. He recalled her words: Some types of love will always be a part of you. No matter what happens.

"I think you should talk to her."

"I tried. Believe me."

"Well," David said, disbelieving that he was trying to help Will Abbott. "You are allowed that last chance dinner. She has to go if you want it. It's in the contract."

Will stood for a moment, his eyes intensely blue against the backdrop of the sky. "First, tell her attorney I'll give her what she wants. Then ask for the dinner."

"But what's the point of the dinner—"

"I want to say goodbye," Will said, interrupting again. "I mean, I know I'll see Hannah again, obviously. We have kids together. But that's Hannah as a mother. I need to say goodbye to my wife. I need to tell her…" He paused and looked at the ground. "There's so much I need to tell her," he said, as he looked back up at David. "Can you just ask for the dinner?"

"I will."

They walked until they reached Will's villa.

Will shook David's hand. "Thank you."

"Good luck, Will,"

As Will retreated down the path, David tried to hate him again.

SIXTY-FIVE

That evening, Jenny held an icepack to David's face as they sat in padded chaises by a tropical pool. Sparkling waters sat on the table between them.

"So you're going to talk to Jack Connors," she said. "Give him the offer."

"I have to. Will's the client and he requested it."

"But you don't want to."

David looked out at the surface of the water and then at Jenny, her face illuminated by the flames of the surrounding torches. "It's not that." David sat up; Jenny removed the ice pack.

David wasn't sure if he wanted to reveal how he felt to Jenny who, without reason, loved him. He had enough flaws without conjuring up more.

Still, needing to talk to someone, David continued, "It's just that this whole case has made me question who I am. Not just who I am but what I've believed in. What I've tried to do. I thought I was helping people, helping men like me not get caught in the cycle I did. And now." David paused, gathering his thoughts. "And now I wonder if I haven't done more harm than good."

Jenny didn't respond. David imagined Jenny felt it too, the weight of his realization. The angst he had caused countless families in the name of justice. The wives, afraid to take him on, stuck in a cycle of "just getting by." Children caught in the crossfire. Men living in bitterness.

"You can't change the past, David," Jenny said, finally. "And who's to say you didn't save someone? Who's to say some man out there doesn't have a better life because of you, because of your counsel? Who's to say all of them don't?"

David stared at the ground. Jenny tipped his head up to meet her eyes. "You gave your clients the best of you. All of them. That's all you can ever do. And the fact that you are sitting here worrying about them, still, shows what a good man you are. You don't have to be perfect. You're human." She kissed him lightly on the lips. "I love you. I don't think you'll ever know how much."

Her words filled the empty parts of him, making David feel whole in a way he had never experienced. How would he ever go on without her?

The next morning, David felt strangely at peace. The idea of giving Jack Connors exactly what he wanted would normally have given rise to a spectrum of negative emotions. But instead, all he felt was happiness. He felt Jenny's small body next to his. He kissed the top of her head and got up to get ready.

When David arrived at the outdoor seating area for breakfast, Jack was already sitting. The ocean, the white sand, the tiny yellow birds which hopped about the patio, all of it created an idyllic scene in which Jack, scowling and angry, seemed out of place. Further down on the beach, black-suited people scurried about on the adjacent lawn area, setting up chairs for what looked like a wedding ceremony.

David approached the table. "Jack."

"David. You wanted to meet?"

David sighed, suddenly not wanting to give Jack the satisfaction of easy victory. He pictured Will's face on the beach, his words echoing in his mind: It's important to me that she gets what she needs. Please. Just do it.

"My client wants to give your client whatever she wants."

Jack straightened. "He's giving in?"

The waitress filled David's mug with coffee. "If you want to put it that way." He took a sip.

"So I just write the agreement. All the terms. And he'll sign it."

"That is what he would like to do."

Jack's face fell. "And you? You're going to sit back and let Hannah Abbott trample over your client? You of all people should know better."

· David cringed. A yellow bird landed on their table. He watched it peck and hop as he continued, "This isn't about me," he said with resolve. "This is about them."

Jack pounded his hand down on the table and the bird flew away. "Suit yourself." He stood up and reached into his pocket.

"Wait—" David said. "He wants the last chance dinner. It's in the—"

"Contract," Jack interrupted. "I've read it. I'll tell her."

As Jack removed a twenty from his money-clip, David felt a sudden need to advocate for Will. "He still loves her," he said. "Could you tell her that?"

Jack threw the money on the table and looked at David, his eyes intense. "What is the matter with you, Dewey?" He looked around the patio area. "Are we on the air? Is that it?"

"We are not on the air. I just thought your client would want to know."

Jack shook his head and left.

David got up and headed toward the hotel, past the wedding area. A few men worked to assemble a large archway at the end of an aisle with noisy drills and hammers. A pixie-like woman with short blonde hair directed their actions.

As he stepped on the lawn, a woman in a hotel robe barreled through the chairs in front of him, upturning the last one. Her straight black hair streamed behind. A short, well-dressed man chased after her. "Wait, Rachel!" he yelled. "Stop! For the love of God, stop and listen to reason!"

The woman continued to run down the beach, finally stumbling into the sand. The man caught up. The woman's mouth moved, but David couldn't make out the words over the drills and hammers. He squinted. David was sure he had seen this woman before.

The man stood over her, his body language neutral. The contrast in their emotions disturbed David more than it would have had they both been yelling. Concerned for the woman's safety, David stepped forward. He recognized her then. The woman was Rachel Goldstein.

The drilling stopped, and David heard Rachel's words loud and clear.

"I will not marry you, Aaron."

SIXTY-SIX

"Rachel. I will give you some time to gather yourself. At 11:30 a.m., I expect you to be at the wedding brunch." Aaron spoke in a calm voice. "You will not make me look stupid in front of everyone important to me."

Rachel stepped forward. "Everyone important to you? I'm going to be your wife, Aaron."

"Exactly. Which is why you need to stop this nonsense."

"You went behind my back. You told me you booked our honeymoon so I could go on a safari. You made me believe it was about me when really it was about you and your business deal. You actually thought I would be okay with you taking clients on a canned hunting trip, that you planned the kill the same lions you and I would see on the tour."

Aaron shook his head. "Business is business, Rachel. I don't expect you to understand. I do expect you to drop this childish obsession with animals. The lions are raised to be hunted."

Rachel leaned forward and shouted. "Exactly, Aaron! It's horrific. Lion farms raise them from cubs not to be afraid of humans. All so they can be more easily shot. Do you—"

Aaron squeezed her upper arm so hard she stopped talking. He leaned closer and whispered. "Rachel, you are causing a scene. I am going to walk back to the hotel now. I will see you at 11:30." He dropped her arm, turned, and walked toward the hotel.

Rachel held her arm where Aaron had squeezed. "Murderer!" she screamed after him. He did not turn around.

Rachel fell to the sand, breathless. She felt unhinged. Had she really just called off her wedding? Over lions? She was insane! She needed someone to talk to. Her mother would be furious; Lexi and Samantha would think she was crazy.

Hannah.

Rachel got up and started to walk in the direction of the path that led to Hannah's villa.

As she neared, Rachel heard people talking inside. She had not thought about other people being there and immediately felt self-conscious in her bathrobe, tear-stained face on display. She stood outside the doorway. This was a mistake.

"Rachel?"

Rachel turned as Hannah walked up the path, camera bag slung about her shoulder.

"Hannah. Oh good." Rachel exhaled.

"What's wrong?"

"Well, I'm not getting married."

"What do you mean you're not getting married?" Hannah pulled her gently toward a small table under a flowering tree. They sat across from each other. "Now what is going on?"

Rachel shared how she found out about Aaron's hunting trip with his work clients on his computer.

"So not only did Aaron invite several work clients on our honeymoon, he actually finagled our plans to accommodate doing this. And he made it sound like he was doing it for me."

Hannah reached out and squeezed her hand. "That's awful."

Rachel smoothed down her hair. "So you don't think I'm crazy?"

"No! Not at all. It's a breach of trust. I understand why you're mad. You have every right to be." Hannah fingered her camera bag. "I know this is really hard, Rachel. But you're supposed to be married tomorrow. And you love Aaron so much. Maybe he will talk about it when tempers settle. Or maybe this will be an area where you agree to disagree. It's just one part of him. I mean, if you love—"

"I don't love him." Rachel exhaled. She had said it. Finally.

"But—"

"I don't love him," Rachel repeated. "It's never been what I made it out to be. What I convinced myself that it was." It felt cathartic to say the words, to finally shed the falseness with which she embodied herself for the past year. She leaned forward and lowered her voice. "I don't even like being around him most of the time. He's so intense. And critical. I feel like I'm walking on eggshells just being in the same room with him."

"Are you sure it's not cold feet? I remember the day before I got married to Will—"

"It's not like you and Will," Rachel interrupted. "That's the problem. I don't have a love like that."

Hannah glanced down. When she looked back up, her eyes glistened. "I don't have a love like that either."

She'd gone too far. Rachel put her hand over Hannah's. "Sorry. That was insensitive. I just liked all the stories you told me. It's the kind of relationship that I want, that anyone would."

"Is it?" Hannah asked. "Do you know Will is so anxious to rid himself of me that he's prepared to give me anything I want? Apparently, he'll sign an agreement with any terms."

"But that's good, Hannah. It's over then. You can go back to your normal life."

"Can I?" She picked a leaf off the table and ripped it in half. "He wants to see me at the last chance dinner. It's his condition for signing everything." She paused again, picking up another leaf. "It's going to be hard to see him."

"When is it?"

"Tonight."

SIXTY-SEVEN

Rachel and Lanie stood in front of the closet in Lanie's airy bedroom; Hannah sat on the plush bed. Rachel pulled a tight green gown out of the closet and held it up.

"No," Hannah said. "I can't see myself in that."

Lanie approached Hannah with a short red dress. "Wear this, Hannah. You'll be pretty as a picture."

Hannah stood up, took the dress, and held it arms-length in front of her. "I'm sorry, Lanie. I just don't think this is something I would wear." She handed her back the dress. "I have to look like myself tonight."

Hannah left the room. When she returned a short time later, she had on a light blue dress, modestly cut, and low, nude sandals. Her only jewelry was a single silver pendant which Rachel knew to be her favorite. Her hair fell to her shoulders in slight waves, her makeup nearly imperceptible.

"You look beautiful," Rachel said.

Lanie shook her head. "Pretty as a peach."

They walked Hannah to the door of the villa. The limousine was already there.

"Well, this is it," Hannah said, turning to Rachel and Lanie. She held out her arms and Rachel and Lanie folded inside.

"Good luck, Hannah," Rachel whispered.

Rachel watched as Hannah's thin figure walked alone down the pathway. It seemed strangely ominous. It was almost as if Hannah were a contestant on the Hunger Games, not a woman about to have a gourmet dinner with her husband of fifteen years.

Hannah turned and gave a quick wave before she closed the door. Rachel watched the limousine until it disappeared into the scenery, knowing she would now have to face Aaron. She had no excuse to stay away any longer.

Rachel pulled on the clothes Lanie had lent her, a surprisingly perfect fit. She said her goodbyes and started for the giant hotel, its impressive structure visible from where she stood. Each step felt heavy. Now that she'd broken up with Aaron, she'd broken up with his whole world. She would miss Sylvia calling her 'doll' and Aaron's father's fond smile. She would miss Aaron's colleagues she had come to know and the few wives she'd been able to connect with. She'd miss the lifestyle and she'd miss parts of Aaron, too. Rachel remembered the look on his face when he showed her Snowball's cat room. She'd felt loved in that moment. Really, truly loved.

A lump formed in her throat; she touched it instinctively. She felt on the verge of crying or yelling or both. She fought the urge to turn around and seek refuge with Lanie at the villa. But she needed to talk to Aaron. She owed him that much.

When she reached the hotel, Rachel climbed on the elevator and took it to the honeymoon suite. She stood outside of the door and remembered the giddy feeling she'd had when she and Aaron stepped into the space for the first time. The first thing they'd done was take a candlelight bath in the oversized whirlpool tub. Before he'd stepped into the steaming water, Aaron had taken rose petals and spread them on the surface.

Rachel squeezed her eyes shut. Had she made a terrible mistake?

Rachel shook the image of Aaron holding the rose petals from her mind and pushed opened the door. The room was empty. Rachel had foolishly expected Aaron to be there, waiting for her. Instead, his things were gone.

Rachel left the honeymoon suite and took the elevator to the lobby. She strode to the bar and looked inside. No Aaron. No one she knew. She walked to the hostess table at the hotel restaurant. A woman with heavy makeup and an elongated face looked up. "Yes."

"Excuse me," Rachel said. "Do you know if Aaron Weiss has dinner reservations tonight? He's a guest here. I'm his fia—" Rachel hesitated, not sure how to identify herself. "I'm his friend."

The woman looked at a list of names on a paper in a thick notebook. "I'm sorry," she said, "there are no reservations under that name." She smiled. "Would you like to make some?"

Rachel shook her head.

Where was he? Where were the guests? She pulled out her cell phone to call her parents; her battery was dead.

Rachel got into the elevator with the intention of going to her parents' room. When the elevator doors opened, she stepped out, realizing too late, that she was in the underbelly of the hotel where the laundry and trash were housed. She must have pressed the wrong button.

The elevators closed behind her. Rachel pressed the up button and turned to wait, leaning against the wall. She gazed absentmindedly at the laundry machines and trash then stood at attention. The custom-built chuppah stood, partially dismantled, in the corner. And next to it, melting in a trashcan, was the ice sculpture Aaron has insisted upon, two hearts entwined.

Rachel stared at the items. A tiny laugh escaped before her breath caught in her throat. It was over. What had she expected? Aaron had made himself clear.

The elevator bell rang, and the doors slid open. Rachel stepped in, taking a final glance at the destroyed chuppah and the melting sculpture.

The elevator arrived on the lobby floor. Rachel walked outside toward the beach where her wedding would have taken place. She stood alone in the vast space which, just that morning, had been set up with perfect rows of white, cushioned chairs. It was completely empty. It felt as if the entire wedding had been a figment of her imagination. Rachel sat in the center of it all, looking up at a perfect, star-studded sky, when she felt a hand on her shoulder.

She whirled around.

Her mother stood over her. "Rachel?"

She looked up and braced herself for the tirade. How she'd ruined her life. How she'd embarrassed her mother. How utterly stupid she had been.

But, instead, her mother sat down and took her hand. After a moment, she squeezed.

"Hannah called me when you came to her villa, love," she whispered. "She told me about your fight with Aaron, that you called off the wedding."

Rachel opened her mouth to speak but a cry escaped instead. Her mother wrapped her arms around her and squeezed. Rachel cried into a shoulder. When she pulled back, her face was wet with tears.

"Oh, Rachel. I'm so sorry, sweetheart." She rubbed her back in tiny circles. "I'm sorry you're going through this. And I'm sorry if I pushed you into it."

Rachel looked at her mother's face etched in the bright moonlight and shook her head. "No, Mom. Don't be sorry. I knew I didn't love Aaron. I kept trying to convince myself that I did."

She stood and reached down to pull her mother up.

"There are parts of Aaron I'll miss and, when I think about those, I feel like I made a big mistake. But then I remember how he made me feel. No matter what I did, Aaron made me feel wrong."

"You're not wrong," her mother said quickly. "If Aaron made you feel unworthy, then shame on him. He doesn't deserve you. And now I don't have to deal with Sylvia."

They started toward the hotel.

"Did you not like her?" Rachel had no idea.

"Of course not. It was Aaron this and Aaron that. What about Rachel? What about my beautiful Rachel?"

Her beautiful Rachel. She couldn't speak, the words caught in her throat.

"Thanks, Mom." It came out a whisper.

"Let's get you something to eat, sweetheart. Anything you want. Size four, no more. Who needs it?" She laughed at her own joke.

As they reached the lobby, Rachel asked, "Hey, where is everyone?"

Her mother paused. "Aaron told everyone he called the wedding off."

Rachel stopped. Her eyes flashed with anger. "For what reason?"

"You're just not the one. As an apology to the guests, he booked a party cruise. That's where everyone is."

"Of course," Rachel said, stepping back. "Of course, it couldn't be Aaron's fault. And you know what else? Not one of my so-called friends, not Lexi or Samantha or any of them, thought to reach out to me to see if I was okay. Nice."

Her mother held out her hand. "Aaron told everyone that you wanted privacy. It was part of his reasoning for the cruise."

"Still. Throwing a party on the day your engagement ends. There's something wrong with that."

"No argument."

They reached the hotel and a doorman held open a heavy door. Rachel and her mother walked through. A few travelers stood with suitcases at the check-in area. A crowd of women sat on plush velvet couches in front of fireplace, a flat-screen television in the corner.

"Oh my God!" one of the women exclaimed. "He's so adorable."

Rachel looked more closely at the television. The last chance dinner was streaming live.

SIXTY-EIGHT

Will stood outside the limousine in a lush tropical garden, beads of perspiration on his forehead. He'd cut his hair short and there was stubble on his face, an older version of the man in Hannah's wedding photo. He turned; there was a shiner on his right cheek.

"He's bruised!" A girlish voice rang out.

Had Hannah done that? Rachel wondered.

Will lifted his hand and wiped perspiration from his forehead. Then he dug them deep into the pockets of his khaki pants. The show's host, Harry Stewart, appeared and shook Will's hand.

"Will."

"Harry."

The camera zoomed in on Will's face. It was unreadable. "Hannah's waiting for you." The host gestured to a pathway. The television footage steeled on a glimpse of Hannah's blue dress before panning back to Will. Rachel's breath caught. Poor Hannah. What she must be feeling right now.

"How do you feel?" Harry Stewart asked Will.

Will shrugged. "I've been better, Harry."

The host's face was etched with concern. "Any idea what the meeting will hold for you?"

Will was silent. The moment stretched on.

"Oh my God. Say something!" a tween girl in front of the television yelled.

"It's really up to Hannah," Will said finally.

Harry Stewart's eyes flashed irritation before he continued, his voice smooth. He put his hand on Will's shoulder and gave a quick series of pats. "Well, America is waiting, Will. We all hope you and Hannah get the closure you need." He stepped back, allowing Will unfettered access to the pathway.

Rachel grabbed her mother's hand.

Will took a step forward, the camera unrelenting in its focus on his facial features. He stopped and closed his eyes. Upon opening them, he smiled, then immediately became serious again.

When he reached the end of the path, the camera switched to Hannah who was sitting alone at a circular, iron-wrought table set with candles. Her back was stiff, her lips tight. She didn't see Will behind her.

"She's such a bitch," someone yelled. Rachel tensed; her mother squeezed her hand.

The camera switched back to Will as he neared the table. Hannah turned. Will ran his hand through his hair. He looked as if he wished the ground would open and swallow him up.

"I'm not sure how to start."

Hannah answered him, her voice quiet. "You could start with an apology."

"Right. Of course. I'm sorry. I can't—" Will looked down then back up again. "I can't believe all I put you through." He pulled out a chair. Hannah nodded. Will sat precariously on the edge, leaning forward, looking down.

They sat in silence, pained faces illuminated in the candlelight. When it was clear Hannah would say no more, Will reached into his pocket and pulled out a note. "You know I'm not good with words," he said, flashing the card. Then he began to read, his voice like a child reading aloud in class.

"Hannah. I don't expect you to forgive me and I will, as I said, give you everything you need to start over. Whatever you need." He emphasized whatever. Rachel held her breath.

"But before we end things, I have to tell you that our times together were some of the be—" He took a breath. "Were some of the best years of my life. I remember when I saw you on the patio with that textbook. I couldn't believe I hadn't noticed you before. And that first night, that first night, I'll never forget it. I think I loved you the moment you fixed my car. And when you went on and on about those ridiculous sandwiches with the French fries in the middle."

He smiled briefly at the memory and the camera switched to show Hannah. No longer stiff-backed and angry, she leaned forward.

The camera back on Will, he looked at his card. "You have to know that—" he started to read again.

Hannah took the note and pulled it gently from his hand. "No card, Will," she said, her eyes on his. "It's me. Just talk to me."

Will got up and walked to the edge of the patio. Turning back, his eyes glistened. "Hannah, I came here tonight to say goodbye. You deserve someone better and I wanted to give you the chance to find that person. I know I should let you go. I want you to find a better man."

He approached her. "But the thing is—I don't think I can. I've been thinking about it all day. And maybe I can be that man, the better man. Maybe it can be me." He paused. "And then I wouldn't have to miss you so much."

No one in the lobby made a sound.

Hannah stared at him.

"Say something!" someone hissed. There was a collective "Shh!" The moment stretched on, far longer than it should have.

Finally, Will broke the silence. "I understand if you can't forgive me. If you don't want to take me back."

Hannah looked down, her expression shielded by the hair that had fallen in her face.

Just do it, Hannah. Just say yes. Rachel stepped toward the television as if she would be able to reach her, to whisper it. Just say yes.

Hannah stood up and took a step toward Will. It was almost as though time had slowed for the show, as though a producer had told them to take forever. She straightened his tie and stood back from him. Hannah took a deep breath; Rachel held hers.

"I don't think you've asked me to take you back yet, Mr. Abbott."

Will looked surprised, then his face broke out into a smile. He took Hannah's hand and bent down on one knee. "Hannah, I love you so much. Would you be so kind as to—" He paused, his words catching in his throat. "Would you be so kind as to stay on as my wife? Will you take me back?"

As the question hung there the camera switched to Hannah. Rachel squeezed her mother's shoulder.

Hannah smiled. "I will," she said. "I will."

He stood up and they embraced followed by the most tender kiss Rachel had ever witnessed. Then the streaming stopped, and the lobby burst with emotion as though each and every viewer had just stood in Hannah's shoes, as if they had all just been the subject of undying love and adoration.

Rachel turned to her mom. "I can't believe that just happened." She had forgotten, in the moment, her own situation.

"And it will happen for you, love," she said. "Someday, it will happen for you."

SIXTY-NINE

Will

Hannah was still holding his hands when the video camera switched off, the bright light replaced by dim moonlight. Will blinked to adjust his vision. Liam, the head producer of the show, emerged from the bushes.

He waved his arms dramatically as he strode toward them. "Keep filming!" he yelled at the cameraman. "Keep filming!"

The cameraman hoisted his equipment back on his shoulder.

Will looked at him. "Come on," he said in a whisper. "I need to talk to my wife."

Liam stopped in front of them. "This is part of the contract." He pushed his glasses back to the bridge of his nose. "I can film anywhere."

"It's actually not," a familiar voice echoed from a distance. David Dewey came into view, holding his phone. "I just pulled the contract up on my phone. Care to see?" David stepped in front of Liam, obstructing Will and Hannah from his view "See right here," David said. "Paragraph 11, subsection 2, part A." David handed his phone to Liam and turned to Will. "Go," he mouthed.

Will grabbed Hannah's hand and led her off the patio and onto the darkened beach.

"This is a website about turtles! Where's the contract?" the producer yelled.

Will and Hannah laughed.

Will picked up speed over the uneven sand, Hannah trailing behind him.

"Wait," she said. She stopped and pulled off her heels. Now unfettered, she ran ahead of Will toward the tree line.

"Oh no you don't." Will ran after her. He caught up and grabbed her lightly around the waist. Hannah fell to the sand and put her hand over her mouth to stop her laugher. Will sat next to her. She stopped laughing; Will searched her face. His regret for the past several months was so intense, it felt like the emotion might pour out of his soul and on to the beach around him.

"Oh, Hannah," he whispered. "I'm so sorry." He put his head on her chest and breathed in her familiar scent. Smelling it felt like home.

She wrapped her arms around him and laid her head on top of his. Ocean waves crashed rhythmically in the background. Will picked up a pile of sand, letting it fall back to the beach through his fingers. He stared at the ocean. "I feel like the most horrible man. I can't believe what I put you through."

Hannah unwrapped her arms and moved back. He adjusted himself to look at her. "Will. I know what I said back there." She gestured to the patio area. "And I love you and miss you and want things to work. But the truth is, I feel humiliated and betrayed. And embarrassed. It feels like the whole world knows you cheated on me." She looked down and then back up at him. "And I never slept with Trent, you know. You didn't even bother to ask me that before you ran off."

Will put his face in his hands. "I know. But everyone told me I was stupid to believe it. And I just kept imagining you with him." He looked up at her. "What did you see in him anyway?"

Hannah picked at the sand then looked out at the ocean and said nothing. Just as the silence became palpable, she spoke.

"Will. I have loved you since I was fourteen years old. When you asked me to Tony Luke's all those years ago, I couldn't believe it. Will Abbott asking me out. No way. I couldn't believe how lucky I was. And it seemed everyone else thought that too. That I was the lucky one." She took a breath before continuing. "And I've always felt like that. The lucky one. The shadow to your sun. That any day you might turn around and wonder, why did I settle for her?"

Will opened his mouth to speak, but Hannah put her hand out.

"With Trent, I was the sun. And he was the lucky one. It just felt good to be the person being idolized instead of the other way around."

Will digested her words. The shadow to his sun? He had never, not once, felt that way. How could Hannah ever believe that he had?

"They were wrong." Will's said, his voice low.

"Who was wrong?"

"The people who made you feel like you were the lucky one. They were wrong." Will stood up and brushed the sand off his pants. He reached down and pulled Hannah to her feet. He took her hands into his, interlocking his rough fingers with her soft ones. He looked into the green eyes of the woman he had fallen in love with fifteen years earlier.

"Hannah. I'm the lucky one. I love you. I love that you're the first person I see every morning and the last person I see every night. I love that you hum when you cook. And that you yell at the Phils when they're losing. I love that you teach yourself Amanda's math lessons in secret so you can help her when she needs it. And I love that you bite your lip to keep from cheering too loud for the kids at their games. I appreciate that you keep me organized. Not an easy task, I know."

Will shook his head, then continued, "And you know the right thing to say to everyone. Always. It's amazing. I love your ridiculous, terrible jokes. I even love your little snores. They used to drive me crazy, but they're like white noise to me now. I can't sleep without them. I can't sleep without you." Will wiped a tear from his cheek with his finger. "Hannah. Are we ever going to be able to get past this?"

He squeezed her hands. A fat raindrop splattered on his arm.

"I don't know, Will," Hannah said. "I don't know if I can get past it."

Will's heart dropped. The rain intensified. He pointed to a small bungalow a few hundred feet away. "I'm staying there tonight. Come back with me. We can talk this out."

Hannah started at the bungalow. Rain pelted her skin and drenched her clothes.

"Please?"

She squeezed her eyes shut then opened them.

"Okay."

SEVENTY

Hannah

They dashed to his bungalow. Will pushed open the door when they reached it, and Hannah walked through. Cool air blasted her wet skin and she rubbed her arms for warmth. She scanned the room. A double bed in a wood frame stood against one wall, with a couch and seating area across from it. An efficiency kitchen sat in the corner.

"You're freezing," Will said. "Wait." He opened the closet adjacent to them and pulled out a thick terrycloth robe with the hotel insignia. He handed it to her. "Remember—"

Hannah smiled and took the robe. "How could I forget? I think I wore that hotel robe every day of our honeymoon."

"I think you stayed in it all day one day," Will said.

Hannah recalled herself wearing the robe on the sunlit deck of their honeymoon suite. Will had come up behind her and put his arms around her. "Good morning, beautiful," he had said.

"I remember," she said quietly.

Will stepped toward the bed and took off his shirt, muscles flexing with the effort. Hannah stared at his bare chest. Her face flushed as though it were her first time alone in a hotel room with a man. She held the robe to her chest. "I'll be right back."

Hannah carried the robe to the bathroom and closed the door. Slowly, she extricated herself from the soaking blue dress then removed her bra and panties, folding them in a neat pile on the sink. She examined her nude body in the mirror. She had stretch marks. And a few cellulite dimples on her thighs. Her stomach was no longer perfectly flat but contained the little pouch she'd gained when pregnant. Her thighs touched at the top.

What would Will think of her now? After being with a woman like Amber?

Hannah shook her head. She shouldn't have to compete with Amber. She looked how she looked after fifteen years of marriage and two babies. She grabbed the robe and wrapped it tight around herself.

When she emerged from the bathroom, Will smiled broadly. "Hannah."

His smile irritated her. How could he expect them to pick up where they left off so easily? She held out her hand. "I'm sorry, Will, but I'm not sure if I can do this. I thought I was getting divorced today but now I'm here." She scanned the room. "It's a lot to digest."

Will's expression changed from happiness to concern. He stepped back from her. "Can I say anything?"

She shook her head. "Not right now. I need to rest." She headed to the bed, then turned to him. "I'm going to sleep, Will. We can talk about this tomorrow."

She slid under the heavy covers and pulled the comforter up to her neck. The rhythmic sound of ocean waves filled the room. Hannah nestled her head on the plush pillow and closed her eyes. Not long after, she fell asleep.

When she woke, it took her a moment to register her whereabouts. Then the events of the day before came crashing through. Hannah opened her eyes and saw Will asleep on the too-small sofa, his legs crunched into an embryotic position. Despite the seemingly uncomfortable space, he was clearly fast asleep, chest rising and falling in a steady rhythm. She'd even heard a faint snore. She'd have to tease him about that.

Did Amber tease him about that?

She registered the internal question with a jolt. Why had she thought that? How could thoughts of Amber infiltrate her psyche so easily? She stared at her husband's sleeping form, willing the thoughts of Amber to vanish.

As if he could sense her staring at him, Will began to stir. He straightened his legs and stretched. When he opened his eyes, Hannah was still looking at him. "Hannah," he said, almost as though he was checking it was actually her.

The unfinished conversation from the day before hung between them. Will sat up and ran his fingers through his hair. Hannah lay back down and stared at the ceiling. She'd been so sure her marriage was over. Was it? Could she really forgive Will? Would she be able to forget about Amber?

She heard the clank of glasses from the kitchenette. Soon after, the aroma of coffee filled the space.

She sat up and watched Will put cream and sugar in a mug and stir. He approached her with it. "I remembered the cream and sugar," he said sheepishly. Hannah smiled briefly. When they first started dating, Will always forgot how she took her coffee. She took the steaming drink. Will sat down on the couch across from the bed.

Neither of them spoke. Hannah half expected Will to bring up the Phillies. He'd often used sports talk as a means to avoid more serious conversations.

"Hannah," he said, finally. "Can things ever be okay between us?"

He looked at her, his expression sincere. She wanted to believe him. Could she? She drew in a breath. "Are you over Amber?

She's so beautiful. I mean I could see why—" She paused, unable to continue.

Will leaned forward and put his elbows on his knees. "Amber is beautiful," he acknowledged. "And she'll find someone. But that someone isn't me." He sat up. "I know that because the person I want to spend the rest of my life with is right in front of me."

Hannah looked down at the comforter. "It's hard to know if you mean that, Will."

He moved to the bed and sat beside her. "Let me prove it to you, then." He put his hand on top of hers. "One day at a time."

Hannah said nothing.

"Start today?"

Hannah thought about how much she had missed Will these past months, about Charlie and Amanda. Didn't she owe their relationship a second chance?

She looked at Will. Love stared back at her.

"Okay," she said softly. "This is day one."

SEVENTY-ONE

David

Two days after the last chance dinner, David stood in the airport at St. John. When the flight from Philadelphia arrived, airport personnel pulled open the door to allow passengers from the plane into the waiting area. A handful of strangers emerged. David craned his neck, looking for his children.

Ryan spotted him first. He waved wildly. "Dad! Hi!" Hailey and Sienna were behind him. The three navigated the crowd.

"Dad!" Hailey said when she reached him

Sienna squeezed his arm. "Congratulations."

"Thank you." David enfolded his children in a group hug. When he looked up, Lauren was standing on the outskirts.

David stepped back. "Lauren. I didn't expect you."

Lauren fingered her sundress and gave him a perfunctory kiss on the cheek. "Well. You know Brett and I broke up, and the kids were going, so I figured—" She stood a moment. "I brought you a gift," she said suddenly. She reached into a giant, straw bag and retrieved a wrapped box. "For you and Jenny." She extended the gift, then took it back. "I guess I should wait for the both of you."

"Let Dad open it," Ryan insisted. He grabbed the package from his mother and thrust it into David's hands. "He'll like it."

David looked at the gift. "I should probably wait for Jenny."

"Come on, Dad," Ryan encouraged. "Just open it."

David took in Ryan's hopeful expression. Jenny wouldn't mind.

"Okay. But if she's mad, I'm blaming you," he teased.

David pulled of an elaborate bow and tore off the heavy paper. He held up the box, took off the lid, and pulled out a paper. It was a gift certificate to a painting class. David looked up.

"We're all going to learn along with you," Hailey explained. "The gift covers the class for five people!"

David stared at the certificate, taking in its meaning. Lauren wanted him and Jenny to take a painting class with the kids.

Lauren stepped forward. "I figured it would be a good way for Jenny to get to know the kids better. They said she liked to paint."

David stared at his first wife, unable to respond immediately to the unexpected gesture of goodwill. Lauren misinterpreted his silence. "Of course, if you don't like it—"

David held his hand out. "No. I love it. It's very thoughtful." He kissed Lauren on the cheek; she grabbed his hand and squeezed.

"I'm really happy for you, David," she whispered.

"Thank you." David put the paper in the box, and they walked to baggage claim.

"I forgot to tell you," Ryan said as they approached the luggage carousel. "Mom said I could keep Bolt."

"Awesome!" David held out his hand and he and Ryan high-fived. "And he's been doing okay while I've been gone?"

"Yes. I've taught him to sit."

David suppressed a laugh and tousled his hair. "I can't wait to see, Ry."

Once they had retrieved their luggage, the five of them piled into David's rental car.

"So," Lauren said as he pulled on to the main road. "Tell us how you asked her."

"I took her to a beach, got down on one knee, and said 'Will you marry me?'"

"That's it, David?" Lauren shot him a look. "Really?"

"Really."

David wouldn't tell her that Jenny had said no when he'd asked her to marry him. She had been too worried about burdening him with her health. David had spent the whole night trying to get her to change her mind. When she'd finally said yes, he'd cheered so loud the hotel clerk called to make sure everything was okay.

"Are you nervous?" Sienna asked. "I mean, today's the big day."

"The only thing I am nervous about is that Jenny will change her mind." David said it in a joking manner but there was a touch of truth to the statement.

David swung the car into the hotel parking lot. He and Ryan went to his room to get ready while Lauren and the girls checked in.

Once they were in his room, David gestured for Ryan to sit on the bed. "I'd like to ask you something."

"Alright, Dad." Ryan turned and looked at him.

"Sometimes, when a person gets married, they ask someone important to them to stand with them at the altar. That person holds the rings and makes sure the groom has everything he needs."

Ryan nodded. "I know, Dad. He's the best man."

"Right. The best man." David looked his son in the eyes. "Ryan, would you be my best man today? It's okay if you don't feel comfortable, but—"

Ryan flew into David's arms. "I would love to be your best man, Dad." David held his son close. Everything was coming together.

They changed into tuxedos, left the room, and got on the elevator. David's heart raced with anticipation. In an hour, he would marry his best friend and the love of his life. He smiled at Ryan.

"You look happy, Dad," Ryan commented.

"I am happy," David responded. He meant it.

He and Ryan walked through the hotel lobby and outside. They headed to the space which had been set up for the ceremony. A white, lace runner ran between two aisles of chairs stopping at a small canopy. At either end of the aisle stood two tall vases of yellow roses. David stared at it and quickened his gait. He was going to marry Jenny.

When he reached the area, David took in the eclectic group of spectators assembled to watch the wedding: an older couple, a few hotel workers, several of the contestants from Divorce House. David's gaze fell to Lauren, Hailey, and Sienna in the front row. He stepped forward to greet them.

"You look great, Dad," Sienna said.

"Thanks, honey. You all look beautiful." He stood back and admired his daughters. They were stunning. Hailey, her hair still short, wore a long, light green dress. Sienna's dress was shorter and aqua blue. Had they gotten them at Lulu's? He smiled at the recollection of their day there.

"Nice night," Lauren commented.

"Yes," David agreed. He adjusted his boutonniere.

Hailey looked at the hotel. "Have you seen Jenny?" she asked.

David followed her gaze, willing the door to open. "No. She said it would be bad luck,"

He looked at his watch. "She should be here any minute." He stepped away but kept his eyes trained on the hotel door where Jenny would come out. He heard bits and pieces of conversations. A bird squawked. He tapped his foot. Where was she? David cursed himself for leaving his cell phone in the room. What if Jenny had been trying to reach him? What if she was sick or hurt? Beads of sweat broke out on his forehead. He took out his handkerchief and wiped them away.

Ryan came up next to him. "Are you okay, Dad?"

"Yes. I'm alright." David wiped more sweat away.

"Do you want me to look for her?" Ryan whispered.

"No, son. She'll be here."

He shut his eyes.

What if she'd changed her mind?

He should go find her. He opened his eyes just as the hotel door swung open.

Jenny stood in a simple white dress. She waved at him.

David's heartbeat accelerated. A lump formed in his throat; he couldn't move. Ryan took his arm and guided him to the canopy. David didn't take his eyes off Jenny. She took her place at the end of the aisle.

The music began and Jenny began to walk toward him.

All David could think was: Oh thank God. My life is here.

SEVENTY-TWO

Jenny stood in the place where, just days ago, Rachel had envisioned herself standing. She wore a plain white dress with no jewelry. Her makeup was barely perceptible. She walked slowly down the aisle, her smile radiant. When she reached David, he pulled her into a hug and said, "You are the most beautiful woman in the world."

Light laughter broke out.

Rachel scanned the crowd for Aaron. Though she didn't regret her decision to break off the engagement, she wanted him to regret it. She visualized what it would be like if he broke through the crowd and declared he would do anything for her love. It would be a Hannah-and-Will or, now, a Jenny-and-David-worthy moment.

The minister began speaking and Rachel squeezed her eyes shut. She had to stop doing this to herself. Aaron was not coming back to fight for her.

She felt a hand on her shoulder.

Aaron?

She turned around. It was Hannah.

"Rachel," she whispered and gestured to an area away from the ceremony.

Rachel followed Hannah to the patio outside the hotel. The stood on the periphery, the wedding still in view.

"I've been trying to reach you by phone."

Rachel shook her head. "I'm sorry, I—"

Hannah put her hand on her arm. "I'm sorry about Aaron."

Rachel shrugged. "Que sera."

"I know this isn't easy for you," she said, leaning closer. "But you know what? I'm kind of glad."

Rachel took a step back and looked at her.

Hannah met her gaze. "You don't need Aaron, Rachel. Or anyone who doesn't treat you the way you deserve. It's better to be single and secure then married and miserable."

"That's easy for you to say," Rachel responded, a trace of bitterness in her tone. "Look how things ended up for you and Will."

Hannah shook her head. "We're not totally okay yet, no matter how it might have looked on the show. There's a lot of emotion still there. On both our parts. But one thing I learned when Will and I were separated is how much I had relied on him for my happiness. I had to find my own way and deal with the kids and the social media and the lawyers."

Rachel shook her head. "Those damn lawyers."

"Seriously," Hannah said, "I made myself better. You will too. You're strong, Rachel."

Strong. It was not a word she'd ever use to describe herself. But she liked thinking of herself that way. Solid and invincible. A woman that tackled life on her own terms. She envisioned herself on a rock, a fortress of strength, arms at her hips. The Wonder Woman of her own life, completely in control.

The minister's voice boomed. "And I now pronounce you man and wife. Ladies and gentlemen, Mr. and Mrs. David Dewey!"

Rachel and Hannah turned toward the couple. David and Jenny locked arms and walked down the aisle to the applause of the onlookers. Jenny smiled broadly; David's eyes looked wet. When they reached the clearing, David turned to his wife, picked her up, and swung her in a circle. "We did it," he said, putting her down.

"We did it," Jenny affirmed, smiling up at him.

Rachel smiled at the Deweys, their joy infectious. Then she braced herself for the familiar pang of jealousy, but none came. Instead, another feeling took root inside her.

Peace.

SEVENTY-THREE

Rachel
five years later.

"Hello…" Rachel knocked on the half-open door. "Hello. It's me."

When no one answered, she stepped into a breezy, two-story room. Hannah's photographs hung in clusters on white walls, their eclectic frames complementing each other and their contents. Natural light streamed in from two-story picture windows, creating a sheen on the hardwood floors. Of course, "the photo" had its own easel in the center of the room. Rachel moved toward it and stared at the image of David and Jenny in the crystal blue waters of St. John, their bare heads touching. The picture had won multiple awards and was most recently used in an advertising campaign by a non-profit, Living Well with Cancer. Hannah had become a local celebrity of sorts, so much so that she'd had enough interest in her work to warrant opening the studio. Tonight was her official grand opening.

"Hello," Rachel called again.

"Aunt Rachel!" Charlie emerged from a back room with a folding table. He seemed taller than he had just last month. He leaned the table against the wall and hugged her. "Mom was looking for you," he said, then yelled, "Moooooooom! Aunt Rachel's here."

Hannah came down the stairs. "Rachel. Thanks for coming." She handed Charlie her car keys. "Can you unload the drinks, honey?"

"Sure, Mom." Charlie took the keys and walked out.

Hannah grabbed her hand. "Good. Rachel. I have to tell you something." She took a breath. "Remember when you told me to get a local news show to cover the studio opening?"

"I remember."

"Well, they're out back."

Rachel looked out the back window. Sure enough, a white Channel 13 news van was parked in the empty lot behind the studio.

"And, well—" Before Hannah could finish, the door opened, Greg Tisbury in its frame. His face burst into a smile.

Rachel frowned. "Greg. What are you doing here?" She hadn't spoken to him since he'd run the piece about Hannah and Will on Trending Now. The show had been cancelled; Rachel hadn't followed what Greg did next.

"Hannah didn't tell you?"

Rachel looked at her friend.

"Greg surprised me," Hannah explained. "When he found out about the news coverage for the studio, he asked to produce the piece. I didn't know he was coming to the studio until today." Rachel looked from Hannah to Greg. It felt surreal.

Greg stepped forward. "I know I screwed up all those years ago. I'm sorry. I betrayed your trust. I sold out your friend. I," he paused. "Well, I'm different now. I want to make amends. I've already apologized to Hannah. Can I," he shifted, casting his eyes down to the floor. "Can I get you a cup of coffee?"

Rachel took him in. He was not college Greg but not the Greg of five years ago either. He seemed humbler now.

"I can't, Greg," Rachel said. "I came to help Hannah."

"I can handle it myself." Hannah picked up the folding table in demonstration.

Rachel glanced at her; Hannah smiled. Was she trying to set her up?

"Just coffee," Greg said.

It seemed harmless. "Alright." Rachel looked over her shoulder at Hannah. "I'll be back in twenty minutes."

She and Greg walked outside. Coffee Corner was only a few doors from Hannah's studio. When they reached it, Greg held the door. Rachel stepped through into the small café. They ordered coffees at the counter and, once served, brought the steaming mugs to a small table by the window.

Greg began his apology as soon as they sat down. "I'm so sorry, Rachel. I behaved like such a jerk. I can't believe how I acted. That I took something you told me in private, something personal to your friend, and made it news." He shook his head. "I'm really ashamed."

Rachel took a sip of coffee. Greg continued. "I mean, who does something like that? I just can't—"

Rachel held up her hand. "It was a long time ago, Greg."

He rapped his fingers on the table. "So," he started. "I hope you don't think I'm a stalker, but I've been trying to keep up with you, with what you're doing."

Rachel blew on her coffee and Greg continued, "I'm impressed. Your own law firm. Collaborative law. Tell me about it."

Rachel took a breath and explained how Will and Hannah's case made her think about the problems with the divorce process. Not long after she got back from St. John, a work colleague had told her about collaborative divorce, a process where attorneys work together like problem-solvers. She'd taken a chance and opened her own firm.

Rachel took a sip of coffee. "And how about you? What are you doing?"

"I produce a local news show in New York and I'm taking guitar." He strummed his fingers.

"You always wanted to do that!" Rachel gushed.

"I know. It's fun."

They talked about old times until their coffee grew cold. As they walked out, Greg asked. "Would you want to see me again, Rachel?"

There was a time when Rachel would not have been able to say yes fast enough. To be with a man, any man, was better than to be alone. It took her years to dispel the notion that coupling up was the only measure of validation.

Rachel had her own money, her own home, her own law firm, and three cats—references to eccentric cat ladies be damned. She didn't want to put herself in a situation where she might slide back into dependence.

But.

She was lonely. It had been five years since her break-up with Aaron. Five years since she had been in a relationship.

Five years was long enough.

She turned to Greg. He smiled crookedly at her.

"I would love to see you again sometime, Greg."

SEVENTY-FOUR

David

David placed the booster seat in the back of the rented minivan. He picked up Faith and placed her in it even though she could do it herself. He liked spoiling her. He'd missed his chance to be the spoiler when his kids with Lauren were young. David was determined not to make the same mistake with Faith. He pulled the seatbelt over her and buckled it. Then he handed her "Bear Bobby," her very loved but rather ragged stuffed dog, along with a sippy cup of apple juice.

"Don't tell your mother," he whispered.

"David. I'm right behind you, you know." Jenny stood holding the diaper bag. "Just one cup of juice," she told Faith. "And a big girl cup next time. And you." She poked David's belly. "You have to stop being such a pushover." She shook her head but her eyes were smiling.

He and Jenny loaded into the van and David drove out of the airport parking lot.

They came to New Jersey twice a year to see David's children and for Jenny's check-ups. The oncologists were repeatedly amazed at her continued remission. "We're going to prescribe living in St. John to all our patients," one had told her.

While the doctor had meant it as a joke, David wasn't entirely sure their lifestyle hadn't been the precursor to Jenny's unexpected recovery. They literally lived in paradise. Jenny taught painting classes a few times a week; David was a public defender on the island, a job with the trial worked he loved.

And Faith. Having a child with Jenny had been a miracle.

"David, it's a left here," Jenny said. "Then the school is on the right, about a mile down."

David followed Jenny's instructions and parked. They got out of the car.

"I'll get the stroller," Jenny volunteered.

"No need. I got it." David pulled open the door and undid Faith's seatbelt. "Princess Faith, your chariot awaits." He bent down to allow his smiling daughter to scramble on to his shoulders for a piggyback ride.

"Honestly, David. You're going to hurt yourself one of these days."

"Probably. But not today. Today, I am a chariot." He galloped ahead; Faith squealed.

They walked to the chairs set up for the ceremony and sat down. Faith busied herself pushing trucks on the grass below; Jenny checked their hotel reservation online. David pulled out the program and looked at the names of this year's Rutgers Law School graduates. He found Amber's right away.

His heart expanded. Jenny followed his gaze. "You must be so proud," she whispered.

Pomp and circumstance sounded from an overhead speaker. David turned and looked at the line of black-robed graduates streaming in from a tree-lined area. He spotted Amber and waved; she waved back and smiled.

"Is that your daughter?" the woman next to him asked.

"Yes," David said without thinking. "My oldest."

"She's stunning. Does she have a job lined up?"

"She'll be working in Washington DC as a child advocate." David was surprised at the level of pride he felt saying the words. "She's one of the top scholars here."

Jenny asked the woman questions about her son; David had been content to talk about Amber.

When the ceremony was over, Amber found them on the lawn. If she was bothered that they were her only guests, she didn't act like it. "Thank you for coming!" She hugged them both, then picked up Faith. "You, my darling, are getting very, very big. You might be as big as your dad."

"No!" Faith said. "Daddy's really big." She held out her hands wide. Amber set her to the ground. Faith whispered to Jenny.

"I think we have to go to the little girl's room," Jenny took Faith by the hand.

David and Amber watched them go. When they were out of view, Amber turned to him. "David. Words can't describe how grateful I am. None of this would have been possible if it wasn't for you."

"No. Amber." David pointed to the diploma in her hand. "This is all you. You should be so proud." He squeezed her arm lightly.

There was a gap in the conversation. Amber knew about Hannah's gallery opening; he hoped she wouldn't bring it up. After Divorce House, Amber had a terrible time getting over Will. To get away from the post-show publicity, she'd even lived with David and Jenny on St. John for a few months. But then she got into law school and her questions about Will had nearly stopped.

"I got you something," Amber said, pulling him from his thoughts. She thrust a small gift bag toward him.

David looked at the gift, then Amber. "Now why'd you do a thing like that?"

"It's just a little thing. Open it."

David reached in the bag and pulled out a mug with #1 Dad on the front. It was identical to the one he'd lost when he closed his office, the one Sienna had given him as a child. There was a note inside.

Dear David,

I saw this and remembered it was just like the one from the office. If anyone deserves a mug like this, it's you. I know I'm not your daughter, but you are still the #1 Dad to me. No one in my life has ever been as good to me as you have been. I'm a lawyer and will be living my dream, all because of you. I promise to pay it forward, even the tuition reimbursement (I know about that now). Sometimes you are hard on yourself for your past. Don't be. You've done everything right for years. You are a wonderful father and I'm proud to think of you as mine. I love you.

Amber

David hugged Amber. "Thank you. I can't tell you how much this means to me." He held the mug. "I'm going to have to start drinking coffee again. You know, now that I have a personalized mug."

SIXTY-FIVE

Hannah

Hannah pushed open the door to her house. The first thing she saw was the note pinned to the bulletin board in Amanda's scrawled writing: "Mom. Wear the black one." She removed the note and held it. Just yesterday, it seemed, the family bulletin board had been home to preschool crafts and field trip permission forms. Now there was a flyer for an SAT tutor and a reminder about the junior prom. Charlie's Xbox password was pinned to the corner on a yellow sticky.

Rufus came up and rubbed her leg. She bent down to pet him. The bulldog had been a Christmas surprise two years ago. Hannah had been the least enthused about the gift but was now the most in love with the dog. Once she'd gotten the studio, Hannah brought Rufus for company. It turned out he was a perfect model for test lighting and angles.

"Come on, boy," Hannah encouraged and he bounded up the stairs after her. Hannah entered her room, peeled off her clothes, and stepped in the shower. The warm water soothed her muscles and she allowed it to cascade over her body. When her skin started to redden, she turned off the shower, toweled off, and moved in front of her lingerie drawer. She pulled out a midnight blue bra with black lace and matching panties and put them on.

Not long ago, wearing lacy, satin undergarments would have been a rare occurrence; now, not so much. Hannah had grown to enjoy the fact that, under a simple T-shirt and jeans, she might have on a leopard patterned bra or beautiful, floral panties. Her body wasn't perfect. So what? She felt pretty anyway.

Hannah lifted the dress off the bed and bent down to put it on just as the door to the bedroom opened.

"Looks like I got here at just the right time," Will called out, shutting the door behind him.

Hannah turned. He smiled at her.

She pulled up the dress. "Oh please. Get your mind out of the gutter and help me zip."

"Buzzkill," Will said in a joking tone. He stepped forward, zipped the dress, then spun her around. "Wow. You look fantastic."

"Thanks." Hannah spied a small package in Will's hand.

He held it out to her. "I got a little something for you as a congratulations. But if it doesn't go, if it wasn't what you had in mind, don't worry about it."

Hannah took the box. She lifted the lid and pulled out a silver necklace with a pendant of a sun.

"It's because—" Will started.

"I remember." She looked at him, surprised. The sun comment she'd made after the last chance dinner had not come up in years. But it must have stuck with Will.

"Just so there's no doubt as to who I think the sun is," he said. "Do you like it?"

Hannah held the necklace. "I love it." She kissed him briefly. "You may just get to help me with my zipper again after all," she teased.

"Nice. But I'll have to hold off for now. I have to get your mom and Walter at the airport." He kissed on her the cheek. "See you at the opening."

After Will left, Hannah fingered the prongs of the sun on the pendant. She wouldn't tell anyone the meaning of it. The sun backstory would just feed into the whole notion that she and Will spent endless hours in love locked adoration; that their every encounter ended in either soulful confessions or passionate sex. Right after the Divorce House finale aired, Hannah understood why people would think that. She and Will had been on the brink of divorce and reconciled on live TV. But it had been five years. Who could sustain that level of intensity?

She and Will had the same life they'd had before the show. There were still kid activities and work obligations and family events. But, in between the busy times, they made time for each other.

It was the little things.

Once a month, they ate at Tony Luke's, just the two of them. Hannah dropped off snacks to Will at his worksite; Will brought fresh flowers to the studio. They got a Phillies season ticket package. They laid together on weekend mornings and just talked— their goals, the kids, and dream plans to get a house at the Jersey shore. The ease of their relationship led naturally to more intimacy. Everything felt as it should be.

Rufus's body leaned against her leg. She bent down and kissed his head. "What a good dog." She opened the door and stepped out, looking toward the kids' rooms.

It was possible that they wouldn't be ready. Or that Will would get caught in traffic. Or that she hadn't ordered enough food. Or that Rufus might, this very second, jump up and leave a trail of slobber on her cocktail dress.

A million things could go wrong. She fingered the sun pendant. But Hannah didn't worry about those details anymore.

SEVENTY-SIX

Will

Hannah's mother, Rose, and Walter piled into Will's car at the airport. As soon as Will pulled out, Walter spoke.

"So, Will. Have your heard about our new adventure?"

"Which one?" Will asked honestly.

"The goat yoga studio?" Walter prompted.

Rose peeked her head through the seats from the back. "It's called Bahmaste."

Will laughed.

"Clever, right?" Walter said. "We have two goats, Buster and Daisy. They stand on people while they do certain positions."

"Wow," Will tried to visualize a goat standing on a woman in yoga pants.

"Of course, there are trainers there," Walter continued. "To make sure everything goes smoothly."

"We can't have Daisy gnawing on a ponytail." Rose made the statement flippantly, but it was so specific that Will wondered if it had actually happened. Will pictured a woman trying to extract her ponytail from a goat's mouth; Walter expounded on the health benefits of the practice.

Will tuned him out. In truth, he was just grateful that his relationship with Rose was back to normal. After Divorce House aired, he, Hannah, and the kids had gone to visit Rose and Walter. The second morning of the trip, Will had woken up first. He'd found Rose in the kitchen making pancakes. She wore an apron with baby pictures of Charlie and Amanda superimposed on flowers with the caption: "Nana's Growing Bunch." Will had been thinking about how much she looked like a doting grandmother when she'd pointed a battery spatula at him and said: "If you ever hurt my daughter again, I'll make sure you regret it." The statement had been so incongruous with the scene that it would have been funny but for Rose's eyes. It was an expression which conveyed a universal message: Don't mess with a mother's love.

As time passed, Rose seemed to accept that Will's love for Hannah was real and her watchful gaze over him waned. Her voice brought him back to the present. "Do you think Hannah would be interested in taking pictures of the goats?"

"I'm sure she would," Will said. "But you can ask her yourself. We're here." Will pulled the car into the parking lot behind the studio.

"Oh. It's so cute," Rose gasped. "Even from the back."

Rose and Walter got out of the car and walked toward the studio. Will stayed back to get more drinks out of the car. As he opened the trunk, he observed the party through the back window.

David and Jenny stood in front of their picture. His children and the other grown grands conversed with older kids that Will guessed were David's from his first marriage. Jess and John stood in front of a painting with their arms linked next to Charlotte, sparkling water in hand. Kat and Scotty, now married with a child of their own, stood with Rachel who held Rufus on a leash.

Will's mother sat toward the back with a little girl on her lap. With her long dark hair and curled up nose, there was no doubt it was Faith Dewey. Constance had the Where is Elmo's Blanket book in her hand—an old favorite of the grands. Will felt a surge of affection for his mother. He knew she would patiently lift every flap in Where is Elmo's Blanket and feign great surprise when the blanket had been in Elmo's bed all along.

Will picked up the case of water and shut the trunk. As he walked toward the studio, he noticed the owners of Jubilee landscaping near their flower display. Just last year, Jubilee had brought Will on as an owner. Initially, he had been hired as part of the landscape design team. But, when Will's "cardinal garden" became the number-one landscape request, the owners offered him a stake.

Will pushed open the door. Hannah spotted him immediately. "Will! You're here." She motioned for him to join her. Will walked toward her group standing in front of Hannah's "family wall," a space dedicated to pictures of the four of them. As he approached, Will took in the dozens of shots. Some were posed and formal, others candid. The cumulative memories contained in them flooded his mind and he smiled.

He reached Hannah and put his hand on her shoulder.

"I'd like you to meet the Petersons," Hannah said. I'm going to take pictures of their adorable son next week."

Will shook hands with the Petersons. "You couldn't have picked a better photographer. And I speak from personal experience."

"Thank you, Will." She squeezed his arm and resumed her conversation.

For the duration of the evening, Will worked to ensure its success. He filled wine glasses, replenished food, and met new clients. He took Rufus over for Rachel and made sure his mother had a ride home. Throughout it all, he stole glances at Hannah. She looked radiant, happier than Will had ever seen her.

When the final guests left, Will shut the door shut tight behind them. He enfolded Hannah into a hug. "I can't believe how lucky I am," he whispered.

"How lucky we are," she whispered back.

They stood in an embrace for a long moment. "I guess it's time to go home," Will said finally.

Hannah left first, Rufus in tow. Will packed up the perishables, got in his truck, and started home. A few blocks from the studio, he saw Hannah's car pulled over on the side of the road.

She had a flat tire.

No way.

Will pulled up behind the car and got out. He sauntered toward her. "Excuse me, ma'am," he said, using his best police officer impression. "You look like you have a flat tire."

Hannah furrowed her brow in mock concern. "I know. You wouldn't happen to know how to fix a flat tire, would you?"

Will smiled. "Of course I do," he said, opening the trunk. "My wife taught me."

Acknowledgments

If you are reading this, it means The Language of Divorce is an actual, published book! Hooray! I have dreamt of being a professional writer since I was eight years old. This is truly a dream come true.

I started this book almost four years ago. My first draft bears little resemblance to this final version. I have many people to thank for helping me turn my initial writing into the book you hold today:

Maria Brown, Kay Weeder, Katie Treese, Jake Treese: As my first readers, you gave me honest input before I submitted this book for publication. Your feedback helped me improve the first draft which, I believe, allowed publishers to believe in the story.

Melissa Nagy: Thank you for your sharing your extensive knowledge of police procedure.

Maria Imbalzano, Maureen Joyce Connolly, and Gerry Bowen: My writer friends – thank you for your guidance and support through this process.

Myra Fiacco, Claire Winn, Milly Thiringer, Brandy Woods Snow, and the FVP family: Thank you for your support and your belief in my novel. When FVP was reviewing my full manuscript, I kept telling my family – this is the publisher I want! You cannot know how excited I was to join your team. It has been a pleasure working with you and being part of such a warm community of writers.

Carla Vonzale Lewis: Wow! Your edits were phenomenal and made The Language of Divorce a much better story. Your advice also helped me improve my writing. I don't think I will ever want to publish a book without you editing it! I cannot thank you enough.

Richard Pike, Charlene Smith, Lori Andrews, Leslie Pike, Cassidy Treese, Kevin Treese, and Katie Treese: Thank you for being so supportive. Sharing the excitement with all of you has made this journey even more special.

Lynn Pike and Dorothy Vanderlippe: I know you are rooting for me and sending support my way.

Jake Treese: Last but not least. You are my biggest fan and this book would not have been possible without your support. Thank you for believing in my dream to be a full-time writer. I am unbelievably lucky to have you in my life. I love you.

ABOUT THE

Leanne lives in New Jersey with her husband of twenty-five years and their three wonderful children. When Leanne is not cheering her kids on in their activities, she can be found running, watching 76ers basketball games, and spoiling her two beloved dogs. Favorite locations include the Jersey shore, Martha's Vineyard, and any place that sells books or coffee, preferably both. A passionate student, Leanne's dream life would include going back to college and majoring in everything.

Leanne is a graduate of Lafayette College and The Dickinson School of Law. She is a former attorney who is now lucky enough to write full-time.

The Language of Divorce is her debut novel.

WITHDRAWN

If you enjoy:

Emotional Journeys ✓
Romantic Themes ✓
Immersive Settings ✓

Check out these other FVP titles!

FILLES VERTES PUBLISHING

www.fillesvertespublishing.com

 @fillesvertespub @fillesvertespub @FVpublishing